# PRAISE FOR

## GUNS & SMOKE

"Guns & Smoke is a triumph of a book with characters who face real & dark internal struggles & who must learn to accept & face their demons."
**-Independent Book Review**

"Sevier & Smith have balanced a dark world with a bright romance. This fresh look at the western genre that grapples with questions of redemption, trauma, & the many wounds of life that love both can & cannot heal . . . We can trust these authors with our hearts."
**-Michelle Cavalier, Cavalier House Books**

"This high-octane dystopian thriller from Lauren Sevier & Abbie Lynn Smith takes readers on an exhilarating journey into a ruined world..."
**-Prairies Book Review**

# PRAISE FOR

**LEATHER & LACE**

"A western-dystopian filled with the kind of angst, drama, and swoonworthy romance that readers will wish every sequel delivered."
**-Independent Book Review**

"Sevier and Smith are masters of their craft, queens of writing concise beautiful prose that manages to weave plotlines together without feeling jumbled or confusing."
**-Emily S Hurricane, Author**

"A genre-bending take on the classic western, this wonderfully satisfying, superbly crafted tale is hard to beat."
**-Prairies Book Review**

# THE FOOL'S ADVENTURE SERIES

Guns & Smoke
Leather & Lace
Chains & Reckoning

# GUNS & SMOKE

## The Fool's Adventure Series
### Volume 1

## Lauren Sevier
## Abbie Lynn Smith

This is a work of fiction. Similarities to real people, places, or events are entirely coincidental.

GUNS & SMOKE

Second Edition

Copyright © 2021 by Lauren Sevier & Abbie Lynn Smith

Written by Lauren Sevier & Abbie Lynn Smith

# TRIGGER WARNING

Please be aware that Guns & Smoke contains dark and possibly triggering themes including graphic violence, language, sexual violence, attempted rape, depictions of child abuse, and depictions of human trafficking.
Remember that your mental health matters.

VEGAS

FLAGSTAFF

SANTA FE

ROSWELL

LAMESA

FORT HOOD

GUNS & SMOKE

To best friends, whiskey, and the roll of the dice...

CHAPTER ONE

# BONNIE

I DIDN'T PARTICULARLY LIKE the idea of killing the handsome, blue-eyed stranger, but he wouldn't be the first. I tightened the laces on my boot, then sank into the shadows between the ramshackle buildings, my eyes never leaving him. He was the most beautiful mark I'd ever seen. On first glance, an easy one, but I look closer than most and could tell immediately this man was more than he appeared. Brushing the red sand off my fingers, I stalked close enough to make out the broad width of his shoulders. A wicked smile curled over my lips as I caught sight of the bag slung over one of those delicious shoulders. *Bingo.*

This part of the Vegas strip was crowded; it was the same in other cities too, dilapidated shops and makeshift markets encroaching on the well in the center of the square. Here in the desert, there was only one God: water. And like the God of old . . . absent too often.

My mark, the blue-eyed man, bypassed the lines of people waiting for their daily ration and walked directly into the middle of the fray. *Fuck.* Almost immediately, I lost sight of him in the crowd. Tugging my hood low over my face, I barreled after him, ducking and twisting through the throng.

"Step right up! Only two brass bits and you can own a piece of the Salt Lake bombs! Rare and radioactive—"

"—all the way from the Borderlands. You've never tasted anything like this!"

"And the Lord sent fire raining down from the sky, in the Culling, punishing us for our sins."

The cacophonous din of the market overwhelmed my senses as I searched for my mark in the crowd. I snorted derisively at the hysterical man preaching on the corner. The Culling wasn't any God-like retribution. It was what happened when greedy, entitled men had access to nuclear bombs. I tried not to get distracted by the mouthwatering scent of rat roasting on skewers, but it'd been a long time since I'd eaten meat. Chewing the cuticle of my thumb instead, I took a steadying breath and paused a moment to remember the details I'd gleaned from my quarry so far.

He was young, early twenties, and handsome. His features were so chiseled it was hard to imagine he was made of flesh instead of stone. The long ridge of his nose led to sculpted lips that seemed carved with precision beneath a pair of the bluest eyes I'd ever seen. They'd caught my notice initially. Their color a striking shade of clear, light blue splintering into dark navy, reminding me of heat lightning. In contrast to his stubbled jaw and corona of golden hair, bleached from too long under the desert sun, his expression had been almost *boyish*.

*Think Bonnie, think.*

What did the details tell me? Pack of supplies over his shoulder, wide-eyed—almost innocent—expression, days or weeks in the desert sun. The realization hit me all at once: he'd traveled here from far away. A dark chuckle escaped my lips as I headed in the direction of the red district. There was one thing almost guaranteed to pique the interest of a man who'd been traveling for that long. *The prospect of sex.*

In my excitement to find him, I grew reckless, something I couldn't afford to be. Crossing the busy thoroughfare hastily, I knocked into a man almost twice my size. My hood flew back, exposing my scowling face as I stumbled on clumsy feet. The man gripped my arm, steadying me. I jutted my chin with a withering glare and a scathing curse poised on my lips. That is, until I noticed the dark crimson ink in the shape of a fist covering his pounding pulse.

My stomach dropped to the red sand at my feet. Immediately I lowered my eyes, letting my long black hair obscure some of my features from his suspicious gaze. The tattoo marked him as a member of the Crimson Fist, a gang of bounty hunters and assassins that controlled this part of the strip. Their only God was money, and I had a hefty price on my head.

"Sorry," I murmured as quietly as I could.

"You look familiar," he said, his grip digging into the muscle of my upper arm. "Do I know you?"

"No," I said, my fingers twitching toward the back pocket of my shorts. "Just here for my rations." He grunted, his eyes trailing to a rough sketch on a wanted poster hung on a wall a few feet away. *Fuck.* His other hand came up to my face, pushing the long strands of hair away. I saw the moment he made the connection: back stiffening, eyes dulling into a hard glare, lips pulled too far away from his teeth. I offered him a pretty smile and flicked the knife from my back pocket into my palm. Before he could raise the alarm, I shoved forward with all my body weight, feeling a crunch as the blade sank deep into the base of his throat.

His eyes went wide, mouth dropping open and shut soundlessly as the warm rush of blood spilled over my hand and down my front. He slumped forward, losing strength in his legs, and before he collapsed completely, I shuffled him toward the entrance of an alley, giggling seductively so any onlookers might think we were just enamored lovers stealing a few moments of privacy.

Once cloaked in shadow, I dropped my arms and let him crumple to the ground. The red sand consumed the crimson puddle rapidly growing around him with each moment that passed. His dark eyes were frantic, hands scrambling toward me as if I would help him. Instead, I placed a boot on his chest and leaned low enough that he could see the apathy in my expression.

"I'm *never* going back," I said coldly. Then the light in his eyes went dim and his arm went still before falling lifeless to the sand.

I tried to pull the knife from his throat, twice, but it was wedged too deep and the hilt was too slick with his blood. Even bracing one foot against his chest couldn't dislodge it. My skin felt sticky now, as his blood started to dry on my hands. I wiped them off on his pants and found a bottle of water strapped to his belt. The son of a bitch forced rations on everyone else but got as much as he could guzzle down.

Looking down at my shirt, I swore. It was completely ruined. There was no way I could walk through the crowds unseen soaked in blood. Peeling it off as carefully as I could, I discarded it next to his prone form. My undershirt was much more revealing, but still covered my left arm and the ugly scar that marked me as a fugitive. I would miss the safety of hiding beneath my hood. Using the last of the man's water, I rubbed as much of the blood off my hands and neck as I could. After checking myself three times, I decided I couldn't get any cleaner.

Rummaging quickly through his pockets, I scoffed at what I found, which was surprisingly little. Three brass bits, a handful of water ration coupons, and a small vial of glowroot with its telltale iridescent blue light.

3

Slipping out of the alleyway as inconspicuously as possible, I kept my silent footfalls near the buildings, letting the darkness obscure me. I should give up now. I knew that. The blue-eyed stranger wasn't a priority, not when the tenuous safety I'd gathered around me had been shattered into pieces. I had a choice to make: look for my mark or get off the streets.

I'd be damned if I lost a knife and my favorite shirt for nothing.

Quickening my pace, I found myself back near the well as I crossed into the red district. Whores with their signature red ribbon chokers perched on stoops, in varying states of undress. Everything in Vegas was for sale, if you knew where to look. I skittered around the lines of people, my hands finding the cool metal and ivory of a gun shoved in the back waistband of my shorts. The gun was dainty and only .22 caliber. An ornamental piece, with a carved ivory handle worn down with age. I knew each groove and line like the planes of my own face. Her name was Selene, and just like me, no matter how diminutive she might be, she was still deadly.

My mind flickered back to the man lying dead somewhere behind me. Maybe I felt bad about it once, the hustle, but that girl had been broken a long time ago.

Turning the corner, a strong gust of wind from a passing wagon startled me. As the dust settled, my eyes fixated on the visage of a man down the lane. A tall, blonde whore leaning alluringly against a post stole his attention, beckoning him forward. It struck me again how handsome he was, all six feet of him lithe muscle. From the width of his strong shoulders to the trimness of his hips. He dwarfed the whore in front of him, which meant he would tower over me.

He held his shoulders back with some internal confidence that leant a slick grace to his movements. I watched as he tipped his chin to the whore, letting her get a glimpse of those pretty blue eyes. He *knew* he was handsome. My mouth curled into a devious grin.

I bit my bottom lip, more curious now than I'd been before. This man was a mass of contradictions. He acted like he knew the hustle, how to con and manipulate; I recognized the signs. Yet, he held his bag in a way that left it exposed to pickpockets and got distracted too easily, as if he'd never had to worry about thieves before.

I had to know more. Get closer.

Taking a few confident steps forward, I nearly fell as the gnarled hand of an undesirable reached from the shadows to grip my ankle. I spared a glance at the woman, her face behind her cowl scarred beyond repair. Like a candle at the end of the night, her flesh looked like at one point it'd become liquid and dripped gruesomely down her face.

Gritting my teeth at the interruption, it was hard not to sympathize with her. Hell, it was hard to *look* at her. Digging into my pockets, I pulled out the water ration coupons and pressed them into her gnarled hand. Then, after a moment, I gave her the bottle of glowroot, too. If anyone deserved to forget for a time, it was her.

"Thhhhank you," she said, the words whistled on a labored breath.

Instead of answering her, I stepped far enough out of her reach that I could continue on my way. When I looked up again, my mark was nowhere to be found. I huffed, wondering why I was still stalking this man when I needed to get off the streets before I became a permanent resident. Like the man I killed. *Fuck this*, I thought to myself, whirling in the opposite direction, ready to head home.

Lightning-strike blue eyes.

Shock and delight warred for control within me, keeping me firmly rooted in place. There he was, less than twenty feet away and closing the distance; he'd flanked me. *He'd flanked me.* That meant he knew I'd been following him . . . but for how long? The possibility of him having known the entire time, leading me on this chase, thrilled me.

The whore from earlier didn't want to give him up so easily. She crossed the space to him, allowing the front of her dress to slip down and expose the swell of her breasts. Trailing her fingers over his forearm, she whispered something close to his ear. What the whore didn't realize yet was that I'd already won this game. His eyes never wavered from my face, a curious spark growing bright within his eyes as a triumphant smile spread wide on my mouth.

Seduction, my favorite weapon, has killed more men than guns ever have. This man, with all his sculpted beauty and countless dizzying contradictions, was *mine.* To tempt, to lure, even to kill . . . if it came to that.

The dust-laden breeze drifted towards me, and I tasted the sand on my tongue, the tang of mineral reminding me that after this I would have to leave. Out in the open expanse, away from the dying civilizations crumbling around me, I knew I'd be safe. For a while, at least. *One last hurrah.*

Slowly, I pushed the long locks of my pin-straight hair over my shoulders to show my face. Aware all the while that his eyes marked each movement. I knew I was beautiful.

Beauty was a weapon, *my* weapon, and I'd cut down more men than I cared to remember wielding it.

I walked toward him, cautiously, noting the nervous bob of his Adam's apple as the space between us began to disappear. My steps were long and lithe, a seductive swing to my hips. *Fifteen feet.* A warning trilled down my spine to stay away, that there was more to him than I could clearly discern. *Ten feet.* The danger forced my heart into a staccato rhythm that exhilarated me. *Five feet.* His eyes were more honest up close, the glint in them devoid of dark intention. That was surprisingly unexpected.

I turned from him then, a hard left, as if I'd never been walking to *him* at all. Twisting between people, I kept him in my periphery.

"Wait!" he called behind me, but I didn't. Instead, I let him chase me this time, twining through the crowds. I'd let him catch a flash of my thigh, a swish of my hips, or a sultry smile before disappearing around a corner or between a group of people.

I was the perfect contradiction to the wasteland surrounding us. My delicate skin, pale and unblemished beneath a shock of long, ink-black hair made my features seem almost doll-like. My body, perfectly on display in my tight undershirt and shorts, highlighted my legs and curves. Athletic, yet curvaceous enough to tempt men to their baser instincts, a hard balance to strike. I knew, intimately, that to this man I would look like a desert mirage made flesh.

Finally, I'd led him to the edge of the red district away from prying eyes. I glanced over my shoulder, halting his pursuit. His eyes flashed back in the direction of the well. Indecision flared bright in his blue eyes; would he follow, or let me get away again?

I faced him then, turning to stare at him plainly, tempting him away from the crowds. I gasped, his handsome face even more devastating up close. A shock of awareness shuddered down my spine. His keen eyes fell to my mouth where I bit my lip. The thrill of danger I'd felt earlier was palpable now, thudding into me with every rapid beat of my heart.

He stepped forward, the heat from his skin a living thing, wavering in the air between us. I assessed him quickly. Sun-darkened skin that ended at his sleeve line, calluses on his palms when he reached toward me. Both signs of hard labor and long hours outside . . . like on a *farm.* I blinked up at him in confusion. I'd never met a farmer before. Farmers stayed isolated near the northern borderlands, a thousand miles away.

*What the hell was he doing way down here?*

I took a step back, reconsidering my trap. He followed. I searched his body with my eyes, looking for the bulge of a knife or gun hidden somewhere. He'd studied me too, the flush on my cheeks, my rapid breaths, and with every evasion, his eyes darkened in desire as his want for me grew.

He weighed his options, his hot gaze lingering around the crescent of my lips, sliding gently down the elegant curve of my neck. Though there were feet between us, his eyes made my skin tighten as if he'd brushed a callused thumb across my skin. A shiver of pleasure forced its way up my spine.

I wouldn't let his pretty face distract me from my purpose. One last conquest. Then I could flee before my past caught up to me. Nodding, I beckoned him to follow me. The seductive smile on my lips spread wide over my face as I ducked around the corner of a building into a dark alleyway. *Here.* I would lay my trap here, away from prying eyes.

A breath. A moment. Then, he was there with me, and I wasn't alone anymore.

Lightning raced across my skin, and I tasted the metallic sting of electricity on my tongue as his eyes met mine. His were dark with lust that mirrored my own. It lanced up my spine and set my pulse pounding in my ears.

*"You're a woman now, Bonnie. You need to use what you have to lure them. Men want soft women, with curves to press into their hands; they want you to be small and enamored with them. Lure them that way, and we'll take care of the rest."* Jones's words rang through my memory, forcing a hitch into my step. I wasn't that girl anymore. I was in control here. No one else, just me. My mark faltered at the sight. This was it. If I didn't act now, this con would have been for nothing.

"We don't have to do any—"

I pressed a single finger to his lips to stop his words, shushing him sweetly. It was better not to know whatever he wanted to say. His lips were soft beneath my fingertip. He nipped at it playfully with his teeth. I pulled my finger back to my mouth and sucked it between my lips, tasting him on my tongue. The gesture seemed to break whatever tenuous hold kept his control leashed so tightly.

His arm snaked around my waist, pulling me close. My hands found purchase against his sun-darkened, taut skin. I shivered in his embrace, my heart hammering against my ribs. I folded into his arms gracefully, as if we were dance partners and we'd rehearsed this a thousand times before. Pushing roughly, I forced him into the stone wall at his back. My hands ran over his chest and down his thighs, searching for a weapon. They lingered greedily as I traced the midline of his jeans, feeling every hard inch of his straining cock for me and reveling in the smooth groan that explorative touch elicited from his open mouth.

I swallowed the sound.

He leaned down to kiss me, but I twisted my mouth away from him, a whore's trick. Instead, I brandished my neck, and he needed no further prompting. His mouth was hot on my skin, and the rasp of his stubbled cheek contrasted sharply with the softness of his lips. The sensation drove my pulse to a frenzied speed, and a whimper fell unbidden from my lips. Strong, calloused hands roamed low on my body, squeezing tight and startling me as I was forced onto my toes. Our hips ground together slowly and methodically, a steady rhythm of small motions meant to drive me insane. *Oh, it was working*. His teeth nipped at the skin of my collarbone, forcing my eyes to flutter open. When had I closed them?

His hands left my hips to slide the shoulder of my shirt over to expose more of my collarbone to his ravenous appetite. He dipped his head lower, his thumb tracing the hard point of my breast through my shirt while he showered my skin with scratchy kisses. A moan wrenched its way from deep in my gut, a husky, breathless noise more animal than human. *Wait*. The sound invigorated him, gave him confidence to continue. He pulled gently behind my knee and hooked one of my legs around his hip. One small change in position and now each of my soft curves was pressed intimately against the tall, hard length of his unyielding body. His blue eyes blazed in the dim light of the alley, reading something on my face that urged him on. *This was supposed to be my trap.*

His hands were buried in my hair now, a thumb tracing over my cheek to land on my bottom lip. I knew what he wanted. Parting my mouth, I wrapped my lips around the pad of his thumb, my tongue flicking against it before sucking softly. A deep thunderous sound rumbled through his chest to shake me down to my bones. His hand in my hair slid to the back of my head, pulling my mouth closer to his. He wanted me to kiss him. He wanted this to be more than a transaction. He wanted me to *want him back*.

I brushed my nose against his, and he stilled. All other motion and sensation forgotten as his eyes landed on my mouth, inching closer to his. I drank in the taste of his breath, a faint echo of the taste of his lips from before. My head tilted to the side, and he brushed the hair away from my face to see me more clearly as I angled toward him. He swallowed down whatever desperate words were on the tip of his tongue, and I took his chin in my hand, mouths open and millimeters apart.

*Click.*

His eyes widened as I pressed the cool steel of Selene to his temple. Shock and fury mingled in his expression until it almost hurt to look at him. *Almost.*

"Sorry pal, you aren't *that* lucky." My voice was more breathless than I meant for it to be. It took a moment to disentangle myself from how fully we'd been wrapped around each other during our embrace. "Do what I say and no one has to get hurt."

My legs trembled as I was forced to carry my full weight again. I slid the neck of my shirt back into place over my shoulder, hiding my skin. Schooling my features into an unreadable mask, I willed my heart to slow down.

Only I knew how shaken I was, how close I'd come to losing control. He stood to his full height, and it took all the strength in my bones to keep steady in the face of him. My gun stayed trained right between his eyes. He towered over me, all long and lean, the shadow of him blocking the scant light from the other end of the alley.

"Toss over the bag," I said, my voice hardened steel. No waver, no hitch, no sign of the fucking breathlessness that'd stolen my senses before. His eyes narrowed in a deep loathing that stung my pride more than I cared to admit. I leveled Selene and brought the hammer back, motioning for him to toss it quickly with a snap of my fingers. He hesitated again, and a cruel smile curled over my teeth.

"Don't pout," I said, earning another hard glare. "You just aren't my *type*. Now, toss it over or I'll put hot lead between those pretty blue eyes and you won't be anyone else's type either." He laughed at me, a short bitter sound. I didn't like it, as if he were laughing at *me* and not his own foolish hopes. Tossing the bag over, he gritted his teeth together, a muscle flexing in his jaw, and he bit back words I was sure burned hot on his tongue. I almost wished he'd say them, that I could hear the ugliness aloud.

*Whore. Thief. Tease. Bitch.*

I heard them all in my head anyway. His eyes were shiftier now, dulled with a predatory glint that reminded me of a mountain lion Jones and I hunted once. My motions were long and slow, keeping Selene trained on him as I slung his pack over my shoulder and backed towards the street.

"Well, it's been fun. Look me up if you're ever in Vegas again. We can *almost* fuck some more." He swore under his breath. A pang of disappointment drifted through my mind at the knowledge that I would never see him again. Just as swiftly as it'd come, it disappeared.

"Jesse?" The voice was small, scared. I whirled, flicking another hidden knife into my palm as a kid looked past me to the barely contained beast of a man held at bay by the vague threat of my tiny gun. *Fuck.* The kid's innocent face crumpled when he saw my knife, and the last thing I needed was some brat's wailing to bring the Crimson Fist down on us all.

"Who's the kid?" I asked through gritted teeth. My gun hand shook, and the echo of horrors in my past whispered towards me, threatening to swallow me whole.

"My brother," he answered, the words a barely veiled threat.

It was the first time I'd heard *Jesse* speak at normal volume; it was a deep sound. Pleasant. Like listening to the rush of water echoing in a canyon. Rough enough around the vowels to be distinctly masculine, but with an oddly calming effect lingering beneath. The kid was blocking my escape, and the longer I stood here indecisively, the more I put myself at risk.

"Motherfucker." I sheathed my knife and offered the kid a placating smile before tucking Selene into my waistband. I held my hands up, palms forward, in a gesture of peace. "Listen, stay off the strip and get outta town. Fast. Whatever you do, keep far away from anyone with a tattoo of a red fist." I pointed to my neck, still red from the attention his mouth had paid to the spot moments ago. "Here." *What was I doing?* He didn't seem to be listening to me, so I fisted my hand in the front of his shirt and pushed him against the wall. He bristled, his muscles bunching tight beneath his shirt.

"You'll get that kid killed if you don't listen. Red fist tattoos, stay *away* from them. Got it?" I didn't wait around to see if he would listen to me a second time. I scrambled back from him and shoved past the kid, ducking around a corner and trying to disappear into the crowd.

"Hey! You!" he shouted after me. Curious stares tracked me as I ran faster. The recognition was worse than anything else; if one of the Crimson Fist caught a good look at me, they'd bring me back to Jones. Or at least they'd try; I'd made my mind up long ago that they wouldn't take me alive. Seconds later, a hard fist yanked me forcefully back. I slammed into a hard wall of flesh, losing my balance. Another hard hand squeezed tight at my elbow, pulling me forward until Jesse's furious blue eyes bore down on me and all my protestations died on my lips.

## CHAPTER TWO

# JESSE

S TRIKING, DARK BLUE EYES stared at me with a mixture of hatred and surprise from beneath the woman's dark eyebrows. The moment lasted a lifetime, before she lowered her gaze to where my hand clenched her elbow. My white-knuckled grip released.

"I'll need my things back," I said, glaring down at her. From the moment I'd noticed the woman across the busy street, I had to find out more, had to know her. She was such a stark contrast to the women I knew. Dark hair and brows above arresting eyes that were a shape unlike any I'd ever seen. I wanted to immortalize the curves of them so I could carry them with me. Her skin reminded me of white sand like on the shores of the lake back home. Clearly, seeking her out had been a mistake.

"Not gonna happen," she said, scathingly. She turned to stalk away, but light glinted off of the weapon she'd just pressed to my head. I yanked the gun from her shorts, brandishing it. She wheeled around, animosity tinting her alluring eyes as she looked between me and the gun. It was a dainty thing, small in my hand. A .22 caliber that I might break if I wasn't careful. It may not have been the most effective weapon to take down a big predator, but it could end a life just the same. The woman straightened, her breasts straining against the front of her revealing shirt. She had a knife in her hand.

A choked sound came from near my elbow. *Harry. Fuck.* I'd almost forgotten he was with me. *Again.* Even after months of traveling, I still wasn't used to the responsibility of watching out for Harry like a parent instead of a brother.

The woman's eyes darkened beneath her deep-set brows; her eyes flashed to my brother and back to me again.

"You see him?" I asked. "I'm the only person in the world he's got, and I'll be damned if I let some two-bit charlatan be the reason he goes hungry." The smooth skin of her cheeks flushed, and her glare reappeared. Never before had someone looked upon me with such contempt. I was certain she hated me. Her gaze wavered as she looked at my younger brother.

"Even trade. My bag for your gun. Otherwise, this is mine," I said, checking the ammunition inside. When we fled from Montana three months ago, I didn't have a chance to bring a weapon. Her attention was almost obsessive as she watched me manipulate the gun.

"You really are clueless," she said, throwing a sarcastic smile at me.

Harry sniffed, a sure sign he was about to lose it. I stifled a sigh, steeling myself for yet another fit from a ten-year-old.

"You just had to go and take all of the fun out of my day, didn't you?" the woman asked, giving a sigh of her own.

Her beauty struck me again. The women in Montana certainly looked nothing like her. Most of them wore conservative clothing. They were fair-haired and fair-skinned. This woman was the opposite. From the tight shorts accentuating her ass, to how her breasts threatened to spill out of her thin shirt, she was different. Seeing her for the first time was like snow thawing after a harsh winter, when the world felt right again after so long of feeling wrong. She cocked her head to the side, brandishing her neck. A temptation. One that had nearly gotten me killed.

"Hand it over, farm *boy*," she said, venom dripping from each word. "Before you shoot something off you might need later." My grip tightened on the handle as she reached for the gun. I lifted it out of her reach, tipping my chin in defiance. I wasn't giving her a damn thing until I got the bag back. Pop taught me that any good poker player knew how to bluff. This woman had obviously never played poker before.

With a roll of her eyes, the woman tossed the bag into the dirt at my feet. She snapped her fingers impatiently. I handed her the gun and snatched the bag up, intent on getting the fuck out of Vegas. We should have never come here. When I'd seen the sign for Vegas, my father's voice had come to mind.

*If you ever have the chance to go to Vegas, Jesse, go. Some of the best times I had were with the guys, playing poker for hours and winning almost every time.*

I didn't know what I expected to find in Vegas, but being robbed and nearly killed wasn't it.

Harry sobbed, pulling me out of my thoughts. The woman eyed him curiously, glancing between us before she put a hand on his shoulder and crouched down to his height.

"Don't cry, kid," she said. Her eyes were alert as she gazed down the street behind me. She let out a defeated sigh, turning back to my brother. "Have you ever had buffalo stew?"

"Who are you?" Harry asked. He took a loud, steadying breath. I grabbed his arm and tugged him away from the woman. He glared at me, shaking me off.

"Bonnie," the woman said, meeting my gaze. Curiosity barely veiled the distrust reflected back at me. "When was the last time y'all ate?"

When my brother looked up at me, I shook my head. We couldn't trust her. This . . . *Bonnie*. She was like a coral snake: beautiful, but deadly.

"Days ago," Harry said, defiance in his eyes as he turned to her. Bonnie didn't respond. Instead, she stared down the road behind me, swearing beneath her breath.

"C'mon, we need to get off the street," she said, putting an arm around my brother's shoulders and steering him away.

When I turned to find what she'd cursed at, half a dozen men brandishing red fist tattoos and guns were thirty feet away, harassing a woman who carried a small bundle. While I didn't trust Bonnie, I didn't know that I could risk our lives running into the men she warned me about.

"We're not going with you," I said, once again reaching for Harry. He twisted away from me.

A scream stole my attention. I turned, watching as one of the men with a red fist tattoo ripped the bundle from the woman's hands. The blankets fell away. A baby. The woman reached for the child, only for one of the men to press a revolver to her forehead. I grabbed Harry as a shot rang out, shielding him from the scene. Before the woman's body crumpled to the ground, people descended on her like buzzards to carrion.

"Suit yourself, pretty boy." Bonnie started to turn but froze mid-step. Her eyes widened; tension snapped her spine straight. She grabbed Harry by the arm. "Change of plans. They saw us. You're coming with me. Now. Keep up." Before I could argue, she elbowed a man out of the way and pressed forward, glancing over her shoulder every few seconds. I looked behind us to find the threat, but couldn't see the men through the crowded street.

Eventually her steps slowed. I trailed a few feet behind them. I was completely out of my element. Vegas was the first city we'd come across. Bonnie certainly seemed right at home as she navigated us through the busy streets. Every now and then, I'd catch her glancing over her shoulder. Sometimes she'd look at me, her eyes trailing the length of my body. Other times, she stared past me, eyes darting wildly as she inspected our surroundings.

On our journey south, we'd traveled inside the backs of farmers' wagons and on foot. Sometimes, people took pity on us and allowed us to sleep in their barns. So far, Vegas was the busiest place we'd been. Half-destroyed buildings lined the concrete street. Dust kicked up around us, as though the desert were trying to reclaim the city. A man was thrown into the street in front of us from a building with a big sign that said *Casino!* Women dressed in shiny, scant bits of brightly colored fabric and wearing feather head-dresses gawked at the man as he climbed to his feet and scampered away.

My brother peppered her with questions about the city and its people.

"Ooh! What's that?" Harry asked, pointing to a woman leaned up against the side of the building. She had a thick red ribbon tied around her neck. Her cleavage nearly spilled out of the confines of her dress.

"Kid, you shouldn't point at people," Bonnie said, glancing back at me. Our eyes met. For a moment, I thought I saw a hint of desire. Then it passed, and she turned away again. I scanned the curves of her body, trailing from the neck I'd kissed down to the hips I wanted to clutch again. Lust flared in my stomach, threatening to boil to the surface. I had to stop looking at her. She steered my brother toward a big, rusty metal building with the word *bar* spray-painted on the side. A single sign hung above the door.

"Who names a bar in the desert the Drowning Camel?" I asked, incredulous. She didn't acknowledge me. Instead, she shoved open the door. A bell rang as we entered. A half-stocked bar lined the back wall. Half-a-dozen tables dotted the room, occupied by a handful of people. I followed closely behind my brother, noting that everywhere Bonnie walked, the stares of the bar's patrons followed her. Some gawked, but most only tipped their hats or raised their drinks in her direction. As if they knew her.

"Where are we?" I asked. With a mixture of contempt and amusement on her face, Bonnie guided my brother onto a bar stool.

"Home, sweet home," she said, flashing a smile as she settled on the stool beside my brother.

What kind of woman called a bar home? Then again, Bonnie wasn't like other women. She leaned over the bar, giving me a perfect view of her ass. It'd felt soft beneath my hand in that alley. I appreciated the view until I heard two glasses clink together. A loud *thunk* sounded as Bonnie set a half-filled bottle of whiskey on the bar. She glanced toward me, pouring two fingers of the amber liquid into a glass.

"You gonna sit down or are you gonna stare at my ass all day?" she asked, lifting an eyebrow. She poured the second glass and shoved it in front of the empty stool next to her. A man walked out from the back, eyes trained on Bonnie. He towered over the bar, his girth almost as great as his height. There were tattoos up and down his amber skin. I probably should have feared him. The man grabbed the whiskey bottle and set it back behind the bar.

"Murph," Bonnie said. "Can you get Beck to bring a bowl of stew for the kid?" She lifted her whiskey, but before she could take a drink, she stopped to stare at the man. He crossed his arms, narrowing his eyes at her. He looked at Harry, then me, then back to Bonnie.

"You wanna tell me about this?" he asked, slapping down what looked like a poster on the bar's surface. Tension seized her shoulders, but she shook it off quickly.

"It's not a very good likeness. They can't seem to get my eyes right," Bonnie said, knocking back the rest of her drink. She leaned over the bar once more and grabbed the whiskey to pour herself another glass. I reached around her to grab the sign.

*Wanted. Alive. Bonnie.* There was a roughly sketched portrait of the woman beside me. I could have drawn her better than that. Beneath that was a list of crimes. *Wanted in connection to acts of domestic terrorism, inciting a riot, and the unlawful freeing of slaves. Suspected in no less than three murders.* My eyes were wide in shock. How could this little woman have done all of these things? This must have been what she was running from in the streets. There was a hefty reward for her to be taken in alive. Five hundred bits of silver.

Murph let out an exasperated huff. He stared at Bonnie with incredulous eyes. I grabbed my drink and tipped it back, reveling in the burn of the whiskey as it ran down my throat. What a day. My brother reached over, snatching the poster out of my hand.

"What's domestic terrorism?" Harry asked.

"It's what you get for being a smartass with a gun," Murph said, staring pointedly at Bonnie. She rolled her eyes and poured me another drink.

"Jealous, Murph?" she asked, smirking at the man.

"Do you know what this means? Not just for you, but for Beck's safety," he said. "If *he* finds her—" The man's voice broke suddenly. Tension filled the air, snapping tight between them. I dared to glance at Bonnie; she glared at Murph.

"If who finds her?" I asked.

"None of your fuckin' business," Bonnie said. Her shoulders relaxed and she leaned against the front edge of the bar, her eyes softening as she looked at Murph. "Nothing's gonna happen to her."

"Yeah, except you're gonna break her heart," Murph said harshly. Then, as if realizing his tone, he lowered his eyes.

"She knew I was gonna have to leave. It just has to be sooner than we thought," she said, running a finger over the lip of her glass. The man looked at me. I ignored him, instead focusing intently on my whiskey.

"Of all the guys you've brought back here, they never had a kid with them before. What's up with that?" Murph's eyes shifted to my brother.

"Just go get the fucking stew!" Bonnie's cheeks flushed. I lifted my glass to my lips to busy my hands as he walked away. *Of all the guys.* Was I just the latest in a string of cons? We sat in silence for a moment before she turned to me. The intensity of her gaze made the hair on the back of my neck tingle. I took my time to sip the whiskey. She still stared at me as I lowered the glass to the bar. I turned to her.

"What?" I asked, quirking an eyebrow. My eyes fell to Bonnie's bottom lip, which she worried between her teeth. I wanted to taste that lip. I blinked, ignoring the tightness in my jeans.

"So, Jesse, from some distant farm who doesn't know how to take the safety off when he's threatening someone with their own gun, where ya headin'?" she asked. Her blue eyes brightened as she poured another finger of whiskey into my glass.

"Why do you care?" I asked before knocking back my drink. I stared back at her intense gaze. After a moment, she gave an exasperated sigh and ran a hand through her dark hair. I imagined running my fingers through the long strands again.

"I'm just tryin' to figure you out," she said.

"Why?" I asked. At the same time, a woman walked out from behind the bar. She was shorter than my brother. Her long, straight black hair grayed at her temples. Lines around her eyes and mouth revealed her age. She fussed over Harry in a language I didn't recognize. Then she turned to Bonnie and took the younger woman's face in her hands.

"C'mon, Beck," Bonnie said, shaking her off half-heartedly.

"I saw the posters. I know Murph worries, but we can keep you hidden—"

"No. Absolutely not," she said, shaking her head. Beck's eyes glistened as she looked over Bonnie's face. I felt like I shouldn't be a part of this conversation, as though it were a tender moment not meant for my prying eyes.

"Please, Little Wolf," Beck said, putting her hands on Bonnie's arms. "Let me do this for you. After everything you did for me—"

"I'm not anyone's hero," Bonnie said sharply, cutting her off. She pulled out of the older woman's grip. "You wanna pay me back? Don't get caught. Or if you do, make sure Murph blows his fucking face off." Her eyes slid to me and she settled back on her stool. I watched Beck disappear behind the bar. Bonnie's eyes felt like daggers as she once again stared at me.

"Enlighten me, then," I said after a long moment, reaching across her for the whiskey bottle. My arm brushed against her breasts as I brought it in front of me. My head was already light from the drink. The scrutiny of her gaze made me nervous. I refilled my glass and topped hers off. Then I set the bottle down and stared straight back at her. "What have you figured out about me?"

"Farm *boy*," she said, her blue eyes piercing into the depths of me. I bristled at *boy*. She seemed quite fond of the word. "That's obvious by the calluses on your hands and the way your tan ends at your shoulders. You spend long hours outside." She paused to glance at my brother before looking back to me. "You've been on the road now for months, judging from the state of your boots. You didn't leave with much, and you've been giving up what little food you've been able to scavenge to the kid. Your jeans are a little too loose." The memory of her hands running along the front of my jeans made me shift uncomfortably on my stool. No woman had ever affected me like this before.

"One of your canteens has a leak," she continued. "Your chapped lips are a dead giveaway." Bonnie's gaze fell to my mouth. Tension snapped tight between us. "I make my living sizing people up. Assumptions have kept me alive so far. It's not personal."

I snorted derisively. "Sure seemed personal in that alleyway," I said. It'd be a lie if I didn't acknowledge that she was the most beautiful woman I'd ever seen. My anger at her wasn't just about being robbed. It was that she used her beauty to play me like an instrument. I'd fallen right into her trap, all because of her pretty face. "Doesn't seem much like living to me."

"It's not. It's surviving. And I'm good at it," she said.

"Could have fooled me," I remarked. She turned on her stool to face me fully.

"Look, I'm no angel, and I don't pretend to be. I'll do whatever it takes so I don't end up in the ground like my mom," she said.

It seemed we had something in common. I knew what it was like having dead parents.

My eyes trailed from the anger written on her face down the curve of her cheek and past her lips. Her thin shirt accentuated her soft curves and breasts. A spot of red dotted the hem of it. *Suspected in no less than three murders.* I opened my mouth to ask her about it, but my brother cut me off.

"This is really good," Harry said. Bonnie's features softened as she turned to face him.

"Beck's a good cook," she said, reaching over to ruffle his hair.

"What's in it anyway?" I asked. I'd learned how hard meat was to come by during our travels. We were luckier than most back home because we raised our own livestock. Bonnie snorted into her glass.

"Whatever Beck could catch this morning," she said, amusement in her eyes.

"Why're you helping us?" Harry asked through a mouthful of stew.

"What can I say? I'm a sucker for a pretty face, handsome," Bonnie said. If that were true, she wouldn't have pulled a gun on me in that alleyway. I scowled into my glass. "How old are you anyway, kid?"

"Ten," Harry said with a sheepish grin. She ruffled his hair again. Then she turned to me and leaned close.

"Look," she said. Heat radiated off of her. "I just wanted to get the kid off the strip. You're not from here, and it's a dangerous place. Not everyone has someone looking out for them." Her breath was hot on my cheek. A shiver went up my spine as desire flared to life in my belly once more. I balled my hand into a fist at my side to stop myself from doing something stupid.

"I'm not sure I want a murderer looking out for us," I said, turning my attention to the bloodstain on the hem of her shirt. "I'm guessing you're responsible for no less than *four* as of today."

Bonnie looked down, pulling at her shirt to see the spot. I caught a glimpse of the smooth skin of her stomach. I swallowed around the lump in my throat, then took a deep pull from my glass.

"That Crimson Fist motherfucker ruined *two* of my favorite shirts today!" Bonnie groaned and stood. Her arm brushed against mine. She smirked, then leaned close. "For the record, it was nice robbing you, farm boy." Then she pressed her lips to my cheek. I felt the softness and heat of them as she stalked away. Her hips swayed as she moved behind the bar. Instead of disappearing as Murph had, she climbed a ladder into a small loft just out of sight.

Harry belched, setting down his glass of water. His eyes were full of amusement when I looked at him. We needed to go. Before I did something stupid. I knocked back the rest of my whiskey.

"Are you ready?" I asked Harry, slipping onto Bonnie's barstool. My vision blurred around the edges as I tried to focus on him.

"What about her?" he asked, glancing toward the ladder behind the bar.

"She's not coming. Just us," I said.

"Why not?"

"She's trouble," I bristled. He looked up at me with sadness in his eyes. I hadn't realized how dark my tone was. I should apologize. Bonnie had clawed her way beneath my skin, and he was taking the brunt of my frustration.

"I like her. She knows her way around. She could help us find Mom and Pop," he said. A rush of guilt flooded my chest at the hope in his voice. The whiskey on my tongue soured.

"What happened to bro-time?" I asked, forcing a smile. "You and me, the great outdoors—"

"I'd like to be able to eat every day," he said. *Ouch.* Even though his words weren't malicious, having a ten-year-old point out your flaws felt like a hot knife to the balls. I stared at the gnarled surface of the bar, trying to force my insecurities back down. It wasn't Harry's fault. I glanced around the room, watching as a man shuffled a deck of cards. My hands flexed on the bar in front of me.

Then, like an idiot, I looked toward the loft. Bonnie. Her bare back faced me. Long, thin marks crisscrossed the right side of her ribs. I couldn't tell if it was a tattoo or something else, something worse. She slid on another shirt, this one less revealing, then disappeared just beyond my line of vision.

The low din of conversation ceased suddenly. The bell at the door rang. Men who'd been talking in boisterous voices went silent. A single mug thudded on a wooden table.

Bonnie came into view once more, just around the edge of the loft wall. Her eyes widened and her shoulders tensed. Fear. She disappeared again as loud stomps followed by the telltale jingle of boot spurs approached.

A young man dressed in a black vest and white shirt appeared behind the bar. The newcomer stopped beside me. He towered as he looked down at me over a pair of dusty aviator sunglasses. He was a beefy man, with tan skin and an ugly scar that crossed over one eye. He had a crooked nose, as though he'd been in one too many bar fights. He tipped his black cowboy hat back as the bartender poured him a shot.

"You ain't seen this girl 'round here, have you?" the man asked, unfolding a wanted poster identical to the one on the bar next to Harry. The page was creased, as though he'd folded and unfolded it a hundred times. I took a modest sip of whiskey before meeting his gaze again. Something about him unnerved me, as though danger radiated from the man in waves. The fear I'd seen in Bonnie's eyes told me that she knew him.

"Depends. How accurate is this drawing?" I asked, pointing to the picture of Bonnie.

"Mostly right. Her eyes are blue, and she's got a large scar on her left arm," he said, lips curling sadistically. He ordered another shot and knocked it back. I caught sight of a tattoo on his neck, a pointed flower in the place where others had red fists.

"How old is she?" I asked. The man regarded me for a moment.

"Best guess . . . nineteen. Who's the kid?" he asked. I glanced at Harry, whose skin was pale. He sat ramrod straight on his barstool. I leaned forward, blocking the man's view.

"Some stray I picked up on the street. Kid was hungry," I lied.

"Well, ain't you a just a goddamn bleedin' heart?" he asked, sarcasm heavy on his tongue. I chuckled. The sound rumbled deep in my chest as I thought of Bonnie. It would be easy to turn her over to him. Five hundred silver bits was a *lot* of money. The purse Mom had given us was lighter than when we left Montana. Turning her over might help my ruined pride. I glanced back to the loft.

Bonnie peered around the wall, her fingertips barely visible. Her eyes were wide. I imagined hearing her pretty voice begging me *not* to do it. I turned my attention back to my drink.

"What are you going to do with the money when you catch her?" I asked.

"Money? Nah. I'm gonna show her *exactly* what happens when a woman disobeys," he said. His mouth curled into a sadistic grin.

I knew enough to understand men like him. No one, not even a murderer and thief, deserved to be raped.

"You know, I think I saw her," I said. He turned his attention to me, eyes narrowing in suspicion. A small crash sounded from Bonnie's direction. The man's eyes flickered toward the sound.

"Had a small handgun. A .22?" I asked, stealing his attention back.

"That's right. Boss is wantin' that gun back. Who're you?"

"Jesse. This .22, did it have an ivory handle?"

"If there's somethin' you ain't telling me—" he said.

"Oh no," I said, chuckling beneath my breath. "I saw her preoccupied with some man in an alleyway earlier." The dark expression on the man's face twisted into something wild and feral.

"Preoccupied?" he asked.

"They were . . . *close*," I said, cocking my head toward my brother, as if to say I didn't want to go into detail with him next to me.

"What'd he look like?" the man's fingers twitched toward the holster on his belt. I shrugged, taking a casual sip of my drink. I gripped the glass tight to keep the man from seeing my hands shake.

"Young guy, lanky, maybe six feet tall? One look at him and you could tell he wasn't a local," I said. "I heard her say something to him though. Something about going north, maybe? I was too busy getting ripped off by a whore on the corner." I shrugged, purposefully looking away to signal the end of the conversation.

"I'll check with the boss," the man murmured. He knocked back the shot and threw a roughly cut brass bit on the counter. He turned to me, sticking out a hand. I considered the action for a moment. I took it. He gripped my hand hard, making me cringe and bite back a cry of pain. He pulled me menacingly close, his rancid breath on my face.

"Most people call me Sixgun," he said.

I didn't expect to be threatened by a gun twice today.

## CHAPTER THREE

# BONNIE

*M*OST PEOPLE CALL ME *Sixgun.*

No, they didn't. Most people called him a monster. Evil hides behind normal faces. Sixgun Ellis's face might be ugly and old, but lurking somewhere within the dark recess of his fucked up mind was the kind of evil that left you defenseless against it.

*He was here to bring me back.*

I'd like to say I was afraid, because being afraid meant my mind was focused on survival. I was numb, as if the inevitable dread of this moment had marinated in my bones. In my mind's eye I saw it all clearly, each move and counter move. Jesse, the man I robbed and humiliated, would stretch out this tentative safety just long enough for me to think I'd get away. Then, inevitably, the lure of money and vengeance would have him call Sixgun back. Then that *monster* would drag me out of this loft and make me pray for death.

I contemplated the gun in my hand. Quick, efficient, *easy.* It would be so easy to pull the trigger and deny Sixgun his prey. I closed my eyes, back pressed firmly against the wall that kept me out of sight, Selene white-knuckled in my fist.

"You wouldn't be lyin' to me would ya?" Sixgun asked menacingly. Here it was, the moment of truth, when an unassuming farm boy showed his true colors. I took a steadying breath and put the barrel of the gun in my mouth, the tang of metal on my tongue.

"Not sure why I would. Just walk a few blocks down towards the well. I'm sure there are others who saw her. She wasn't exactly *subtle*, if you know what I mean." Jesse's lie was easy and confident. My eyes opened at his words.

*He lied for me.*

I peered around the corner to stare down at him from my hiding place. I drank in every detail. His shoulders were relaxed, his expression casually disinterested. He was a world class liar, no hint of deception to be found. Sixgun must've thought the same; he grunted in acknowledgement and turned back to the liquor in front of him.

"I don't like liars; you better not be one," Sixgun threatened. Jesse's stare hardened in the outlaw's direction, his jaw set firmly.

"Duly noted," he said before Sixgun shoved off from the bar and sauntered out, the noise returning in a riot of sound the moment the door clanged shut.

My mind buzzed as I looked down at the gun still in my hand. *He lied for me.* Flicking the safety on, I grabbed my pack and a few things from my makeshift room in the loft before swinging my legs out and dropping heavily onto the floor. *I was alive, because he lied for me.*

I couldn't seem to grasp the idea that a stranger I'd *robbed* made the decision to save my life. Fear barreled into me as the shock receded. We had to get the fuck out of here. *Now.*

My pulse pounded hot at my neck and in my ears. There was no time for hesitation. Springing into action, I marched towards Jesse and the kid, reluctantly nodding in appreciation as I slammed my fist on the bar twice. My signal to Murph that Sixgun was gone.

I shoved Selene into Jesse's hand and jerked my head to the side, a clear indication that he was supposed to follow me. He stood there dumbly for a moment before getting the hint and scrambling after me as I crossed behind the bar and around a corner.

"Stay here for a second," I said quickly. I climbed the short ladder to my room, reaching into the small crawl space where I'd been sleeping and pulling down my bedding. It was thin but mostly intact, and I rolled it quickly, tying it down to my pack.

"Look, Bonnie, we have to go—"

"Are you stupid?" I asked bluntly, watching the muscle in his jaw flex with the force of his clenched teeth. "You can't just leave; he's probably watching that entrance." I opened my pack and tried to check a list of essentials in my mind. Compass. Map. Flask. Med kit. Rations. My hand wrapped around the cool metal of the M9 at the bottom.

A beretta, military issue from before the Culling. Much deadlier than the dainty Selene I'd entrusted Jesse with. Selene could scare people, but she wasn't much use in a firefight. This gun had seen deserts around the world and still looked like sleek, black death. I chambered a bullet with a noticeable *clack, clack* and tucked it into my waistband. I tried not to overthink why having it on me spread warmth to my fingers and stilled the slight tremor in my hand.

"We're just going to take our chances on the main road. I mean, he wasn't looking for *us*, anyway." Jesse said, eyeing the new weapon warily. I rolled my eyes and tossed my hair over one shoulder.

"Kid, did you hear the dumb shit your brother just said?" I asked, turning my attention to the rapt ten-year-old who'd been watching my every action obsessively. "Repeat after me: Never. Take. The. Main. Road." I punctuated each word as Jesse's glare hardened. I swung my head back in his direction with a mocking smile. "Besides the fact that there are *three* gangs operating out of the strip who monitor the main roads for easy marks, like you, that Crimson Fist goon saw you with me on the street. You won't make it out of Vegas alive if you do that."

He bit his lip, hard, with the force of shackling the unkind words in his furious eyes. Maybe part of me just *really* wanted to see the sanctimonious farm boy shed his saintly manners. I sighed and put a hand on his chest before I even thought about it. It was just like in the alleyway. A shock of desire thudded into me like a hammer at the contact.

"I can admit," I said begrudgingly, "that I might have been wrong about you." I dropped my hand from his chest and lowered onto my knee in front of the kid, unhooking the knife from my belt. He scoffed behind me.

"I figure I was right about you." His words were hard and stung more than they should have. A tense silence descended between us before his voice broke through. "If we can't go out the front or on the main roads, how are we supposed to get out of here?" I snapped the knife onto the kid's belt. His eyes brightened with the small act of trust. I stood tall, shaking off the biting insult.

"Kid?" I asked, eyes trained on Jesse. The kid squeaked in response, startled by being called into the conversation. I held my hand out to him. "Give me the leaking canteen." He fumbled with the strap around his chest and shoved it over his head, handing over a canteen with a leak high up on it. The metal was too bent and compromised to mend, so I tossed it across the room into a barrel Murph used as a garbage container. Jesse made a strangled noise and lurched towards the steel barrel.

"Leave it," I said as his furious blue eyes blazed at me from across the room. "I have a better one to replace it with."

"Why would you do that?" He crossed his arms over his chest in defiance.

"Because I'm taking you with me."

His eyebrows rose so high they disappeared into his sandy hair. Heat crept up my neck as I remembered how his lips had felt on my skin. "Or you're taking me with you. Either way, we're sticking together and getting the fuck outta Vegas. How's that sound?" His arms dropped noncommittally to his sides, and he let out an aggravated sigh I took to mean he was on board with the plan. However begrudgingly.

"Murph! Beck!" I called again, turning back towards the bar, where they were gathering as many supplies as they could possibly give. It was too much. Beck walked forward with tears in her eyes.

"Please don't leave again, Bonnie," she said, sniffling and wrapping her arms around me in a crushing embrace. I twisted myself out of her grasp a moment later, no good with the sentimental stuff.

"Here, it's not much. I'll pay you back for the water rations somehow," I said, pressing the few brass bits into her hand and digging in my pack for a wad of crumpled ration coupons. Not nearly as many as she'd sacrificed for me. Taking the extra pack Murph handed to me, I began to stuff supplies in. As many as I thought Jesse could feasibly carry.

"Keep out of sight until he comes after me, a week or two at least." My words were directed at Murph, who nodded solemnly.

"I owe you, my li—"

I cut her off. "You don't owe me anything." Beck got overly emotional at times. "The supplies are enough."

I handed the loaded pack to Jesse. It was infuriating to see how easily he slung it over one shoulder and carried the load. She began to cry softly, wiping at her cheeks as I ignored her sorrow. Jesse's eyebrows knit together, trying to reconcile Beck's attachment to me, or maybe my cold, disaffected attitude. Either way, I was leaving, and I wouldn't be looking back. I never looked back.

True to my word, a moment later I handed Jesse a full canteen. This one, leak free. He looked at it before securing it to his new pack with an odd expression on his face. There was an echo of the attraction from that alleyway in his eyes now. As if he saw the mirage instead of the woman for a moment before it fell away again and he remembered he hated me.

"Why did you rob me when you have all these supplies?" he asked, but I had no intention of answering that question. I gave him a disarming grin and pulled the M9 out from my waistband.

"You ready?"

He held up Selene unenthusiastically and followed me out through the kitchen to the back door. The kid was between us, smiling so wide it was a wonder his face didn't break in half. I cleared the area, the M9 held confidently in front of me as we exited into an alleyway, not unlike *our* alleyway from earlier. I wanted to spare a quick glance at Jesse but decided it was probably better if I didn't. As we crossed the alleyway, I looked down at the kid and really assessed him for the first time. He was pretty young to have already had a run-in with a guy like Sixgun.

"Hey, kid, you scared?" I asked him, hoping he was tougher than he'd looked earlier today. He shook his head but wouldn't meet my eyes. I stopped and pulled his chin up until he was forced to look at me dead-on.

"Is that man going to hurt Jesse?" he asked. His eyes were wide and more innocent than I'd ever been. An ache for the little girl I was so long ago started throbbing in my chest. I lowered myself to his level again and stared him down. Kids appreciate honesty, or at least I used to when I was one.

"No one is gonna hurt you or Jesse, not while I'm around. Got it?" I said. He nodded, looking more sure of himself already. Standing back up I took a moment to adjust the strap on my pack and beat the ravenous memories away before they swallowed me whole. I didn't have time to get distracted by things I couldn't change.

"You get scared, grip the handle of that knife. When we get outta here, I'll show you how to shoot a gun so you won't ever be scared again," I promised. His smile was blinding.

It'd worked well enough for me anyway.

"Where are we going, Bonnie?" Jesse asked, his oddly calming voice grounding me to the moment. He said my name a lot now that he knew it. As if he were testing it out on his tongue. I wouldn't admit how much I liked that.

"To get horses," I said, my voice clipped.

"Well, where are the horses?" he retorted, just as clipped.

"Close," I said, smiling at him. The attraction I'd felt for him earlier in the alleyway hadn't subsided as I'd thought it might. In fact, the more time I spent with him, the stronger it grew. Maybe if he was lucky, I'd give him a roll in the hay before sending him off into the sunset. Glancing over and watching him glower at Selene, I decided probably not.

"Harry's not going anywhere until I know what we're walking into," he said, the stern expression out of place on his handsome face. My brows furrowed deep as I looked over the kid. He had a uniquely sunny disposition, oppositional to my own, but he definitely didn't look like a *Harry*.

"What kind of name is that for a kid?" I asked, unable to mask the disgust in my tone. "I'm sticking with 'The Kid.'" I blew a wayward strand of hair from my eyes before motioning towards where the alley met the street. It was busy, but the congestion of people had slowed considerably from earlier. Still, a few men milled about, their conversation too muffled to make out. We'd be more visible in the open.

"The stables are just there." I pointed to the building. From the front it didn't look like much: a large sliding door that was more rust than aluminum at this point and the hint of a faded number seven. Ironic, as it didn't seem that the place had been particularly lucky.

"How are we *getting* these horses?" Jesse asked, his tone pointed. I scowled in his direction and shrugged.

"You could just try to outrun Sixgun on foot instead, since you don't like my plan," I said, too sweetly. He didn't respond.

"Well?" I asked, taking sick pleasure in watching him run frustrated hands through that sandy hair of his. Briefly I wondered what he would do if I ran my fingers through his sun streaked locks. Stamping down the distracting thoughts, I refocused on our goal. He waved me forward, the gesture overly wide and sarcastic. It was time to get the fuck out of Dodge before my past caught up with me.

My hands were sweaty, and I wiped them on my shorts. Running every scenario through in my mind, I shifted my weight on my feet somewhat nervously. Jesse fiddled with a ring on his finger, and I could tell he felt it too. A sweet tension in the air indicating that danger was present. Without any indication, we both leapt into action at the same time, rushing forward through the busy street and dodging wagons and large groups, The Kid dragged behind Jesse by a hard grip the former had on his little arm. In no time at all, we burst through the door, and I swung it shut, flicking the lock closed before facing the blustery face of the heavyset man behind the counter.

"What the hell do you think you're doing, bustin' in here like that!" he shouted, his face ruddier the more he yelled. A brief touch to Jesse's forearm was all it took for him to understand my simple command. *Wait here, I'll take care of this.* He just held The Kid back with an outstretched arm as I turned to the man behind the counter, a familiar swing to my steps that showed off my hips as I approached. I bit my bottom lip and settled a pouty expression on my face as I leaned over the counter, letting him get a good, long look down my top.

The idiot liked the view so much, it was easy enough to pull the M9 from my waistband and press it to his temple. He made a startled sound that was something between a squeak and a wail but reminded me distinctly of a squalling piglet. I brought my face close to his, eyes hard, and spoke softly as if I were trying to ease his worries.

"I know who you've been selling to," I said, watching his eyes widen in horror.

"I-it's you! From the posters," he stammered, recognition settling into the corners of his scowl. My smile was eerily detached; it was sick how much I liked the fear on his face.

"If I hear that you've sold so much as a horseshoe to the slavers again, you'll *wish* I killed you. Got it?"

He nodded furiously, but I didn't trust anyone, much less a piece of shit like this guy. I brought my gun down hard, the satisfying thud against his skull reverberating up my arm. He crashed to the straw-covered floor, his mass of flesh jiggling before he lay still, conveniently hidden from view behind the counter. Jesse and The Kid stared at me, scandalized.

"What?" I asked defensively. "You act like this should be a surprise or something."

Jesse chuckled, as if he saw me clearly now. Shame like thick smoke swirled around my skin. Instead of responding, I turned towards the rows of stables and began to look through the horses. They were all the finest quality, well-fed, long-limbed, energetic. Satisfaction pulsed deep as I thought about stealing from this man who equipped slavers in the area. I tossed my pack to the dusty floor at my feet, assessing the options. We'd need horses that were fast, but more importantly, horses used to desert conditions. Then I spied her, tossing her head defiantly in her stall. A gray paint mare who danced on her feet as I approached. She had a wildness inside of her that I admired immediately.

I stared her down for a moment, and she came closer, shoving her nose into my hand and demanding a scratch. Just like that, she was mine. I pressed my face into her neck and let her nuzzle me, drinking in the warm animal scent of her. She started prancing again, and I knew what she wanted right away. To stretch those long legs out across the open desert. The same desire passed through me, to be out of this suffocating city and rushing across the vastness of the world.

"Can I name her?" The Kid asked beside me, though I wasn't sure when he'd gotten there. I stepped back to find her tack, allowing him to stroke her long muzzle.

"Sure," I said, forcing myself not to smile. "But it'll have to wait until we're on our way." He nodded, not paying attention to me at all. I couldn't blame him for being fascinated by the mustang. She was beautiful. He wandered down the stalls for a while, staring at the horses in each one before returning to his brother's side.

"What about the other ones?" he asked. Jesse ignored him and kept gathering the tack he would need.

"Jesse, what about the other horses?" He tried again. "Jesse!"

"Not now, Harry. Just let me finish this," Jesse snapped, frustrated. The Kid grumbled before crossing to me. I paused and gave him my full attention as he reached my side.

"What about the rest of them?" he asked, and I looked down the long rows of horses. Some stamping impatiently, others nickering or tossing their heads. All of them, like my mustang, caged against their will and longing to be set free. I breathed out an ironic laugh. I guess sometimes it took a precocious kid saying something obvious to see what was right in front of you.

"You're a genius, Kid. You know that?" I asked, ruffling his hair affectionately. "Start unlocking the stall doors while I tack this one. We'll use their escape as a distraction." He grinned wide, running to the end of the row and beginning to unlock stable doors as quick as his feet would carry him. Leading my mustang out of her stall, I started saddling her, my movements mechanical. From the corner of my eye, I noticed Jesse doing the same.

The stallion he chose was a rust color, nearly four hands higher than mine. A massive creature that I worried may not fare well in the harsh climate, but I held my tongue. The corded muscles along his flank shifted with his movement, glinting like copper in the scant light. My hands fumbled as I tightened my pack down on the back of the saddle. We needed to *leave*. The stablemaster wouldn't be incapacitated for long. The thought of Sixgun closing in sent adrenaline racing through my veins, forcing a jittery clumsiness into my movements.

I mounted quickly, leading the mustang towards the metal door Jesse wrenched open. I'd carefully averted my eyes from the muscles bunching and straining against his shirt as he'd done it. Horses spilled into the street, galloping in every direction. Surprised shouting rose louder with each horse that galloped into the streets; people scrambled out of the way of the stampede. We made our escape in the ensuing chaos.

The silence between us was deafening as I led them through the twisting alleys and back roads. We ducked our heads anytime we came close to the main road. Jesse kept his mount close enough to mine that our legs brushed when the alleys grew too narrow. Time stretched thin, and my heart pounded with every corner we rounded. What had been only the matter of a few hours seemed infinitely long with the threat of death hanging over us.

My first deep lungful of air came as soon as we cleared the congestion of the city and made our way into the red sands of the desert beyond. A dry, dust-laden breath grounded me in ways I hadn't begun to analyze. I clicked my tongue and dug in my heels as a wild grin unfurled on my mouth and I let my horse run loose over the hard-packed earth.

Elation thrummed through me the farther we got from the dilapidated city and the people who lived there. Unlike most, I didn't fear the open desert. It welcomed me like an old friend, enticing me further. The arid air whipped my hair into knots and tangles that would be hell to work through tonight, but I didn't care. I knew how to stay alive out here, and the farther I got from that city, the surer I was that I would survive another day.

It was a long time before we slowed, though I'm sure my horse would've gladly kept up the pace. Bone-deep weariness took hold of me, as if I were a wet rag that'd been wrung dry. The sun dipped low toward the horizon, setting the land ablaze in a wash of vibrant red and purple light. Before long, it would be too dark to see, so I slowed my mount and found high ground to make camp. The Kid's eyes were half-lidded as he swung down from Jesse's horse. The temperature began to dip, but soon it would plunge down to a cold that could seep through your skin if you let it.

We were all so spent that we didn't talk about how to set up camp, instead just working together with stiff motions caused by sore muscles from the long ride. I built the fire, blowing the ember until it caught in my hands and feeding it until it became a flickering furnace to beat back the chill in the air.

Jesse and The Kid began unwrapping rations to eat. Meanwhile, I rolled out my bedroll and took stock of our supplies so far. Now that the adrenaline was wearing off, my mind wandered to memories I'd rather keep buried. They clawed at me, sharp and dangerous, threatening to shatter my self-control. I needed to keep busy and distracted in order to keep ahead of them. Usually I beat my demons back with the mindlessness of alcohol and sex. I didn't have enough whiskey to drown the darkness raging inside of me.

When I had nothing left to do, I allowed myself to look over the campfire at Jesse. The firelight made shapes and shadows flicker in angles of his face. He really was chiseled perfection. I wondered again why he did it. Why had he lied for me in the bar? I pulled my flask out of my bag and unscrewed the cap, taking a long pull and relishing the comforting burn of the whiskey, greeting me like an old friend. It slid down too easy, the burn settling into my blood and warming me from within.

The Kid stared at me again, so I passed him the flask. Jesse's eyes snapped to the motion, a protestation poised on his tongue.

"Just a sip, Kid. To keep you warm," I said. Jesse didn't say anything as his brother tipped it back and spluttered a moment later. He handed the flask back, red-faced, and wrapped himself in his bedding, asleep in moments.

The quiet magnified my loneliness. Seeing the two of them together reminded me how alone I'd always been. My mind wandered back to that alleyway. His hands were hard, but his mouth hadn't been. He'd tried several times to kiss me, to get me to want him back. The truth was, I didn't kiss him because I *did* want him back. Too much. I stood, crossing to sit next to him on the opposite side of the fire. He didn't ask, but his eyebrows rose high enough to imply his question.

I handed him the flask and he took it, fingers brushing against mine. He passed it back after a moment, his eyes fixed on my face. Why was this so hard all of a sudden? The silence between us grew into a thunderous roar, thick with implications from the day. It was smothering the breath from me, until I couldn't take it anymore.

"Why'd you do it?" I asked, turning to meet his gaze head-on. "Why did you lie for me back there?"

He blinked, slowly, as if he didn't understand. "Because it was the right thing to do," he said, matter-of-fact. That was it. No other explanation. He expected nothing. He gained *nothing*. He said it with a certainty I'd never felt before. I chuckled, a breathy sound. Jesse was an honest-to-God upstanding guy, maybe the only one I'd ever met.

"You have no idea what you've done," I said, handing the flask to him again. "That lie saved my life. Now, I owe you a life debt." He took the flask but otherwise seemed ambivalent to everything I'd said.

"You gave me a new canteen; let's call it even," he said, taking a sip of whiskey.

"A life debt isn't something settled by a new canteen, farm boy," I said, watching as he began to roll his sleeves up his muscled forearms. I didn't avert my eyes this time, watching as the movements made his muscles flex beneath the fabric.

"But I have another idea." I bit my bottom lip to stop the wicked grin from giving my thoughts away. "I could guide you through the desert. I know it better than most and, like I said, I'm good at surviving."

"Is there another option?" he asked, clearly not thrilled with the idea of traveling with me for any real length of time. Not that I could particularly blame him. He took another long pull of whiskey.

"We could finish what we started in that alleyway," I said. He choked on the drink. He sputtered unattractively before I pulled the flask from his shaking hand. His eyes fell to the movement, watching as I screwed the cap back on.

"I thought you said I wasn't your type," he said, his voice gruff but his eyes suddenly bright in the darkness.

"You aren't." I leaned close enough that I could feel his breath hitch. My finger trailed up his denim-clad thigh, stopping just shy of where I'd felt his desire for me earlier. "But after a day like today, we could both use a good fuck." His Adam's apple bobbed. "One night. Then we part ways in the morning and you never have to see me again."

He didn't answer right away. Instead, he reached out to brush a long strand of my hair behind my ear. His thumb traced a path down my jaw as he considered.

"One night?" he asked.

"I don't do repeat performances," I said with a noncommittal shrug.

"If I choose the guide option?" Jesse asked, the warmth from his body seeping into mine.

"Oh no. I never mix business and pleasure. One-time offer," I said softly. Our mouths were close enough that his warm breath fogged against my skin. A shiver worked its way down my spine. His thumb brushed my bottom lip and his eyes darkened. Was he remembering how I'd refused him in the alleyway? He'd wanted me to kiss him then, to taste me. I brushed my lips against his softly, showing him in my own way that I wanted that too. His hand slid easily to the back of my head, and he pulled me closer.

"What'll it be, farm boy?" I asked, my heart hammering against my ribs.

He didn't answer. Instead, his eyes were hot on my mouth. He leaned toward me slowly, as if afraid I would get spooked if he moved too fast and brought his lips down on top of mine. He kissed me slow, his mouth firm, so there was nothing messy or awkward about it. I wasn't prepared for just how *good* he tasted. A moan escaped my lips, and he drank it down. My hands buried in his sandy hair as I'd imagined earlier that day. It was thick and surprisingly soft. He pulled back to look at me, his eyes tracing every detail. My fingers tangled in his hair, breath coming sharp in the cold air, cheeks flushed. I had no idea what he was searching for in my expression.

Whatever he found there made him kiss me again.

## CHAPTER FOUR

# JESSE

R ATIONAL THOUGHTS ABOUT OUR journey flew away. All I could feel was the heat from her skin and her breath on my neck. I wanted to kiss her again, so I did. Her lips were softer than I imagined. I tipped her chin up, deepening the kiss and tasting the whiskey on her tongue. She balled a hand in the fabric of my shirt.

It would be easy to lose myself in her for tonight. I'd never had a one-night stand before. Back home, if I found a girl I liked, things happened on repeat. Over the years, I'd been with a few. Like the girl from the dairy in the next town who came to the market every other week. Then there was Clara, the girl I was meant to marry. They were both probably dead now.

With Clara, it was sweet kisses and unspoken promises.

With Bonnie, it was fire and chaos.

Where her hands trailed, heat followed. I moved on top of her, gripping her hip hard. There was something about her curves I found absolutely irresistible. I pulled my mouth away from hers, flicking my tongue across her jawline, then to the sweet spot beneath her ear. Bonnie's back arched, pressing her breasts into my chest. My mouth traveled down her shoulder and across the swell of her chest. Eventually my teeth nipped one of her collarbones, eliciting a sharp intake of breath from Bonnie.

I didn't know if the temporary satisfaction of fucking her was worth our safety. We had a long way to go to New Mexico, and I didn't think I could handle another two months wandering aimlessly through the wilderness. If I accepted her offer to be our guide, at least we would survive.

Life was meant for living, and Bonnie made me feel alive.

Bonnie yanked my head back to hers, her hands trailing beneath the edge of my shirt, tugging at the fabric. I rolled on top of her, hooking one of her legs around my waist and showing her exactly what I wanted.

Her eyes blazed up at me. The heady glaze in them reminded me of the alleyway. My breath caught in my throat at the memory. She'd looked at me with the same expression moments before she put a gun to my head. She might have killed me if Harry hadn't appeared. She admitted that she was a criminal. She might kill me now. I couldn't trust her.

As much as I wanted to explore every inch of her body, I knew I couldn't.

My movements stilled, and I shifted back onto my knees, our heavy breaths no longer mingling. I stared at her for what felt like an eternity. Then, I stood, watching confusion flash across her face. I righted my shirt, tucking it into the top of my pants.

"You should get some sleep. We've got a long way to go . . . *guide*." I couldn't help the satisfied smirk that crossed my face. I'd show her what it was like being left hot and bothered. I also couldn't stand there staring at her, because if I did, I'd finish what we'd started and get myself into trouble all over again.

For the first time since I met her, Bonnie was speechless. It looked good on her.

I wandered out into the desert, just far enough that I no longer felt the heat of her body or the fire. The cold air soothed my blazing skin; I willed my heart to slow. The temptation was still there. I let out a long, low breath. This was a business transaction. She didn't want me, not really. I knew what she wanted. She wanted to forget the trouble that followed behind her. I was just a distraction. I couldn't let her get past my defenses. I needed to be more careful going forward.

Exhaustion weighed heavily on my shoulders as my excitement abated. I closed my eyes, an image of her handling that man back at the stable in Vegas flashing through my mind. It had been nothing less than impressive. She'd managed to size him up in seconds and dispatch him without another thought. Had she decided within moments how she was going to take advantage of me in that alley?

I had respect for her, for how she conducted herself. Seeing people that could jump into action without hesitation was new for me. In Montana, people often paused before jumping into potential danger. It was part of why I never fit in. I often found myself longing for foolish adventures and dangerous places.

Maybe the differences between us weren't so vast.

I finally had the chance to reflect on this crazy day, especially that man in the bar. Sixgun. Who was he, and why was Bonnie running from him? What kind of danger did that put all of us in? I would have never turned her over to him, but that didn't stop me from wanting to know more about the things she'd done.

The fire had faded to embers by the time I returned to camp. Bonnie, thankfully, was asleep. At some point, Harry shifted to her side, resting his head on her stomach like a pillow. I settled across from them, adding another branch to the fire and stoking it for a while. Only when my eyelids grew heavy did I settle down, using rolled-up clothes as a cushion beneath my head.

Though my body was exhausted, my mind wasn't quite ready to settle. I thought of home, of Mom and Pop, of our simple life.

On snowy nights, Pop sat with Harry at the piano, correcting him when he hit a wrong note. Mom rocked in her creaky chair next to them, eyes closed as she hummed along, never stopping even when the notes weren't right. I sat by the fire, drawing places in my sketchbook that I wanted to see when I left Montana. Anywhere had to be better, right?

I craved the routine of my mundane, Montana life.

My eyes snapped open at the sound of Harry's whimper from the other side of the fire. I frowned, knowing this trip wasn't easy for him either. Had he spent more time doing hard labor on the farm, he might have been able to adjust to this easier. The first few nights on the road, he would wake up begging for Mom. I wasn't good at comforting him. I wasn't good with him at all, really.

Bonnie ran her fingers through his hair. The whimpering lessened, and eventually Harry settled back down.

I could never find the words to tell him what I'd found when I went back to that night.

*The two-story house was reduced to a pile of ash. I approached it, imagining what it had looked like before. I passed through the smoldering foyer into the living room, seeing the framework of the piano slouching against the wall. I stepped cautiously through the soot, until I saw a charred boot in what used to be the kitchen. My knees went weak as the acrid stench of death consumed me. My parents wouldn't have wanted him to know.*

Crackling from the remnants of the fire brought me back, reminding me we weren't in Montana anymore, and our lives had completely changed.

Exhaustion eventually sent me into a light sleep.

It wasn't long after the first twinge of daylight that a sharp boot made contact with my ribs. I swore, eyes snapping open to find Bonnie standing over me.

"Mornin', sunshine. We've got a long way to go," she said. She gave me a wide smile, her eyes full of amusement at my pain.

Without a word, I sat up and rolled my neck to one side and then the other to get rid of the ache from sleeping on the hard ground. As I stood, I felt her eyes on me again.

"What?"

"You gonna tell me where we're headed?" she asked.

"Well, Harry and I—"

"The Kid," he said.

"What?" I asked.

"Call me 'The Kid,'" he repeated.

"That's stupid," I said. The color drained from his face, and I was pretty sure he was about to cry.

"Jesus, fine. 'The Kid.'" I threw my hands in the air, still feeling Bonnie's gaze on me. "Roswell, New Mexico."

Bonnie tossed a roll of paper and a pencil to me. "Can you mark it?"

Silently, I unrolled the paper, finding a map of the southeastern part of the country. I found Vegas, then ran my finger across what I assumed was our current path. I scanned the map, finding New Mexico, then Roswell, I put a thick 'x' on the page.

"What's in Roswell?"

"Family," I said as I handed her things back to her. That was all she needed to know. I had a feeling it didn't matter where we were going, as long as it put plenty of miles between us and Vegas. I crossed to my horse, making quick work of his blanket. My brother hovered near my elbow. I ignored him as I hauled the saddle up onto my horse's back.

"Can I help?" Harry asked.

Roswell felt like a million miles away as I remembered my mother's desperation from that night.

*"Jesse!" Mom's voice was barely more than a hysterical whisper. She shoved me toward the door, thrusting the bag at me. She gripped my arm so hard it hurt. "Go to Roswell, New Mexico. To the military base. Look for your uncle. Michael Kincaid."*

*"Uncle? I don't have an—"*

*"Go!" Then she slammed the door in my face. We ran into the woods, the crashing of our footsteps muffled by the blaze behind us. Then I heard it. Mom's screams. The crack of gunfire. Then silence, except for the fire that tore my world apart and our harried footsteps as we fled into the night.*

My parents had secrets. What else did they neglect to tell me before the world crashed down around us?

"Jesse!" Harry grabbed my arm, shaking me from the memory.

"Jesus, what?" I asked, running a hand through my hair.

"I wanted to help with the saddle," he said, frowning.

"Kid, why don't you handle the bedrolls for me?" Bonnie asked. She stared at me curiously as my brother stomped away.

"What?" I asked.

"Nothing," Bonnie said.

Shortly after, we set out at a brisk pace to extend the distance between ourselves and Vegas.

"What about 'Horse?'" Harry asked a while later. The sun was getting high, and sweat beaded on my brow. There was sand in every crevice of my body.

"No," Bonnie said.

"Pony?"

"No," she said.

After a pause, Harry offered, "Mustang?"

I couldn't help the chuckle that came from my lips at Bonnie's annoyed expression.

"No," she repeated, glaring at me.

"Maple?"

"No, damnit. You can't name a horse after a tree, Kid." Their arguing didn't help much, but at least I was entertained at my brother pestering her instead of me for once. If she would just agree to a name, maybe he would shut up.

"Well, why not?"

I opened my mouth, preparing to tell him to stuff it, but Bonnie cut me off.

"You can't just pick a name outta thin air. Names have power. You shouldn't give one lightly. Take me, for example," she said, sitting up straighter in her saddle. I gazed over at her again, watching her roll up her sleeves. It was the first time I'd truly looked at her that day. Bonnie no longer wore the short shorts and revealing shirt she had in Vegas.

Instead, she wore jeans and a button-up that didn't show her cleavage. It was such a jarring contrast, I wondered how I didn't notice sooner.

"What d'ya mean? Didn't your mom name you?"

"If she did, I don't remember. I don't even remember her. Not really," Bonnie said.

"Well, then how'd you get the name Bonnie?" Harry asked.

"Why don't you give it a break?" My tone warned him he was pushing too hard. We had a long way to ride today, and I couldn't have our guide exhausted before the sun was high in the sky. I was grateful he was in better spirits, but he needed to shove it. Harry looked up at me, blinked twice, and then turned back to Bonnie.

"It's a long story. Probably not the best for a ten-year-old to hear." Her hands gripped her reins tighter. There was something else there. Not that it was long or a troubling story. She didn't want to talk about it because it brought her discomfort. Did it have anything to do with the wanted posters?

"I like stories. Please, Bonnie?"

I'd admit, I was curious, but I wouldn't be asking any questions. I'd leave that to Harry.

Bonnie turned to look at us, her eyes meeting mine and then shifting to my brother. They were full of reluctant affection.

"Alright, fine. I'm not good at tellin' stories, though. So don't blame me if it's awful," she said.

"That's okay. I've already heard all of Jesse's stories. He's really bad at it," my brother said.

"Hey!" I chastised.

Bonnie met my gaze, and once again, I found amusement on her face. I could also see dark spots beneath her eyes and the way that her shoulders slumped forward when she didn't think I was watching. Her exhaustion was clear as day. Did she get any sleep last night?

"I was named after Bonnie Parker, the most famous female outlaw who ever lived," she said. That was when Harry snorted and burst into laughter.

"Jesse was too!" he said between breaths. Bonnie met my eyes again.

"What?" she asked.

"His name is Jesse James, the most famous outlaw in the Old West!" Harry said, obviously excited at being able to reveal that my parents had, in fact, named me after a murderous outlaw.

A smile played across Bonnie's soft lips. I had to stop looking at her. Well, her lips, really, because they brought back memories of kissing her last night, which then made me imagine her soft curves beneath my hands. I cleared my throat, shifting uncomfortably in my saddle. Harry's fit of laughter eventually subsided.

"I was a lot younger than you when my mom was murdered. The guy who raised me said I wouldn't speak for weeks after he found me. I don't really remember much, but he said all I did was cry myself sick every night." The sun glared down at us.

"Let's head over there," Bonnie said, pointing to a red rock formation nearby. "We can wait out the heat of the day and keep going when the sun sets behind that ridge." I followed her gaze, seeing the line of mountains to the west. I was relieved to have a break. My back was aching by the time we stopped the horses in the shade. It wasn't much cooler, but at least my skin was no longer burning.

"Do you know anything about Bonnie Parker?" she asked Harry as we dismounted. He shook his head.

"Well, the only thing that would get me to stop cryin' was when I heard stories about her. When things got scary or hard, or we didn't have enough to eat, he'd tell me, 'Be my Bonnie girl,' and it worked. I'd buck up and deal with whatever was happenin'. Eventually, that became my name," she said.

We neared the rock formation. I felt like I needed to say something, after she'd given us a kernel of her history, but words wouldn't come. She'd said 'the man who raised her' instead of 'father.' I leaned against the rocks, pretending to be focused more on tying my boots than the story of her namesake.

"But what happened to Bonnie Parker?" Harry asked. Could he never be satisfied?

"She lived a long time ago, when the world was almost as bad as it is now. No one had anythin' and it was hard to survive. They called it the 'Great Depression.'" She snorted derisively, pausing to stretch out her back. "Like anything could be as depressing as this shithole."

"Tell me more. Please?"

"Harry," I said, but Bonnie took it in stride. She ruffled his hair. It wasn't the first time she did that either.

"She got married really young. Her husband would leave her for months and months. Until one day, he didn't come home. She worked odd jobs to survive, but it was a lot like it is now. Women weren't allowed to do anything without a man." She rolled her eyes.

"Then she met Clyde Barrow. It was love at first sight. Bonnie and Clyde. For a while, they were the most fearsome pair of outlaws the world had ever seen." Her eyes were alight with wicked fervor. Bonnie nudged my brother with her elbow.

"Bonnie even got caught once," she said. "Until she talked her way out of it. She was good like that, like me." She paused. We could both see my brother's wide, curious eyes wanting to know more.

"Rule number one of being an outlaw, Kid: don't fall in love. Bonnie Parker did and wound up dead for her trouble. Shot full of holes on some backroad in the swamp."

Silence fell. I couldn't help but stare at her, wondering what *her* story was. The Bonnie she was named after was infamous; even I knew her name. But this Bonnie, I wondered, what was her true story? Who was she running from and why? What kind of people raised her? Who had she loved before?

I was so lost in my thoughts I didn't realize I was still staring at her, and she stared right back. After a long moment, she averted her gaze.

"C'mon, Kid, let's kill some stuff. We're stuck for a while. Might as well make good on my promise and teach you how to shoot," she said.

As if sensing my protest, Bonnie stood, my brother walking alongside her.

"What're you scared of?" she asked him, putting her hands on his shoulders to square him in front of a tall, crooked cactus. I reached to my waistband, double checking that the .22 was in place in case anything went wrong. I didn't like this. By the way she kept glancing at me, Bonnie knew it.

"You can't face your fears if you don't admit what they are, Kid."

"Fire," he said. My knees turned to sand, and my stomach churned. "I'm scared of fire."

Any further protest I had washed away at his words. He was afraid of the fire. I was afraid of what lay beyond the smoke.

"You see that cactus?" Bonnie asked, leaning down to his level. I narrowed my eyes at her words. What was she getting at?

Harry gave one swift nod.

"It's the fire. When you have a gun in your hand, you don't point it at anyone or anything you aren't prepared to kill. It's not a toy. Got it?" He nodded once more, his back and shoulders tense. I felt that tension all over me; I was wound tighter than a bowstring.

"Here," Bonnie said, handing him the large gun. She positioned his grip properly. "Use both hands. Hold it tight and level it right at the heart of what scares you most. The gun is an extension of yourself."

It was like when Pop taught me to shoot. We weren't facing our fears then. We hunted for survival, not for protection. Bonnie continued her instructions, bringing me back to the middle of nowhere, surrounded by the endless desert.

"See this line down the barrel of the gun? It's called the sight. That's where you look to aim." Harry adjusted his stance and lifted the gun, peering down it. Bonnie clicked her tongue.

"Keep both eyes open and soften your elbows. Remember to breathe in deep, look down the sight, and follow through. You do those three things and you'll never miss."

The empty click of the gun sounded.

"Good. Now we're gonna take the safety off, and you're gonna do it again. This time, the cactus is the fire. Take control of the fear so it doesn't control you."

My brother exhaled a ragged breath, narrowing his eyes slightly. The next thing I heard was the piercing sound of a single shot and my brother hollering in victory.

His joy was a sweet sound, compared to the horrors that had destroyed our lives that night. I'd rather hear him excited over something like this than the crackle of flames, the moaning of splintering wood, or the cries of animals being slaughtered. In a way, Harry's shot into the cactus brought my life full circle. After all, this journey began when a gunshot stole my quiet farmer's life.

## Chapter Five

# BONNIE

The Kid whooped and hollered, shaking his shoulders and hips in wild motions while brandishing the M9 above his head. I caught myself smiling at him before plucking the gun from his hand quickly. Stamping it down, I turned my back on his pouting face.

"I told you it wasn't a toy," I chided him, his pitiful groan wafting towards me on the faint breeze. As soon as I turned from him, my mood plummeted. The Kid had done the near impossible and beaten back the memories that had hounded me since our run-in with Sixgun yesterday. Jesse's eyes were on me again as I crossed to the horses. He watched me with near-obsession, as if waiting for me to make a mistake and prove to him that I was the same as Sixgun. He was going to be disappointed.

There wasn't anyone as evil as Sixgun, except perhaps Jones.

The Kid crossed to Jesse, talking too fast to make much sense in his excitement. Jesse nodded absentmindedly, and my hands shook as the memories clawed their way to the surface.

*"You can't cry when they touch you. Just fucking pretend to like it, okay?" Jones snarled, his lips twisted in disgust as I wiped the tears off my cheeks.*

*I nodded, taking a deep breath and straightening my shoulders. Ten was old enough to start helping the crew run cons. It was. Jones said so. He snapped impatient fingers, and one of the newer guys, probably mid-40s with a sagging gut, stepped forward. His lumbering bulk reached out to touch one of my too-thin, too-pale arms. Instantly my face screwed up, and tears ran in salt tracks down my cheeks as I recoiled. He sighed, turning to Jones with an open-handed gesture of helplessness. Jones, however, wasn't having any of it this time.*

*"I told you to stop crying!" His harsh words startled me, forcing me to sob harder. His hand reached out and tangled in my hair at the base of my neck, dragging me across the room to a trunk he kept in the corner. Throwing the lid up he tossed me inside, not for the first time.*

"Bonnie!" The Kid's voice snapped me from my thoughts, but I didn't think I could take looking at his sweet, innocent face right now. Instead, I inspected the red rock we'd settled in the shade of; a large crack scored the surface, running almost all the way to the top. My hands shook harder. I needed something to distract me from my dark thoughts.

Without looking back, I bent over and began unlacing my boots. Sliding my feet out, I reassessed the rock. It was tall. Tall enough that a fall from that height could seriously injure me. I studied the path I would take, tying my hair tightly away from my face.

"What're you looking at?" The Kid asked, stopping next to me and shielding his eyes from the sun.

"Just trying to see the best way to climb to the top," I said, shrugging.

"Why?" Jesse asked, the word tumbling from his mouth before he had the good sense to stop it. I looked over my shoulder at him, his eyebrows knit low in bafflement. Last night he'd turned me down, and I still didn't know why. When the unfulfilled promise of his mouth and hands and body left me cold, the nightmares came to haunt me. Jesse wouldn't be the distraction I needed to get through the nights, so exhaustion would have to do.

"It's a long way to Roswell; we'll need more water for the trip. I wanna see if there are any settlements nearby where we can resupply," I muttered, crossing towards the craggy surface of the rock and finding my first handhold. My arms weren't strong, so I used my legs to push up onto the surface as Jesse began untying his boots and swearing below me. He crossed to my side and found a handhold with a black expression on his face.

"What're you doin'?" I asked, the words an exasperated sigh.

"Isn't it obvious?" he retorted, finding another handhold and pulling himself higher on the rock than me. I ground my teeth together, my legs straining hard with the next push that helped me catch up.

"I don't need your help," I said. He made an incredulous sound in the back of his throat, a mix between a scoff and a grunt. He was taller, longer, stronger than me and able to climb more quickly. Before long he passed me again and I gritted my teeth against the urge to curse at him as I pulled my way up. The heat of the sun reflected onto my skin from the surface of the rock, and sweat beaded at my temples. I'd caught up with Jesse again, but it wouldn't be long before he made it to the top.

I didn't like the idea of him looking down on me.

His forearms flexed from the strain of climbing, and the sight pulled my focus just long enough for my recklessness to get me into trouble. The stone crumbled beneath my hand. I slipped, heart plummeting to crash somewhere near my ankles. A cry escaped my mouth before I could stop it. Jesse's arm shot out, wrapping around my waist before I slipped to the craggy rocks below.

I couldn't tell if I wanted to thank him or slap him.

His skin was hot, and he repositioned his arm to keep me in the cage of his body as we made it the last few feet. His breath was hot on my neck the whole time, and I was sure he could hear the racing of my heart through my chest. Awkwardly, we scrambled over together, knees and elbows knocking into each other until we were both sprawled on the flat surface. I looked at Jesse; he looked how I felt. Flushed and gasping for breath, an echo of his passion-glazed face from the night before. I hadn't imagined his naked lust for me; it was hard for a man to mask when he wanted a woman, especially with his hips pressed so hard against mine. Why hadn't he taken me up on my offer?

Part of me, the part I furiously ignored, wondered if he could tell how broken I was. If he looked at me and saw the scars I hid from the world. If he could tell that I wasn't half as brave as I pretended to be. His rejection still stung. I could feel it like a splinter, working its way through layers of my skin.

"Why did you follow me up here?" I asked, my words angry. He rose onto an elbow, his blue eyes dark with fury.

"To keep you from plunging to your death and stranding us in the middle of the desert without a guide." He spat the words.

"I told you, I didn't need your help," I said, shoving onto my feet.

"You did, actually," he countered, rising to his feet and towering over me. The truth in his words rankled my nerves. I turned away with a disgruntled scoff. The wind cooled my feverish cheeks, and I shielded my eyes from the glare of the sun as I looked out to the horizon. With my bare feet flat on the stone beneath me and the desert laid out before me in a riot of color, I could practically hear the earth breathing beneath my feet.

The sky was set ablaze, swirling violently with color as I scoured the hills and hollows searching for signs of people. A column of smoke rose in the distance, far enough away that it was a good indication of a town or settlement, not just a lone campfire. I pulled the map from my back pocket, marking the direction and distance as I worried my bottom lip with my teeth. I'd thought of thirteen insults while mapping the area. Glancing at Jesse, the harsh words poised on my tongue faded into smoke. He was staring openly at the landscape in wonder, the awestruck expression transforming the hard lines of his face into a peaceful look I didn't recognize.

"A great and terrible beauty," I said, instead of the hateful insults I'd planned. My words seemed to break the spell he was under as he blinked himself into awareness. Pity. I'd never seen him more handsome than he'd been moments before.

"Yeah, the most beautiful things tend to be the most terrible," he said, offering me a sarcastic grin. The words had a playful lilt in his oddly calming voice, but they brushed against the raw edges of wounds that would probably never heal.

*Terrible.* I couldn't deny it. How many men had I lured for Jones over the years? How many died because of it? I looked down at my hands, red dust settling into the lines of my palms like tiny rivulets of blood only I could see.

"Yeah, they do," I agreed softly. Tucking the map back into my pocket, I made towards the edge to start my descent. Legs hanging over for a moment before Jesse spoke again.

"Who was that woman back in Vegas? Beck," he asked, startling me at the abrupt change in conversation. "Does she have something to do with why you're on the run?" It seemed The Kid's curiosity was infectious today. A sad smile feathered across my mouth before disappearing again.

"Beck's . . ." I trailed off, unsure how to explain our complicated past. "I looked out for her once, and it cost me." Unconsciously I tugged at the sleeve of my left arm, making sure the knotted scar was fully covered.

"Okay, what about those men with the red fist tattoos? Are they coming after you too?" He crossed his arms over his chest. I sighed, though his questions weren't unwarranted. I motioned for him to sit next to me.

"The Crimson Fist," I explained, tightening my hair tie. "A gang of assassins and thugs. No job they won't do as long as you can pay for it." He sat, eyes dull as he took in the information. "You saw the bounty on my head. If they found me they would bring me in." He turned to regard me plainly.

"What about the people you've killed?" he asked. *Ah, finally, the real questions he wanted answers to.*

"What about them?"

"How do I know we'll be safe traveling with you?" he asked with no levity in his eyes. I laughed, a bitter sound.

"I only kill for one of three reasons, farm boy. A threat to my freedom, safety, or someone I care about. Don't do those things, and you won't have to worry about me killin' you. But, make no mistake, I've got people comin' after me. Traveling with me isn't exactly *safe*." A flirty smile slid over my lips to mask the too-vulnerable moment between us.

"What if they catch you?" The words pushed through a scowl on his lips. As if he'd asked the question before deciding if he really wanted to know the answer or not.

"Don't worry. They won't take me alive," I said, the shock in his eyes forcing a chuckle from my throat as I pushed off the edge and began to make my way down the face of the rock. By the time our feet hit the sand, The Kid had worked himself into a frenzy. He had so many questions about Bonnie Parker and my childhood that the only way I knew to deal with him was to put him on Jesse's horse and keep riding for the remainder of the afternoon.

The heat slid around my shoulders and slicked against my skin, sinking deep enough that the exhaustion I'd craved earlier settled into my bones. I wanted water, but knew I needed to start rationing now. I'd grown too comfortable in Vegas, having a place to sleep and food every night. I'd have to retrain my body to ignore thirst, hunger, and pain.

We didn't make it much farther before the sun began to set and it was time to set up camp, but I hadn't pushed them at the same grueling pace of the morning either. The need to keep my hands busy trembled through me as we stopped moving.

"Hey Jesse! Look what I found," The Kid called from somewhere behind me.

"Get that thing away from me!" Jesse shouted, a note of terror in his deep voice. I turned, watching as The Kid chased Jesse with hands clasped around a tarantula. Jesse stumbled, swearing, as The Kid cackled gleefully.

Without words, I built a fire, rolled out bedrolls, tied horses down, tended them, and on, and on, and on, until there was nothing left to do except stop for the night.

When I finally sat, The Kid sidled up to me, more questions I couldn't answer poised on his too-curious mouth. The tarantula crawled across his knuckles and down his wrist casually. Wasn't he tired yet? Jesse passed the food he'd unwrapped toward me, but I shook my head, stretching my arms above me and groaning as my muscles burned with the effort. My shirt was stiff with dried sweat, and I rose to find a new one in my bag.

I walked into the darkness to peel the shirt from my sand-covered skin, keeping my back to the fire as I shoved the clean fabric over my shoulders and shuffled out of my jeans before pulling my soft cotton sleep pants up over my hips. Was there anything that felt better than clean clothes? I didn't think so.

Once I'd finished changing, the boys were settling down for the night. Slipping into my bedroll wordlessly, The Kid dragged his bedding across from Jesse's side of the fire next to mine without asking. He shoved himself between layers of blankets before curling up beside me.

I opened my mouth to tell him to go sleep next to Jesse if he was cold, but the look on his sweet, sleeping face made the words die on my lips. Whatever remnants of a heart I had left tugged sharply at the sight. I ran my fingers through his hair, marveling at how the flickering firelight made it change colors. That was how I fell asleep, brushing my fingers through his hair and staring at his innocent face, wondering whether, if someone had protected me when I was his age, I would have turned out differently.

The heat of the next day was brutal. As much as we sweat, our shirts were never wet for long. The sun beat down, baking the moisture off our skin. I pushed them hard, even harder than the day before. Just the simple knowledge of a settlement ahead made me yearn for a shower. I daydreamed about the water, sluicing down my back and ridding me of the layer of dust and sand that'd inevitably found its way onto every inch of my skin.

By mid-afternoon, the heat was making me crazy. I glanced over at the boys; my eyes lingered on The Kid. His eyes were glazed, and his body swayed in front of Jesse as we rode. Jesse stared hard towards the horizon, mesmerized by the way the heat of the day could wave and flicker in the air.

"We need to find a place to stop," I said finally, my voice an unattractive croak. I licked my lips, even though I knew it would only make them crack and bleed. My thirst was a living thing, trying to claw its way out from my dry throat. But I'd bested this beast before.

We settled in a small thicket of shrubs. My head swam, and my body shook as I dismounted, the lack of food and water taking its toll. I should have eaten the night before. Silently I cursed my lack of endurance. I fought against my thirst, taking only one swallow. I could've downed the entire canteen. Conservation was key until we came upon the settlement.

Passing the canteen to Jesse, I thought over the route again. I'd pushed them hard, but if they could keep up the pace for a little while longer, we could make it to the smoke column by nightfall. I glanced at Jesse, noticing dark circles beneath his eyes and how unfocused he seemed today. He hadn't slept again last night. Even though he hadn't said anything, I recognized the signs. Something bad had happened back on his farm. He was running from it as furiously as I was running from Sixgun. It didn't matter that he hadn't said anything; I knew what it felt like to have your past chase you into your dreams. I also knew his body couldn't handle much more stress today. The Kid wandered off, probably to relieve himself, and Jesse turned to face me.

"How much farther?" he asked, screwing the cap back on the canteen. His voice sounded as anxious as I felt; we were both ready to be out of the open expanse of desert.

"Not far," I said, my eyes sliding away from him.

"How far is not far?" he asked again, irritated.

"We could make it by nightfall if I pushed y'all, but . . ." I trailed off, biting back the words I knew would wound his pride.

"But what? Can't you just answer a fucking question?" he asked, pushing off of the ground to stand. My anger flared bright, nerves shot and body shaking from exhaustion.

"You can't make it through the fucking desert like this!" I shouted, pressing a finger into his chest to punctuate my point. The color drained from his face, and he fisted his hands at his sides as the hot words spilled from my mouth.

"Excuse me?" he asked, angrily. I ran frustrated hands through my hair and gritted my teeth.

"You haven't slept in days; earlier I thought you were gonna fall off your damn horse," I said, ticking one of my fingers before barreling on. "The Kid isn't used to the heat, and it's taking *way* more outta him than it ought to. And you both don't seem to have any concept of rationing. So, we need to find high ground, make camp, and eat some dinner before either of you keel over and don't get up again!" My chest heaved as my anger subsided into a steady pulse. His eyes darkened as they scoured my flushed cheeks.

"If we do that, will you actually eat tonight?" he asked, an accusatory tone turning the words into an insult. They shocked me all the same. He noticed how little I'd eaten?

"What do you care?" I asked him, arms crossing over my chest defensively.

"I don't!" he shouted. A moment of silence pressed heavy between us before his eyes hardened at me. "I just don't want you to die of a heatstroke and leave us stranded in the *fucking desert.*"

Heat rose in my cheeks, and I ground my teeth together as I realized he thought I was *weak.* My arms shook as I clenched back the urge to hit him in his smug face.

"I'm used to going hungry," I ground out, infuriated past caring about what came tumbling out of my mouth next.

"I guess it's settled, then," he spat, a muscle twitching near his jaw.

"Fine!" I shouted again, hands flinging wildly into the air. "I can't wait to get to Roswell and be rid of you."

"Then fucking *guide us there!*"

The urge to stomp my boot into the hard-packed sand beneath my feet was nearly impossible to quell, until I heard the sound of a rattle in the bushes. My anger fell away like a heavy blanket, my senses sharpening in an instant. I knew that sound.

"Which way did The Kid go?" I asked, panic softening my voice as my eyes dropped to the shrubs at our feet, searching furiously for any sign of the snake nearby. I picked up a branch and snapped it until I had one long length of wood with a forked end. Jesse motioned in the direction the rattle was coming from.

"Shit." I swore. Jesse's hand gripped my upper arm tight, and he spun me to face him. "Don't panic." I shook off his hard grip and then led him slowly toward The Kid, whimpering as he faced down a furious-looking rattlesnake. Jesse tensed beside me, and I pressed a hand to his chest, a silent command to let me handle it. The snake curled, fangs bared, preparing to strike. Raking in a deep breath, I crouched low and walked forward as slowly as I possibly could.

"Kid," I whispered, breath coming hard, pulse rushing in my ears. "Don't move a muscle. You don't wanna scare the snake." He nodded so slightly I could barely tell he moved at all.

"Screw the snake," Jesse hissed, his panic making my heart slam against my ribs. I glared at him, and his voice died in his throat. Calmly I positioned myself behind the snake, crouching low. I sucked in a nervous breath, then struck. The next moment it was twisting and jerking below the forked part of the branch, and I snapped at The Kid impatiently.

"My knife, Kid."

He hesitated, wavering on his feet at the sight of the snake.

"Now," I growled, stepping on the head of the snake with my boot to keep his jaw shut and fangs sheathed. I held my palm flat, and The Kid pressed my blade to it tenderly. "Rule number two: never go anywhere without telling your crew."

He nodded furiously, backing away until he reached Jesse's side.

I made quick work of cutting the head from the body, relief flooding through me like a heatwave. I bent down to retrieve the long body from the ground, turning to them with a wicked grin.

"Good goin', Kid, you found dinner." The disgust on their faces deepened the smile on mine. "Don't knock it 'til you try it," I said with a chuckle. As I led the way back to camp, The Kid ran up to me, asking a thousand questions about snakes. I told him everything I could remember, ruffling his hair as he carried his snake with a reverent expression in his eyes.

Jesse was quiet, which could've meant a thousand things. We barely knew each other, after all. I didn't want every conversation with him to turn into a shouting match like earlier. I noticed an aloe plant and cut off a long leaf with my knife. Without asking, I split it open and moved towards Jesse, pressing the slimy insides to the back of his neck where the sun burned him the worst. His eyes fluttered closed at the relief it provided.

"I get that you don't trust me," I said. His eyes opened to regard me carefully. "I wouldn't either, considering how we met." I shifted nervously on my feet. "I gave you my word. That might not mean much to you, but out here . . . it's pretty much all we have left of value. I won't go back on it."

I didn't wait to see if he was going to respond; instead, I turned towards camp and showed The Kid how to prepare the snake for dinner, giving him the rattle when we finished.

In his excitement, he threw his arms around my neck and pulled me abruptly into a tight hug. The contact was startling and unfamiliar. I was shocked into stillness as my mind raced. How did someone react when a child hugged them so tightly? I patted him affectionately on the shoulder until he finally released me. Jesse's eyes glowed at me from across the fire, amusement etched deep in the angles of his face. He was laughing at me.

I cleared my throat and focused on the task at hand, trying to hide the blush on my cheeks. Soon enough, we were sharing what was left of the bread and the roasted rattlesnake. Jesse eyed his warily while The Kid ate with gusto. I tried not to let the satisfaction of a full belly show on my face but failed miserably. It was no time at all until The Kid leaned forward, more questions glinting in his bright eyes.

"How do you know so much about the desert?" he asked, shaking the rattle. I sighed, licking the last bit of flavor from my thumb before leaning back and contemplating my answer.

"Beck, mostly. She grew up around here and used to teach me survival skills when we both ran with the same crew." I offered him a soft smile.

"What about guns, and how you knocked out that guy in Vegas? Did she teach you all that too?" My mood darkened, and I heard the echo of my younger self, sobbing in that dark trunk. The chill crept in, and a shiver raced down my spine. Instead of answering, I just shook my head. His questions always turned just personal enough to keep the specter of my past close.

"How about I tell you about crater beasts instead?" I noted the amazement in his eyes as he shuffled closer. "You know about the Culling, right?" He nodded, so I picked up a small stone and cleared the sand in front of me. "When the bombs dropped, they made craters in the earth," I explained, letting the stone fall from my hand to the sandy ground. As it made impact, a puff of dust rose and rolled from the place the stone had fallen, showing a miniature crater. Picking the stone up, I tossed it to The Kid, who fumbled but caught it.

"Inside the craters, strange plants and beasts grow wild, fed on the radiation from the bombs." I let my voice soften, adding an air of mystery as I leaned real close to him. "Creatures the likes of which no one's seen before. No two alike, and they all have a ravenous taste for human flesh." He gasped, and I leaned back from him as his eyes widened. "Wild gator dogs with tail spikes as long as Jesse's arms and skin so hard even bullets can't pierce it."

"Have *you* seen a crater beast?" he asked, his words coming in puffs on the cold air. I shook my head, and disappointment dropped his shoulders low.

"If I'd come face-to-face with a crater beast, I wouldn't be here to tell you about it, Kid," I said, chuckling and ruffling his hair affectionately.

"Well, I'd stick 'em with my knife!" he said, realizing he didn't have it and ducking his head sheepishly. I handed it over, hilt first, and watched as he snapped it carefully in place. He checked three more times that it was still there before bedtime. The temperature dropped so rapidly I could see my breath fog in front of me as he settled into his bedding for the night. I tucked the blankets up around his chin.

Jesse's eyes were on me again; without acknowledging him, I could tell. His gaze felt like the brush of his calloused hands on my skin, a startling awareness that'd become too frequent. His eyes were *always* on me. It'd grown comfortable, to be watched so closely by him. Familiar.

"You should try to get some sleep tonight," I said softly into the darkness, knowing he'd heard me. I turned my face into my bedroll and let exhaustion drive me into a deep sleep.

The next morning, I woke before the sun was up. I shot nearly off my bedroll and clutched my left arm, a cold sweat breaking out on my skin. *It was just a dream.*

The Kid grunted and rolled over from my movements, blinking sleepily into wakefulness. I took a steady breath and gave him a smile, shaking off the tremors from the nightmare that haunted me. He grumbled at the early hour, but when I stood and began packing up camp, careful not to wake Jesse, he helped.

The sun peeked over the horizon, the sky lightening with the telltale signs of morning. It would be daylight soon, and we needed to get on the trail before the sun was too high. I hated to wake Jesse, though, knowing how little he was sleeping. After a long moment, I decided it was time and walked over to him while The Kid finished tying bedrolls to saddles.

I knelt down, brushing a long lock of sandy hair from his forehead as he breathed deep and even. He looked so serene, the harsh lines of his face softening into that peaceful expression I'd noticed the day before. His hand reached out to grip mine before I could pull it back, and my heart leapt into my throat. He dragged my palm to his chin and then to his mouth, pressing his lips unconsciously against the pulse on the inside of my wrist. He inhaled deeply, drinking the scent of my skin into his lungs. His eyes cracked open to lock on my face, flushed from being caught touching him while he was sleeping. Confusion flittered in those brilliant blue eyes of his, settling into recognition. It was a pity; he almost looked happy to see me before he realized who I was.

"Sorry," I said, fumbling over the word and pulling my hand out of his grip. "T-the sun is up and we need to get goin'." I rocked back onto the balls of my feet and turned towards the horses before I could embarrass myself any further. Swinging up onto my mustang, I tried not to notice the way he stretched as he stood. Or the line of flesh that peeked from beneath his shirt near the line of his jeans when he moved that way.

What was *wrong* with me? When did I start stumbling over words or blushing over the sight of a man's stomach? I continued to beat myself up silently during the ride that morning, until the air dried out and the sun's unrelenting blaze battered all thoughts of anything but the heat.

The smoke billowed high just beyond the next hill. Close enough to withstand another hour of the heat. The direction of the wind changed, whipping past my cheeks and bringing with it a scent that stilled my heart. I pulled on the reins, stopping my horse short as the acrid stench wafted over me. It was char and rot and something sweet enough to curdle your stomach. A scent you never forgot. I turned to Jesse to suggest an alternate plan, but the words died on my tongue.

His knuckles were bleached white from his furious grip on the reins of his horse. His body so tense I felt sure he would snap in half. Without a word or a glance, just the tight lines of his body, I knew he recognized that scent too. The smell of burning human flesh.

*Fire.* The Kid said he was afraid of fire when I taught him to shoot. Jesse's eyes snapped to mine, fierce and determined. A mask of bravado I knew intimately, meant to cover the worst hurts that would never heal. We'd seen this smoke two days ago. This wasn't just a single funeral pyre, but a tragedy.

There was nothing I could say to Jesse that would lessen the pain of remembering whatever they'd run from. So I nodded and tucked the collar of my shirt up around my nose, digging my heels into the side of my mount and moving forward.

We needed supplies to get through this desert. No one said it would be easy. I made them both a promise: to help them survive. No matter what lay beyond that hill, I was going to keep it.

CHAPTER SIX

# JESSE

"W HAT *IS* THAT?" HARRY asked, turning up his nose to the heavy air. I didn't respond. The desert fractured; Bonnie and The Kid, the tan soil and dark smoke, it all disappeared. Instead, the Montana night enveloped me, returning me to the place I was born.

*I shivered against the night air, wishing we could light a fire. It wasn't safe. We would have to wait until the spring sun came up to chase the chill away.*

*"I want Mom," Harry said through chattering teeth. We didn't have time to grab our jackets before leaving in a hurry.*

*"Tough," I said as we rounded the trees that led to the church where Clara's father preached on Sunday mornings. My first thought was to go to the church for help.*

*It was burning. Everything was burning.*

*Flames crackled and wood groaned. My heart twisted at the thought of Clara and her family. Had the same men that burned down our house come here? The roof of the church caved in, sending sparks into the night sky. Smoke rose in giant plumes, blotting out the full moon just above the horizon.*

*Had Clara and her family gotten out in time? Their house was connected to the church. I broke into a sprint, barely conscious of my brother's attempt to keep up. My boots crunched through gravel until I neared the double front doors of the church.*

*Chains. A padlock.*

*Heat radiated from within. I couldn't get any closer, or it would burn me. Harry's feet skidded, sending a spray of rocks into the air. I stuck an arm out in front of him, looking into his eyes. The fear in them was mirrored in my chest. They couldn't have escaped.*

*"Come on," I said, pulling him away from the burning building. Our feet sank into the soft dirt of a freshly planted field as the horizon lightened.*

*"I'm not going," Harry said.*

*I walked for a minute before realizing that he sat in the middle of the field, arms crossed. Obstinate as ever. I doubled back, shaking my head in frustration.*

*"Come on," I said. We couldn't stay here. If those men came back, we couldn't outrun them.*

*"I'm not going," he repeated.*

*"Then I guess you'll starve, won't you?" I'd been on edge the entire night. There was a bone-deep weariness inside of me, but we had to keep moving. We had to get as far away from our home as we could.*

*"We have to go back for them," he said, voice cracking. His bottom lip trembled. Emotions welled in my throat, words threatening to spill out. I balled my hands into fists at my sides. How could I tell him they weren't there anymore? Harry needed comfort, but that was something I couldn't give him.*

*"They're not there," I said, the words clawing out of my throat.*

*"How do you know? How do you know they didn't run into the woods to wait until those guys left?" Harry asked, a hint of hope in his small voice. He sniffed and wiped his nose with the back of his hand. I couldn't answer him.*

*"I wanna go back," he said.*

*Without a word, I walked past him and back the way we came. My brother was stubborn, more stubborn than even I could be.*

*I'd be lying if part of me didn't want confirmation either.*

*The silence threatened to choke me. It would take hours to walk the ten miles to get back home. With each step, dread consumed me. The lead weight in my stomach grew heavier. We barely spoke. Harry asked me the same questions over and over: Why? Who? What do they want? I didn't have the answers.*

*By the time we reached our land, the sun was fully up, highlighting the tragedies of the night before. The fields smoldered. The animals were slaughtered and left in the pasture. The house was a shell of its former glory. The only thing left untouched was the barn. That was the last place I'd seen Mom as she'd watched us escape into the woods.*

*Not two minutes later, I'd heard her screams.*

*Then, a gunshot. Mom went silent.*

"Harry, I want you to stay here," I said, my voice more certain than I felt. I crouched behind a thicket of bushes, watching for movement near the house.

"But—"

"You don't know if anyone else is there. I can check faster if you just stay here," I said gruffly. The words came out quiet, but firm enough that my brother shut his mouth and nodded. I'd sounded just like Pop.

My stomach churned as I approached the house. The life my parents had built for us was gone. This was the one place I'd ever called home, and now it was little more than ash and soot.

The red brick chimney stood as though little had happened to it. The stone steps and concrete foundation were intact. Cautiously, I stepped onto the front porch, where two rocking chairs were set up to watch over the crop fields. The chairs rocked on a gentle breeze. The exterior was made of thick logs. While scorched, they remained mostly intact. The front door hung off of its hinges, smoke drifting out. The walls inside were crumbling. No longer was there a separation of the small foyer, living room, or kitchen. Soot and ash rained around me from the sky above, which flashed a brilliant blue, beautiful and clean, as though tragedy had not struck. I stepped forward, scanning over the charred ruins of our life. There was no sign of them. Until the wind kicked up and sent a stench unlike any other my way.

My heart dropped as I saw Pop's charred boot—still attached to his leg. I stifled a scream. He wasn't alone. He was holding onto something. No. Someone. Mom. My knees hit the concrete. I gripped my stomach, unsure if I wanted to cry or vomit. I'd hoped I wouldn't find them. I'd hoped I could leave here thinking they escaped.

Unfortunately, I couldn't be that ignorant. I knew they were dead. I knew. Still, I came back.

Anger and devastation coursed through me. Why would anyone want to hurt my family? They couldn't just be . . . gone.

I turned away from them, clutching my stomach as the contents spilled across the charred concrete. I heaved until I couldn't anymore. When the sickness abated, I gathered myself. I had to do something for them. I couldn't leave them like this.

It took a long time, but I found a shovel and dug a shallow grave. By the time I finished, I found Harry whimpering against a tree.

"Hey. Hey, I'm here." I put a gentle hand on his shoulder.

"I th-thought you left me—"

*"No, I'm here. I'm sorry." I crushed him into a hug against my chest, grateful that he'd listened to me for once.*

*"You stink," he said.*

*"I know."*

*"Were they there?" he asked. Frowning, I shook my head, silent. If I opened my mouth, no doubt I would hurl the truth out.*

*After a long moment, I said, "C'mon, let's get going."*

*I didn't have the heart to tell him that our father died holding our mother.*

*"Where'd you get Pop's ring?" Harry asked, pointing to my left hand.*

*"Oh. He gave it to me at the market," I said, the words bitter on my tongue. It was an easy lie. Too easy. In a matter of hours, my life had been completely upended. My father died because he refused to abandon my mother. It would haunt me for the rest of my life.*

That was the first time I smelled burning bodies. I knew that now.

"Jesse?" Harry's voice tugged me back to the present nightmare.

A shiver ran down my back as I looked toward Bonnie. She pushed ahead while I was lost to memory. I glanced down at Pop's ring, the one thing I had left of him. For a brief moment, I considered telling Harry the truth, but the words died on my tongue. I couldn't kill the hope in his eyes every time he spoke of reuniting with them. He'd already been through too much. I'd carry this secret to my grave if I had the choice.

Instead, I tugged my shirt up to cover my nose and dug my heels into my horse's sides. I couldn't bear the thought of putting the truth on my brother. That night possessed my dreams. Our travels were hard enough; he didn't need anything else to keep him up at night. We followed after Bonnie.

The closer we got to the top of the hill, the larger the column of smoke was. It nearly blotted out the sun. The pungent air grew even heavier. Bonnie swore. When I turned in her direction, my heart dropped into my stomach.

Just beyond the bottom of the hill was a giant pit in the ground on the edge of what looked like a town. At the sight of the fire, Harry's shoulders tensed. People milled about, carrying long shapes draped in fabric, then tossing them onto the fire. Bonnie's eyes searched me, the unasked questions heavy between us.

When I finally looked at her, I thought I saw something in her eyes. Sympathy? Recognition? What horrors had she seen to know what they were burning?

I averted my gaze, afraid to speak. Guilt rose in my throat like bile, the truth threatening to spill out.

We rode closer. The mass pyre wasn't just a pit in the ground. It looked like a dried-up lakebed. Houses lined a street nearby, which led further into the town.

"Might want to stay here," I warned Harry as I climbed down from the horse. When he opened his mouth to protest, I gave him a stern look. His shoulders sagged, but he stayed put. I pulled my shirt up even more, balling the fabric around my nose and mouth. A man barked orders ahead.

I called out to him in a brief greeting to get his attention. The man turned, his features showing exhaustion and maybe even sickness. There were gaunt lines on his face; his skin appeared yellow in the hazy light.

"What?" he yelled.

The fire roared ahead, crackling every second. I didn't want to get any closer. I couldn't.

"What's going on here?" I yelled back.

The man still couldn't understand me. I pulled down my shirt, sputtering as the full stench of the pit assaulted my senses.

"Why are you burning bodies?" I asked, quickly covering my mouth. The air grew heavier the closer we got to the fire.

"Plague," the man said.

Suddenly, Bonnie was at my side, pulling me back from the man by several feet. Her eyes conveyed a warning, which I knew better than to ask about.

"Where from?" Bonnie asked. I glanced over, silently grateful for her presence. Our eyes met, but I turned away, remembering how easily she'd sized me up in Vegas. I was afraid of what she'd see in my face, what secrets I might reveal.

What happened to my parents was my burden to bear. I couldn't share it with anyone else. Least of all Bonnie. She would only judge me for my cowardly actions.

"Water supply is infected. Everyone in town's either stricken or run off afraid of being stricken." Suddenly it dawned on me. The people here were infected. My already rankled nerves hit an all-time high. I shifted, bumping into Bonnie. As I tried to pull back, her fingertips brushed against my arm. The contact grounded me, like a cool rain after a hot afternoon of work.

"Anyone know the cause?" I asked him.

"Plagues don't need explanation. But I don't suppose the two of you would be able to understand that. We learned about them before the Culling, in school," the man said.

Mom once told me that kids used to go to places for learning, instead of being taught at home like Harry and me. I longed for the chance to go, to make friends, to have a life outside of the farm. Because we lived in such an isolated area, of course we wouldn't know about illnesses in other places. Our remote location back home leant a sense of safety as well as health.

"Where were you when it happened?" Bonnie asked the man suddenly. I looked over at her. "The Culling."

What did it matter? The Culling happened over twenty years ago. You couldn't change the past.

"Seattle," he said, the hard lines around his eyes and mouth softening. The flames kicked up, ash raining down around us. I needed to leave.

"Not far from the coast; it always rained there. Never thought I'd miss the rain," the man said. I frowned.

Neither did I.

"Do you know where the nearest clean water is?" I asked. The man eyed me suspiciously, glancing quickly to his covered wagon. That was all I needed to know. The nearest safe water wasn't close, and he would shoot me before he spared any of his own.

"I suggest you move on, unless you wanna meet the business end of my gun," he said, resting a hand on the weapon at his hip.

"Thanks," I said.

I was grateful that Harry stayed with the horses when I returned. I ruffled his hair before climbing up. He was quiet, which was a refreshing change for once. I hauled him up as Bonnie rejoined us and climbed onto her mount. She'd recognized the smell of burning bodies just as I had. Not for the first time, I wondered what horrors she'd known.

The sooner we got away from here, the better. A cold sweat broke out across my forehead and down my spine. My vision wobbled, and all I could do was grip the reins to ground myself.

Silence settled around us as I tried to shake the remnants of the burning bodies from my mind. My head ached. Unsure if it was due to the past dredging itself up or my concern about our water supply, I shoved all of the thoughts away. I needed to remain sharp if we were going to push ahead at the grueling pace I expected from Bonnie.

We rode together past the remains of houses. A cobblestone street marked what I assumed was once a town square. The few people milling about eyed us suspiciously, as though they were afraid of catching something from *us*. We cantered past a fountain taller than me on the horse. Useless coins littered the bottom of it. Before my brother had a chance to ask the question I was certain was on his lips, I motioned down the lane. The edge of town wasn't far.

By the time we reached the desert once more, the silence unnerved me. I took a long pull from my canteen, noticing how much lighter it was. Harry took it from me, nearly draining the rest of the water. Though Bonnie had put something on the back of my neck to help with the sunburn, I could feel the skin heating up again. I appreciated the instant relief it gave me then, but I didn't think it would help us now. It was going to be another long, hot day.

What I wouldn't give for a shower.

We set a demanding pace once more. Every now and then, Bonnie would pull out the map and adjust our direction, but I never asked how far we were from the next stop. I wasn't even sure if she knew.

The afternoon sun came, burning down on us from above and flashing up at us from the asphalt highway. Sweat barely had time to form on my skin before it disappeared, evaporating in the heat. Harry was unusually quiet as I steered around a cluster of broken down cars. I wondered if we should stop but thought against it. Shade was nowhere to be found. Only once in a while would a cloud float over the sun and give us a momentary reprieve from its harsh rays. If we stopped, we might not start again.

I looked at Bonnie, seeing the same exhaustion on her face that I felt in every inch of my body. I was glad she'd eaten, but I could tell it wasn't nearly enough. Matched with what little water we had and how far we had to go, I knew that she was just as worried as I was. We needed to stay focused.

"Why don't you tell Bonnie about that time you broke your arm?" I asked Harry, ending the silence. He liked to listen to stories but rarely ever told them. Maybe he thought he didn't have any good ones to tell.

"Nah, I'd rather hear Bonnie tell a story. She's good at it," he said. Her knuckles turned white as she gripped the reins of her horse.

"I'm all outta stories, Kid," Bonnie said, her tone as dry as the desert.

"I can tell you about that time Pop and I killed a bear," I said. It was probably the only good story I knew. Even though Harry insulted my storytelling, I needed to stay sharp. Focusing on anything other than the heat and our dwindling water supply would do no good.

"Pop killed it. Dumb bear ran you up a tree," Harry said, voice dull. My cheeks flushed as I glanced at Bonnie. She hid a secret smile as my embarrassment was laid out for her.

"Fine. Bonnie's out of stories. I'm no good at telling 'em, and you don't want to tell one. Seems to me there's only one thing we can do now," I said, forcing a playful edge into my voice. "I spy with my little eye something . . ." I looked around, finding only the vast expanse of desert before and behind us. Shit. "Something—" There was something blue glinting from inside of Bonnie's open saddlebag. "—blue."

Harry looked around, confused.

"The sky?" he asked. I turned my eyes upward. Because of the heat, the sky looked more white than blue.

"Nope," I said. Harry grunted. He never liked the game when I was the one spying things. Maybe I made it too hard for him, but at least I had fun.

"Those mountains?" He pointed north at a ridge of peaks in the distance. Because they were so far away, the snow caps looked blue.

"Wrong," I said, punctuating the word with a grin. Was that twinge of satisfaction a bad thing?

"My eyes?" Bonnie asked, her voice teasing. I turned toward her. She batted her lashes, blue eyes never leaving mine. The intense stare she challenged me with made my heart race faster. It reminded me of the glaze in her eyes that night by the fire. Need burned low in my belly, almost as if it had never fully gone out and was just waiting for the first chance to consume me. I swallowed hard, forcing my eyes forward.

"You're as bad at this game as you are at telling stories," Harry said, aggravated. He crossed his arms over his chest. The game was all but over. I opened my mouth to tell him what I'd seen, but then he leaned forward in the saddle.

"That water!" He pointed ahead of us. In the distance, there was a large expanse of water, maybe a mile ahead. The sun gleamed off of its surface, creating a rippling effect.

"Holy—" I dug my heels into my horse.

"Stop!" Bonnie shouted. I ignored her. We were so low on water that my fear of running out was enough to get me chasing after anything. We raced ahead, my horse reaching its fastest speeds yet. But the water never seemed to get closer. If anything, it moved farther away. I tugged at the reins, slowing my horse to a stop.

The sound of Bonnie catching up to us stole my attention.

"Idiot. It's a mirage," she said. "A mirage is the way the light and heat hit the sand. It makes it look like a damn pool of water."

Bonnie was right. I was an idiot. My cheeks burned. I clenched my jaw and stared ahead, refusing to acknowledge the insult.

Silence overtook us as I increased our pace. Not quite breakneck speed, but enough to where talking wasn't easy. The sun began to descend in the sky behind us, though there was little relief from the high temperatures. I purposefully avoided talking to her. I'd like to see her in the woods in Montana, see if she could handle the terrain. My headache returned with a vengeance.

By the time the heat broke, the scenery began to change around us. The expanse of dry ground gave way to greenery. It was refreshing to see actual colors. The obscure mountains from earlier were getting closer the farther east we went. We didn't speak as we veered south. Bonnie and I had unconsciously developed a system of hand gestures to indicate direction.

The heat gave way as we reached a line of lush trees. The shade wasn't cool by any means, but it wasn't nearly as hot as the rolling desert. Partnering the long trek with my exhaustion, I had to be imagining things. My mind was messing with me. The trees eventually gave way to a luscious green field: tall stalks of corn in neat rows almost as far as I could see. It reminded me of home.

Beyond the field were buildings made of wood and brick. People milled about on the streets. It was too good to be true. Maybe I'd died.

"Is that—?" Harry asked, weariness in his voice. He was seeing it, too. I glanced at Bonnie, her wide eyes confirming that I wasn't imagining things this time.

"Yes," she whispered, her voice hoarse. If I wasn't dehydrated, I was sure just the thought of a place to stay, a hot meal, and maybe even a shower would have sent me salivating.

"Flagstaff," I read from a giant, dilapidated billboard lining the road. It was as good a place to stop and stock up as any. We couldn't go farther even if we wanted to. The horses were pushed to the brink of exhaustion from our hard traveling.

The evening temperatures were much cooler than the desert; the air was more saturated than dry. When we reached the edge of town, the sun was descending closer toward the horizon. I hopped down from my horse, leading it by the reins. People bustled down the streets, lighting lamps and carrying large bundles.

This place was happy. Music echoed down the lane just beyond the houses and shops. People took in our haggard appearances but didn't seem to be bothered by our presence. I saw a three-story building ahead with a sign that said *inn*. We tied the horses near a large watering trough just outside of it.

"I'll be right back," I said, climbing the steps and pushing open the door to the place. It could have been a beautiful room once. Instead, paint chipped from the discolored walls, the floors were littered with dirt and debris, and the innkeeper appeared bored out of his mind.

"Have a room?" I asked. His gaze trailed the length of my body, eyes narrowed when he looked back up at me.

"Have payment?" he asked.

"Of course. Depends on if the room is worth it." Which I highly doubted, by the look of this place. I was tired, thirsty, hungry, and not in the mood to tolerate bullshit. What little money I had, I needed to save. We had a long way to Roswell. The thought of parting with the brass and copper bits in the bag before we got there filled me with dread.

"We just need a place to shower." I turned to look out the window, watching as Bonnie and my brother talked near the horses.

"That's a nice ring," the innkeeper said.

"No." I balled my hand into a fist and released the tension a second later.

"What about that little pistol you have in your pants?" he suggested. My jaw dropped at the man's words. What did he just say? Was he propositioning me? The innkeeper eyed me up and down, before letting out a booming chuckle.

"The *other* pistol?" he asked.

I reached to my waistband, pulling the gun from its spot.

"I'll let ya shower. Just give me the gun." I stared down at the ornamental details of the handle. It wasn't much of anything, really. If I squeezed it too hard, I bet it would fall apart anyway. I glanced toward the window once more, where Bonnie was smiling at something Harry said. The gun was of little use to us with the M9 she carried. She would understand bartering for a shower, right?

"Fine. But don't tell the woman outside." I placed the gun down on the countertop. He slid a key over to me, instructing me on where to find the shower. Without thanking him, I went back outside.

We took turns taking showers. My brother first, then Bonnie. As she walked out of the bathroom, I couldn't help but notice the flush in her cheeks. It reminded me of the fire, when I'd had my hands all over her. She'd come to life beneath me that night, her skin soft and supple, her body mine to consume. Droplets of water dripped from her long, dark hair, sliding down the curve of her neck, a neck I'd tasted. I averted my gaze, brushing past her to take my turn. The cold water did nothing to stifle the image of Bonnie's body writhing beneath my touch by firelight. It was only then that I realized I was alone for the first time in months.

Wrangling a ten-year-old through the wilderness allowed very little personal time. The memory of Bonnie's lips, hot on mine sent my heart pounding. My skin flushed, remembering her nails scratching across my skin. The mirth in her eyes sent my skin burning through the spray of the cold water. *Goddamn it.* Why did she have to be so fucking sexy? Water sprayed over my face. If I didn't get a handle on *this*, I was sure it would turn to steam. I reached down, determined to take control of myself. What must have been nearly an hour later, I dressed in my change of clothes and shaved the scratchy beard from my face.

Refreshed, I made my way back to Harry and Bonnie. As I approached, the most beautiful sound trilled on the stale air. Laughter. Her voice wasn't hard like I was used to. In contrast to the harsh lines of her face and normal condescension in her tone, Bonnie laughed. My brother removed the towel from his head, and his hair stood on end.

Stifling a smile, I pulled out our broken comb and helped him fix it. My eyes met Bonnie's. For the first time, hers were tranquil. There wasn't a scowl on her face or any of the normal sarcasm behind her expression. She looked as beautiful as her laughter sounded. I wondered if she realized how gorgeous she was.

Bonnie opened her mouth to say something but was cut off by shouting outside. Immediately, my guard went up. What now? We rushed outside. Night had fallen, but the town hadn't gone to sleep. Throngs of people, more than we'd seen earlier, passed us, heading in a single direction. I glanced toward my companions. Bonnie had the usual suspicion on her face, but my brother's eyes were alight with wonder.

Might as well join them and see what the excitement was about, right?

From far off, a banjo sounded, along with singing and cheering. We rounded a bend in the trees, which opened up to a large field surrounding a bonfire that shot straight into the sky. The faint outline of a nearby mountain framed my view; the sky glittered overhead with stars.

Flagstaff was better than any of the other settlements we'd traveled through since leaving home.

We found a tree to tie off the horses and wandered toward the bonfire, eventually settling down in an empty space. Bonnie rationed out what little dried meat and cheese we had. I waited to see that she actually ate before digging into my own meager portions. Vaguely, I thought that we needed to make plans for the next leg of our journey, but my attention was stolen by the performers. Men and women in ceremonial Native headdresses danced around the fire. They chanted in a language I didn't recognize.

The smell of roasting meat wafted over on the breeze. People walked and talked and danced. They celebrated. What it was, I didn't know. I just knew that I hadn't felt a sense of community in a very long time. These people knew how to live.

It was such a contrast to my recent travels that my senses were in shock. The music hurt my ears at first, reminding me of when Pop would play the piano off-key. Bonnie hummed along beneath her breath. She probably didn't realize I could hear her. Her eyes were bright with unfettered joy; I recognized that feeling within my chest. Harry broke the moment, suddenly peppering Bonnie with questions again.

The crowd around us cheered, and the music stopped. The performers took a bow and exited the scene.

A woman sitting nearby leaned toward us. "You're such a lovely young couple," she said over the crackle of the fire.

"We're not a couple," I said quickly, my eyes wide.

"Where are you from?" the woman asked.

"Montana," I said.

"You're a long way from home. Where are you heading?" The woman's kind eyes and quiet voice leant a sense of comfort to me. She reminded me of the older women at the market. The ones that would smile at you like they knew more than you did but didn't want to hurt your feelings for saying so.

"Roswell. Just gotta make sure our horses can hold out that long," I said.

"You should take the train. It's not as fast as the electric trains when I was young, but they travel well enough. It stops in Santa Fe. You can ride south to Roswell from there." I turned to Bonnie as the woman excused herself and wandered away.

"What did she say?" she asked me.

"That we should take the train. There's a stop north of Roswell." I watched as Harry wandered toward the musicians, who started a new, livelier tune. Like my parents, Harry got all of the musical talent. Even before he could reach the keys, Pop would set Harry in his lap, pressing the pedals while my brother beat out a tune. Pop loved it. With time, Harry could play dozens of songs from memory, without missing a single note.

Even Montana didn't have this sense of community. Everyone was so spread out that it was hard to gather. During the winter months, the weather could be harsh, so we were always inside. During the spring and summer, there was always work to do. But for a moment, I allowed myself to wonder what life could be like, being surrounded by dozens of people, everyone taking part in the work so you didn't have to do it by yourself.

"What do you think?" I asked Bonnie after a moment. She shrugged noncommittally, watching the couples that floated toward the fire to dance.

It was nice not being at odds with her. It was nice not being on edge every second. Silently, I compared Bonnie to the image of Clara in my head. Sure, there were the physical differences. Clara was tall, blonde, and delicate. Bonnie was soft and small, with dark hair and mystery swirling around her. I always thought Clara was my type. But she wasn't, not really. She was the type everyone else thought I should be with.

It wasn't until Vegas that I knew I'd been wrong all along.

"So how do you know what burning flesh smells like?" Bonnie asked, finally looking at me.

I knew it was only a matter of time before she asked. I stared at the fire, not wanting to answer. It would have been easy to lie, but I couldn't find the words. Instead, I saw the charred remains of my parents. I stared toward the bonfire, willing the lead ball of grief in my stomach to go away. She shifted more in my direction. One of her hands inched toward mine on the grass.

"It's not a smell you forget," she said.

Why couldn't she get the hint and leave it alone?

Bonnie's hand moved across the short distance. Our fingers tangled, and the contact almost undid me. It wasn't hard or rough, it was almost . . . sweet.

"I was twelve when a fever struck a town near our camp. It spread fast, mostly killing children and the elderly. It wasn't safe for me, but that didn't matter much to anyone back then. Four days. It took us four days to drag them all out and burn them," she said.

My stomach flipped at the thought of having to make the decision to burn the bodies. I understood now why it was necessary to stamp out the disease before it spread.

Bonnie fidgeted beside me. As usual, she couldn't keep still. She pulled her hand out of mine. She looked up at me, her mouth slightly open with an unasked question resting on her lips.

"Can I have Selene?" she finally asked.

Selene? Who was Selene?

"The gun, farm boy. Every good outlaw names their gun." A smile found its way to her pouty lips.

Selene. The gun that I no longer had. Her brows furrowed at my hesitation. It was sad. Because we'd been getting along for once. We were just two people, enjoying music and the company of others.

"I'd give it to you . . . if I still had it."

CHAPTER SEVEN

# BONNIE

*I* LIKE THIS SONG. The music distracted me enough that I chuckled at Jesse, holding out a flat palm for Selene. When, a moment later, he still hadn't given her back, I glanced at his face, and my heart stopped. There was no hint of humor in his expression. My breath stilled. My demons raged towards me, setting my hands and body to trembling.

He couldn't be serious.

My hand dropped, and so did any fragile sense of safety that'd enveloped me since entering this town. I shook my head disbelievingly, refusing to meet his eyes. *This is what you get for trusting him.* The unkind thoughts echoed endlessly. I *knew* better. I'd allowed myself to believe Jesse was decent. That he wouldn't use me like every other man in my life. That he didn't have it in his poor little farm boy heart.

I was a fucking idiot.

Shoving onto my feet, I stared at him and hardened my heart to his handsome face.

"How could you do that?" I asked, cringing at the desperate edge to my voice. *I trusted you.* The words froze on the tip of my tongue, desperate to tumble from my lips. Instead, I turned towards the horses, unbuckling a saddle bag and pulling out the M9. I tried to control the fear settling deep in my stomach. It thrashed, threatening to spill what little I'd eaten. Jesse moved to my side in a moment, the familiar heat from his eyes burning against my skin.

"What are you doing?" he asked, voice strained. I chambered a bullet, fixing him with a dull stare. There was only one thing to do now, and Jesse had no part in it anymore.

"Where is she?" I asked, a hard command. Jesse's eyes fell to my gun, taking a tentative step back. "You have no idea what you've done. Now, I don't want to, but I'll make you talk." My eyes hardened to ice as I raised the M9 to his chest. His face fell, hurt flashing in his eyes before confusion replaced the emotion.

"I traded it for the showers. It's just a gun," he said, hands raised and shoulders tense. I dropped the M9 and shook my head, my lips pressed into a hard line.

"Just a gun?" I asked, eyebrows knitting together. "*Just* a gun?"

"Yes, a gun. It's barely even functional. There's nothing that special about it," he said, incredulity driving the dagger of his words deeper. I didn't know why it felt like he was talking about me, but I clenched my teeth against the surge of emotion. I didn't have time for this.

"A gun I trusted you with," I said, and he stilled. His hands dropped to his sides. He moved as if to take a step towards me. *No.* I needed to put distance between us. I turned on my heel and marched back up the lane towards the inn. He trailed behind me, but I didn't acknowledge him. Gritting my teeth, I pushed my hair behind my ear and took a steadying breath. Why did I feel like this? Disappointment, anger, betrayal, they all roiled in my gut, clawing up the back of my throat until . . .

At the steps to the inn, I whirled to face him once more.

"That gun belonged to the man who raised me," I said, shoulders tight as I braced myself for the confrontation. "Not that it matters, right? You know, congratulations, farm boy, you conned the con artist." A derisive laugh bubbled up from my chest. "You had me convinced that you were decent. That there were actually decent people left. I'm so *stupid.*"

"Bonnie, slow down," he said, hands extended as if he wanted to touch me, but I shook my head to deter the action. "Just help me understand—"

"What's to understand? I *trusted* you, and you fucked up. Just like everyone else," I said, turning and taking the steps two at a time before kicking the door in, M9 extended. The innkeeper shouted as I crossed the room in three long strides. I pressed my forearm against his throat, shoving him hard against the back wall and placing the barrel of the M9 to his temple. His eyes widened, his face turning a ruddy purple that accompanied his lack of oxygen. Jesse barreled through the door, swearing and running angry hands through his hair.

"Where's my gun?" I said, a snarl ripped from somewhere dark within me. The man's mouth opened and closed. I pressed my forearm harder against his windpipe. "You can tell me and live, or I can kill you and find it myself. Your choice." He smacked a desperate hand against my forearm, but I used my body weight to anchor myself to the ground, and he couldn't budge me. Just like I was taught.

Tossing his head back and forth, he finally pointed a shaking hand to a drawer below the counter. I dropped my arm, watching as he fell heavily to the floor, gasping in relief. I slammed open the drawer, yanking Selene out and shoving her into my waistband. Sweet relief pulsed through me now that she was where she belonged.

"Bonnie, look out!" Jesse shouted as the innkeeper swung the butt of a shotgun at my head. I ducked, and the strength of the swing knocked the innkeeper off-balance enough that I was able to change my grip on the M9 and bring it down on his temple. Hard. The blow forced a shock of pain up my arm. The man crumpled to the dirty floor in a heap, and I shook the pain off my knuckles, swearing. Pulling the shotgun out from beneath the innkeeper's prone form, I tossed it to Jesse, watching as he caught it easily. Confusion and unasked questions were dark like storm clouds in his eyes.

"You'll need that to get to Roswell," I said. Promise or not, I was *done* helping Jesse. I turned my back on him and walked outside. I made my way quickly down the front steps. The familiar need to run burned through my veins; my past clawed against what little sanity I had left. The news of this incident would get back to Jones eventually. He'd come here, to this happy place, and he'd raze it to the ground. Heat pricked in the corners of my eyes, but I clenched my jaw tight, forcing myself to ignore Jesse bursting through the door behind me.

"You can't leave us like this," he said, catching up to me more easily than I thought he would. I'd forgotten how fast he was, like how he'd caught me back in Vegas. He stalked beside me, his long strides easily keeping up. Even if he didn't reach out to me, I felt the desperate thud of his feet like a plea at my back.

"Oh, yeah? Watch me. I need supplies, but I've done without them before," I said, refusing to meet his eyes. Tension rippled in the air, crowding between us, around us. I refused to acknowledge the promise I would be breaking. Conflict snapped tight between us as he blocked my path, his composure threatening to break like storm clouds as angry words dangled on the tip of his tongue. My hand clenched tight as the urge to slap him flooded through me.

"Stop them! They robbed me! Don't let them get away!" the innkeeper shouted, holding his hand to his bloody temple. Whatever we'd been about to scream at each other died in our throats as we moved in a synchronized sprint towards the horses. Before we knew it, the seemingly friendly townspeople were leveling weapons at us from every direction. Jesse, unused to staring down the barrels of dozens of guns, stopped cold. I ducked below the arm of one pursuer and kept running.

My heart hammered against my ribs as a man grabbed my shoulder, his hands bruising me in his grip. I slammed my elbow into the soft part of his torso. He bent over, gasping for air, before I forced my feet forward again. As soon as I'd twisted out of his grip, another man slammed into me from the side, his hand grappling against me as I tried to get the M9 high enough to get off a shot. His scrambling hands gripped my shirt tight, and the sound of fabric ripping was punctuated by my inhuman growl of desperation.

A shot rang out, the M9 pointed high in the air. My would-be captor stilled, and I leveled the gun at his head.

"That one was a warning," I said, bearing down on the man. "Don't fucking touch me." My voice was too raw, too small. My sleeve was ripped so badly the fabric bunched around my elbow, exposing the scarred, knotted flesh from my shoulder to nearly my forearm. It felt like it'd exposed more than that, more than what I wanted to show anyone. It took me too long to notice the dozens of guns trained on me. My breath came sharp, and I bit my lip to stop myself from letting out the pitiful sound building in the back of my throat.

I kept my weight on the balls of my toes, ready to change direction or sprint at the faintest opportunity. I scanned the faces of the crowd. None of them were familiar, but that didn't matter. I couldn't get caught now.

The crowd stilled. A woman whispered to a man holding a Ruger on me; she pointed, and his grip wavered. The crowd parted, and another woman walked into the circle of weapons, her back hunched by the weight of her advanced age. She seemed unconcerned as I leveled the M9 in her direction to stop her.

"Leave them alone!" The Kid's voice, high and clear, rose above the crowd. He shouldered his way past a man in torn jeans to run towards me, flinging his arms around my waist and burying his head in my stomach.

My heart thudded painfully in my chest as I looked down at him. He hadn't run to Jesse; he'd run to *me*. I wrapped an arm around his shoulders and twisted my body around, trying to protect him as best I could. Whatever happened, I would do my best to keep him safe.

"Put the gun down, Bonnie," the woman said. Panic rose like bile into my throat. I shook violently, lurching away as she stepped forward. Fear coursed in my veins, freezing me from within.

"I won't go back," I said, my voice barely a whisper. My thoughts shattered and reformed, one name pulsing through to the surface. *Jones.*

"I was right. It *is* you," she said, her words a reverent prayer.

*"No one leaves me, Bonnie. Not unless it's in a pine box." Jones's words were calm as he wiped my blood from his hand. "Isn't that right?" His pale fingers wrapped slowly around my throat, resting there. So that I could feel the threat in them. He held my neck tenderly, sweetly. The fear in my eyes a drug that calmed his madness for a moment. "What will happen if you try to run from me, Bonnie?" he asked, tobacco on his breath.*

*"You'll kill me."*

The words he spoke that night resounded through me, a truth I would never be able to escape. No matter how far or how fast I ran, he was there. He was *always* there. He was so deep inside of me that sometimes I wondered if I was even a real person, or just the twisted creation of his fucked-up imagination. Hot tears welled in my eyes, and I gasped in a hot breath.

"I *can't* go back," I said, turning the M9 and pressing it hard against my temple. The Kid gripped me harder. I squeezed my eyes shut, tightening my grip on the trigger. I took a deep breath, a sense of peace stilling the tremors in my hand. Anything would be better than going back; the sweet release of death was a kinder fate than what Jones had in store for me.

The woman made a strangled sound. Large hands wrapped around the gun at my head. My eyes shot open to find Jesse, pulling the M9 out of my grasp slowly, his blue eyes dark with concern and shock. I opened my mouth to say something, anything, but the words wouldn't come. He handed the gun to the woman before burying his hands in my hair, cradling them on either side of my face. I blinked hard, refusing to let the tears fall, the image of his face wavering in my vision.

"What's your name?" he asked. I couldn't see anything but his eyes, couldn't feel anything but the warmth of his hands.

"Bonnie," I breathed, desperation dimming within me. *Bonnie.* My name was Bonnie, and I was stronger than this. He nodded softly, a relieved hitch in his breath.

"What are you?" he asked. My fragile strength flared bright between us, and I swallowed down the urge to fade into the darkness.

"I'm an outlaw," I said, my voice stronger. His thumb brushed my jaw, the touch grounding me to this moment, to his unwavering faith in the strength I'd painstakingly gathered from the shards of the broken girl I used to be.

His hands dropped away, and I stood tall, fingers buried in The Kid's hair as I turned to face the threat of the townspeople, head held high. The way I did everything.

"Beck said you were spirited, Little Wolf," the woman said, eyes crinkled at the edges in kindness. She reached out slowly to touch the raised skin of the scar on my arm. I flinched from the touch, and Jesse was between us in a moment. *Little Wolf.* Only Beck called me that.

The whispering I'd noticed earlier grew louder.

"That's her, from the poster!"

"Beck said that she—"

"She's way too small to have done all those things."

I shook my head, trying to wrap my mind around the sudden turn of events. The weapons raised against us were lowered or put away. The Kid disentangled himself from me and looked up at the woman. Jesse's eyes were still hot on me.

"They mean us no harm," the woman announced. The townspeople began to move away, curious eyes still trailing me.

"I've wanted to meet the tenacious young woman my old friend told me so much about," the woman said, her kind eyes warming as respect shone through her dark gaze. I didn't like that look. It came with expectations I wouldn't be able to live up to. The innkeeper pressed forward, wiping his bloody temple with a dirty rag.

"They robbed me, Quanah! I demand you do something," he said, glaring at me and sucking a sharp breath into his chest to make himself appear larger. I rolled my eyes.

"Is this true?" Quanah asked.

"No," I lied. The innkeeper opened his mouth to argue, but I thrust my chest forward, and he stumbled back on his feet, fear flashing in his eyes. Grinning, I looked at Quanah. "Well, yes." I worried my bottom lip with my teeth. "But he doesn't want *anything* to do with this gun."

Quanah raised an eyebrow, clearly asking for an explanation. Glancing at Jesse, whose attention was rapt, I refused to lower my gaze again. The shame of the truth burned the air from my lungs.

"It's *his* gun," I said. Quanah's body snapped tight with tension. "It's Jones's gun." The words tasted like ash on my tongue.

"I see," she said, understanding weighing down her features. "Well, this is my town. You'll be safe as long as you choose to stay here. After what you did for Beck, it's the least I could—"

"Stop that," I said. She fixed puzzled eyes on me. "I'm not some hero. Stop talking like that."

"Come, there's food and dancing by the fire. Your friends are welcome too." She motioned us forward. The Kid, distracted by a stall where a smiling woman painted eager children's faces, ran off to join the line and get his own markings. "Tonight you'll stay with me, and in the morning, I'll arrange for passage on the train to Santa Fe." I wasn't sure how to respond, so instead, I followed after her as she kept walking.

"We're not friends," I said, unable to comment on the uncommon generosity she showed us. Quanah turned, fixing me with a knowing stare that forced me to squirm on my feet.

"No?" she questioned. My eyes swung to Jesse, the shotgun slung over one shoulder, distracted by a pretty girl giggling in his direction.

"No," I confirmed.

"Shame. I've been around long enough to know there aren't many men walking around who can fill out a pair of jeans like he can," she said, and my mouth dropped open in shock.

"What?" she asked. "I'm old; I'm not dead."

She left me, disappearing into the crowd. Now alone, I spared a glance at Jesse, my eyes trailing the backside of his jeans and realizing she wasn't wrong. He was still talking to the girl from earlier, so I moved towards the stalls. My fingers trailed along a row of windchimes that tinkled merrily. The woman behind the counter stared for a long time at my exposed arm, and I tugged at the ripped fabric, pulling it up to my shoulder only for it to fall back to my elbow once more.

"Here." The woman ducked to the back of her stall and returned with a bundle of fabric. She handed it to me with a soft smile on her mouth. Unfolding it, I found a new shirt. The print was more colorful than what I normally wore. The sleeves were shorter than I preferred; the bottom of my scar would show.

"You can change behind here." She indicated the back of her stall, where another brightly patterned piece of fabric hung.

In moments, I was changed, looking too conspicuous for my comfort. The next stall had beautifully carved pieces of wood, and the one after that was filled with stones and beads of all colors and shapes, etched with trees and animals. Beautiful. My hand reached for a medium-sized bead, so blue it was nearly black. It was carved and etched into an intricate design that reflected the light of the fire as it rolled on my palm.

"Keep it," a deep voice said from beside me. I glanced over to see a man staring down at me. He was too skinny, his arms and face gaunt.

"I can't pay for this," I said, handing it back.

"I didn't ask for anything. It's a gift," he said, placing it in my palm before turning his back. A gift. I'd never gotten a gift before. Stifling a smile, I carefully placed it in my pocket so I wouldn't lose it. The sound of Jesse's laughter carried toward me in the warm night air, and my eyes searched the crowd for him. There were two women near him now. One leaned in close, an insinuating smile curved on her pretty mouth. His grin was wide and bright, an easy confidence relaxed around his shoulders.

It was clear in this moment how different we really were.

These people, with their gifts and generosity, welcomed him like a lost friend. Meanwhile, I stood apart, my loneliness driven to lower depths. This happiness, this peace, wasn't meant for people like me. I longed for the ease and comfort Jesse felt around others. He looked more handsome than I'd ever seen him. Whole and happy.

The girl who laughed with him whispered something in his ear, and he nodded, pulling her by the hand onto the dancefloor. She folded easily into his arms, as if she were meant to be there. I forced my eyes away from him and to the baskets of fruit at a nearby stall. A crimson berry caught my attention. I pressed a brass bit into the woman's hand, and she gave me a dozen wrapped in a cloth. As I walked, I popped the first one into my mouth, stopping short as the flavor burst bright in my mouth. I closed my eyes in pleasure as the sweetness coated my tongue.

My eyes were drawn again to the dance floor; Jesse and his partner transfixed me. I stood and watched them as I finished the berries. They were like birds, twisting and tumbling through the sky. Elegant and perfectly synchronized, as if the steps were predetermined.

Jesse's eyes found mine from over his partner's shoulder, and my cheeks flushed hot as he caught me staring.

As the swell of the music crested to an end, Jesse stepped away from his partner and walked to me with purposeful strides. His partner looked after him with disappointment and confusion. I pointed towards her as he crossed the distance between us.

"What are you doin'? Didn't you see the way she was lookin' at you?" I asked, but he didn't acknowledge my words. Instead, he took my outstretched hand and pulled me forward until I was stumbling after him onto the dance floor.

"Jesse!" I hissed, trying to tug my hand out of his. He entwined our fingers together and pressed forward. "No. Jesse, no!" But my protests went ignored as he turned to lock his sky-blue eyes on my heated face. Couples swayed around us as we stood still, hearts hammering.

"You are the most infuriating person I've ever met."

"I get the feeling you haven't really met that many people," he said, his hand hot against mine. He stepped closer, and I swallowed my trepidation down.

"Wait, I can't do this," I said, and he stopped, his thumb making a circle on the back of my hand.

"Do what?" he asked, his words hot. The implication of them lingering in the air around us. I squeezed his hand gently.

"Dance," I admitted, feeling even more foolish as the teasing smile spread across his face. His eyes dropped to the dust between us. I thought he would leave me to find his previous partner again. Instead, when his eyes met mine, his smile softened into an expression I'd never seen before.

"At least you don't have big feet," he said. I laughed. His eyes brightened at the sound.

"Okay. But you can't laugh at me," I said, hardening my stare at him. He schooled his features into a stoic expression.

"I wouldn't dare," he said, biting back a grin I saw anyway. He stepped close enough that I could feel the heat from his skin seeping into mine. "I'm going to put my arm around you." His voice was low in my ear, the breath causing goosebumps to rise on my skin. Swallowing hard, I nodded softly in consent. His arm slid around me, pressing me close to his chest and keeping me trapped in the cage of his strong arms.

The music changed tempo, and my eyes dropped to our feet as Jesse started to lead us. His hand tipped my chin up so that I was staring into his eyes again. I barely started before

I stepped on his foot. Cringing, I tried again, only to stumble backward a step. The heat in my face crept down my neck.

"This is stupid," I said. "I don't even know why people do this." Jesse was unfazed by my clumsy attempts and clear frustration. Instead, his hand moved to my lower back, and the other caught my free hand.

"Because it's fun," he said, his unique brand of conviction clear in his tone.

"Fun? I look like an idiot," I retorted sharply. He breathed a laugh into my hair.

"Yeah, well, you're pretty terrible," he admitted, and my flush deepened. I shrugged in response, trying hard to seem as if I didn't care.

"When was the last time you did anything fun?" he asked. The question surprised me. I took a moment to think about it. Jesse watched every emotion cross my face as the moment stretched between us.

"Well, probably when I robbed you," I said. His answering smile made something warm in my stomach flip. His arm tightened around me, and I suddenly realized how tall he was compared to me. His hand, on the small of my back, was impossibly large as it fanned out on my skin. How had I not realized how big he was until now? I was dizzy with the scent of him, somehow shuffling even closer, our hips pressed tight, and we swayed together.

I pressed my cheek to his chest and leaned against him, allowing him to lead us through one song and straight into another without breaking.

"I shouldn't have traded the gun," he said quietly. I closed my eyes, not wanting to admit how good it felt for him to hold me.

"I know," I said, not forgiving him right away. "You shouldn't have."

"I'm trying to apologize," he said, a familiar edge to his voice that meant we were about to fight again. I pulled back to look into his eyes.

"Yeah, you just suck at it," I said, biting my bottom lip to stifle a grin.

"Well, you suck at talking to people," he retorted. I chuckled at the abruptness. "Has anyone ever told you that?" There was a playful lilt in his deep voice.

"No, actually," I admitted, pressing my forehead against his chest briefly. "No one's been brave enough to say it to my face before." He ducked his head, his arm tightening around me. "Or stupid enough."

"You know, you're kind of nice when you aren't too busy calling me an idiot," he said, chuckling into my hair. We rocked softly together to the music. I'd lost track of the song, humming beneath my breath.

"It was my fault," I finally admitted. "I shouldn't have given her to you."

"Why did you?" he asked, his words hot in my ear. I shrugged, not sure myself. Why had I trusted him? I'd given him Selene before we left that bar in Vegas, before I even knew him. Like blinking, or breathing, I'd just done it.

"You told Quanah that it belonged to a man named Jones. He was the man who raised you and gave you your name, wasn't he?"

I faltered, stepping on his foot and swearing as my eyes dropped to the dust. He noticed all that? He tipped my chin up to his gaze again, eyes studying my expression and seeming to find something that interested him. Was he remembering what I'd said before pressing the M9 to my temple?

"Yeah," I said finally, breaking the intense stare. "He has a habit of naming things he thinks he owns."

Jesse made a sound of disapproval in the back of his throat. The song ended, and instead of dancing through to the next one, I dropped my arms and stepped out of Jesse's embrace. The chill in the air washed over my skin and forced a shiver down my spine.

"If I get caught and I'm brought back, that gun is the only thing I have to bargain for my life," I said. The words hit Jesse like a physical blow. Before he could respond, The Kid ran up, face painted brightly and wearing a ceremonial headdress.

"Guys! I wanna be a Comanche!" he said, excitement alight in his eyes. I dropped to a knee in front of him and turned his face back and forth to admire his paint. "Quanah said that anyone who wants to join the tribe can. Can I, Jesse?" He bounced on the tips of his toes.

"Let's see how you feel about it once we find our uncle," Jesse said, his voice full of affection. Quanah stood behind The Kid.

"Sorry to cut your evening short," she said, her eyes flicking between Jesse and me suggestively. "But I'm an old lady. I can't stay out as long as I used to. Follow me back to the house so I can get you settled for the night." She held her arm out for Jesse to help her up the lane. She winked at me over her shoulder and squeezed his arm tight. I tried to stamp down the chuckle, but it escaped anyway. Jesse turned confused eyes on me, but I shook my head.

"When do I get my gun back?" I asked, but she ignored me for a long moment until The Kid was distracted by a man who came to retrieve the ceremonial headdress.

"When you arrive in Santa Fe," she said, eyes hard. "You won't need it until then, I can assure you."

I swallowed the arguments poised on my tongue.

"Be a dear and help me up these stairs," she said sweetly to Jesse as we stopped in front of a house. She leaned on him a little *too* much, which amused me to no end. The old harlot.

My eyes rose to the wooden two-story house, and my breath caught in my throat. Stone steps led up to a wide porch cocooning a seafoam green exterior, flower boxes overflowing with wildflowers at every window and lanterns twinkling on the front porch and in windows. I didn't know people could live like this. I didn't know that a building could look *loved*. The Kid rushed to me, gripping my hand tight and dragging me forward behind him as we climbed the steps together.

"C'mon, Bonnie, I wanna hear another story before bed," he said. I stumbled through the threshold, and everywhere I looked, there were bits of Quanah's personality on vibrant display. The kitchen had herbs hung and drying from the ceiling, giving the air a sweet, earthy scent. Bits of color in fabric tapestries and pieces of art saved or restored from before the Culling hung in every available inch of space on the walls.

"It's not much," Quanah said, taking off her shawl and hanging it over the back of a worn blue armchair. "But it's home."

I swallowed a lump in my throat. *Home*. I'd never had one. Not really. Not like this.

"Your room is upstairs and to the left. It's not very big, but it's clean, and the bed is comfortable," she said, shooing us upstairs with an impatient flick of her wrist. At the mention of a bed, my exhaustion from the frantic journey seemed to weigh my limbs down with weariness.

"Thank you," I said softly. Quanah nodded, offering me a small smile before jerking her head towards the stairs, where Jesse and The Kid disappeared. This night had been emotional and strange. So I followed behind them, listening as The Kid chattered the whole way about the story I'd *promised* him. Running my hands over my face, I turned into the room and nearly slammed into Jesse, who stopped just inside the doorway.

He stared into the room, at the one bed that engulfed the space.

I swore under my breath at the old woman's mischievousness. Jesse's eyes slid to mine, a question in them. Shifting from one foot to the other, I sighed deeply.

"I'll sleep on the floor," he offered.

"No." His eyes flew to my face, wide in surprise. "How long has it been since you've slept in an actual bed?" I asked, but I didn't wait for his answer. "We'll just share it." I shrugged, trying for nonchalance.

Jesse crossed to the washbasin in the corner and soaked a hand towel. Snapping at The Kid, he shuffled over on jittery feet, barely able to keep still long enough for Jesse to wipe his painted face clean before darting off again. I tore my eyes away from the brothers and busied myself by pulling the sheets down.

I sat on the corner of the mattress, unlacing my boots and wriggling out of my jeans. The Kid was less graceful as he flung his shoes and sweater across the room haphazardly. Sliding under the quilt, I raised a single eyebrow at Jesse across the room.

"Well?" I asked, and he turned his back before pulling his shirt off in one smooth motion. I pressed my face into the pillow to get the image of his strong shoulders from my mind. He crossed the room to climb on the bed on the other side of The Kid, who was already beneath the covers.

"I don't want you to sleep next to me. That's weird," The Kid said, shoving Jesse's chest until he stood again and gave a pointed glance to the floor. I sighed deeply and pulled up the corner of the quilt in a reluctant invitation.

"Hurry up, farm boy, before I change my mind," I said, ignoring the flutter in my stomach as the mattress dipped behind me and the heat from his body forced a tremor through me. He shifted, and I twisted the opposite way, trying to put distance between our bodies.

"Bonnie, I need to—"

I nodded, turning until his arms were around me and his body pressed flush to mine. I was cocooned within his embrace so that we could both comfortably fit on our half of the bed. His breath fell hot on my neck, and it reminded me of how good it felt when he pressed his mouth to the skin there.

"Bonnie?" The Kid said, a welcome distraction from the nearness of Jesse's body. I made a noise to let him know I was listening. "Will you tell me the story of your scar?" I stiffened in Jesse's embrace, and in response, he held me tighter, his chest pressing flush against my back.

"That's not a bedtime story," I whispered, my voice an unattractive croak.

"Please, Bonnie," he whined, and I nodded softly, taking a deep breath to gather myself. I swallowed hard, turning to stare up at the ceiling instead of looking directly into The Kid's innocent face. The thought of lying didn't even occur to me.

"Someone hurt me," I said, my voice smaller than I'd imagined it would be. "Bad."

"Why?" The Kid asked, his voice quiet as my fingers found his hair, and I ran them through his blonde locks to calm the tremor in my hands.

"I was being punished," I said, and Jesse's arm tightened almost imperceptibly around me.

"Does it hurt?" The Kid asked. I sucked in a pained breath, pressing my lips to the top of his head.

"Not tonight."

CHAPTER EIGHT

# JESSE

S HOUTING WOKE ME FROM a dreamless sleep. I blinked awake. Laughter trilled on the air, floating up to our room. Harry. To no one's surprise, he was already awake. Maybe, just maybe, I could capture a few more moments of sleep, before whatever trouble of the day came.

I closed my eyes, stretching my back, only to realize there was a very soft, very warm body pressed up against mine. I ran a hand over her arm, letting it rest at her hip.

She smelled like rain in the forest. Being in the desert so long, I'd forgotten the scent. A bitter tang of ozone muted by the sharp sting of pine.

Bonnie buried her face in my chest, her breaths even. There was peace in her expression, a peace I so rarely got to see. The lines that normally showed her aggravation or amusement at me were gone, replaced by the serene look of an untroubled woman. Whereas the last time we'd been this close together, there was heat and urgency, now, I took my time to trace her slightly rounded cheeks with my eyes. I wanted to put a pencil to paper, to capture the serene expression on her face. To remember what she looked like when her problems were far away.

Last night had been hard. Bonnie didn't hesitate to put that gun to her temple when we were surrounded. I'd recognized the fear in her eyes. She didn't want to die, but she wouldn't go back to Jones. My eyes flickered to the yellow and pink shirt she wore, where the bottom edge of her scar stuck out. I trailed my fingers up her arm, pulling the bottom of her sleeve up to inspect it. My heart dropped into my stomach; anger pulsed through my chest.

Jones had carved his name onto her body.

Her bitter words last night came back to me in a flash. *He has a habit of naming things he thinks he owns.* The violence she'd been ready to commit only made more sense now, after she'd said the gun was the only thing she could use to bargain for her life. No wonder she was willing to put a gun to her own head to escape the tortures waiting should he get his hands on her again.

No one deserved that.

All I'd ever known was safety and security, but what had growing up looked like for Bonnie? She had no family, seemingly few friends, and she pulled cons on people to get by. But when threatened with going back there, she seized up like a caged animal, ready to do whatever it took to save herself.

I brushed a stray lock of dark hair out of her face, for the first time able to stare at her plainly, without fear of her staring back. I trailed my fingertips over her cheek, marveling at the softness of her porcelain skin.

Why did I feel like I needed to protect her?

Bonnie wasn't my responsibility. I knew that. I also knew that no one deserved to live a life like she had. Even if I didn't know the details, I knew that she'd been through worse things than I could ever imagine.

I *wanted* to protect her. I never wanted to see that look in her eyes again.

That thought scared me.

I disentangled myself from Bonnie, sliding my arm from beneath her head. I moved at a painstakingly slow pace so I didn't jostle the bed and wake her. She rolled over, her back to me. I let out a low breath. I needed some space. The lines between us were blurring. I wasn't supposed to care about her, wasn't supposed to want to protect her. Having her in my arms made me forget that. I forgot last night when we were dancing, and I nearly forgot this morning. I needed to think. To breathe. After slipping on my boots, I left the room, closing the door silently behind me.

Harry's voice drifted up the stairs as I descended. Something about crater beasts. Quanah stood at the wood-burning stove, sizzling sounds coming from the pan near her hands.

"Coffee?" she asked, smiling in my direction. My face lit up, and I didn't have a chance to answer her before she handed me a steaming mug. I cradled it in both hands, staring down at the dark liquid. Then I took my first glorious sip of sinful heat.

"Where did you get this from? We haven't had coffee in Montana for years," I said.

"We aren't far from Mexico. Men come through the Borderlands once or twice a year selling the beans at decent prices. I'm not surprised it doesn't make it that far north. Coffee is a commodity these days," Quanah said, giving me a knowing smile.

I looked back to the pan in front of her. Bacon. My mouth watered at the smell. The last time we'd had any was over a year ago. Our last hogs were slaughtered by a pack of wild dogs, and none of the meat could be salvaged.

Harry was unusually quiet. I turned to look at him, finding him smiling into a hand-crafted mug.

"What's in that cup?" I asked.

"Coffee," he said smugly.

"Who gave you coffee?" I asked, narrowing my eyes at him. My brother's gaze gleamed as he looked to Quanah.

"No one," he said, grinning. He lifted his cup, drained it, and set it back on the table.

"It's mostly milk," Quanah said in a quiet voice. I wasn't going to argue with a woman who commanded an entire town.

"Want to go for a walk with me?" I asked my brother. His eyes lit up, and he bounded from the table.

"Train leaves in two hours," Quanah called after us.

When we stepped onto the front porch, the town was bustling. People rubbing sleep from their eyes walked by, heading in the direction of the fields. Some dragged makeshift wagons. Children walked lazily behind their parents. As we moved into the street, low voices bid us good morning.

Light blues and pinks streaked through the sky. The clouds caught the colors and reflected them back to the world below. The main street was made of packed dirt and lined with houses on one side. A flash of holding Bonnie in my arms passed through my mind as I spied the remnants of the bonfire in the open field. A wagon pulled by two ponies passed us, the driver greeting us and complimenting the weather.

"I like Quanah," Harry said as we walked. I looked down at him, seeing that familiar wide-eyed excitement he got when talking to Bonnie.

"I bet you do," I said, shoving my hands into my pockets. He glanced behind us before turning back to me.

"I like Bonnie, too," he said.

"Who wouldn't?" I remarked, chuckling to myself.

"I think you like her. *A lot.*" Harry's tone changed. Was he . . . teasing me?

"I don't know what you're talking about," I said.

A shrill whistle sounded nearby. Harry covered his ears, looking up at me with wide eyes. Together, we turned toward the sound. A rusty engine blew steam into the air as it settled on the tracks. The brakes screeched and passengers spilled out on the platform. People shouted, but I couldn't make out the words. Immediately, Harry wandered toward the engine.

"Beauty, ain't she?" an older man said from beside me. "Trains used to be nice to ride on. But now, we make do with what we have."

The man's eyes glazed over, as if he were lost in a memory.

"How old were you when the Culling happened?" I asked, noting the gray in his hair. His skin was rough from long exposure to the sun. He reminded me of . . . well . . . me. I knew the bone-deep burn you felt after harvesting crops all day. The exhaustion written on his face reminded me of how nice it was to fall into my bed after working in the fields.

"I dunno. Maybe your parents' age," he said, scratching at his beard. "Tragic how all of those people died, but I'm sure you know about that already."

"My parents never talked about it. Anytime I asked questions, they went quiet," I said, watching as the conductor of the train invited Harry into the engine car.

"Dark times," the man said. "Sometimes it's best to forget."

I wasn't sure that I agreed with him. Mom said the reason she taught us history was to do better than those that came before us.

After fifteen minutes of pestering the conductor with questions, I managed to pry Harry away and steer him back to Quanah's house. He broke into a run, beating me inside the house by a few minutes. I took my time, enjoying the quiet before the day started.

When I made it inside, Harry sat next to Bonnie. Each had a mug and plate in front of them. My brother looked up at me with a grin as Bonnie poked at her plate with her fork.

"Bonnie's never had bacon," he said with a grin.

"What?" I blurted, earning a dirty look from Bonnie.

Quanah handed me a plate loaded with bacon, eggs, and potatoes. It smelled heavenly. I considered taking the empty chair next to Bonnie, but the silent threat in her eyes stopped me. Instead, I leaned against the counter. Through the rest of breakfast, Harry told the women about the train, including a long tale about the conductor, who said he was once a circus performer. While I doubted the man was being honest, Harry was excited about it. I could give him that, after all we'd been through.

After eating and finishing another cup of coffee, I walked upstairs to check the room for our stuff, even though we'd left everything except what we were wearing last night on the horses. Bonnie's boots were on the floor next to the bed. To the naked eye, they seemed small and delicate, but I knew better, remembering sharply how they had squashed my toes last night.

I went about the room, picking up my brother's sweater and any other wayward items. Before long, the door opened, and Bonnie walked in. A grin broke across my face.

"How was the bacon?" I asked. Bonnie shot daggers at me with her eyes. My smile widened.

"Shut up," she said. Her hard features softened as she took a step toward me.

"Oh, come on, you can't expect us *not* to think that's strange," I said.

"Says the guy who got run up a tree by a bear," she countered.

"At least I know how to dance."

"At least I know how to take the safety off of a gun."

"That gun wouldn't have done any damage if I had," I said.

"It sure stopped you in that alleyway, didn't it?" she asked.

Was the room getting smaller? Because Bonnie stood closer to me, whereas before, she'd been across the room.

"Speaking of that alleyway . . . robbing me was your idea of *fun*?" I shot back, grinning. She'd admitted it last night when we were dancing.

"Yeah, farm boy, *fun*. That's all it ever was meant to be," she said, her eyes glittering at me. Her cheeks pinkened; it looked good on her. "Besides, I hadn't robbed anybody in a while."

"You're as bad at lying as you are at robbing people," I said, tipping my head in challenge.

The room must have gotten smaller, because Bonnie stood mere inches from me now. The heat of her skin warmed my own, and a familiar flash of desire passed through her eyes. I wanted to kiss her. Like I kissed her that first night by the fire. I leaned forward an inch. She moved closer to me, breath hitching in her throat. Then I stopped.

She might shoot me if I tried.

This was Bonnie. A murdering, one-and-done type of woman. Even if I did like her, I didn't want just one night.

"Train's leaving soon. I'll get the horses," I said, but Bonnie moved faster.

"I'll get 'em," she said, shoving her feet into her boots and crossing to the door.

"I don't mind—" I said. But she was already gone. I stood there, staring after her, regretting my decision not to kiss her.

I gave Bonnie ten minutes to get away from the house, because if I didn't, I might have tried to remedy that. Then I joined Quanah and Harry downstairs. The former shouldered a pack of her own.

"You're coming with us?" I asked.

"Yes. I'm due to visit Santa Fe, so I thought I would go with you on your journey," Quanah said with a knowing look. Maybe she was joining us to help ensure our safety. It seemed like something she would do. The three of us set out on foot from Quanah's quaint home toward the small train station. As we walked, Harry started again, his words faster than I could keep up.

"Did you know that my Pop killed a bear once? Yeah, it chased Jesse up a tree!" he said as we neared a cargo box. The sliding door was wide open, showing the space full of metal crates and wooden boxes. Quanah rolled out a blanket and took a seat near the head of the car. Harry sat beside her, talking about our adventures.

I gripped the door handle, preparing to swing up into the car. A woman cried out, and panic gripped my heart.

*Bonnie.*

People milled about, blocking my view of her. I followed the sound of her voice down the long line of cars, weaving between people trying to get onto the train. I shoved through a sudden swarm of people. When I broke through the gathering crowd, Bonnie was struggling with a man who towered over her in height. I sprang into action, sprinting toward her.

"Get off!" she yelled. The guy twisted her arm behind her back. He struggled as she kicked him, but he succeeded in pulling her from the train. Adrenaline raced through my veins at the thought of him taking her. All rationale escaped me.

*Protect her. Protect her. Protect her.*

I swore, sweat already beading across my forehead and down my neck. The brakes let out a blast of air, kicking up dust. The train was preparing to leave. Most of the crowd dispersed, either climbing onto the train or walking away from it. We had to hurry. The guy was a little older than me and wore a dusty cowboy hat. He continued to wrench Bonnie's arm behind her. With his other hand, he held a knife to her throat.

The train's whistle screeched. My already hammering heart beat an erratic rhythm.

"You know what Jones is gonna do to you, huh?" I barely heard the man say over my own pounding pulse. "He's gonna slice you open. He's gonna rip your fingernails off one by one." The man focused so intently on Bonnie, he didn't see me coming. I took pleasure in the crunch of his nose as my fist slammed against his face. He released Bonnie, hands covering his bloody nose. She staggered toward me, eyes wide and full of shock. I moved her behind me with one hand, placing myself between them.

The train workers shouted last call.

"We need to go," I barked over my shoulder. I grabbed her hand and turned to run for it. A sharp pain exploded behind my knee. I stumbled, nearly knocking Bonnie over. When I turned, the man smiled. Blood flowed freely from his mouth, spilling over onto his ochre skin. When he grinned, his teeth were stained red. A shiver ran down my back.

"Who's this?" he asked, advancing with the knife in hand.

I cursed myself for forgetting my shotgun.

"Bonnie got herself a boyfriend, huh?" The man lunged at me. I was faster. I batted his arm away, grabbed him by the head, and ran him face-first into a thick, metal flag pole. The man staggered, glaring at me as he grasped his bearings. Was he some kind of superhuman? I couldn't believe that after two blows to the head, he was still standing.

"That the best you got?" he shouted, blood spackling my face.

Bonnie grabbed my arm, trying to pull me away. I turned to her, distracted long enough for the man to slice my leg with his knife. I hissed in a sharp breath. While he smiled, I brought my other leg up, kicking him in the gut. He fell flat on his back. I knelt into his chest and punched him in the eye. Then I lifted my other fist and punched him in the other eye.

I didn't consider myself an angry person. I rarely lost control. But it'd be a lie if I said I didn't enjoy the crush of his face beneath my hands. I hadn't suffered through a thousand miles of wilderness, dehydration, and damn near starvation for this man to take away our chance at making it safely to Roswell.

"Jesse! Stop!" Bonnie's voice cut through the noise raging in my head. She grabbed me, holding me back from delivering the next blow. My knuckles were covered in blood, some his, some mine. I could feel the sharp sting of the cuts on my hands and leg.

"Time to go," Bonnie said. Her blue eyes were sharp on mine, and I couldn't read the emotion behind them.

"Right," I said, standing. The guy remained sprawled out on the ground. He laughed.

"We need to go. Now." Bonnie grabbed my arm, yanking me away.

The train was already moving, picking up speed with each second. People stared at us from the windows, watching as we raced alongside the train.

"Who was that guy?" I shouted breathlessly.

"Faster!" she screamed, out of breath and incredulous at the same time.

I tried my damndest. I might be able to make it, but Bonnie, I wasn't sure. When faced with a choice between getting on the train with Harry or staying behind with her, I didn't want to fathom it. Harry absolutely needed me, but *we* needed Bonnie. My muscles screamed as I sped up, somehow managing to grab the handle on the side of the car and climb up. Bonnie wasn't as fast as me. I'd known since I'd chased her out of that alleyway. Bracing myself inside the cargo car door, I leaned out, extending my arm to her.

"Grab on!" I shouted. She ran, staring up at me. For a second, I thought she might let us go and remain behind. That she would rather stay behind with that madman than come with us. Fear shot through me. I didn't know what I was doing in the desert. I needed her. My brother needed her. I couldn't leave her. I didn't in Vegas, and I wouldn't now. The air whipped past as the train gathered more speed.

"Damnit, Bonnie, trust me! I've got you!" I screamed. My eyes pleaded with her. While it was tenuous at first, I trusted her now. I needed her to trust me back.

A second later, her small hand fit in mine, and I yanked, using my entire weight to pull her into the car. We tumbled together, eventually coming to rest against some metal crates. Chests heaving, both of us out of breath and no doubt coming down from a high, I looked at her.

"That was fun," I breathed, chest rising and falling in heaves.

Bonnie's eyes were wild. I wished I knew what was going through her mind, because in the next second, she laughed. It was a booming sound that came all the way from her belly. Reality sank in that we could have died jumping onto a moving train, and then I burst into laughter. How had my life become so crazy since Bonnie walked into it? She exhaled loudly, an attempt to compose herself, but it failed. As soon as our eyes met, we burst into another round of roaring hysterics.

"You're insane," she finally said.

"Me? None of this started until you came along," I shot back. Both of us remained flat on the floor.

"Yeah, you're right," Bonnie said, groaning as she sat up.

Finally, I turned my attention to Harry and Quanah, who looked at us like we were crazy.

"What?" I asked, unable to stop the grin from creeping over my face. Harry's eyes lit up, and his mouth hung open, as though he wanted to say several things but couldn't form the words.

"That was a nice right hook," Bonnie said, respect in her eyes.

"You know, fighting bears and all."

That sent us into another fit of chuckles.

Over the noise, Harry said, "Did you see that? Quanah, did you see Bonnie and my brother jump into the train? That was so cool!"

"Yeah, I mean, we could have died, but I'm glad we could entertain you," I said.

Bonnie snickered, which made the stupid grin on my face even wider. Were we nuts? Probably. Did I care? I looked over at her; the mirth in her eyes mirrored the bright feeling in my chest. Nope.

We took out Bonnie's med kit to tend to the wounds on my hands and leg and Bonnie's collarbone. As the adrenaline faded, the last half hour played through my mind again. That guy put a knife to her throat. He was trying to take her.

"Who was that guy?" I asked. She turned toward me, eyes clouded.

"No one important," she said darkly.

"I think I have a right to know," I said. Bonnie spared a glance at The Kid and Quanah before shifting her gaze to me.

"Will Ellis," she said, pressing a hand to the shallow cut on her collarbone. "Sixgun's son. He's a part of Jones's crew."

"Is that the Crimson Fist?" my brother asked with wide eyes. Bonnie shook her head.

"Jones is head of the Hanged Men," she said to him.

"Hanged Men?" he repeated.

"Yeah," Bonnie said. "Once you're in, the only way out is at the end of a noose."

*Oh.* I'd be lying if I said a flicker of fear didn't pass through me. The man I'd met in Vegas had been threatening enough. Now, I'd beaten his son.

"You two should go down to the next car. Talk a little," Quanah said, glancing at Harry. "This one owes me a story about a rattlesnake." The woman gave me a knowing smile, then turned her attention to Harry, who was more than happy to have it.

I motioned with my head to Bonnie, and we walked through the sliding door together. The next car over was quiet as we entered. Windows lined both sides, showing the open desert spread out around us. Mountains rose above the northern horizon and rolling deserts splayed out to the south. Booths sat in neat rows on the right side of the car, many occupied by women staring at us.

My mood instantly brightened as I saw the fully stocked bar across from the booths. A young man with long, black hair and skin like the desert during sunset worked behind the bar. Women tried to catch his gaze from across the car. A woman at the bar lingered, handing him money for her drink before rejoining her friends. She winked at the bartender as I walked up.

After ordering a bottle of whiskey, I brought it and two glasses to the farthest booth from the women playing cards, plunking it down on the rough surface of the wooden table. Nothing matched in the room. The booths seemed to have come from different places. Our table had initials carved over the surface. I poured us each a glass, glad that Quanah had the good sense to allow us a moment to gather ourselves.

"So," I finally said while pouring my second glass. "Do you think I killed him?"

Bonnie looked up at me, confusion on her features. Then, slowly, it seemed to settle in.

"I doubt it. Will is *resilient*," Bonnie said. She didn't speak with hate or anger. Her voice was almost devoid of emotion, coolly indifferent. It was a stark contrast to how she described the men from her life. I watched her for a long time, waiting to see if she would expand, but she didn't. She stared at her glass.

"He was your friend," I said. Bonnie brought those pretty blue eyes back to me.

"Friend. Lover. Enemy. Whatever he was doesn't mean a damn thing now." There was a bitter edge to her words. *Lover.* The word struck me in the chest. Why did it hit that hard?

"Did you love him?" I asked, staring at my glass.

Bonnie laughed. It was so genuine I looked up at her, watching as she stared back with incredulity in her eyes.

"Love him?" she asked, and shot the rest of her drink. "Did I love him?" Bonnie sighed, pressing her fingers to her lips in quiet contemplation. "Yes, in a way." She motioned to me with her glass. I refilled it. "But not in the way you mean."

"Then . . . what way?" I asked, forcing any emotion or feeling from my voice.

"I needed him, to make me feel like I was in control again," Bonnie said. She turned her piercing stare to me.

"What about you, farm boy? Have you ever been in love?" she asked.

I sipped my whiskey, enjoying the burn as it went down. That was a fair question. What did love even look like? Love was the look in Pop's eyes when he'd dance with Mom to whatever song Harry played off-key on nights at home. Love was the gentle way she chided Pop when he ripped his clothes or needed a new pair of boots. Love was the little things, the big things, and everything in between.

"I could've been," I admitted, an image of Clara flitting through my mind. "I was engaged."

Bonnie's brows lifted on her forehead. "Yeah? And what happened to this fiancée?"

I poured another round, pausing only to look at the bottle to gauge when we'd need a new one and concerned over whether I'd have enough money to pay for it.

"She's dead," I said, frowning. The church and their small house burned the same night as mine. I had no doubt she died the same way.

The conversation had taken a darker turn than expected. I didn't want to talk about Clara or Montana. I wanted to find that high again, feel the adrenaline in my veins. I didn't want to go jumping on and off moving trains again, but I wouldn't mind something to take my mind off of my troubles.

Bonnie seemed to be searching for something to keep herself entertained as well. When I looked up at her, she looked at the bar. Subtly, I glanced that way, finding the bartender smiling back. When I turned to her, there was a rosy flush in her cheeks. Envy bubbled up inside me at the heat in her eyes. I wanted her to look at *me* like that.

Either she wasn't good at hiding her feelings, or I was more in tune with them than I realized. I leaned toward her, pretending to reach for the bottle of whiskey instead of blocking her view of the handsome bartender.

A round of loud giggling sounded through the car. I turned at the noise, finding five women crowded around a table, playing cards. I reached into my pocket, jingling the handful of brass bits I had left. I leaned across the table, capturing Bonnie's attention.

"We're low on money," I said, smiling. "I think I'll go play a round of cards."

Bonnie's brows lifted, but she didn't speak. Instead, she lifted her glass as I rose to my feet. I carried my half-empty glass with me, sauntering slowly toward the women. I had no doubt I looked like some greasy vagabond compared to the prim and proper tone emanating from their fancy dresses and hats.

"Hi there," I said, trailing a hand over the back of the booth. "Got room for one more?"

When the sun finally started to set and the bar car turned orange from the light, I couldn't tell how many hands of poker I'd won. My pockets were a lot heavier, and I was quite drunk. I'd kept an eye on Bonnie. She sat for a while by herself but then wandered to the bar.

I was proud of myself. The women I'd beaten were lovely. Two of them wanted to take me back to their car, but I didn't want that. All I wanted was to go back to Bonnie and laugh about how I'd taken their money. Maybe have a drink or two with her. The rest of the women seemed amicable, except one who I thought would stab me if she had a knife.

"Thank you for the wonderful time, ladies," I said, grinning as I stood from the booth. I placed a hand on the back of it to steady myself, trying to find Bonnie.

There were a few things I wanted to tell her. Like how this morning, when I woke up and it was just us, I should have kissed her. I should say to hell with our little arrangement. Or tell her that we could find a quiet car somewhere and *finally* finish what we started back in Vegas.

Bonnie, however, sat in one of the booths, talking to the bartender. Well. Jealousy flared bright in my chest, sending me a step backward. I was confused. How was I supposed to tell her anything when she looked at that bartender like she'd looked at me in that alleyway? I straightened and left, somehow making it back to the car with Quanah and Harry. Both of them were asleep. I took my cue from them and found the least dirty spot to settle. The drink heated my veins. Every time I nearly fell asleep, the train jerked me awake. At some point, I passed out.

The train jolted to a stop after dark. I started awake, still drunk, and scrambled to my feet, reaching for my shotgun at the first sign of trouble. Quanah sat quietly beside my brother.

"A slight mechanical problem," she said. "You should get some rest."

Right. I looked around for Bonnie. Harry and Quanah were accounted for, but she wasn't. Should I have left her earlier? Was she in trouble? It didn't seem like her to stay gone.

Instead of settling back down, I moved to the door of the car, blinking rapidly and willing my vision to settle long enough for me to get to her. I reached for the handle of the bar car, pulling it open an inch. Sounds from inside stopped me mid-action. I peered in through the crack. The only thing visible in the darkened car was the moonlight outside. It highlighted the desert landscape, and revealed a silhouette seated on the bar. Long, dark hair whipped behind her, her neck arched. I could make out the curve of Bonnie's chin, her jaw, even the soft slope of her nose.

Bonnie moaned, her voice echoing throughout the empty car. Her body shuddered in pleasure, sending fire burning low in my belly.

The bartender's head wedged between her legs, his hands gripped around her creamy thighs. Bonnie's hands fisted his scalp, sending an intense flare of jealousy through me. I started to move into the car, intent on replacing the man and showing her what I could do, but her voice filled my mind.

*One night. Then we part ways in the morning and you never have to see me again.*

Bonnie had made it clear what she wanted, and it wasn't me. I wanted to punch something, or someone. I wanted to feel the rush of anger like this morning when I beat that guy's face in. How could she choose *him*, someone she didn't know, when I was right here? I slammed the door, not caring if she saw me. In fact, I wanted her to know I'd seen her. I turned my back, repeating over and over again that this was a lost cause and that I couldn't wait until we got to Roswell.

The train picked its course back up after another hour, but I was long asleep, the image of Bonnie's body writhing beneath the ministrations of another man haunting my dreams.

Someone shook rocks in a glass. Light spilled into the car, heating my skin. When I opened my eyes, a shadow stood over me. It was too bright, too loud, too *everything*. I sat up, blinking to steady my vision. Harry stood in front of me, shaking that stupid rattle Bonnie'd given to him.

"Mornin'," he said with a happy smile. The incessant noise continued. I yanked the rattle from him, meaning to toss it out of the car. Then I noticed we'd stopped. The Kid let out a strangled shriek and shouted my name. I threw the stupid thing back to him, moving to the open door.

"Where are we?" I asked, my throat scratchy and dry.

"Just outside of Albuquerque," Quanah answered as she appeared from another car. "We should reach Santa Fe tonight."

By the position of the sun, it had to be almost midday. Either that, or I was hallucinating. How had I slept so long? I glanced around the car.

Still no Bonnie.

I clenched my jaw, staring outside at the cactuses lining the tracks. I gripped the metal handle, the one I'd used to climb onto this stupid train and steady myself to help Bonnie. Above the trees I saw the ruins of a city. Tall half-collapsed structures marked Albuquerque in the distance. Behind it, a mountain towered, framing the city. I wondered if Bonnie had ever been there.

Jesus. Why did she consume me?

Probably because all I saw the entire night was the scene in the bar car, over and over. I relived it continuously, like I was tied up and being forced to watch. She was laughing at me. She had to be laughing at me, because I was so stupid. *She* didn't get jealous because I was flirting with those women last night.

Then again, I didn't fuck any of those women like my life depended on it either.

I needed to get out of my head. I needed to do something.

As fate would have it, the door to the car slid open, and in walked Bonnie, hair flowing over her shoulders, eyes clear, and a smile perched on her lips. When she saw me, she stopped, her eyes widening for a split second before flickering away.

"It's time for some lunch, Harry. Would you help me to the dining car?" Quanah asked. He led her away, leaving me alone with Bonnie. I couldn't look at her.

"I'm glad at least *one* of us had a good night," I spat, then jumped out of the open car door. I couldn't be alone with her. I didn't trust myself. I needed fresh air. I needed to get the fuck away from her. Her feet slammed into the dirt behind me. She grabbed my arm, yanking me to face her.

"What the fuck is that supposed to mean?" she asked, fury written in her eyes.

"Oh, I'm sorry, did that guy literally *fuck* your brains out? Because that's a stupid fucking question. I thought you were smart," I said.

Before I could blink, Bonnie slapped me. More than one pair of eyes turned toward us at the crack of her hand on my face.

"I'm *not* stupid!" she shouted, not seeming to care about the commotion we were causing.

I touched my cheek, startled by her sudden reaction. She took a half step toward me, her chest puffed forward and hand balled into a fist, as though she wanted to hit me again. She considered it, then relaxed her fist.

"Not that I owe you an explanation, farm boy," she said, running her fingers through the long, dark strands of her hair. "But you seem to have a hard time grasping the concept of a sexually empowered woman. So, before you start putting your *meek little dairy maid* standards on me, maybe you should shut up and listen." She was shaking, and so was I.

"I was The Kid's age when Jones started forcing me to help the crew run cons. The *same* con I pulled on you," she said. A lump formed in my throat; I struggled to swallow around it.

"Only, the kind of men who're lured by ten-year-old girls into dark alleys don't have your *gentlemanly* tendencies." She pressed a finger to my chest and bucked up to me, forcing me to take a step back.

"It was never about Will, or that guy last night, or you. It was about *me*. My body. My pleasure. My *choice*." She turned then, her entire body shaking. Fury was in her eyes; my shoulders deflated. Silence stretched long between us, but she didn't walk away.

"I already told you: you aren't my type," she said.

"And that Will guy is?" I said, my voice quieter than before.

"Yeah. He's a piece of shit. Fucked up and broken, just like me." Bonnie turned to face me, a sad smile on her lips. She let out a dark laugh. "You aren't like that. You're *way* too good for someone like me."

Then she walked away. I watched her climb into the car and out of sight.

It hit me then, standing alone on the side of that train, that she and I had an agreement, but that agreement didn't give me rights over her. It wasn't my place to judge her or shame her for her decisions. That's what they were. Hers.

Just like I could have fucked one of those women yesterday.

The difference was that I had feelings for her, and she didn't give a shit about me.

CHAPTER NINE

# BONNIE

HAD IT ONLY BEEN an hour? It'd felt like a hundred years. The train rocked before
dragging forward and gaining speed. *Finally.* The silence was stifling. Even The
Kid was too wary to speak. No doubt due to the glares shot like shrapnel between Jesse
and me anytime either one of us accidentally caught the other's gaze. Quanah, frustrated
with her multiple ignored attempts at conversation, shuffled out of the train car on stiff
limbs. I noticed her lumbering form through the small window of the car door.

The car door . . .

*I needed this. I could feel the tremors of my past like a sluice in my mind, gashing open
wide and threatening to drain the humanity from inside my skull. I let him kiss me, his
mouth too eager as his large lips crushed against mine. It was too harried to be considered a
good kiss, too greedy. I didn't care. This wasn't about indulgence. It was a necessity.*

*Will's words echoed louder and louder in my mind. Reminding me of all the things Jones
would do when he caught up to me. It'd been so close. Too close. Will's hands had been on my
skin. His blade pressed into my throat. Had it been his father, that blade would've dragged
along my body until I begged for death.*

*I needed to sink into mindlessness. Needed the heat from this man's skin to burn away all
the darkness inside of me. I pushed him away, hard. His eyebrows knit together in confusion,
until my hands dropped to my zipper and I stripped from the waist down. His eyes sank to
the place between my thighs, hungry. I pulled myself up on top of the bar and spread my
thighs shamelessly. A clear indication of what he should do next.*

*"You are so—"*

*"Shut up," I said as he neared me, his hands slipping over my bare legs. Another clouded
look of confusion. "I can't imagine you're someone else if you talk." I pressed my hands to his*

*shoulders until he dropped to his knees before me. I tried to order my thoughts, to imagine some other handsome stranger to distance myself from this, from everything. His breath on my inner thigh made me shudder. My eyes closed, and I tried to find the mindlessness I craved. At the first touch of his mouth against my flesh, an image of Jesse flashed in my mind.*

*No. I shouldn't be thinking about him. I knew that, but my body disobeyed me.*

*Those lightning strike eyes darkened in pleasure as he pressed me to the ground beside the fire. His smug smile on the top of that red rock in the desert. The scent of him lingering in the sheets of the bed we'd shared. How I'd touched myself that morning remembering the echo of his arms wrapped tight around me.*

*The mindlessness grew into something else, not an escape anymore, not sweet oblivion. I chased the sensation, desperate for more. I buried my fingers in his hair and dragged him against me.*

*Jesse's hips pressed too close to mine as we danced. His eyes lingering on my skin. Always lingering. How I felt those obsessive glances like fingertips all over my body.*

*More. I needed more. There was no mindlessness here. It was too real, too visceral, too fucking good. I moaned, unable to contain it. My body jerked on its own as I teetered on a knife's edge of something reckless.*

*A slam forced my eyes open to stare at Jesse's furious gaze before I shattered, gasping his name into the night. My pleasure rolled through me and left me feeling weak and spent. By the time I finished, Jesse was gone.*

*The betrayal in his eyes, however, lingered. No matter how I tried to forget, no amount of mindless pleasure would let me.*

Shame heated my cheeks in a furious flush as Quanah slammed the car door shut. She crossed to me with a stony look of understanding that felt like she could peer into my mind. Quanah handed me a steaming mug of herbal tea without comment or question.

Jesse sat in the corner, eyes carefully averted, using a small pocketknife to clean his fingernails as I leaned against one of the crates. The Kid settled down near me. I took a sip of the tea and grimaced at the bitter taste.

"What is that stuff?" The Kid asked, and I didn't know how to answer him. Naturally, he didn't let it go until I sighed deeply and fixed him with a too-honest stare.

"I like you, Kid, but I don't want one of my own." I raised my glass in a toast and took another large gulp, choking it down. The taste wasn't pleasant, but necessary. The angry words from earlier crowded the space between Jesse and me. There were things I said that I didn't mean, others I couldn't take back.

*I fucked him because I feel out of control when I'm with you.*

I couldn't say that, though. I closed my eyes against The Kid's incessant talking and remembered how it felt, waking up after Jesse held me all night. Surrounded by his scent on the sheets and the echo of his warmth on my skin. I'd woken up alone, sure that at some point I'd been tangled in his long limbs.

I'd never felt safer.

Maybe if I were a different person, that wouldn't scare me so much.

"Bonnie, what's rule number three?" The Kid asked. I blew some hair out of my eyes and turned to face his maelstrom of curiosity.

"Rule number three: keep your word," I said, draining my cup and standing on the now-thundering train car, the vibrations forcing me to continuously shift my balance to stay upright. "Outlaws may steal, lie, or cheat." I ruffled his hair affectionately. "But if we make a promise, we keep it."

"Like the promise you made in Vegas?" he asked. The air shifted wrong in my throat, and my eyes widened. How did he know about that? My pulse thrummed in my ears at the thought that The Kid had heard my not-so-decent proposal to Jesse.

"When you promised nothing bad would happen to me or Jesse while you were with us?"

I breathed a sigh of relief. My eyes softened at his innocent expression. My fingers ran through his beautiful blonde hair, like sunlight reflecting around his face.

"Yeah, Kid, I meant that promise," I said softly, my eyes sliding over to Jesse and offering a small, conciliatory smile. He didn't smile back, but something tense around his eyes relaxed. I half stumbled towards the open car door, looping my hands through the bar at the top for stability and watching as the sun dipped lower in the sky and the desert raced past. The light was fading quickly now, and sooner than I wanted to admit, we would be in Santa Fe.

Then Roswell.

"You can stay with us," The Kid said, stealing my attention from the desert landscape.

"What?" I said, blinking to clear my vision. I couldn't have heard him correctly.

"When we find Mom and Pop, you should stay with us! Jesse and Pop won't let Sixgun hurt you," he said, the idea catching like a spark and burning into a blaze of excitement on his face. I stared, open-mouthed, unsure how to respond. My frantic gaze shot to Jesse, a silent plea for help, but there was a dark expression in his eyes that stilled my words. What could've possibly made him appear so guilty?

"Mom's gonna like you a lot; she always talks about how she wished there were more girls around, and you can sing while Pop plays the piano and—"

"Kid," I said, crossing the car to kneel down in front of him. "Listen—"

But I never got to say what I wanted. A high-pitched screeching resounded around us, and the car lurched as if stopping too quickly. I slammed backwards and slid a foot towards the open car door before the momentum of the train righted itself. Before I could stand, Jesse was there, having crossed the space in a few long strides. His hands were on my arms as he helped me stand.

I searched frantically for The Kid, who was crouched near Quanah, helping her into a sitting position. She groaned at the quick movements.

"More mechanical trouble?" Jesse asked Quanah, but her eyes were wide and panicked. A soft shake of her head sent my heart hammering against my ribs.

"We shouldn't be stopping yet," she confirmed with worried words. I swung towards Jesse with a plan already forming on my lips.

"I'll check the other car," he confirmed before I even had a chance to speak. As I began to step away from him, I realized our hands were gripped tightly together, fingers entwined unconsciously. *When did we start holding hands?* I offered a gentle squeeze before dropping them and making purposeful strides toward The Kid.

"What's going on?" he asked, but I shook my head, gripping his arm tight and dragging him behind the metal crates on the far side of the car.

"Nothin' good," I said, eyes scanning for danger before falling to his fearful eyes and trembling lips. "Rule number four: always listen to your commanding officer." His bottom lip stopped wobbling as he nodded. "Stay here. Okay?" He opened his mouth to protest, but I gripped his shoulders tight. "Stay hidden. Stay quiet. No matter what you see or hear, you don't come out unless me or Jesse come get you. Got it?"

He clenched his teeth and nodded again. Fear rolled off of his tense shoulders; his hands shook as he white-knuckled the hilt of his knife. *Fuck.*

"Give me your knife," I said. He gripped the hilt tightly. I pulled Selene out of my waistband and offered her to him on an open palm. Reluctantly, he unsnapped the knife from his belt and handed it over.

"Remember, that's not a toy," I said. He cradled Selene to his chest and sat behind the crates, eyes wide in understanding. I stood and began to make my way across the space.

Now that The Kid was settled, I needed to find Jesse and—

"There you are, Bonnie." His voice was deep, slick with deadly intention, and too familiar. *Sixgun.* Frantically I unsheathed the knife and brandished it to the open car door and the darkness beyond. My heart crashed to my feet, and I struggled to breathe. Seeming to materialize from within the shadows themselves, Sixgun Ellis stepped onto the train car, his spurs echoing against the metal floor with each hateful step.

His smile was carnivorous, lips pulled back too far, exposing too many gleaming teeth in the dim light. Tipping up his black cowboy hat, he smirked at the small knife as my only defense against him. Heat pooled in the corners of my eyes, and I blinked it back, hard.

"Put the blade down," he commanded. His hand rested easily on the silver gun at his hip that'd given him his name. The need to run was desperate within me; my muscles burned with an ache to burst into action.

"I'm not goin' back, Sixgun. Not alive. You'll bring my corpse back, but not me," I said, voice raw. I turned the knife, pressing the blade to my throat. He laughed, a triumphant guffaw that put me even more on edge.

"I have a feeling you won't be doin' that," he said, smacking his lips and letting out a low whistle. The car door slammed open, and three men dragged Jesse in. He fought against their hands, wrenching his arms as hard as he could, trying to get free. They slammed him onto his knees. My arm fell down to my side, my knife forgotten.

"Bonnie—"

His anguished cry was cut off as one of the men slammed the butt of his pistol against Jesse's cheek. He cocked the hammer back and placed the barrel flush against the back of Jesse's head. I wavered, lurching a half step towards him with a strangled shout before catching myself. *What was I planning on doing?* Sixgun held all the cards, and with a glance at his self-satisfied grin, it was clear he knew it too. Sixgun whistled low, his spurs clanging against the floor as he walked a few paces closer. My eyes never left Jesse; unspoken words rested on my lips, but the opportunity to speak them was wrenched away.

"This is the same bastard from Vegas; imagine my surprise to see you still runnin' with him." He clicked his tongue in disappointment as he crossed to Jesse. "That's not like you at all." Sixgun pulled out a large Bowie knife from his gun belt, the metal glinting in the sparse lamplight as he reached towards Jesse. Not *that* knife.

"No!" I cried. I adjusted my grip on the hilt of the blade in my hand. "Leave him alone," I growled, watching as amusement flicked across Sixgun's face.

"Now, why would I do that? You know I don't like it when other men touch my masterpieces," he said, rounding on me, his madness flaring bright in the dark pits of his eyes. I swallowed down the fear that clawed its way up my throat and spared a glance at Jesse.

The choice was clear to me now. It was my life, my freedom, my dignity . . . or theirs. I couldn't have both. I sucked in a terrified breath and steeled myself against the choice. I had a promise to keep, and only one way to keep it.

"What if I go quietly?" I asked.

"No!" Jesse shouted, lurching forward so violently, one of the men holding him fired a warning shot. The sound blasted through the air, everyone flinched, and Sixgun swore. How stupid did you have to be to fire a gun in a metal train car? In their distraction, Jesse renewed his struggle, and I forced my eyes away from him.

"Will you let them go?" I asked, voice steadier than I felt.

"It's a deal," he said. His sneer deepened as I dropped the knife, defeated. He advanced on me like a mountain lion striking down its prey. Sixgun's thick fingers knotted themselves into my hair.

"Attagirl," he said, fisting his hand tight against my scalp until my eyes watered. He dragged me forward, stumbling, and threw me bodily to the ground. I landed hard, my shoulder screaming in pain as I stifled a groan at the impact. Quanah cried out in protest, and Sixgun snarled at the interruption.

"You promised. Now let 'em go," I said, catching my breath as Sixgun meticulously began to undo his ornate belt and slip it through the loops on his jeans, one loop at a time, painfully slow.

"I said I'd let 'em go. I didn't say *when*. I think they should see what happens when you forget your place," he said, leaning down to crowd me. I rose onto my elbows and spat in his face, watching with pleasure as he scraped the saliva from his cheeks.

The back of his hand cracked hard against my face. My teeth cut into the soft skin of my mouth, and I tasted blood. Pain flared bright behind my eyes, and I blinked to clear the black spots from my vision.

"Don't you fucking touch her," Jesse said, his deep canyon timbre laced with a deadly tone I didn't know he was capable of. Sixgun's expression hardened as he turned to regard Jesse for a few long moments. Whatever he saw in Jesse forced a glint of malevolence into his dark eyes.

"'Cause that would *bother* you," he said, testing the words out on his tongue. Like he couldn't understand why seeing someone hurt could possibly be hard to watch. "I wonder what'll bother you more: when I split open her skin, or when I fuck her while she bleeds."

His tongue darted out to wet his bottom lip. I trembled in the face of his depravity. Fear cloaked me; I breathed it down into my lungs, and it sank into my skin. I wasn't Bonnie the outlaw anymore. I was a scared little girl hiding helplessly beneath a bed, trying not to scream. Sixgun's hands came down on my body, and my flesh recoiled from his greedy fingers. He started to rip at my jeans, and I kicked out against him, but he pressed a knee against my chest until the pressure built and I couldn't breathe.

"I wonder if it bothers you that other men have touched your masterpiece," Jesse said, spitting blood onto the metal floor. "Because I've had my hands *all* over her." Sixgun stilled but didn't turn to face Jesse. "I don't think she's *your* masterpiece anymore."

Sixgun's dark eyes held no remorse, no empathy, no spark of human emotion. He leaned down until I could feel his rancid breath in my mouth.

"Is that true?" he asked, something unhinged in his tone. I couldn't speak. Heat gathered in my eyes, and my mouth opened wordlessly.

"Of course it's true," Jesse said, giving a bitter laugh. "You should ask the bartender she fucked last night." A muscle in Sixgun's jaw twitched, an indication he'd been pushed too far. Sixgun whirled to Jesse, knife flashing, and I screamed.

"No! Sixgun, *please*." My words were calming, pleading, begging. The fear that'd paralyzed me a moment before spurred me into action now. I crawled, scrambling over the metal floor on hands and knees until I could wedge myself between Jesse and Sixgun's knife.

I was close enough that Jesse's ragged breath feathered against my shoulder, and I could still feel the point of the knife, a prick of pain against my skin. I closed my eyes, trying to steady my breath. Jesse's chest was pressed against me, flush against my back, his hot skin and hammering heartbeat resonating into my body by proximity. My fingers twitched at my side, the tips of them brushing against Jesse's. He inhaled at the small contact. He slid his hand against mine in return as if to say, *I'm here.*

I opened my eyes, fixing a determined stare on the monster in front of me.

"I fucked her, too. I've been fucking her since Vegas," Jesse said, his voice tinged with desperation. "She's *my* masterpiece now."

"He's lying," I said, breathing slowly and deeply, hoping Sixgun would mirror me. The madness slowly receded from the corners of his eyes, but a calculating glint replaced it, his attention rapt on Jesse. Catching Sixgun's interest would be the death of him if I didn't intervene. I had to do something, anything, and I needed to do it fast.

"He didn't fuck me, but Will did," I blurted. Sixgun's eyes snapped to me, unbridled rage curling on his lips. My heart skittered and skipped, racing so fast it was a wonder it could still beat at all.

"What did you just say?" he snarled. I grit my teeth against the urge to make myself small in front of him. To cower.

"Why're you so upset? Because your son *ruined* your masterpiece?" I asked, glancing pointedly at his belt. "Or because he made me scream louder than your little *knife* ever could?"

"I'm gonna shut that whore mouth of yours!" he shouted, bringing his belt down against my shoulder. I flinched, the blow landing across my back. It knocked me off balance, and I fell. Sixgun wrapped the belt around my throat and tightened it before I could even blink. I gasped and choked, blood pounding in my temples and in my face as my whole body jerked and twisted with the lack of oxygen.

He squeezed harder, until the edges of my vision began to turn black. I beat my fists against his arms. I was on my back now, Sixgun straddled on top of me as my legs kicked uselessly beneath him and my nails clawed at the unyielding leather around my neck.

This was it. My vision began to fade in and out. My muscles slackened, and the fight drained from me as my eyes fluttered closed of their own accord.

"Not yet, bitch," Sixgun snarled, and the belt loosened. I arched up, sucking in sharp breaths in sweet relief. My eyes snapped open, and I coughed uncontrollably. I scrambled backwards, rolling onto my stomach and dragging myself inch by inch away from Sixgun as I fought to drink air into my lungs.

His boot slammed into my shoulder, and I cried out. He dragged me by my ankle and yanked me bodily until I was on my back beneath him again. I turned my head so I wouldn't have to look at him, squeezing my eyes shut tight as his thick fingers brushed my hair away from my face almost tenderly.

"Open your eyes and look at him!" he shouted, yanking my hair until I did as he wanted. Jesse's blue eyes were aflame, stark and devastating, like the heat of a lightning strike.

"We'll make him see whose masterpiece you are, won't we?" he breathed softly against the shell of my ear, as if he were talking to a lover. His fingers drifted down my neck and lower, to my collarbone. Everywhere he touched, I died. Until his exploring fingers found the bottom of my scar and he folded my sleeve up to expose the entirety of the knotted flesh to his hungry gaze.

"So much beautiful pain," he muttered, salivating. He swallowed, his desire straining against the front of his pants. His trembling fingertips brushed against my scar. He moaned, bringing his face close to the pink lines on my skin, tongue darting out as if he could taste the memory of my pain on my flesh.

"I'm going to do it to every inch of you. Every bit of your pale, perfect skin, knotted and angry. Just like this." His words were insane, eyes too wide, too focused on the skin in front of him.

"You'll do no such thing," Quanah said, her voice a lantern in the darkness of my mind. Sixgun turned to find the double barrel of Jesse's shotgun wielded by a broad-shouldered man in dirty blue jeans. My eyes widened, noticing twenty well-armed people who'd come to our defense. Sixgun and his men slowly raised their hands in defeat. One of Quanah's men grabbed Sixgun by the scruff of his neck and shoved him into the corner with the rest of his hired thugs.

My head banged back to the metal floor. Relief coursed through me; a pitiful sound wrenched itself from the back of my throat. I clenched my jaw tight, but it escaped anyway. I pressed the heels of my hands against my eyes. My lips trembled, but I refused to cry. Hot tears tried to sweep me away, but I pressed my hands down harder. I clenched my teeth until I thought my jaw might break. I wouldn't give him that.

Jesse's hands were on me the next instant, shocking my body into sudden awareness. It was the distraction I needed to help me ground my emotions and swallow down those poisonous tears. His hands were gentle. He cradled my head, checking for wounds. I blinked, his concerned expression the first thing I could clearly see. He didn't speak; he didn't have to. Tonight would stay with both of us always.

Wordlessly he reached down to me, pulling me onto my quaking feet. I leaned against him heavily. He pulled the belt from around my neck and tossed it away. His arms held me up, held me together. I pressed my cheek against his chest, content to hear the steady thump of his heart. Proof that he was alright, that we were both alive. I sighed in relief, sinking into the warmth of Jesse's arms. He buried his nose in my hair and inhaled deeply.

"What are you?" he whispered tenderly. A gentle reminder that soothed the raw edges of my fear and stilled my trembling hands. I raised my head from his chest, casting him a grateful glance before schooling my features into a mask of cool stoicism.

"I'm a goddamn outlaw," I said, my voice thin and scratchy. The Kid whimpered from his hiding place. Though I didn't want to step out of the strength of Jesse's arms, the urge to confirm The Kid's safety won out.

"Kid," I rasped, calling for him as loudly as my ravaged throat could manage. He rushed at me from behind the crates, nearly knocking me over as he flung his arms around me and crushed me in his embrace. He sobbed into my shirt in great, gasping breaths. My fingers ran through his hair until he calmed enough to peer up at me, his face red.

"None of that now," I whispered against his hair. "I'm alright. We're all alright."

Quanah crossed to us and reached out as if to brush my hair away from my face, but I recoiled from the touch. The train moved forward, unsettling me on my already-unsteady feet. Jesse wrapped an arm around my waist to balance me.

"There's a place for you in Flagstaff, Little Wolf," she said, her kind eyes making me deeply uncomfortable. "It'll always be there, if you want it."

Flagstaff wasn't where I belonged. As peaceful as it'd been. I couldn't say that out loud, so I just shook my head, ignoring the disappointment in her expression.

"I can't ever repay you for what you did tonight," I managed to croak, but Quanah waved away my concern.

"There's no need for that. Not after what you did for Beck," she said, and I nodded as understanding passed between us. Even. We'd call it even. For now.

The train rolled for a few minutes before it slowed again, pulling into Santa Fe. The lights of the city were too bright through the car door compared to the darkness from before. The Kid finally unwrapped himself from around me, looking to Jesse for an indication of what came next. Sixgun's wild laughter trilled on the cool night air.

"This isn't over," he said, grinning tight, eyes flashing towards The Kid. I shoved him closer to Jesse and held a hand out to Quanah impatiently.

"We're in Santa Fe," I told her, eyes hard. "Give me back my gun." She opened her mouth to protest, but my hard glare stilled the words.

"I'm going to tear you apart from the inside out, then stitch you back up again," Sixgun said as the cool, comforting metal of the M9 fell heavy in my hand. "You can run, but I won't stop."

"Bonnie—"

Whatever warning Quanah wanted to give me, I had no room for. Revenge pulsed hot in my blood. Crossing to Sixgun, I chambered a bullet with a loud *clack, clack*. He jutted his chin, and all I could see were his ravenous eyes and greedy hands that'd been all over me. My skin crawled in the places he'd touched me, and I heaved a breath.

"You don't have the guts," he said, confident I wouldn't be able to end his life. I wasn't as confident. I *wanted* to kill him. I wanted to watch as the life left his eyes. I wanted to bury him so far down he would never be able to touch me again.

A shot rang clear and high; Sixgun dropped to the floor of the car. He clutched his bloody knee, screaming in anguish, as blood seeped through his fingers and splattered on my shirt. A satisfied smile stretched languidly over my mouth.

"Have fun chasin' after me on that leg," I said as loudly as I could manage. I turned my back on him, chin high, ignoring the scandalized expressions from the onlookers in the car. A familiar face stared incredulously from the back corner. The bartender from last night. I hardened my expression and turned from him to face Jesse, ready to leave this place.

This night of horrors had *finally* come to an end. Quanah moved to Jesse, pulling him down for a kiss on the cheek and a motherly pat on the shoulder.

"Don't stop listening to your heart," she told Jesse cryptically. "It hasn't led you wrong so far."

"And you," she said, her head swinging around to me. "You could listen to yours a little more, you know." I rolled my eyes. The Kid hugged her tight, and I realized I'd be a little sad to leave her behind. I hoisted my pack over my shoulder and Jesse retrieved his shotgun, both of us eager to leave the bleeding madman far behind.

"Don't worry, we'll take him to the end of the line," Quanah said as we disembarked. Jesse reached a hand out to help me down. I didn't let it go afterwards. Before long, we found ourselves alone again. Just the three of us against whatever was waiting for us next in the darkness.

Right now, with Jesse's hand in mine and The Kid close at my heels, I felt like we could take on anything.

## CHAPTER TEN

# JESSE

S ILENCE SETTLED AROUND US like a heavy fog as we walked from the train station into the main strip of Santa Fe. Bonnie's hand clutched mine; it was hard to think about anything else. I didn't know what it meant. That she clutched onto my hand like a lifeline, that she ignored the bartender on the train. Confusion rippled from the small contact. The Kid led Bonnie's horse on her other side.

I wanted to talk to her, but I couldn't find the words. Even if I did, I wasn't sure they would be words of comfort. We could all use a little comfort. After tonight, I didn't want to imagine the other horrors Bonnie had seen at Sixgun's hand. I didn't want to think about that man ever again.

The cussing and fighting up the street in Santa Fe was a welcome change to the silence. Some of the tension relaxed in my shoulders. When did rowdy towns become normal for me? Either way, I was glad to be away from the train.

I sidestepped a man lying drunk in the street, guiding Bonnie around him with our joined hands. Harry paused, staring at the man with wide eyes. I motioned my head to keep him moving. Without a word, he fell in line, still leading Bonnie's horse.

We looked rough; I knew that before the onlookers stared at us. I could still feel the barrel of that man's gun against my head. Blood crusted at the corner of my mouth. All that mattered was that we were alive.

A fight broke out in the street, making the horses whinny. My horse tossed his head. I reached up to comfort him, dropping Bonnie's hand. I grabbed his bridle and whispered hushed words to calm him. Just one night here and we would move on.

"Home, sweet home," Bonnie said. The words startled me after not hearing her voice for so long. We walked the horses toward one of the buildings. I focused on tying mine to a post by a watering trough; The Kid followed my motions.

"This looks like the least rowdy place," Bonnie said.

Up the street, men laughed and fought. Women sauntered in front of the buildings. The one we stopped at wasn't quiet, but it would do.

"Yeah. Right," I said, shifting uncomfortably as I checked the knot on my horse's lead. I wanted more than anything to give Bonnie comfort, peace, but I wasn't the person for that. That would imply some sort of bond between us. Something more than just guiding us through the desert. Something I didn't think she would accept.

Bonnie led the way into the wooden building. Inside, over a dozen men drank, played cards, or danced. Two women sat in a corner, one playing a guitar and the other a fiddle. A lively tune filled the air, every other note punctuated by the stomps of the dancers.

As Bonnie marched purposefully toward the bar, I took in the sight of the woman behind it. Her black hair was shaved on the sides, and she had facial piercings. She saw Bonnie, and a lascivious smile crossed her features. She tightened her black suspenders, pulling the front of her shirt to show her cleavage.

"Hey, got any vacancy?" Bonnie asked. The woman plucked a toothpick from her mouth and leaned forward on the bar.

"Yeah, you can stay in my room, sugar," she said.

Jealousy blazed once more, reminding me of the last bartender, of the things I'd seen, of the fact that *I* hadn't been the one doing them to her. Bonnie, however, was unfazed by the woman's suggestion.

"Look, I just need one for the night. Do you have any available or not?" Bonnie asked, exasperated. The edge to her voice brought back that urge to protect her. I balled my hands into fists.

"We got one," the woman said. "How ya wanna pay? I got a few ideas if you don't have any money." She flashed another lascivious smile at Bonnie. I'd had *enough*. I fished out more than enough money for the room and slammed it down on the bar. She turned toward me, blinking, as though she hadn't noticed me.

"The room, please," I said through clenched teeth. We'd been through enough today.

The bartender picked up a key from the wall behind her, then tossed it onto the counter. It bounced off of the polished wooden surface and hit the floor. Bonnie moved to reach for it, but I stuck out my arm, stopping her. I grabbed the key, narrowing my eyes in warning, trying my damndest not to think about the last bartender that made a move on Bonnie.

"Jackass," the woman muttered as we turned to walk away. My shoulders tensed. Pop always said you shouldn't hit a woman, but tonight I wanted to make an exception.

"C'mon, let's get some rest," Bonnie said, ignoring the bartender's smug grin. She gripped my arm, warning in her blue eyes. She was right; a fight would do me no good.

By the time we shuffled upstairs and into our room, which thankfully had two beds, The Kid was already stripping his clothes off. I stole a glance at Bonnie, vague regret flashing through me at the thought of sleeping alone tonight. I rifled through the pack, sorting the food Quanah gave us. There was plenty of dried meat, hard cheese, sunflower seeds, and apples. I couldn't remember the last time I'd had apples. I tossed one to Harry and offered one to Bonnie, but she declined.

She stripped out of the bloodstained shirt; I turned my back to give her some semblance of privacy while she changed into sleep clothes. When she was finished, I lifted my eyebrows at her, pointedly staring at the food. She needed to eat *something*. Bonnie rifled through my pack. She ripped a piece of bread from the larger loaf and shoved it into her mouth. She arched an eyebrow with enough attitude that I could almost hear her say *there, you happy?* Nodding, I gave her a grim smile.

Through his crunching, Harry asked Bonnie questions about Sixgun. Lines creased across her forehead as Bonnie squinted, exhaustion written in her eyes. Her shoulders slumped as she moved to the wash basin on the nightstand. From the corner of my eye, I watched as she dipped a rag into the water. She walked over, handing it to me before climbing into one of the beds. My brother joined her a moment later.

"What's this for?" I asked her.

"You've got blood on your mouth," she said, settling into the blankets.

Right. I'd forgotten. I wiped my face, wishing I could as easily erase the memory of Bonnie's terrified eyes as Sixgun forced her to look at me.

"What does your scar say?" my brother asked.

"Get some sleep," I said. He finished the apple and tossed the core at me, grinning.

Within minutes, the two of them settled in. I extinguished the oil lamp on the table, then sat down with my back to them. My shoulders slumped as I leaned forward to rest my elbows on my knees. I ran a hand across my face, knowing the exhaustion would take me the moment I put my head down.

That it had only been this morning when Bonnie slapped me seemed insane. I felt like I'd lived a lifetime since then. While I was emotionally drained, I didn't think I could rest. I needed to do something physical, something to combat that helplessness welling deep inside me. It went all of the way back to Montana, when I couldn't help my parents. I'd barely managed to keep Harry safe. If I couldn't protect them, what good was I? If Bonnie or The Kid had been killed on the train, I wouldn't have survived. I'd already put us at risk trying to protect her.

It was the right thing to do, and yet, it was useless. *I* was useless.

It didn't take long for Harry's soft snores to fill the room. I glanced toward the other bed, finding Bonnie's eyes closed as though she were asleep. I tugged my shirt off, realizing that as much as I wanted to find a distraction, I wouldn't leave them. Not tonight. Not like I had on the train. I untied my boots, then set them aside and placed my shirt on top. Finally, I lay back on the mattress. It wasn't nearly as comfortable as the one at Quanah's home.

Then again, I'd held Bonnie all night. There wasn't anything as comfortable as that.

That thought scared me. She wasn't mine. She didn't want me. Not like I wanted her. The feeling of her body against mine haunted me as I fell asleep.

*The world was burning. Smoke surrounded me. It filled my lungs, choking me. I stumbled forward, blind, only the blaze ahead guiding my path.*

*"Mom? Pop!" I yelled. I pulled my shirt up to cover my mouth and nose as the flames grew closer.*

*"Jesse?" Mom's panicked voice echoed. "Jesse! You have to leave! You have to leave now!"*

*"Mom?" I wheeled around, but she wasn't there.*

*"You have to protect him, Jesse!"*

*"I am," I said. The words felt false on my tongue. Had I really protected my brother since that night? Since Vegas, all I'd done was put him in danger. Fire licked across my skin. I hissed and recoiled, stumbling over something. My ankle crunched beneath me as I landed hard on the charred ground.*

*When I turned to see what I'd tripped over, I found Harry, lying perfectly still, his eyes wide open. They were dim and unseeing, no curiosity lit within.*

*He was dead.*

112

*"Farm boy." I picked up my head, fighting back the tears threatening to spill over. Just beyond the flames, Bonnie came into view. Like the devil standing in the flames of hell.*

*"Bonnie! Help me!" But she just stood there.*

*"I can't, Jesse," she said. A loud crack came from above. Flames rained down, singeing my clothes and skin. I looked to Bonnie, but she turned her back.*

*"Where are you going?" I shouted over the roaring flames. She turned to me again, sorrow in those blue eyes of hers.*

*"I was always going to leave, Jesse. You know that," she said sadly. Her eyes were full of regret.*

*Wood groaned as she disappeared. I looked up, watching as a wooden beam split apart and came crashing down.*

Darkness greeted me when I snapped awake. Where was I? I blinked rapidly, then sat up, looking for Harry. My eyes adjusted to the dim light. Two figures curled together in the other bed. Harry. Bonnie.

*Bonnie.*

I pressed my palms into my eyes until they hurt.

Harry was safe, I'd been dreaming, but what did it mean? I couldn't forget how she'd looked at me before disappearing. That was what Bonnie was always going to do. Leave.

My chest tightened, forcing me to rasp in short breaths. I rolled out of bed, struggling to get to my feet and across the room. I shoved open the window and stuck my head out, gasping in the night air. Cold sweat covered my skin. My hands shook as I ran them over my face.

It was just a dream.

When my breathing finally slowed, I crossed to the basin of water. I splashed tepid water on my face, letting the droplets fall down my neck and onto my undershirt. I crossed back to the window and sat on the sill, staring out at the busy street.

The cool desert air filtered into the window. While my panic subsided for the moment, my hands still shook, and a leaden weight settled in my throat.

*Just a dream. Just a dream. Just a dream.*

The words echoed over and over. I thought back to Flagstaff, when she held the gun to her head and said she wouldn't go back. When it came to choosing between her safety and ours on the train, though, she brokered a deal to protect us. She was willing to give

113

herself up so we could escape. That she was willing to go back to Jones meant more to me than even I knew. It was no small thing. I'd never find a way to thank her.

The bed creaked from the other side of the room, and footsteps padded toward me. It wasn't my brother; he had heavier feet. She sat beside me on the windowsill.

"It's our last night together," Bonnie said softly.

Her skin glowed in the orange streetlight. She looked up with wide eyes. We knew that there was an end date to this little agreement. I just wasn't ready for it.

"Yeah," I said, turning back to the window. "How's your throat?"

"I'll survive. I always do," she said, fumbling with something in her hands. When I looked over at her, she opened her palm. She held a beautiful glass bead, covered in intricate carvings. It was incredibly dark. I took it from her, holding it up to the light. It was more blue than black, like her eyes. "Something to remember me, or trade, if you're ever in a pinch."

Rolling the bead between my fingers, I sighed. How had this come up so quickly? The long days in the desert made our tenuous agreement feel like it would stretch forever, though it hadn't been that long. It was strange that I knew her so well, and yet she was still a mystery to me. There were so many things that I wanted to know, but couldn't find the words to ask.

"I don't want what happened on the train to be the last thing you remember about me," Bonnie said, breaking the growing silence between us.

"I didn't think you cared what I thought," I said, averting my eyes back to the bead in my hand. I lifted it and gave her a nod. "Thank you."

"I recognized the guilt in your eyes when The Kid mentioned your parents," Bonnie said, gazing out at the street. I slipped the bead into my pocket to avoid looking at her. "What happened to them?"

She missed nothing. I tried to keep that guilt to myself; it was my burden to bear, my bad news. I didn't want anyone else to have to deal with it, least of all The Kid. I swallowed hard around the lump in my throat. Willing the sadness lying heavy like a stone in my chest to go away.

We sat together, watching as a couple kissed in the street. Regret flashed through me. I should have kissed Bonnie before we left Flagstaff.

"It's okay if you don't wanna talk about it," she said. "I didn't talk for a long time after my mom died. Some things there aren't words for. But, if you feel like talkin', I promise,

I'll listen." She reached over, grabbing my hand. A comforting warmth spread up from my fingertips at the contact. I stared at our joined hands, wondering when holding her hand had become such a natural thing for me.

"You're not easy," Bonnie said, breaking the lumbering silence. I looked at her. "You wanted to know why I robbed you in Vegas. I didn't rob you because I thought that it would be easy. Or fun," she added, with a shaky laugh. She let out a sharp breath, pulling her hand out of mine so she could run both of hers through her dark hair. "Most people, they're easy to figure out. With a glance I know exactly what they want and how to exploit it. But you—I couldn't tell what you wanted, and *I* wanted to prove to myself that I was up for the challenge of finding out." A smile lit up her features.

"And I thought it would be *fun*," Bonnie said with a crooked grin. "So, that's why I robbed you. You're different than I thought you would be."

"I wanted to be. Different," I said with a nod. "I didn't like the country life. I was better than the farm. I did the work, but I wanted out. Because I wasn't like them." A wave of devastation crashed over me. I swallowed around the lump in my throat, willing it down. My eyes heated, filling to the brim with tears. I didn't want to cry. Not in front of Bonnie.

As if sensing it, she lifted her small hand to cradle my cheek. I covered it with my own. Tears spilled over. Bonnie swiped them away with a gentle caress of her thumb. In her eyes, I found more empathy than I'd ever expected. Especially after the hateful glare she'd given me this morning.

Bonnie squeezed my hand. I watched her gaze lower to our joined fingers. Then I took a steely breath.

"I'd give anything to see them again. Mom. Pop . . . Clara," I said, the words shaky.

"What happened to her?" Bonnie asked, muted curiosity in her eyes.

"Same thing that happened to my parents. Fire." My throat constricted at the memory of the church in flames. I looked at the lump in the bed that was my brother. "The Kid thinks they're still out there. I didn't have the heart to tell him they burned alive. I buried them. I just . . . I don't understand why someone would attack us. They were farmers. Clara's father was a preacher. There was nothing special about any of us."

"Well, you were special enough to rob, farm boy," Bonnie said with a small grin.

Gunfire popped up the street. People shouted incoherent words. Then balls of light flew into the sky, exploding in bursts of brilliant reds, whites, and blues. *Fireworks.* I'd never seen them before, but Pop had told me stories about them. He said he got burned once because a fuse burned up too quick. I let out a shaky breath.

When I looked at Bonnie's face, she seemed distant. She looked at me, but I recognized the glaze in her eyes, the one indicating that someone was stuck in the past. The hard lines of her face disappeared, replaced by the soft slopes that I recognized. It was the first time I'd allowed myself to openly stare at her while she was awake, without fear or judgement.

I'd been wrong about her. I knew that now. I let her wound my pride in Vegas, but I could see it. She was strong. She was smart. She was beautiful. I would hate to see her go.

"What happened to yours?" I asked. Bonnie's attention focused on me, but her expression was difficult to read. She pushed off of the windowsill and walked across the room. When she came back, she held a hair comb adorned with opalescent pearls and dark blue stones. That must have been what I saw sticking out of her bag when we played I Spy. I took it from her, turning the elegant piece over. The comb was beautifully crafted. Shiny crystals between the other stones sparkled beneath the light filtering into the window.

Bonnie settled down beside me, sitting closer than she'd been before. She leaned into my shoulder.

"I was younger than The Kid when I asked her for this. I annoyed her for hours, begging her to play with my hair," she said, her expression glazed over in memory. A frown crossed her face. "She clipped my hair back, then we heard men shoutin' outside. The windows broke, and she told me to hide underneath the bed and be quiet.

"I saw four pairs of boots. She screamed. Next thing I knew, she was on the ground and they were ripping her dress . . ." Bonnie shuddered, and her words faded into silence. I wrapped an arm around her, tucking her beside me, in case it offered her some comfort. I couldn't imagine witnessing something like that now, much less when I was younger than my brother.

"When they were done, they put the barrel of a pistol to her temple. It was the first time I ever heard a gunshot," she said, wringing the comb between her hands. "Even though I promised to be quiet, I screamed. They dragged me from under the bed and took me away. I never had a dad. At least, not one I remember."

When Bonnie looked at me, she said, "I try to remember her now, but things have faded. I can't remember the way her laugh sounded or the way she smelled. But I remember her eyes; she had my eyes."

"They're beautiful eyes," I said, smiling gently. *You're beautiful*, I wanted to say, but the words remained, twisted on the tip of my tongue. She didn't want me. Not like that, and it wouldn't be fair of me to place that on her shoulders. It wasn't her fault that I had developed feelings for her.

Bonnie still looked at me, her eyes clouded as I set the comb on the windowsill beside me. She reached to cup my cheek, pressing her weight against me slowly. What was she doing? Her breath was soft on my lips as she brushed her nose against mine. My arm around her tensed. Her eyes fluttered closed, eyelashes feathering against my skin.

It was hard. It was *so* hard to be this close to her and not tell her how I felt.

"You should get some sleep," I said, pulling away. I put my hands on her arms to steady her, then stood. I could have taken advantage of the situation, but I wouldn't. It was our last night together. Even if things had changed since Vegas, kissing her now would only hurt me later.

One night with her wouldn't be enough. I'd rather never know what being with her was like than watch her ride away knowing I could never have her again.

"You, too," she said, her voice soft.

I brushed her dark hair behind her ear and pressed a gentle kiss to the crown of her head. At least we would leave things on amicable terms tomorrow. It was the best I could hope for.

Neither of us moved for a long time. I didn't want to go back to my nightmares, and I could tell she didn't either. Wordlessly, we moved together to my bed. Bonnie climbed in first. She didn't look at me, and I didn't know that I would have said anything if she did. I slid beneath the sheets behind her, not caring that there wasn't distance between us. She scooted back against my chest. I wrapped an arm around her, burying my face in her hair. I relaxed into the embrace, her scent snaring my senses and bringing me as close to home as I would ever be.

Bonnie laced her fingers through mine, holding me as though she were afraid of letting me go.

## CHAPTER ELEVEN

# BONNIE

J ESSE WAS BEAUTIFUL WHEN he slept. I didn't know a man could even *be* beautiful, but Jesse was. He had impossibly long, dark eyelashes I hadn't noticed until they fanned against his cheek. His mouth, as sculpted as the rest of him, was swollen from sleep. It made him look painfully kissable. I ached to run my fingertips over his stubbled jawline. I'd been lying there for too long, afraid to wake him, just watching him breathe.

He didn't kiss me last night.

I couldn't understand it. Today was our last day together, so we could've spent last night tangling the sheets around us. I'd never made the first move before, unless it was a con. Being rejected by Jesse had never crossed my mind. Now, I had been. *Twice.*

His oppressive heat surrounded me. As he stirred into wakefulness, I wriggled my hips against him. A not-so-innocent gesture he could write off as morning stretching. Bleary, blue eyes cracked open to focus on my face. His hand gripped my waist, and I shivered beneath his welcome touch. He ran a hand down my side. I arched my back in another innocuous stretch and pressed my breasts against the hard planes of his chest in encouragement. His eyes widened, and he muttered a soft *sorry*. His hands fell away from my body and left me wanting more.

Then he turned his back.

I watched as he shoved himself to sit on the edge of the bed, running his fingers through his hair vigorously. *Nothing.* He threw his shirt on and began to lace his boots. I buried my face in the pillow that still smelled like him and fought the urge to scream into it.

Since last night, all I'd been able to do was imagine his mouth hot on mine. The feel of his hard hands on my hips. I clenched my thighs together, hoping the pressure would ease the warmth flooding between them. Without raising my head, I heard Jesse waking The Kid and helping him to dress for the morning.

"C'mon, let's let Bonnie get dressed," he said in his deep canyon timbre.

"Don't take too long," he called softly.

I grunted into the pillow until the door snapped shut with a *snick*. As soon as he was gone, I threw the offending pillow at the door and fell back onto the mattress with a frustrated huff. The warmth from before turned into a mind-numbing heat settling into my blood.

I slipped my hand beneath the waistband of my sleep pants and closed my eyes. I'd touched myself like this the last time I woke up after sleeping in Jesse's arms. Then, it'd been a quick way to dismiss him from my mind. Now, much like on the train, I recalled memories of Jesse in startling clarity as fuel for my passion.

*That day in the alleyway, the night by the campfire, the way he moved our bodies together as we danced in Flagstaff . . .*

I bit my lip so hard I could have drawn blood. My skin burned, and a restlessness raged out of control inside me. I opened my eyes to catch sight of my mother's hair comb on the windowsill. Suddenly I couldn't feel the rising tension anymore. The heat still raged, driving me to insanity, but not delivering the swell of pleasure.

*His eyes in the darkness, flooding with tears. His hand on mine as my heart broke open for him. The way he'd looked at me when Sixgun forced my eyes open. As if he would burn the world down to keep me safe . . .*

This wasn't working.

Even my imagination was a pale facsimile of Jesse. Giving up, I threw the covers off and pulled open my pack, searching for something clean and not bloodstained. A smile crossed my face as I changed, slipping quickly into my shorts and the tightest shirt I owned, cut low enough to catch Jesse's attention for sure.

If I was going to burn, so would he.

In moments, I was packed and ready, taking the steps two at a time. Jesse glanced up from tying his pack to his horse's saddle, and something in his expression shifted. A second later, the flash of shock and desire was hidden behind a careful mask of cool indifference.

*Not even the shorts?*

I crossed to my mustang, tying my pack down, albeit a bit too forcefully. The heat pulsed within me now, making me uncomfortable and flushed.

"Can I ride with you, Bonnie?" The Kid asked. I blew the hair out of my face in frustration and waved him forward.

"Sure, Kid," I said, helping him into the stirrup so he could swing his leg over before climbing on after him.

"We still have to name your horse," he said, very seriously. I smiled, the edge of my bad mood dulling. Clicking my tongue, I started off on the trail out of town, Jesse trotting along beside me silently. The morning was quiet and still, as if the whole world was waiting for something to happen. Of course, after only ten minutes, The Kid's voice cut through the relative peace.

"Bonnie?" he asked. "Can't you stay with me and Jesse?" His words were small, and something painful twisted deep in my chest as I squeezed my arms around him a little tighter. I shook my head softly, watching his shoulders slump as he let out a long-resigned sigh.

"Rule number five: never overstay your welcome," I said, but The Kid didn't take the bait. "Besides, I have worse people than Sixgun after me. I need to disappear if I have any chance of outrunning them."

"Worse than Sixgun?" he asked, incredulous. I laughed, ruffling his hair affectionately.

"You know who's worse than Sixgun?" I asked, watching as his insatiable curiosity blazed to life again.

"Who?" he asked.

"Crater beasts. Have I told you about the panther scorpions yet?" I asked. He flicked an uninterested wrist in my general direction.

"Quanah already told me about them," he said, and I feigned hurt.

"Oh, okay. So I guess you don't wanna hear about the great snapping lion turtles?" I asked, until he begged me to describe the beast. I'd kept my eyes carefully trained away from Jesse as he spit sunflower seed shells during the ride. Truthfully, I was still upset with him from last night.

My thoughts took a dark turn as the merriment ebbed and flowed. I'd told Jesse more last night than I'd told anyone. Part of me wondered if now that he knew me, saw me clearly, he couldn't handle my brokenness. Maybe what he saw was so ugly, he didn't want me. As soon as those thoughts came, The Kid was asking for another story and lifting my mood again.

"Hey, Bonnie?" The Kid asked. I should've probably been annoyed at his questions, but honestly, I was grateful for the time with him before we parted ways. I would miss his inquiring mind.

"Where are you going to go?" he asked, worrying his bottom lip with his teeth, eyebrows furrowed low over his eyes.

"I was thinking about St. Louis," I said with a shrug. "Word has it the gangs were chased out a few years ago. Not havin' to run may be the closest I ever get to an apple pie kind of life."

"Me and Jesse could come too!" The Kid exclaimed, nearly unseating himself from the saddle. Jesse choked on a sunflower seed. I would've glared, but I refused to look at him after last night.

"Sorry, Kid, but I think it's best if you do a little growin' up first. Besides, you know better than anyone it takes a lot of hard work to become an outlaw," I said. He nodded, deep in thought.

"What about Eagle?" he asked. "Your horse. What if we name her Eagle?"

"What's an Eagle?" I asked, confused. Jesse laughed, and I looked at him for the first time this morning, hating how handsome his stupid face looked when he smiled. The heat that'd been muted during the ride flared bright and burned deep when he smiled at me. I bit my bottom lip hard, silently willing the flush in my face to dissipate. *I'm not blushing. I can't be blushing.*

"It's a bird," Jesse said. "Or it was. Our mom taught us about them."

"Yeah, that's a great name, Kid. Eagle. I like it," I said, my voice clipped through my fight to regain control of my senses. *What was wrong with me?*

Flustered again, I twisted the reins until my knuckles were white. I needed to *do* something. Anything. To stop thinking about Jesse and how badly I wanted to kiss him. Sucking in a deep breath, I fixed Jesse with a flirtatious smile. He raised a bored eyebrow at me, obviously too used to my particular brand of coercion.

"Hey, Jesse," I said, my voice low and husky. "Wanna race?" I bit my lip. The Kid whooped and Jesse's answering smile nearly unseated me. His playful grin would highlight my dreams for weeks to come.

"You're on," he said. Before I could even think about it, I dug my heels recklessly into my mount. I let out a cry as the air whipped past, whistling in my ears. Eagle was born for this; I'd known since the first day I laid eyes on her. Leaning down, I urged her faster, keeping The Kid in the cage of my arms as he hung onto the saddle horn for dear life.

The thrumming of the wind, the merciless pounding of Eagle's hooves beneath us, and the synchronicity of the telltale beat of my heart connected me to this place, this moment. It was here, racing towards the unknown, that I came alive. That I remembered what life could feel like.

Just when I forgot we were racing at all, I caught sight of Jesse's mount from the corner of my eyes, nosing ahead. They were a sight to behold, Jesse bent low over his stallion, the both of them long and lean. The sun glinted off of his horse's legs like burnished copper, and Jesse's eyes shone as bright as a cloudless sky. I caught his gaze, wild and disastrous, racing together toward some inevitable culmination.

We were the same. We were wild, untamable things. We were *free*.

Together we crested the hill, slowing down, Jesse's stallion having taken the lead in our race. Jesse threw his head back, crying out in victory. The Kid scrambled down from Eagle's saddle to pepper him with wide-eyed questions.

"You win some, you lose some," I said, gulping in unsteady breaths.

"I wanna ride with Jesse!" The Kid exclaimed, but Jesse wasn't looking at him. He hadn't stopped staring at me. I couldn't break the intensity of his stare. I gulped. Squirming in my saddle as the unbearable heat stirred to life within me again. He stared at me like this wildness we'd touched had unchained something inside him, something that'd been there all along. Something I was responsible for. When he stared at me like that, I was naked beneath his scrutiny.

I wanted to be naked beneath his body.

Forcing my gaze awkwardly to the reins and readjusting my grip, I was able to close my eyes briefly and remember where I was. *Get a grip.* Jesse answered some of The Kid's millions of questions, smiling at him affectionately. Suddenly, I realized how close I was to saying goodbye to them.

They weren't friends, not really, but they were as close as I would probably ever come. I would miss them. Shielding my eyes from the sun, I peered out over the horizon, my breath stilling at the sight before me.

Spread out below us, a lake carved out its own basin from the red rock surrounding it, the water still and perfect like glass. It was a shade of blue so deep it was almost black, and reminded me of the bead I'd given Jesse last night. *When he wouldn't kiss me.* The bitter thought swelled in the awe of the moment.

I led Eagle down the path, marveling at the intensity of the colors of this place. As if life had burst forth in a kaleidoscope, almost too vibrant to look at directly. Most of the trees and shrubs had pale green foliage and branches that were short and wiry. The lichen clinging to the stones, however, was an emerald green so dark it reminded me of shadows in the forest. With the red rock looming around on all sides, the sounds were rounded in an ethereal way. Echoing endlessly back. Insects buzzed and chirped in a symphony of sounds, the quiet hum of life ever present. I led Eagle through a tuft of small purple flowers blooming in patches, almost obscuring the path. As if this place were completely forgotten, unknown to anyone. I thought, perhaps, this was the closest I would ever get to heaven.

The thud of hooves catching up sounded on the gentle breeze. I dismounted quickly, letting Eagle drink her fill of the water, causing ripples on the surface. I laughed, the sound incredulous. Without hesitation, I pulled my boots off. For the first time since I could remember, I felt like maybe life could be about more than just surviving.

In one slick motion, I pulled my shirt off and tossed it on top of my boots. I turned to make a sarcastic remark, but the words died. My body was shocked into sudden awareness. Jesse's eyes were liquid heat, roving my curves with unmasked lust. Every nerve ending crackled like electricity inside my skin. The Kid splashed in the water, but I was burning alive.

I licked my lips, as they'd suddenly gone dry. The motion brought his eyes to my mouth, and my pulse hammered in my ears. He swung off of his horse and slid onto his feet.

"You comin', farm boy?" I asked, breathless, popping the top button on my shorts. I took a bracing breath to steady myself. He'd rejected me last night, and I wanted him to regret it. Instead of fighting another losing battle against my traitorous body, I turned away and slid my shorts down over my legs. Picking up one of my boots, I whirled and threw it at him, nearly catching him in the chest, since he wasn't paying attention to anything other than the view.

"What was that for?" he asked, focusing back on my face.

"For being a creep," I said, a playful grin on my mouth.

"If you didn't want me to look, you should've kept your clothes on," he said, dropping my boot. I backed slowly into the water until it was halfway up my calves.

"Who said I didn't want you to look?" I asked, enjoying the shock on his face at my blatant flirting. I turned to walk farther in, until the water was waist high, then dared a look back. I'd seen Jesse shirtless before; we'd glimpsed each other during changes in dark rooms or by dim campfire light. Nothing had prepared me for this.

Jesse tossed his shirt off, and the air shifted wrong in my throat, choking me. Beneath the midmorning sun, every ridge and hollow in his labor-hardened body was on clear display. His lower abdominal muscles dipped towards the midline of his jeans. Desire pulsed hot within me, throbbed in every part of my body.

I wanted to run my tongue down every groove and ridge on his chiseled torso. I wanted to wrap my legs around him and ride him like Eagle at a full gallop. I wanted to see that playful grin of his staring up at me from between my thighs. I wanted—

Realization slammed into me, cooling my feverish skin better than the lake water ever could.

I didn't *need* Jesse. I didn't need him to help me regain control of my body. I didn't need him to distract me from nightmares or memories of my past. I didn't need him to dull the sting of my loneliness. I wanted him.

I *wanted* him.

I wanted him to keep holding my hand. I wanted him to annoy me until I ate at night. I wanted to wake up next to him again tomorrow. I wanted him to *want me back*.

Hot tears welled in my eyes. I ducked beneath the water so he couldn't see. Because it didn't matter how much I wanted Jesse. Today was our last day together, and I couldn't have him.

## CHAPTER TWELVE

# JESSE

T HOUGH I KEPT A cool mask on, I couldn't help but wonder *why* Bonnie wasn't speaking to me today. What had I done to piss her off? I thought after our conversation last night that things would be easier. Instead, she seemed determined to drive me crazy. From the short shorts she wore to how she bit her bottom lip when suggesting we race.

Didn't she know how she affected me? I tried to be indifferent, but by the time we got to the lake, I was dying. Especially watching her unclothe so seductively. I remembered the soft curves of her body and how she molded beneath my touch.

I'd wanted her then, but not nearly as much as right now.

All we had was today. When we got to Roswell, our arrangement would end. Maybe I could let myself enjoy it. Bonnie ducked beneath the water, and I slid my boots off, then my jeans.

The Kid splashed near her, calling for Bonnie to watch him. He flung himself backwards, sending up a large wave. When was the last time we went swimming? Though he was normally carefree, something about splashing around in the water reminded me of his youth and innocence.

We deserved a break after everything we'd gone through.

When she turned away, I adjusted myself before heading in. The water cooled my hot skin, a beautiful reprieve from the burning sun overhead. When the water reached my chest, Bonnie swam toward me, eyes alight with mischief. The expression caught me by surprise. She was usually serious, her eyes always alert with the next job, the next step. I hadn't yet seen her look playful. I liked this side of her.

Her hands slid onto my shoulders, and I narrowed my eyes playfully at her, wondering what she was doing. If she tried to kiss me, I couldn't deny her again.

Then she shoved me under.

The water burned my eyes and throat. I came up to the surface sputtering, intent on seeking revenge. She tried to swim away from me, but I grabbed her around the waist, dragging her back against my chest. She was different today, as though her hard exterior had melted away and she felt free.

"Not so fast," I said, chuckling. I lifted her out of the water and tossed her away from me. When she surfaced, she splashed me in the face, grinning. I grinned back.

"Let me jump from your shoulders!" The Kid exclaimed. I ducked beneath the water. He climbed on my shoulders, and I shot up, sending him into the water. He resurfaced, smiling and begging to be thrown again. So I did. Again and again until he tired of it and swam farther out into the lake.

I liked seeing them like this. It was a welcome change of pace. And a good way to delay Bonnie's departure.

"This was a good idea," I said to her.

"Do I have any other kind?" she asked with a flirtatious smile. Bonnie usually didn't flirt; she belittled, insulted, and teased me at every opportunity. Instead of answering, I darted toward her.

"Jesse! Don't you dare!" she warned, but I didn't listen. Using both hands, I dunked her beneath the water. She came up sputtering. I only felt slightly bad.

"Jerk," she grumbled, still smiling at me.

"Tease," I said, remembering the heat in her eyes as she'd undressed in front of me, as though it was *for* me.

"Flirt," she said.

"You started it."

"You *liked* it."

"Keep telling yourself that, sweetheart," I said, lifting my eyebrows suggestively.

"Maybe I will." She bit her bottom lip and moved toward me. My gaze fell to her mouth, to that damn lip. She had no idea how much I wanted to bite that lip. I reached my hands beneath the water to grab her hips, but before I could act on my impulses, The Kid swam up.

"Guys!" His eyes were wide with excitement; his mouth opened to say something. I put my hand on top of his head and shoved him beneath the water, holding him there before squaring off with Bonnie again.

"Jesse! Let him up," she said.

"In a minute, we're not done," I said. Bonnie grabbed my forearm, but I didn't move.

"You're gonna kill him!"

"He's fine. Now, where were we?" I asked with a smirk.

"Let him up or I'll stop arguing with you." Though her features were serious, I could tell by the look in her eyes that she enjoyed every second of it.

"Somehow I seriously doubt that." One of the most enjoyable things about us was the playful banter. Even when it wasn't playful, sparring with her was the highlight of my day. Bonnie pushed against my ribs, sending me backward. I let go of my brother and he resurfaced, gasping for air.

"You could have killed me!" The Kid said. His face cracked into a grin, so he couldn't have been *that* mad.

"No. Way. Jesse James is *ticklish*?" She darted for me again, and I squirmed away.

"I'm not ticklish. You're just getting handsy," I said, unable to wipe away my grin even if I wanted to. She reached toward me again, but I caught her hands, trapping them in my own. I moved a step closer to her. Bonnie couldn't touch the bottom, but I could.

"My hands never bothered you before," she said, her voice deeper. Her eyes darkened as she looked at me.

I didn't kiss her last night. Every time I didn't kiss her, I regretted it. I was tired of regretting it. I tipped my head toward her. One of the horses whinnied, breaking the moment. Bonnie slipped out of my grip, murmuring something about tying them off. I watched her swim toward shore. Water slid down her body; the sun glinted off of her skin, highlighting her better features. Specifically, her ass. I'd appreciated it many, many times since meeting her, but seeing it barely clothed almost undid me. I cupped my hands together, then splashed water over my face. I needed to calm down.

"Jesse! Throw me!" my brother shouted. I turned my attention from Bonnie, who was tying the horses to a nearby tree.

"Not right now, Kid," I said. Harry narrowed his eyes at me.

"What?" I asked.

"You called me Kid," he said with a grin.

127

Honestly, I hadn't noticed. It came out so easily.

"I guess I did," I said, sparing another glance at Bonnie, who stroked Eagle's mane. I appreciated the curve of her hips for a long moment.

"Why don't we grab some food?" I called out to The Kid.

I didn't know when it became my responsibility to make sure everyone ate or drank or slept. But I didn't mind. Especially if it got me closer to a nearly naked Bonnie.

"Nah," The Kid said, swimming away. Bonnie's back still faced me. Our time grew ever short. I wondered if maybe she was glad for the delay, but then again, I could have just hoped she didn't want to leave us. Something scaly slithered past my leg. I saw movement in the clear water. Fish.

"Hey, Bon," I called. "Ever been fishing?" My voice carried over the silent oasis. She picked her head up from Eagle to look at me.

"No. Why would I? I grew up in the desert, idiot," she said. A smile crossed her face. I walked through the mud and onto the warm bank.

"It's easy," I said, grabbing the large knife she'd given to Harry. She scoffed at me, but I ignored it.

"Hey, Kid! Guess we get to teach Bonnie something for once. Want to do some fishing?"

My brother hollered and headed for the shore. When I glanced at Bonnie, there was a scowl on her lips, but her eyes glimmered at me. I smirked before searching through the sparse trees that dotted the shore of the lake. I cut a couple of branches into sturdy lengths, then got to work.

Twenty minutes and a lot of ingenuity later, I had a couple of rough looking fishing poles. The Kid stood nearby, bouncing on the balls of his feet.

"These don't have a fancy reel like the ones Pop had. We'll have to work at it," I said.

"You look like Pop," The Kid said suddenly.

The words smacked me in the chest. "What?"

"When you smiled like that." My brother grinned, then bounded off toward a small rock embankment on one side of the lake. I didn't have a chance to digest the words.

"C'mon," I said, grabbing Bonnie by the wrist.

"Now who's getting handsy?" she asked with a grin. I flashed a smile at her as we joined The Kid on the hot rocks. Though the underside of my thighs burned, it was nothing compared to the flush of my skin as Bonnie slid down beside me, her leg against mine.

I was keenly aware of the contact, to the point that I forgot I was supposed to be doing something. Vaguely, my mind registered faint scars crisscrossing her ribs on one side. I looked at her; she stared back through her eyelashes. My brother said something, which shocked me back to the moment.

"Want a go?" I asked Bonnie, holding the rod toward her.

"Oh! Jesse! I got one!" The Kid shouted beside me. I didn't have a chance to question the barb on Bonnie's tongue and the mischief in her eyes.

"Okay, keep a steady grip, don't pull too hard," I said. I leaned toward him, ready to offer a hand if needed. "Remember, slow and steady."

"Like the tortoise," he said, giving a curt nod. I wasn't surprised that he remembered. His favorite bedtime story was the one about the tortoise and the hare. I was more surprised by the memory of Pop, the first time he brought Harry fishing with us, and the way he'd used the story to teach him how to handle a fishing rod.

"Yeah, bud," I said. "Just like the tortoise." The Kid's tongue stuck out of his mouth as he leaned back, focused on pulling the fish out of the water.

Then the rod snapped in half.

He blinked, staring at the piece in his hand. His face turned red, and he stood.

"This is stupid," he said, throwing it to the ground. The stick bounced off of the rock and into the water, sending ripples cascading across the glassy surface of the lake. He stalked off.

"Well," I said. "Kids." I wanted to comfort my brother, encourage him, but I didn't know how. I wasn't Mom or Pop. I'd never been good with him. We'd managed to regain a sliver of our past. I got comfortable enough to think things could be like they once were. I knew he really wanted to catch one, and maybe he felt the same disappointment I did.

"He just wants to be good at something," Bonnie said in a low voice as we watched Harry plant himself on the sandy shore, legs tucked beneath his chin. "He looks up to you." I turned to her, surprise and confusion warring in my chest. "He just wants to feel included."

I'd never thought of it like that before.

It made sense. Any time Pop invited him to join us, whether we hunted or fished or just tended the farm, he was excited. I'd brushed it off, bitter about the differences between the way our parents raised me and the way they were raising him.

All he wanted was to be a part of it, whatever *it* was. Why didn't I see that before?

"It's not like it was," I said, lowering my gaze to the fishing rod in my hands. "It never will be. Maybe it *is* stupid, trying to make things like they used to be."

"It's not stupid," Bonnie said. I looked up at her, surprised by the compassion in her eyes.

"No?" I asked. Her eyes softened as she looked at me. She placed a hand on my thigh, gentle, almost innocent.

"Show me," she said, her voice full of certainty.

Something changed between us. Something significant. After all we'd gone through in our short time together, it was inevitable we'd find ourselves on the same side.

"Okay." The word felt stupid coming from between my lips. I put an arm around her, placing the rod in her hands. The scar on her arm caught my attention. Lines of angry pink skin spelled out the name of the man who'd raised her. Anger coursed through me, remembering how Sixgun had owned carving the word into her skin.

"Keep a firm grip on it," I said, tucking her in front of me. My chest was hot against her back. An effect of the afternoon sun, I tried to convince myself. I leaned forward, perching my head above her shoulder.

I guided her hands to toss the line into the water. She took in a sharp breath. My pulse pounded in my ears.

"Like this?" she asked, breathless. I nodded.

"Just like that," I whispered, hoping she couldn't feel my hardening cock at her back. This was the closest we'd been since that first night.

That fire within me, the one that smoldered for her, began to burn.

Bonnie turned her head in my direction, her hot breath hitting my cheek in short bursts. I'd wondered if her reaction to me in that alleyway was all show. Based on her quick breaths and the flush on her skin, I had a feeling that wasn't the case. Heat surged as the fire inside of me raged; the need I'd stamped down broke past my carefully curated walls. I couldn't hide it anymore. I didn't want to.

"Eyes forward," I said, gulping. Bonnie didn't listen to me. I tilted my head back to look at her.

There was heat and desire and downright longing in her eyes. Her hot breath caressed my lips, reminding me of last night, of how she'd wanted to kiss me. I'd wanted to, even more than I had in Vegas. I lifted one hand to her cheek, gently cradling her face as her eyes fluttered closed and her lips parted.

One kiss wouldn't end the world, right?

I tipped my head down, pressing my lips to hers slowly, gently. There was heat, but there wasn't urgency. The desperation in her last kiss outside of Vegas was gone, replaced with a vulnerability that I didn't think she'd ever show me. I ran my tongue across her bottom lip, and Bonnie obliged, opening her lips beneath mine. I groaned against her mouth.

One kiss might not end the world, but it could certainly kill me.

## CHAPTER THIRTEEN

# BONNIE

I WAS DROWNING. I was trembling. I was aching. I was dying.

My fingers buried in his lake-water-slickened hair. Droplets freed from the ends by my mussing to rain down on my feverish skin. His tongue slid against mine slowly, as if we had all the time in the world and all he wanted to do with it was savor me.

I don't know what happened to the fishing pole, if it fell into the water or rolled into the shrubs. There wasn't room for anything but Jesse. He filled my vision, his taste causing a slick heat to grow bright within me. He groaned against my mouth, and I gasped into his. The rumble of his groan shuddered through my whole body.

*Stop, Bonnie.*

But I couldn't. His hand slid from my cheek to the back of my head, fingers tangled in long dark strands of my hair. The heat in my blood raged until my bones melted and my body grew pliant in his arms. Jesse didn't grab at me, the way most men did. Instead, his hands held me steady, pressing along my spine until there was no space left between us. My heart slammed against my ribs so hard I was sure he could feel the galloping rhythm through my skin. In all the nights of passion I'd shared with beautiful strangers, I'd never felt like this before.

Naked.

Sure, they'd seen me naked, but that was just my body. Jesse saw *me*, all my scars and jagged broken pieces. Maybe for him it was how little I was wearing, but for me, this kiss was the first I'd had with all my guards down. It was just me kissing him now. Not Bonnie the outlaw or Bonnie the vixen. Just a broken, lonely girl who'd never felt safe or cherished until right now in his arms.

"Hey! Stop kissin' already! I'm hungry!" The Kid shouted, and we both stilled, neither breathing. Jesse pulled away, hunger burning low and steady in his blue eyes. I dropped my arms, chest heaving, as the realization of what I'd done sank into my feverish skin. I'd broken all my carefully crafted rules for a taste of him.

"We're coming," Jesse shouted back. He turned to me, his hand sliding to the small of my back, leaning forward as if he would kiss me again. Panic flashed through me suddenly. I pushed away from him, putting space between us. Gulping in air that didn't make me dizzy with his scent. Dread unfurled within me, like tendrils of ice, forcing a shiver down my spine.

*What was I doing?*

"Bonnie." His voice was that deep canyon timbre, soothing, as if he could read the panic on my breath. Maybe he could. "That kiss—"

*Tell him. Tell him how much you want to do it again,* an insidious voice whispered in the back of my mind. *Don't run away, you fucking coward. Coward!*

I stood and retreated swiftly, fear and longing and loneliness mingling into a cocktail of emotions that triggered the familiar urge to run. Before I got more than a few steps, Jesse gripped my upper arm. His fingers clenched tight around the knotted scar tissue that'd long since lost feeling. My past crashed into me, like a tidal wave of darkness.

"Don't touch me," I said, wrenching my arm from him. The claws of that darkness dug deep inside and left me raw and shattered. I covered the knotted scar with my hand, as if to hide it from his sight. Jesse's eyes had been soft when he looked at me before; now they were wide and concerned. He held his hands up, as if to calm a spooked horse.

"Talk to me," he said. *How?* In a few hours, none of this would matter anymore. I wouldn't matter anymore. Not to him. I'd ride away into the night, and he'd never see me again. He would find another farm girl to marry and think about me on lonely nights. The broken girl who'd outsmarted him once and probably wound up dead somewhere along the way.

"Why?" I asked, my words hard and bitter. "All I've *been doing* is talking to you. Yet you can't seem to hear anything I'm sayin'. How many times do I have to tell you that I'm not your type before you get it?" Confusion dimmed the bright shine of his blue eyes. His hands fisted at his sides, and he took an angry step forward.

"Then why the hell did you try to kiss me last night? Why'd you climb into *my* bed?" he asked. I clenched my teeth to keep the words I wanted to say locked tight within me. *I feel safe with you.* I'd be gone in a few hours; I couldn't tell him that. I couldn't leave that piece of me behind. I had so few left already.

"Maybe I thought you'd stop looking so wounded after I fucked that guy on the train. Did you ever think of that?" I said, the words ugly and untrue. I wanted to hurt him as much as it hurt me to leave him. His hands fell to his sides, shock stealing his words.

"I'm not some charity case," he said, the deep timbre of his voice hinting at barely veiled anger. He looked away, taking a steadying breath before turning back to me.

"I don't care about what happened on the train," he said, his voice deeper and calmer than before. Without thinking, I snorted derisively.

"Sure you don't, farm boy," I retorted, my words designed to wound his pride. "That's why I had to stop you from starting a bar fight with that woman hittin' on me in Santa Fe, right? Because you *don't care.*"

"Yeah, well, she—"

"Of course, I must not know what I'm talkin' about. I had my *brains fucked out,* after all," I said, each word bitter like poison on my tongue. "It's kinda funny, you callin' me stupid when all you've done since I met you is stupid shit. The mirage, letting your brother almost get killed by a snake, giving Selene to that skeezy innkeeper, telling Sixgun you fucked me . . ." I ticked off each instance on my fingers, arching my eyebrow in a clear challenge.

"Excuse me for trying to save your life," he said, condescension dripping from his tone.

"No one asked you to do that." I huffed in frustration. "The only thing a hero is good for is dyin' young. I don't need *anyone* to save me. I never have, and I never will."

"Then I should've just turned you over to Sixgun in Vegas!" Jesse shouted.

Each word thudded into me like the point of a knife. I gave myself up for him. Something I swore I'd *never* do. I'd like to think I kept my face indifferent, but that'd be a lie. My expression screwed up, hurt and betrayed, before I could stamp it down.

"I guess it's a good thing you'll be rid of me soon, then!" I spat, my heart falling to my feet as I fought the tears in my voice. I only half-succeeded.

"I guess so!" he shouted back.

"Fine!" I yelled. Because I was too angry to think up anything meaner.

"Fine," he said, the muscle in his jaw twitching as he clenched his teeth together.

I turned my back so he wouldn't see my face fall. I walked down the path towards the lake, and The Kid was on his feet as soon as he saw me. I clenched my feelings down tight, because he noticed everything. I crossed to the horses and unbuckled one of the saddle bags. The Kid already had questions poised on his lips.

Pulling out a pair of jeans and sliding them onto my damp legs, I hopped up and down to get them over my hips before zipping them. After that, I pulled on a long-sleeved shirt with a conservative neckline. Certain that I didn't want to feel exposed in front of Jesse.

"Why are you mad at Jesse?" The Kid asked, but I ignored him the best I could as I shuffled into my clothes. "Is it because you kissed him?"

Heat burned my cheeks. "I didn't kiss him, *he* kissed *me*," I corrected, the words snapping tight, but The Kid didn't care. He just barreled on with his endless questions.

"Or did you miss catching a fish too?" he asked. It seemed so stuffy all of a sudden. "It was the kissing, wasn't it?"

"Rule number one, Kid!" I screeched. The sharp tone of my words reverberated around us, echoing back to my ears and making me cringe. The Kid's face fell, eyes wide and fearful, as if he'd never seen me before. I regretted the harsh words instantly, tugging him to my chest and pressing a kiss to the crown of his head. After a while I began to gather our belongings and tie everything down for the afternoon ride that would separate us forever.

In the hours that followed, I kept my distance from Jesse. The Kid swam, we ate in silence, and before long, we were riding towards Roswell. I paused briefly, looking over my shoulder as the sun set behind the ridge of the lake, knowing that as horribly as the day had ended, I'd never forget this place. The sun dipped low, and my heart thudded in my throat every time we turned a corner.

Would this be the turn that led us into Roswell? Would this be the last time I saw The Kid smile or heard him complain? *Were those the last words I would ever say to Jesse?*

If I hadn't been so lost in my thoughts, I would've noticed sooner. The night was too quiet, too still. The closer we got to Roswell, the more my sense of unease grew. I couldn't see the glow of any lanterns or campfires, couldn't hear anything beyond the howl of coyotes in the distance. The moon was bright enough to make out the shapes of buildings as we rode closer. Buildings overgrown with spindly plants, the shards of broken windows glinting like jagged teeth in the moonlight.

"Where's this base of yours?" I asked, trepidation in my voice. The Kid cracked open bleary eyes as we stalled the horses somewhere on the north side of the town. Jesse, however, didn't acknowledge me at all. He was looking around the town, knuckles bleached white against the reins in his fist. *I guess he isn't talking to me.*

He swung down from his horse and walked until we reached the center of town. Once we'd reached the main thoroughfare, it was clear this place had been abandoned long ago. The buildings here were crumbling, faded scorch marks on the shop fronts and the skeletal remains of awnings that might've been colorful once. Now everything was awash in gray moonlight, everything except the orange glow of a single lantern.

Fear settled into a hard knot in the pit of my stomach, the hairs on the back of my neck standing on end in warning. Despite my misgivings, Jesse pushed toward the light. An old woman sat outside the ruins of a shop, a knife moving in her hands as she worked, hunched over in the dim lamplight.

"Excuse me." Jesse's deep voice startled me in the silence of the night. The woman didn't acknowledge him at all. I stared at her, my eyes assessing for potential risks. The only thing I could clearly make out was the knife in her hand. No hidden guns or weapons.

"Jesse," I hissed in warning. He was too close to avoid a stab if she were to attack him. He didn't even turn in my direction, insistent on ignoring me. I clenched my teeth together to stop the angry words resting on my tongue. My eyes fell to her face, the silver of scar tissue reflecting the moonlight as she kept her eyes downcast. Dread flooded through me, cold and unsettling.

"Hey, lady!" The Kid shouted, trying to gain her attention.

"Hush," Jesse snapped paternally, earning a grumble from The Kid.

"Excuse me," he said again, leaning closer to the woman. My heart was in my throat, my hand gripping tight to the handle of the M9 as I clicked the safety off.

She lifted her head, and Jesse took a startled step backwards. Half of her face had been burned away at one point, now hardened into silvery scar tissue. Where she'd once had hair was only hard, marred flesh. One of her eyes was sunken too far into her skull, an eerie, unseeing white film covering it. The burns were violent and ugly, reminding me of another violent and ugly scar. The memories yawned open in the blackness of the night surrounding us. *Let's remind her where her loyalties lie.* Jones's voice filled my mind.

"We're looking for the Air Force base near here. Do you know where it is?" Jesse asked, and she nodded, seemingly unable to speak as she tried to gesture with her crooked fingers. "Can you show us?" He realized quickly he wouldn't be able to understand her game of charades.

I didn't like this. I didn't like this woman, or her scars. I didn't like the idea of taking her with us.

"You can ride my horse," Jesse offered. My eyes snapped to his face, furious words poised on my tongue. "Kid, ride with Bonnie."

It was the first time he'd acknowledged me since our fight. His eyes were hard, unyielding, and as The Kid shuffled out of Jesse's saddle and scrambled over to climb up mine, I scoffed at his blatant command. I was under no obligation to ride with them to the base. If it weren't for The Kid, I would've told Jesse to go fuck himself back at the lake.

"I hope you know what you're doin', farm boy," I said, a warning and a threat. Then, because I couldn't help myself, I added, "It's not *smart* to trust an undesirable."

He'd already turned away, shoulders bristling at my tone, and let the woman lead us forward through the night. The clop of hooves against crumbling asphalt echoed eerily in the silence of the night. We continued on that way, until we couldn't see the buildings of Roswell anymore.

She kept riding into the thick of the wilderness, turning off the asphalt path and leading us into strange woods. Another half hour and my grip on the M9 was punishing. With each turn, the dark shapes of water-starved trees like skeletal hands crowded closer. As if beckoning us back the way we came.

Turning a corner, the woman stopped Jesse's horse with a tight pull of the reins, and Eagle pranced away from a makeshift fence in the distance. The bioluminescent blue glow of hundreds of glowroot plants, clustered together like constellations in the night sky, forced a sound from my throat I didn't recognize. Fear, thick and suffocating, robbed me of speech. My stomach thrashed, threatening to empty itself. The old woman scrambled down, motioning with arthritic hands and opening her useless mouth to say something to Jesse. It was clear what lay beyond the fence.

The destroyed remains of the base, sunken deep into a crater.

My heart hammered in my throat, strangling me and stealing my breath. My hands fumbled as I knotted the reins, shoving them into The Kid's hands. I prepared to leap from my saddle at the first sign of danger.

"Where is it?" The Kid asked, his voice small and scared. As if he too could sense the threat beyond that rickety fence. The woman's hands flailed more dramatically, and Jesse's eyebrows furrowed in concentration, as if he were still trying to understand her garbled warning.

Then we heard it.

The rumble of a growl, clicking and terrible, rising louder than thunder from beyond the confines of the fence. The sound unraveled me with each bass-like tone, shaking violently into my bones like an otherworldly death knell.

"Get on your horse," I whispered to Jesse, praying for the first time in my life that he would finally listen to me. He stood still, frozen. A flash of yellow eyes in the darkness, too large, too tall for a normal beast.

"Now!" I shouted, the word wrenched from somewhere primal. The creature, still obscured by darkness, slammed against the chain link fence as Jesse shot into motion. The M9 was in my hand, but I couldn't shoot what I couldn't see. Eagle reared back, nearly unseating me and The Kid.

I dug my heels into Eagle's flanks as Jesse swung up onto his horse. The old woman ran in the opposite direction, a significant limp hindering any progress she could have made. A piercing screech reverberated in the air. The beast slammed into the fence again, shattering the metal with a twisted clang.

A thought penetrated the fear pulsing in my mind: we'd never know if the old woman survived, since she couldn't scream.

Adrenaline flooded through me with each rapid breath and pounding beat of my heart. Eagle shot forward, her survival instincts driving her to new speeds. Underbrush ripped beneath jagged claws, too close to us. My head swiveled around, searching for any sight of the beast. A flash of yellow eyes in the darkness, closing in on Jesse's right flank. *No.*

I yanked the reins hard, forcing Eagle to close the space between us. The beast was black as pitch, barely noticeable in the dark until it peeled back its lips to extend white fangs as long as Jesse's arm.

"Hard left!" I shouted, hoping Jesse understood my hurried command. I pulled up on Eagle's reins and let Jesse cut in front of me. I extended the M9 to the creature and squeezed off a shot.

I missed. Or the beast's hide was too thick for a bullet to penetrate. Another predatory screech lit the night. I shoved the reins at The Kid.

"Hold her steady, Kid!" I shouted over the rush of blood in my ears and the frantic whistling of the wind. The fangs glinted in the moonlight, gaining on us, and I did the only thing I could do. I shot at it. Again and again and again. The gunfire echoed before an inhuman howl lit the night. The thud of the beast falling nearly forced Eagle to stumble.

My ears rang as I took the reins from The Kid, veering Eagle off the path. We rode hard, for so long that I worried about Eagle's endurance and pushed her past her limit, twice. Until finally, we were so far away from where we'd seen the beast that I slowed us.

My pulse still pounded in my ears. I didn't know if I was terrified or furious or relieved. I slid off the saddle onto quaking feet. My whole body thrummed with the need to run. My eyes caught sight of Jesse, tying off his horse.

Before he could register the fury hardening my features, I was across the space, shoving him with all my weight until he was forced back a few steps.

"What the *fuck* was that?!" I shouted, punching him solidly in the chest. I shoved him again, but he didn't move. "You're so stupid!" I yelled, raising my fist to hit him again. He caught it easily in his hand, staring incredulously as it trembled in his firm grasp.

"Why are you shaking?" he asked, his voice softer than I'd thought it would be. Concerned.

"Why the fuck do you think?" I said, yanking my hand out of his to run it nervously through my hair. Before I'd even realized I'd moved, my arms wrapped tight around him, face buried between his shoulder and neck. I hugged him tight as relief flooded through my entire body. He was warm and here and *alive*.

"You could've died," I whispered against his neck. My breath shuddered as the air shifted strangely in my throat.

His scent filled my nose and eased the panic lingering from our near-death experience. After a moment, his strong arms wrapped solidly around me, and he held me tight. Pressing me as close to him as I could get, his fingers in my hair. I couldn't tell how long we stood like that. Long enough for my heart to stop pounding and for me to feel safe again. As safe as I always felt in Jesse's embrace.

I pulled away first, my arms dropping from around his shoulders. The cold night air rushed into the space between us and raised goosebumps on my skin. His eyes were bright and piercing, unasked questions on his mouth. His gaze dropped to my lips the same way they had before we'd kissed at the lake.

"W-we should probably set up camp," I said, stumbling over the words. I stepped away from him. After the disaster of our last kiss, it was probably best to keep my distance. Besides, I hadn't quite forgiven him for what he'd said earlier.

The Kid waited for me, saddlebags untied from Eagle and bedrolls already set out. Mine and his, anyway. I ruffled my fingers through his hair, smiling down at him proudly.

"Bonnie?" he asked, and I took Eagle's reins to tie her down near Jesse's horse as The Kid followed behind. "I helped you shoot that crater beast, didn't I?" I nodded, exhausted already. "Do you think that makes me a *real* outlaw?"

I fixed him with a thoughtful stare.

"Kid, I think you're more of an outlaw than I am some days," I told him, cuffing his chin affectionately. "No fire tonight, and we take watch in shifts. You think you can help set up the rest of camp?"

He nodded, schooling his face into a serious expression that was nearly comical before getting to work.

I noticed Jesse from the corner of my eye, his broad shoulders shifting beneath the thin material of his shirt as he unpacked with The Kid. I didn't know how to be like this with anyone. There was something undeniable between us. Barely caged in like that crater beast, looking for an opportunity to break free. This feeling was dangerous. It would consume me if I let it.

The Kid was too wound up to fall asleep straight away, so as usual he looked to me for entertainment.

"Tell me a story, Bonnie," he said, tucked up to his chin in the bedding to stave off the chill without a fire to warm him. I sighed, so exhausted I couldn't make my thoughts line up to form one.

"I can't think of one right now," I said, running my fingers through his hair. It was starting to curl at the ends.

"Tell us about the undesirables," Jesse said, his voice troubled. In the moonlight, the hollows of his face seemed deeper, the lines around his eyes furrowed in guilt. Was he thinking about what happened to that old woman? "Back there. You said not to trust them, but I've never heard that word before."

"I need to make my way to Montana," I said, snorting derisively. Jesse didn't smile; instead his eyes clouded in confusion until the joke registered. He barked out a laugh, the sound too sharp, as if he'd laughed against his better judgment. Clearing my throat, I pulled the blanket of my bedding up higher on my lap. "You saw. Undesirables are deformed, or touched by the Culling. Some people, the superstitious ones, claim they spread disease. All I know is, they live on the fringes. In the burned-out, forgotten places. They're called *undesirables* because no one wants them."

"That's just *wrong*," Jesse said, a hard glint in his eyes. I shrugged, leveling a stare at him.

"All I know is, I've lived on the fringes before, or been close enough to see how bad it can get. That old woman was nice enough, but not all of them are sweet ol' ladies. If you get hungry enough, or desperate enough, you'll do just about anything to survive. So next time, don't get so close when one has a knife in hand," I said, before tucking The Kid's bedding up to his shoulders and following suit. I stared up at the stars for a while, until The Kid's sleepy voice muttered beside me.

"After you leave us, will we ever see you again?" he asked, but I didn't answer. He was already out cold anyway. Before I knew it, I fell fast asleep, feeling weightless and warm like we were back at the lake. Floating.

*"Bonnie," Jones's voice said, roaring through my mind. "My Bonnie girl." There were hands on my arms, pinning me down. A blindfold was ripped from over my eyes, and I saw clearly where I was. Jones's tent, being held down by two crewmen as Jones lazily lit the end of a fat cigar. The smoke was too sweet and stifling in the heat.*

*"You know why you're here, don't you?" he asked, grinning too widely. This was when he was the most dangerous. When he was enjoying it. "Beck's missing. A little birdie told me you had something to do with that." The man on my right turned away, and I noticed he was wearing a familiar dusty cowboy hat. Will? Will wouldn't have ratted me out to Jones. He couldn't have.*

*A hard hand yanked my chin up to meet Jones's dark gaze. The calculating glint in his eyes assessing me, finding all my weak spots and ready to crack them open wide. My bottom lip trembled, but I held my tears back. He got angry when I cried.*

*"Not my Bonnie girl," Jones said, his words slick and mocking. "She would never betray me. She knows what happens when people betray me." The back of his hand cracked against my cheekbone. I bit back a cry of pain.*

*"When I first found you, you were just this wild-eyed, half-starved brat. I made you into what you are. I can unmake you just as easily. Let's see how long it'll take you to break," he said, his grin twisting into a scowl as I begged for mercy I knew he wouldn't give.*

"No! Please!" I shouted, shooting up from my bedroll and grasping at my left arm. My eyes were wild. I gulped in air as if surfacing from deep water. *It was just a dream,* I reminded myself. I pulled up the sleeve of my shirt and felt the hard ridges of the healed scar. No blood. No water. Just the memory of what had happened that night pounding through me. My head fell into my hands as I reminded myself that I'd survived that night, which meant I could survive this one too.

"You okay?" Jesse asked, his voice startling me. He was leaning forward, as if he'd been moments from coming to me when I woke suddenly. If he'd asked me that a couple weeks ago, I might have resented his kindness. I knew him better now. I shook my head, an easy answer to a complicated question. I didn't know if I'd ever be okay.

I stood, retrieving my flask from one of Eagle's saddlebags before crossing to Jesse. I sat next to him, my hands shaking so hard I almost couldn't twist the cap off. Wordlessly, I handed it to him.

"It had to do with your scar, didn't it?" he asked. I nodded, still not recovered enough for words. After passing the flask a few times, my hands stilled as the whiskey warmed my blood. I studied his handsome face in the dark. The moonlight caught on the high points of his face, the sharpness of his jaw. It was a real shame he hated me, because I could have used a good fuck to distract me from the ugliness in my mind.

"Want to talk about it?" he asked.

"Not really," I said, my voice an unattractive croak.

"If you didn't want to talk to me, then why did you come over here?" The edge was back in his voice, like earlier at the lake when things got ugly. He sighed and took a large swallow of the whiskey before trying again, this time calmer.

"It seemed *bad*," he said.

"It was," I responded in a clipped tone. He scoffed, shoving to his feet. *It's hard for me to talk about!* I wanted to shout, but the words wouldn't come.

"Fine. If you're going to stay up, then I'm going to sleep," he said, but I made a strange noise in the back of my throat and reached forward to grab his hand. I didn't want him to leave; I didn't want to be alone in the dark with my past. He stared down at our hands, then at my fearful face.

"Do you know what waterboarding is?" I asked, in a voice I barely recognized. I'd never felt so small and unsure before. He sat again, in one fluid motion, entwining his fingers with mine. I bit my lip, trying to think of where to start.

"You've met Sixgun," I said, my eyes on my boots. Jesse squeezed my hand reassuringly. "But, he's just a thug. A crazy thug, with certain *appetites*, as you saw. He's nothing compared to *Jones*. It's Jones who runs things."

He shuffled closer, until his thigh was pressed against mine. Heat emanated from his body.

"He was in the military before the Culling. Black Ops. They trained him to be ruthless, cunning, cruel. The perfect weapon."

I shivered, and he wrapped his arm around my shoulders, never rushing me.

"They trained him to interrogate enemy soldiers and terrorists in black sites all over the world. And he's *good at it*. Waterboarding is . . ." I choked on the words, hardly able to say them. "It's drowning on dry land. Brought to the brink of death, over and over and over again." Silence blanketed us both. There was nothing but the truth of the monster in my mind on the night air between us. My breath fogged in front of me. I wasn't sure if he heard me at all. Not until he put his hand on my jaw and raised my face until I was staring into his eyes.

"Why would he do that to you?" he asked, angry. Angry like he was on the train, the kind of anger that could break the world apart if I let it. I swallowed down my trepidation.

"Jones sees something he wants, and he takes it. That's what he did to Beck. He saw her and he took her," I said, feeling stronger now with his eyes on mine. "He had her for *years*, and every night I could hear her cry when he was done with her. It was like I was back under that bed, watching it happen to my mother, over and over again. Until one day, I couldn't take it anymore. So I helped her escape. Jones's one rule is that the only way out of the crew is at the end of a noose." I swallowed down the last of my trepidation, wetting my lips as the rest of the past came pouring out like dark blood, staining the night in shades of violence.

"This was around the time Will and I were . . . *together*. I hurt him when I told him it didn't mean the same thing to me that it did to him. I guess I underestimated how *much* I hurt him, because he saw me helping Beck and he ratted me out. When Jones found out I'd betrayed him, he lost it. He tortured me until I told him everything. Which, thankfully, wasn't a lot. Then he let Sixgun *remind* me where my loyalties lie." Jesse pressed his forehead into mine. I closed my eyes and drank in his scent, soothing my jagged edges with his warmth. Like leather and desert dust and something all his own.

"Sometimes, at night, it's like I'm back there. Drowning over and over again, then Sixgun carving into my skin. I feel weak and powerless, just like my mom was that night," I said. Jesse shifted until I was nestled against his chest. I could hear the steady thump of his heart against my cheek. *Safe.* I was safe when he held me.

143

"Sometimes at night," he said into my hair, "I can still smell the ash from the fire, and something else, something worse." I squeezed his hand tight, and we stayed like that for a long time, silent. At some point, Jesse disentangled from me and crossed to my bedding, pulling a blanket around both of our shoulders to stave off the chill. He was the first one to break the comfortable silence that'd settled between us in the long moments after.

"I didn't mean what I said earlier, about turning you over to Sixgun. I was just . . ." He struggled for the words.

"Hurt?" I offered, and he nodded. "I know. I have a talent for pushing people away."

"I still shouldn't have said it," he muttered near my ear, his arm tightening around my shoulders to hold me closer.

"Do you really think I'm stupid?" I asked.

"No, I think you're the smartest person I've ever met," he said, with all the conviction with which he said everything else. I smiled against his shirt. "Did you really climb into my bed because you thought I was upset about the train?"

"No," I croaked, hiding my face as best I could. "I don't have nightmares when you hold me."

"I don't have nightmares when I hold you either," he admitted.

So I let him. I let him hold me all night. We didn't speak, we just leaned against each other until the sky began to lighten and the shadows of our pasts seemed to fade into the distance. The Kid stirred, and regretfully, we had to disentangle from each other.

I moved first, stretching my arms over my head and crossing to Eagle's saddlebag to pull out my map. Jesse's eyes followed me; I felt them on my skin. A few moments later, he crossed to me as I stared down at the map, biting my nail and studying the familiar lines.

"So, your uncle clearly wasn't in Roswell," I said. He ran a weary hand over his face.

"Nope," he said.

"Got any ideas what to do now?" I asked. He shook his head. "Okay, well, we can figure it out." I unfolded the map and spread it before us so I could look at the entire area. "As far as I can tell by the stars last night, we're about here." I pointed to an area on the map, and Jesse ducked his head to see it more closely. "If your uncle was in the military and his base got bombed, what would he do?"

I tucked some wayward hair behind my ear and bit my nail again. My eyes traced the familiar symbols and lines on the map. Places I'd marked in my travels with Jones. Trading posts, craters, dangerous places, and military outposts.

"He'd probably travel to the closest military base, for backup or a commanding officer. Right?" I asked. Jesse stared at me with warmth in his eyes, and it was incredibly distracting. "The closest one is here." I pointed out the place I'd marked.

"Fort Hood, Texas," he said as The Kid finally dragged himself off the ground, his bedding still around his shoulders as he shuffled on weary feet over to us. "Yeah, let's do it."

"It's a long way, farther than we've come so far," I said, rising onto my feet and doing a mental inventory of our supplies.

"I thought you were leaving," The Kid said. I stilled. That was right. I was supposed to leave them now. The deal we'd struck outside of Vegas didn't apply anymore.

"Rule number six, Kid," I said, and he looked up at me expectantly. "Pay your debts. If you wanted to get rid of me so badly, you should tell your brother to stop saving my life."

Jesse stared at me with an unasked question on his lips.

"The train, remember?" I said.

He smiled, all the way to his eyes.

"You're coming with us?" The Kid asked, and I nodded, watching as he blinked himself into wakefulness and started running around camp in his excitement. We gathered our things and mounted up again. I locked eyes with Jesse as we started out for the morning's ride together.

Something had changed between us last night. Something I was through running from.

## CHAPTER FOURTEEN

# JESSE

FORT HOOD. YET ANOTHER mystery location where my uncle might or might not be. My mother's instructions loomed over me like a falling tree, heavy and unyielding. It hadn't occurred to me that Michael Kincaid wouldn't be in Roswell.

I appreciated Bonnie's quick thinking, because I didn't know what to do.

Even as we set out, Fort Hood our final destination, I couldn't help but wonder if this was all for nothing. What if we traveled all this way, and when we got there, nothing? Mom would never steer us wrong intentionally.

"Not sure about Eagle," I said a while after we set out, "but my horse's shoes are pretty worn. We're gonna need to find a blacksmith soon."

"Shouldn't be too hard to find. Probably would be good to give them a couple of days to rest, too," Bonnie said, eyes narrowed as she stared out across the vast desert.

We pushed the horses forward at a steady trot, not wanting to drive too hard. As the heat of the day wore on, my eyes lingered on Bonnie more often, watching nearly every move she made. Like a moth drawn to the flame, I was hooked. In such a short time, I'd learned more about her than I'd ever thought I would. Not to mention the hot and cold between us.

One second, she could be kissing me, and the next, hitting me.

Bonnie was infuriating, but she was also tantalizing. I couldn't control myself around her. Back on the train, I'd thought I was done with it. I'd thought I could shove those feelings down and fight my way through to Roswell, long enough for her to ride away.

Except she wasn't leaving.

What did that mean? What did the kissing mean? What did the small pieces of herself that she'd given to me mean?

Now that she was leading us to Fort Hood, the questions kept coming, and my mind kept racing. I didn't know what to feel. I was glad she wasn't leaving us but, at the same time, worried what that meant. Rescuing her on the train was a flimsy excuse for her to stick around, and we both knew it.

By the middle of the day, we stopped long enough to take inventory of our supplies and eat a quick bite. The food from Flagstaff wouldn't last forever. We rationed what little we had left.

After another half hour of riding in relative quiet, I glanced over at her again. Her shoulders were relaxed. While she wasn't smiling, she wasn't scowling either. I missed seeing her smile, especially when she thought I wasn't looking.

"I'd give just about anything to be back at that lake," I tossed over at her. Before our argument, it was the best day I'd had since leaving Montana. "Maybe we'll go back some day." The words tumbled from my mouth without thought. Of course we wouldn't. Because one day, Bonnie would be gone, and it would be me and The Kid again. Without her.

"Say we go back," Bonnie said, breaking through my dark thoughts. "What would we do there?"

A smile crept across my face. There were plenty of filthy things I'd like to do to her at that lake. Although none of those things were appropriate to say within earshot of my brother.

"Anything. Everything," I said, turning to face forward. "That's the beauty of it."

I felt Bonnie's eyes on me. When I turned to look at her, a smile rested on her lips.

"If you had one day," I said, "one day that you weren't on the run and didn't need to pull cons on people, what would you do?"

Bonnie paused, thinking over her answer. She was quiet for so long, I thought she might not answer me.

"I think I'd sit in a room all day and read," she said, her voice dreamy. Her eyes seemed to glaze over.

"Why in the world would you want to do that?" I asked. Her shoulders straightened, tense. I'd offended her, but she tried not to show it. She turned forward.

"Why not? What would you do?" she asked, her tone masked.

"I'd go to Hershey, Pennsylvania," The Kid chimed in. "Mom said they had a chocolate factory." I smiled, remembering how much he loved sweets.

147

"I'd go to the ocean," I said. "Mom once told me that Pop took her there before we were born. There was water as far the eye could see. Gotta be better than this desert anyways."

Another two days passed before we came upon the first sign of life. While Quanah gave us more than enough food for the trip from Santa Fe to Roswell, none of us could have prepared for how much longer we had to go. Water supplies were frighteningly low. I would take barely a sip, just enough to wet my tongue, before passing the canteen over to one of the others.

I had to make sure they had enough. I trusted that if anything happened to me, Bonnie would press on, and she would take care of The Kid. My faith in her surprised me. We weren't just a couple of strangers leaning on one another to get through the night anymore.

It was more now. Much more.

Each night, we'd roll out our bedding, and by morning, Bonnie's stuff would be tangled with mine. We tried our best to keep watch during the night, but there were plenty of times one or both of us fell asleep when we shouldn't have. Having her in my arms was the most natural thing in the world. The nightmares that had plagued me since Montana ceased to exist. The desert was still exhausting, but either I'd become used to the harsh conditions or could handle them better when I was well rested.

On the days I woke up before her, I would study the lines of Bonnie's face, committing the arch of her eyebrow and the pout of her bottom lip to memory. I imagined drawing her untroubled expression, so I could keep her long after we went our separate ways. I wanted to remember how warm and soft she felt; I wanted to capture her likeness so a part of her would always be mine.

As the sun descended behind us on the third day of endless desert, we crested a hill that opened into a large valley. Not far ahead, a stone structure stuck a few feet out of the ground. A man stood by it, a small wagon beside him. In the wagon were water jugs.

A well. I watched the man tug on the rope to pull the bucket up, then dump its contents into one of his containers. I climbed down from my horse.

"Excuse me," I called. "Can we use your well?" My throat ached; the words came out scratchy. He looked us over for a moment before nodding.

"You three look rough," he said, passing the bucket to me. I lowered it into the well.

"Been a long ride," Bonnie said from beside me. I lifted the bucket and filled my canteen. As I gulped the water, Bonnie took over lowering the bucket into the well.

"Where are we?" I asked.

"Almost to Brownfield," the man remarked.

"Do they have a blacksmith?"

"Naw. Nearest one is in Lamesa." He pointed toward the southeast. "'Bout half-day's ride."

"Thank you," I said to the man, watching as he started off away from us.

"Best be careful; there's slavers out in these parts," he said. "You won't make it to Lamesa before nightfall. If ya need somewhere to sleep, you can use my barn." He pointed to a large building not far off. It didn't look much like the barns I was used to, but I appreciated the man's offer.

After filling our bellies with water and topping off the canteens, we set off to the barn. We tied up the horses for the night and climbed into the hayloft. The Kid fell asleep in moments, and Bonnie curled up beside me seconds later.

A rooster crowed, waking me from feverish dreams starring Bonnie. I kept my eyes shut, wishing I could fall back asleep, to a place where I didn't have to hide my feelings for her. One of the horses let out an annoyed chuff. I opened my eyes, finding myself face-to-face with the woman featured in my dreams.

Bonnie's dark hair covered half of her face from view. I reached up, tucking the dark strands behind her ear so I could get a better look at her. Her lips were swollen from sleep. Her chest rose and fell against me as she clung to my side, resting in that spot where she fit so well. The rooster crowed again, interrupting my peaceful study of how the shadows played across her flawless skin.

I caught the scent of freshly baked bread. My eyes flashed toward the ladder, where a basket rested. I tried to lift my arm. Bonnie inhaled sharply and turned toward me, her arm wrapping around my waist. She buried her face in my chest.

"Five more minutes," she mumbled incoherently. Pieces of wheat-colored straw stuck out, stark against her black hair. I chuckled, not hiding my amusement as I plucked one out.

Bonnie stretched her arms above her head, pressing her breasts deliciously against my chest.

"What're you doin'?" she asked, her voice thick from sleep.

"You have hay in your hair," I said, pointedly picking out another piece.

"You tryin' to turn me into a farm girl?" A sleepy smile crossed her face, sending my heart fluttering in my chest.

"You don't have what it takes," I said with a sarcastic grin. Bonnie snickered beneath her breath, her eyelids growing heavy.

"Like it's that hard," she said, yawning. She moved her head back into the crook of my shoulder, her sleepy breath hot on my neck. "Besides, I'd have you teach me."

The words vibrated against my neck. I tucked my arm around her. Very suddenly, I realized that her body was solidly against mine, my hard cock embarrassingly apparent against her leg. I slammed my head back into the hay, willing it to go away. This was the last thing I needed.

I stayed that way for a couple minutes more before nudging Bonnie awake. I got up to inspect the basket near the ladder. Sure enough, someone had left bread and cheese for us. The bread was still warm. We feasted on it, for once glad to have something fresh for breakfast. Then we set off toward the southeast.

Even after a night of rest, I could sense my horse's exhaustion. Bonnie was right. They needed more than one night if we were going to make it to Fort Hood in one piece.

By the early afternoon, we spied buildings in the distance. We reached the outskirts of town and navigated through dilapidated neighborhoods. Most of the houses were either crumbling to pieces or boarded up with symbols spray-painted on them. None of it made sense to me. I glanced toward Bonnie.

"Gang markings," she said, her voice quiet. I grabbed my shotgun and laid it across my lap.

No one bothered us. We eventually made our way to the busiest part of town: a single road paved with red bricks. Old buildings lined either side of the street. People standing outside of bars or walking down the street stopped to look at us, but, for the most part, no one seemed concerned with our presence.

We located the blacksmith, who said it would take two days to get the horses shod.

After securing a room at an inn, we sat down in the bar, poking around at our bowls of some kind of stew. Honestly, I would have preferred rattlesnake. My brother's interest in the town had renewed his vigor, and he chattered away at us.

A pretty blonde woman with a red choker around her neck sauntered down the staircase at the back of the room. She caught sight of me and winked. The blonde woman back in Vegas had worn a ribbon just like that around her throat.

"She's a whore," Bonnie said matter-of-factly as she sipped her whiskey. I glanced at her, not sure if that look in her eyes was anger or fatigue. I turned back to my bowl. The last thing I wanted was for Bonnie to think I was interested in that woman. Then again, there were no promises between us. I may have wanted more with Bonnie, as afraid as I was of admitting it, but I still didn't know where she stood.

"Well," I said, my appetite gone. "We're stuck here for a couple of days. Anybody have any ideas on what to do?"

For months, all we'd done was run. Now that I had the chance to sit, I didn't know how to handle it. Our days were filled with nothing but the desert and each other. What did one do when they weren't running from murderous psychopaths or crater beasts? Could we ever have a life like they did in Flagstaff, with celebrations and bonfires and dancing? I stole a glance at her, watching as she picked through her own stew. I realized how much I wanted to dance with Bonnie again.

"Let's go shoot some stuff," The Kid said. I turned to look at him.

"Like what?"

"I dunno. Birds?"

"That's not a bad idea, Kid. You need to learn how to shoot a moving target," Bonnie said.

"I saw some shops on the way in. We could check them out," I suggested.

Because it was getting close to sunset, most of the stores were closed for the day. We settled for a relatively vacant area of town, where dozens of black birds sat atop old electric lines. I threw rocks at the birds, sending them flying up into the air, and Bonnie and The Kid would compete to see who could shoot the most.

She always let him win.

When we swapped places, with The Kid sending the birds up, I lost to her every time.

Night fell as we entered the inn. My brother rubbed his eyes, climbing up the stairs ahead of us. As usual, he didn't hesitate to strip down the moment we were inside. He peppered Bonnie with more requests for stories, but we were both tired of entertaining him.

I'd noticed the band setting up in the bar on our way in. The last thing I wanted to be doing right now was sleeping. By the alert expression in her eyes, I thought Bonnie felt the same way. I tried not to watch her. I tried to push my thoughts of her away. Just because we'd come to some sort of peace didn't mean that my feelings for her had resolved themselves. Once The Kid was snoring, I gave her a smirk.

"Want to have some fun?" I asked. Her eyes lit up. She slid her hand into mine as we left the room, locking the door swiftly behind us. I kept a firm hold on her hand as we moved through the crowded barroom. It had become such a natural thing to touch her that I didn't realize until we reached the bar that I'd been holding it at all.

The band played a merry tune. The bar's patrons sang and danced along in front of the small stage in the corner. A man playing a fiddle stood at the front of the band, singing bawdy songs. Every now and then, he broke off to tell a joke or give an anecdote that sent the crowd howling.

It was nice to be around people again. Bonnie and I settled down on two barstools, taking shots of whiskey for a while, not talking. Honestly, the only thing we truly had in common was The Kid, and whatever this *thing* was between us. Of course, neither of us wanted to talk about *that*. I worried that if I even broached the topic with her, it would put an end to whatever *this* was.

Bonnie wore her short shorts again. How I hadn't noticed before was beyond me. I took the time to admire the way they accentuated her ass as she walked to the bathroom.

"Hey," a man said from beside me. I glanced over at him. He couldn't have been much older than me. He had a gold tooth, and I could tell by the whiskey on his breath he was quite a few in. "Listen, that woman with you?" He motioned with his head toward where Bonnie'd left.

Jealousy, hotter and brighter than what I'd felt back on the train, flared up. I didn't realize that I had to worry about Bonnie sneaking off with another guy.

But I was now.

I scowled at him, grabbing his drink on the bar.

"What's it to you?" I asked. I downed the rest of his whiskey, reveling in the burn as it went down.

"It's a simple question. Yes or no?" His eyes flashed at the empty glass in my hand. I didn't care. I set it back down hard.

"And if I said no?" I asked, motioning to the bartender for another.

"She's hot. I figure I could get her out of those shorts in five minutes, tops," the man said.

I lifted my eyebrows. A smile crossed my face. Oh, I had to see this. I lifted my glass in salute to him, waiting with baited breath for Bonnie's return. Doubt crept back in, hot and bitter in my mouth. What if she *wanted* to give in to the other man's advances? She sauntered back a few minutes later, and I ordered her a fresh drink. I leaned in close, placing a hand on her leg. Her blue gaze fell to where my hand rested on her bare thigh.

"The guy on the other side of me wants to get you out of your shorts," I said with a smirk. "Tried to bet me he could do it in five minutes."

Bonnie's brow furrowed as she pulled back from me. At first, I thought I saw disappointment when she looked at me, but it faded quickly, replaced with bald fury. That look was dangerous. I checked to see if she had the M9, and was pleased to see that she didn't. Then again, it might be fun to see her shoot the guy.

Doubt crossed my mind again. What if she *wanted* the guy to get her out of her shorts? She was, after all, wearing the same outfit from Vegas. I couldn't help but trail the curve of her shoulder with my eyes down to the low neckline of her shirt, which revealed the faintest patch of smooth skin.

"Five minutes, huh?" she asked. Bonnie was furious. It was clear as day by the straight set to her shoulders and the barely veiled anger in her voice. Relief formed in my chest; for once, that fury wasn't directed against me.

"Hey," she said, her voice loud above the music. She turned to the guy. "So you bet you could get me out of my shorts in five minutes."

The man's smile faltered before he leaned back against the bar. His friends were making snide comments but overall egging him on. Bonnie leaned toward him, giving him the same smile she'd used to lure me in.

"Big, strong man like you . . ." The words fell from her lips slowly, seductively. "I bet you could do it in three."

The man's friends whooped as Bonnie ran a finger down his chest. She pulled away, flashing *that* smile again.

"Put your money up," she said when the noise settled.

"What?" he asked, his brow furrowed.

"It's a bet, right? Put your money up on the bar, and take my shorts off in three minutes or less. You do it, you get all of his money and me for the rest of the night." Bonnie motioned to me.

"This is a trick, right?" the guy asked, incredulous. "You'll just slap my hands away and he'll take all my money." That sounded like a good plan to me, but I wasn't about to invade Bonnie's hustle.

"I won't touch your hands," she said, her tone serious. "Unless you aren't as much of a big shot as you told your friends, that is." She shrugged her shoulders at him, glancing from me to the guy's buddies. His friends started shouting over one another, encouraging him to take the bet.

"Okay, fine!" The guy slammed down a purse that sounded full of money onto the bar. He moved toward her, smirking.

Bonnie kneed him squarely in the crotch, watching with cold eyes as he fell to the floor, groaning, and clutching his injured appendage.

Then she stood there. For three long minutes.

"Listen here, pal. If a woman wants to fuck you, she'll be excited enough to take her own pants off," Bonnie said, standing over him. "And she won't be fucking you a second time if you only last three minutes."

The music stopped, and eyes stared at her from all around the bar. She brushed her long, dark hair over her shoulder and turned to me.

"Well, I think I'm gonna call it a night. Don't stay out too late," she said, stepping over the man, who groaned and clutched his bits. She reached out and grabbed my shot, taking it, then slammed the glass on the bar. Before she turned to head back upstairs, she grabbed the money bag.

I barked out a shocked laugh, watching the short shorts accentuate her hips as she disappeared up the stairs. As soon as she was gone, though, the adrenaline and humor faded. I was sorry to see her go.

Long after Bonnie went to bed, I stayed downstairs, playing poker. If we were planning on staying at inns, we needed to have money to pay for it. The blonde whore from earlier came down the stairs again, catching my eye as often as she could from across the room. Most of the patrons were either passed out drunk or leaving for the night. As I bowed out of my last hand of cards, the whore crossed the room to me.

"Hiya, handsome," she said, pressing herself against me, her accentuated breasts in my direct line of vision.

"Hi," I said, trying to brush past her to get back upstairs. I was drunk, and tired, and ready to curl up next to Bonnie. The whore grabbed my wrist.

"Now wait a second," she said. "You've been eyeing me over your cards all night. Look, I'll cut you a deal because you're so handsome. Half price." She batted her eyelashes at me.

"No thanks," I said, once again moving to the stairs. I heard an aggravated sigh come from between her lips.

The room was dark when I wandered in. I kicked off my boots and pulled my shirt over my head. Maneuvering in the dark half-drunk probably wasn't a good idea. I moved toward the bed where Bonnie was, only to stumble over our bags. I flew forward, headfirst into the bedpost.

"Son of a bitch," I said in a whisper as I landed in a heap on the floor. I covered my face with my hands, willing the ringing in my ears to go away.

"Jesse?" Bonnie said sleepily.

"I'm fine, go back to bed," I murmured, picking myself up off of the floor. I climbed into the bed beside her a few minutes later, only vaguely aware that I smelled like whiskey and a whore's perfume.

I woke up to a pounding headache. The bed was cold, and that was when I realized I was alone. How had I slept through Bonnie and The Kid getting up? My brother was as quiet as a bull in a china shop. Must have been the whiskey. I tried to sit up and immediately fell back onto the stiff mattress. As I rolled over onto my side, I noticed that my pillow didn't smell like Bonnie.

How long was I out?

Within minutes, I dressed and headed downstairs. Bonnie and The Kid were sitting at a table in a corner, eating breakfast. A waitress came by and dropped a cup of coffee for me as I sat down. I murmured my thanks, before looking up at my companions. They stared at me.

"What?"

"Who'd you fight?" The Kid asked.

"What?" I asked again.

"You've got a shiner, farm boy," Bonnie said, amusement glittering in her eyes. I picked up a spoon, wiping it to see my reflection. Sure enough, there was a dark line beneath my eye. I wished it was because I'd gotten in a fight with somebody. I didn't acknowledge it; instead, I set the spoon down and picked up my coffee. When I looked at Bonnie, she had a knowing expression in her eyes.

After breakfast, we wandered into the streets of Lamesa. People milled about, going in and out of shops, stopping to talk in the street. Somehow, it reminded me of home. Of market day, when the people back home came together. I'd loved the sense of community we had. I'd take it over isolation in the desert any day.

"What about this one?" The Kid asked, stopping in front of a large window. There was a mannequin dressed in head-to-toe cowboy gear. I turned to ask Bonnie her thoughts, but she'd wandered across the street and disappeared into another shop.

"Yeah, let's do this one," I said, opening the door.

Once inside, he headed straight for the back. The shopkeeper watched him closely. I stopped at a rack with a sign boasting *like new jeans*. I grabbed a pair in my size and then continued on to the back of the shop.

"What ya got, Kid?" I asked.

In his hands, my brother held a wide-brimmed cowboy hat. A beautifully woven band in blues and greens was around the base of the crown.

"Can I get this?" he asked. I nodded; my winnings from last night would be more than enough to pay for it. I picked up a brown hat with the sides flipped up. The Kid didn't realize how smart he was. Hats would help keep our skin from getting burned.

We paid the shopkeeper and wandered back outside at the same time as Bonnie crossed the street. She had a couple of wrapped packages in her hand.

"What did you get, Bonnie?" The Kid asked. Her eyes flashed to me as I put my newly purchased hat on my head. She gave me a teasing smile, mirth in her eyes.

"I needed some new clothes, Kid. Most of my stuff is ripped up or covered in blood," Bonnie said. She took the hat from my head and put it on her own.

"Nice hat," she said, running her fingers over the brim. When she handed it back to me, her lips pursed as if she were trying to hide a grin. Her eyes glimmered as I put it back on my own head.

"Thanks," I said, shoving it into place.

"I got one, too. I'm gonna put my rattle on it," The Kid said proudly. Bonnie flashed a smile in my brother's direction before once again turning those amused eyes on me. She lifted a hand, flicking the brim of my hat.

"Wouldn't wanna hide those pretty blue eyes," she said with a grin. I stared at her back as she turned and walked beside my brother. If I didn't know any better, I'd think Bonnie just gave me a compliment.

We continued through the main drag, stopping only to get ice cream. The street vendor claimed it was the best in town. I think it was the only in town, honestly, but the cool treat was a welcome relief in the heat. We reached the far end of the main strip. Bonnie tensed beside me, and I turned to see what she was looking at.

In a narrow alleyway, a woman crouched on the ground, clutching her arm to her chest and rocking back and forth.

"What's wrong with her?" The Kid asked.

At the sound of his voice, the woman looked up. Her hair was long and stringy, like it hadn't been washed in months. Her skin looked gray, and her lips were stained blue. Her mouth moved, but I couldn't make out any sound. We needed to go. The last time I'd gotten close to someone strange, it almost didn't end well. I put a hand on my brother's shoulder and steered him back up the street.

"What was that?" I asked Bonnie in a quiet voice minutes later. My brother was once again distracted by the ice cream cart. I passed him a couple of bits and told him to have at it.

"Glowroot," she said. "Remember that glowing plant at the crater? People distill it. It's got this weird glow, and stains your lips blue when you drink it."

"Why would anyone drink that?" I asked, horrified at the idea.

"To forget. If you'd seen half the shit people out here have, maybe you'd understand," Bonnie said. "Sometimes you need something stronger than alcohol to get the job done. Once you're hooked, there's no going back."

I'd heard of drunks. Almost everyone knew someone addicted to alcohol. By the sound of this glowroot, it was much worse.

The afternoon sun dipped behind the buildings. We stopped off at the blacksmith, who confirmed the horses would be ready in the morning. On our way back to the inn, we stocked up on whatever supplies we could: jerky, more apples, and some bread made that morning. We bought bullets, and I purchased a new pocketknife. I noticed Bonnie eyeing the strawberries. She bought a small container of them. Even though we'd just filled up the canteens, I bought an extra one and filled it up too.

It was dark by the time we took our haul to our room. We unloaded our packs and reorganized them to make sure everything fit. At the bottom of mine, I found the small bag I'd toted from Montana. It was the first time I'd looked at it since Vegas. I dumped it out in front of Bonnie, who sat on the bed chewing a strawberry. She offered me one, but I declined, instead focusing on the remnants of our old life.

There were three books Mom had packed: an old bible, a grammar book, and a copy of *The Grapes of Wrath*. Mom made me read it when I was fifteen. The worst book I ever read. Well, skimmed. There was no way I could get through hundreds of pages of that garbage. I tossed the book to the side and picked up the bible.

My breath caught in my throat when I flipped open the first page.

*Jesse. Never forget where you come from. Mom.*

I ran my fingers over her words, closing my eyes. I could almost hear her say it. Almost. Like a long-lost memory, it wafted around in the depths of my mind. I couldn't quite hear her voice. I clenched my jaw, forcing back the sadness threatening to take hold. The Kid couldn't see me upset. He'd ask too many questions. I closed the book, smoothing down its leather cover. Pop's name imprinted on the front.

"What's that?" The Kid asked, rounding on me. He reached over and picked up the grammar book, making a disgusted face when he read the title.

"The books Mom put in the bag," I said, and then cleared my throat in an effort to force my emotions down. "Do you want it?" I motioned to the grammar book.

"Nope," The Kid said.

Well, no sense in keeping something that would only weigh us down. Before we met Bonnie, I'd tried to trade them for food. No one wanted them. I put the two books on the side table, more than happy to leave them for the next guest. But not the bible. The bible was mine.

After repacking our bags, I sat on the edge of the bed, trying to think about anything other than the bible I'd packed away. How had she known to pack a bag? Or was that something she did in the moments leading up to our escape? How would she have known to write a note in it for me?

There were still so many questions I didn't have answers to.

"We spent a lot of the money I won last night," I said, standing from the bed. "I'm gonna go play some more poker." I didn't bother waiting to see what Bonnie would say, if anything at all. I needed to breathe. I needed to forget my humble beginnings for a while, because if I didn't, I might lose my mind.

Bonnie didn't follow me, and I was relieved. I didn't think I could handle her looking at me tonight. I smoothed down my shirt before walking to the bar and ordering a drink. I downed it in a single gulp, then asked for another. Once my glass was refilled, I sauntered over to the table I'd played at last night. A couple of the men were new, but the others looked at me with hatred in their eyes.

"Got room for another?" I asked. I dragged an empty chair over before any of them could respond.

No one said a word. They shuffled the deck and dealt me in. After a few hands, some I won and some I lost, a crowd gathered around the table. The pretty blonde whore planted herself on my knee, and I made a show of letting her pick my cards. Most of playing poker was bluffing, and I was damn good at it.

People kept buying me drinks. The blonde whore kept putting her hand against my chest and whispering in my ear. I didn't hear most of it, but it was nice to have her soft, warm body within an arm's reach. She moved herself to sit squarely on my lap during the last game of the night.

By the end of it, I'd nearly cleaned out the others. It was late, and I was sufficiently drunk and ready for bed. I let the woman take me by the hand toward the stairs. I stumbled on the first step. She stopped, laughing a cute, high-pitched sound, then threw my arm over her shoulders. We made it onto the second-floor landing, laughing together.

Lamesa was an alright town.

"Where's your room, cowboy?" she asked, putting a hand on my chest. She took the hat from my head and placed it on her own. An image of Bonnie doing the same thing earlier flashed through my mind. I snatched the hat back. She looked up at me expectantly.

"What?" I asked, eyes wide.

"Your room," she said. Her hands gripped the front of my shirt.

"Nah, we can't go in there," I said. The words weighed heavy, like lead, on my tongue.

She glanced to her left, then to her right, and shrugged. Then she shoved me back against the wall. Her lips found mine. Her mouth was hot and wet, the kiss uncoordinated. She reached her hands beneath my shirt, raking her nails across my stomach. The touch sent goosebumps up and down my arms.

My eyes closed, and there was Bonnie from my dream the other night. Dressed in her short shorts, nothing else but a white tank top on, water cascading over her breasts and nipples straining against the fabric.

All I'd wanted was Bonnie, to touch her in ways that would make her squirm and moan, to taste every inch of her. To do to her what that bartender did. All thoughts of control left me. My cock strained against my jeans. She struggled with my belt buckle. I reached down, helping her to unlatch it. Then she peeled the layers off of me, settling them at my knees.

It had been too long since I'd experienced release. I'd stamped the feelings down for weeks now, out of obligation. I'd denied myself the carnal pleasures I'd once enjoyed. My entire body pulsed. My heart pounded in my ears as she took me in her hand. I shuddered at the warm touch, fisting my hands into her hair.

Then she took me into her mouth. I couldn't stifle my groan even if I wanted to.

I knew that I wouldn't last long; I never did after such a long bout of celibacy. My head slammed back against the wall, and I clenched my jaw, willing myself to hold on, to savor it, because I didn't know when I would have the chance again. She set a steady rhythm. I fisted her hair, thrusting my hips forward.

Fireworks exploded behind my eyes as my release took me. I groaned out Bonnie's name; the only other sound in the hallway was the pounding of my heart as I raked in a sharp breath. Her movements stilled, and I let out a shuddered exhalation. I grabbed her by the shoulders, pulling her to stand in front of me.

The flash of blonde hair sent my heart plummeting.

"You're not Bonnie," I murmured, suddenly sober.

She leaned into me, her lips an inch away from mine. "I can be whoever you want me to be, cowboy, long as you pay." She was stroking me again, and I was half a second from losing it. I shuddered at her touch.

"No," I said, shoving her more roughly than I should have. She clambered back from me, shock in her eyes.

As quickly as I could, I pulled my pants up and retrieved my forgotten hat from the floor. "Sorry," I murmured, moving past her to the door of our room. I fixed my belt right before I entered the dark room, shame filling my chest.

## CHAPTER FIFTEEN

# BONNIE

I COULDN'T SLEEP. IT wasn't just the absence of Jesse's warmth, it was the haunted expression in his eyes when he'd left. I knew the echo of that pain. I didn't follow him, because I knew better than most that sometimes the only way through was by drowning it.

The night wore on, and the sounds of the rowdy bar below reminded me of my childhood. Long nights in places like this, searching the crowds for Jones's next mark. It was just as comforting as it was unsettling without Jesse's body next to me, a reminder that I wasn't alone anymore. It was nearly daylight, and Jesse hadn't returned; a pit in my stomach yawned open, and I bit my nails down to the quick.

Then I heard him.

A high-pitched giggle, then Jesse's deep canyon timbre moaning in the hallway. *No, it couldn't be.* I slipped out from beneath the quilt on the hard mattress and padded on bare feet to the door. Cracking it open, I peered out to watch as Jesse fisted his fingers in the hair of a blonde whore kneeling before him.

As quietly as I could, I shut the door again, my stomach dropping to my feet. Jealousy and anger swirled inside of me, threatening to unravel me completely. I bit my bottom lip hard as I stared at the bed. The one I'd assumed I would be sharing with Jesse tonight. I ran my hands through my hair in panic. *Think, Bonnie, think!*

The door clicked open behind me, and Jesse stumbled in, obviously drunk and buckling his belt. I froze, my entire body strung tight. Sucking in a sharp breath, I attempted to calm my obviously stricken features. Either Jesse was too drunk to comment on my expression or he didn't care enough about the hurt and jealousy raging within me. He only met my eyes for a moment before crossing with heavy steps to the bed we were supposed to share.

"Come to bed," he said, his voice slurred at the edges. My stomach roiled at the thought of lying next to him after what I'd seen. My thoughts fractured, justifying and vilifying his behavior all at once. Still, being cradled in his arms like something precious to him would undoubtedly break me.

"I think I'd rather get ready to leave," I said quietly. He contemplated the quilt on the bed, seeming to pay no attention to me. I crammed my feet haphazardly into my shoes as I prepared to flee.

He wasn't trying to stop me. Didn't even spare a glance in my direction. He slumped onto the bed, struggling to shove his boots off before lying down as I shuffled into my jeans and fled the room like my life depended on it.

Once I was in the hallway, alone, I slumped bodily against the wall he'd been moaning on moments before. The shock receded from my mind, and all that was left was an emptiness I hadn't expected. I stumbled downstairs to the bar and sat heavily, but waved the bartender away when he offered me a whiskey.

I wanted to feel this.

Resting my head in my hands, I thought about Jesse. He was handsome. I'd known that since I'd first laid eyes on him, but he was *so* much more than that. When we met, he'd put his own safety at risk, even though all I'd done was wrong him. And while he was good at the hustle, he'd never lied to me.

My mind flashed to the ugly words shouted between us over the last few weeks and the quiet admissions beneath the cover of darkness. A rueful smile twisted onto my mouth. There were so *many* times it would've been easier for him if he'd just lied to me, forsaken me, abandoned me. Instead, Jesse had been kind when it was easier to be cruel, honest despite the steep price of the truth, and vulnerable even though I'd done *nothing* to encourage soft affection between us.

Still, every time I closed my eyes or blinked, all I could see was his face, slackened in passion, his fingers knotted in another woman's hair. A sharp ache in my chest ripped wide within me, like an open bleeding wound.

*Is this how he felt seeing me on the train?*

The thought knocked the wind out of me. Heat built recklessly in my eyes. I sniffled back the tears threatening to fall. I couldn't just sit here. I couldn't just—

I stormed out into the dim light of dawn. Walking in the cold air, I watched my breath fog in front of me as I focused on the steady thud of the ground beneath my feet. My world narrowed to the burn in my muscles and the jagged edges of the frigid air in my lungs as I gasped in chestfuls.

Why wouldn't he be with her? She was uncomplicated. She was beautiful. She wasn't constantly making mistakes or yelling at him. She sure as fuck wasn't putting him in danger. I looked up and noticed I'd made it all the way to the other end of town, staring out into the vast expanse of desert beyond. A place that used to welcome me like home, that used to make me safe.

Now, without Jesse, all it did was make me feel alone.

My breath heaved raggedly, my chest rising and falling in shuddering waves. I raised my hand to my face. Incredulously, I wiped away hot tears that streaked down my cheeks. Something cracked open wide within me. I couldn't remember the last time I'd allowed myself to cry. There was no stopping it now.

This was my fault.

I was a *fucking* coward. I was a coward on the train. I was a coward at the lake. I'd been a coward every single day since I'd lured him into that alleyway. Too fucking scared to tell him I wanted him. That even though I hadn't been ready before, I might be now. That just the *thought* of him with another person devastated me in ways I couldn't begin to understand. The image came again, his eyes closed tight with his fingers clenched in her flaxen curls.

The thought sobered me. I mopped at my eyes with my sleeve before turning and making the long, winding trek back to the inn. The sun had barely risen by the time I got there, despite my best efforts to delay my return. I nervously touched my hands to my face, as if that could somehow hide the blotchiness on my pale cheeks. I sat at the bar again, signaling the bartender for a cup of coffee, which he provided with a slosh.

The bitter heat steadied me, and I wondered how long I would have to wait until Jesse and The Kid woke up. A high-pitched giggle sounded behind me. Familiar and devastating. Closing my eyes for a moment, I braced myself and turned to see the woman. Younger than me, pretty, with warm brown eyes and freckles splattered on her cheeks. Her pretty smile faded into a weary expression as she left her customer's room.

Worrying my bottom lip, I dug in my pocket, pulling out a few bits from my jeans pocket. I walked over to her slowly, pressing the money into her palm without a sound.

She looked up at me, startled, before her warm brown eyes welled with tears. I didn't know if she knew who I was, or why my face was tearstained. All I knew was that she'd had a harder night than I did. I wouldn't blame her or Jesse for the way I was feeling right now.

"Take the night off, okay?" I said. She sniffled, turning her back before disappearing out the front doors.

"Bonnie!" The Kid exclaimed from behind me, taking the steps two at a time. He bounded over to the table in the corner where we'd been taking our meals and sat in the seat he liked next to the wall. I retrieved my coffee from the bar before joining him.

Moments later, Jesse stumbled in, eyes bloodshot as he slumped into a chair across from me. The sight of his mussed blonde hair and pale skin tugged at my conscience. I slid my coffee over to him, our fingers brushing briefly. Whether I had blotchy, tear-stained skin or not, he still looked like shit.

"Bonnie—"

I turned my attention on The Kid, a clear sign I didn't want to talk about the night before.

"Mornin', Kid," I said. It was all the prompting he needed to carry me away with conversation. Shooting birds, crater beasts, rules of being an outlaw—all his chattering started to blend together, but I nodded along anyway.

"Can we talk?" Jesse asked, reaching across the table to place his hand over mine. The warmth of his hand and the brush of his thumb against my skin shuddered through me. My jealousy clawed hot and ugly up the back of my throat, like bile. I had to remind myself that I wasn't what he wanted. He liked pretty blondes, preacher's daughters, innocent and undamaged women, or at least the appearance of them. I wore my scars like armor.

I pulled my hand away, pressing my lips together to stamp down the tears that wanted to rise again. I cleared my throat and schooled my features into a careful mask of indifference.

"You don't owe me an explanation," I said, meaning every word. He didn't do anything wrong. If I thought that, I'd be a hypocrite. There were no promises between us. He didn't owe me his loyalty or fidelity. If I could be sexually empowered, hell, so could he.

"I'm gonna stock up so we can head out before we waste too much daylight," I said, my words soft even though I couldn't quite meet his eyes.

I threw myself into preparations. Keeping my hands busy and my mind driven to distraction. I traded with a man on the corner and managed to haggle a good price for a worn green tent and a harmonica for The Kid. He seemed to like music. Hauling everything down from the rooms, I brought it over in several trips to the stable, where Eagle and Jesse's horse were rested and freshly shod. Sighing, I started to tie down the bags and tack the horses. I took care to pack everything tight enough to make it easy to set up and break down camp each night.

It was when I was nearly finished that Jesse walked into the stable behind me.

I didn't have to turn to see if it was him. I felt his eyes on my skin, the way I always could. They lingered around the curves of my shoulders, as if he were trying to read my emotions through my body language. Good luck. I could barely keep up with them myself. My breath hitched, and I crossed to the table in the corner, keeping my back to him. My hands shook as I fiddled with a brush I'd used on Eagle's coat in an attempt to keep them busy.

*Why isn't he saying anything?*

The silence stretched long between us, pulling my raw feelings taut within me. The thud of his boots in the dust unsettled me. I gripped my shaking hands on the edge of the table as he approached. Slowly, so slowly. Each step echoed the painful thud of my pulse. Until I felt his familiar, comforting heat licking against my skin, relaxing the tense set of my shoulders. He was so close, his scent made me dizzy, something warm like leather and desert dust and yet, still uniquely *him*.

"What d'ya want, Jesse?" I asked, my voice more breathless than I wanted it to be. He inhaled languidly, his breath close to my ear. As if he were drinking me deep into his lungs the way I had seconds before. His hand covered mine on the edge of the table. I sucked in a breath at the startling contact.

"She was pretty," I said, my voice a garbled choke. He stayed silent, his thumb making a firm circle on the back of my hand. My fingers flexed in response, entwining with his slowly, methodically. So that I could feel every second of friction. I didn't know that you could feel so much with just the tips of your fingers. I didn't realize it could make your heart pound in your chest like the rapid tempo of a Comanche drum.

"Would it make a difference if I told you I was thinking about you last night?" he said, his words raw. Wrenched from somewhere painful inside of him. My breath shuddered audibly, and hot tears welled in the corners of my eyes.

"It's none of my business," I said. Even to my ears, the words sounded false.

"What am I supposed to do?" he asked, sounding smaller than I'd ever heard him before. As if the words were being raked over broken glass. "I can't have you."

Something shattered inside of me, my resistance crumbling to nothing.

"Why not?" I asked with an edge of desperation, whirling to find myself trapped in the cage of his arms. "Why can't you have me?"

"I'm not your type, remember?" he asked bitterly, his mouth turned down into a scowl. I scoffed, ducking beneath one of his arms and taking a step away from him. Only one. Because Jesse's fingers were still tangled with mine and he didn't let me walk away. He gripped my hand tight, yanking hard enough to spin me around to face him. He was furious, his mouth set in a hard line.

"Don't run away from this," he demanded.

"Fine," I said, turning on him. "I'm not *your* type, farm boy."

He blinked, trying to clear the confusion clouding his eyes. I tugged my wrist out of his hot grasp.

"You . . . you're *good*," I said, trying to explain. I ran a frustrated hand through my hair. "Good, and honest, and kind. I'm not like that. I'm fucked up and broken. I won't apologize for it, because it's who I am. That won't change."

"Change? Who asked you to?" Jesse asked. "I know who you are, Bonnie. You *robbed me at gunpoint* when we met. You're ruthless and difficult and downright fucking mean sometimes—"

"Well, then, why don't you—"

"Shut up," he said, with enough conviction in his deep canyon timbre to make me actually shut my mouth. He dragged a weary hand down his face, scratching at the stubble on his chin. "You have all these goddamn *rules*. But all you're doing is using them to keep me at an arm's length. Is that what you really want?"

The truth of his words hurt, physically, like slices into my skin. I'd had the thought myself only that morning. How lonely I would be without him. His eyes grew soft, and he walked toward me again. I felt the table at my back.

"The rules are just the basics of survival out here—"

"Tell me what you want," he said.

"They don't mean anything. It was just supposed to be a distraction for The Kid," I said.

The defiant and cowardly parts of me raged at being faced with my own shortcomings. There was comfort in familiar pain. Even though loneliness ached, there was a kind of safety in the knowledge of it. Better to hurt in familiar ways than to be surprised by new ones.

"Not *those* rules. Your proposition. One night only. One time offer. No repeat performances," he said, repeating my own words back to me. For a long moment, neither of us spoke. His words tilted my entire world on its axis. That now-familiar heat built in my eyes. *Goddamn it.* He was right. His blue eyes pleaded with me as he stared me down with an expression of open longing. No games. No teasing. No bullshit.

"What if . . ." The words tumbled from my lips haphazardly, before I could think to stop them. I bit my bottom lip hard, wondering if I was making a huge mistake. His eyes dropped to my mouth, and the look in them was positively *feral*. He shuffled closer, strong arms like thick columns of muscle, caging me once more within the frame of his body. His shoulders hunched as he bowed in anticipation of my next words.

"What if I wanted more than that?" I asked, my words barely a whisper. "What if I made an exception for you?"

His hands were on my body before I could blink. Sliding along my waist and then lifting me onto the table so that I was eye-level with him for maybe the first time. His chest heaved, each breath forcing me back onto my forearms as he leaned forward. His fingers brushed gently against my jaw to push my hair away from my face as his eyes dropped to my mouth.

He hesitated, heart thundering, with a wild kind of vulnerability in his eyes. His mouth slid down and hovered over mine, drinking in my ragged breath. I could taste him on my tongue. His eyes were liquid heat, a desperate question hanging in the infinitesimal space between our open mouths. The charged silence between us screamed one thing.

"Are you sure?" he whispered against my mouth, finally breaking the stalemate. Each time we wound up here, I'd run. As far and fast as I could from admitting what I knew now with absolute certainty. *I have feelings for Jesse.* The kind I couldn't quite define. Overwhelming, terrifying, inevitable. I didn't answer him.

I kissed him. He barely had time to register that I'd moved before I sealed his mouth to mine in a savage kiss. His surprised exhalation was muffled against my lips. It didn't take long for him to catch up, one of his arms wrapping around my back to crush our bodies together. I opened his mouth with mine in a flurry of teeth, and lips, and tongues. My fingers buried deep in his thick hair, and I pulled him closer.

I wanted to erase the taste of that woman from his mouth, to claw the memory of her away from his skin. He pressed closer to me, and my thighs opened so he could settle his hips between them. My need for him was a living thing, throbbing out of control and stealing my senses. Reaching deft hands down to his belt, I made quick work of the buckle, the clink of it echoing between labored breaths. I hooked my legs around his hips and writhed against his thick cock, eliciting a thunderous sound from deep in Jesse's chest.

"Would you guys stop kissin' already?" The Kid shouted from the open doorway, stilling us both. "Every time y'all kiss, you end up fighting, and I don't wanna hear it all day!" He flung frustrated hands into the air.

I laughed against Jesse's mouth, and it was then I realized how ridiculous this must've looked to The Kid. The both of us, half on top of a table, my legs hooked around Jesse's hips and breathing so hard we may as well have run after another train. Jesse leaned his forehead against mine, gulping down a calming breath and groaning in regret.

"He has the *worst* timing," Jesse said. I laughed again, my lips and the skin around them feeling swollen. He pulled away from me slowly, letting me down onto solid ground.

"We're comin', Kid," I said, shrugging at Jesse in disappointment before turning to our horses. Jesse fumbled with his belt as we led them out together. I reached out for his hand, and he tangled his fingers with mine. I smiled at him, and his eyes glinted at me with an expression of barely veiled desire. A mirror of my own.

"We're gonna have to name Jesse's horse next!" The Kid exclaimed and I nodded, not really hearing anything he said. I dropped Jesse's hand with a squeeze before mounting Eagle and settling myself in the saddle.

The road before us would lead to Fort Hood, but the path I was on was leading me to a place I'd never been before. It was terrifying and exhilarating. Jesse was quiet as we rode out that morning, but the heat burning low in his eyes made one thing abundantly clear.

Whatever was happening between us wasn't fading away; it was only getting stronger.

## CHAPTER SIXTEEN

# JESSE

I COULDN'T STOP LOOKING at her. Even hours later, as the afternoon dragged forward, my pulse pounded like a drum each time I glanced Bonnie's way. The fire that burned inside of me yearned for her. As The Kid prattled on about our time in Lamesa, all I could do was watch her. I wanted to capture the way her dark hair shone in the bright sunlight. My hands twitched as I imagined tangling my fingers in it again.

Every time she would catch me staring, whether it was at the curve of her hip or the smooth expanse of her neck, Bonnie smiled. The heat in her cheeks sent my heart racing, and my jeans grew tight.

The heat of the afternoon became oppressive. Then again, it could have been that satisfied glint I'd catch in Bonnie's eye from time to time.

*What if I made an exception for you?*

Her promise from this morning left me jittery. I felt like a child again; anticipation grew with each passing hour. I couldn't wait for The Kid to go to bed. I imagined getting lost in the taste of her skin while peeling off her jeans.

"Jesse?" my brother asked.

"Huh?" I choked out. My gaze flicked to Bonnie. A secret smile perched on her lips. She turned her eyes from me, the black curtain of hair blocking her features from my gaze.

"Buttercup?" Harry asked. I turned my attention forward. Bonnie snorted in amusement. I couldn't tell if it was at me or The Kid.

"What?"

"Your horse," Bonnie said. When I once again glanced toward her, her eyes glimmered. She was laughing at me.

*Oh.* The horse. Why were we talking about the damn horse?

"His name?" my brother prompted.

"We can't name him after a flower," I said, the words gruff. "He's too powerful for that." The Kid's face fell. I'd declined at least a dozen names already. His brow furrowed as he sat in front of Bonnie. He flung his hands wide and huffed dramatically.

"Then you think of something," he said.

"Who said I wanted to name my horse?" I asked teasingly. I sat straighter in my saddle, tipping my hat back. "Jesse James and the Horse with No Name."

"That has the makings of a tall tale, farm boy. There may be hope for you as an outlaw yet," Bonnie said. A wave of heated satisfaction shuddered through me. I didn't look at her. I didn't trust myself *not* to say something stupid.

"Jesse can't be an outlaw," The Kid said matter-of-factly. I looked over at him with a brow lifted.

"Why not?" Bonnie asked.

"He doesn't follow *any* of the rules," he said. My mouth hung open at the blatant disdain in his eyes. Bonnie stifled a laugh by biting her bottom lip. That *damn* lip. She met my gaze before sitting straighter in the saddle.

"You have a point, Kid," she said.

With a click of my tongue, I dug my heels into No Name's sides to pick up the pace. *I don't follow the rules?* Well, they weren't wrong, but that didn't mean I had to admit it.

The sun continued its long descent toward the western horizon behind us. We didn't stop for most of the afternoon. Instead, we opted for walking the horses at a lazy pace and ate in the saddle. We left Lamesa too late and were too *distracted* this morning to make any real progress. By the time we stopped to make camp, my back and shoulders were tense from riding. I tried not to watch Bonnie as we moved about the camp. Tried, and failed. She spent time with The Kid, showing him how to set up an old tent.

While I set out the bedrolls, she watched him take the tent down and put it back up until he could do it by himself. His chest stuck out with pride as he turned to me with a grin on his face. I smiled at him. For a moment, I saw myself at his age, learning how to take apart the car Pop had kept in the barn. Remembering him was normally hard, but right then, it was like looking at a mirror. Except *I* was Pop, and Harry was me.

Life would never be the same, but that didn't mean we stopped living it.

Bonnie crawled inside the tent with him. I stoked the small fire I'd built, straining to hear what story she'd decided to tell him tonight. Instead, all I heard were muffled voices and the crackle of the fire. I settled back against our bedrolls. We'd stopped laying them out separately at all now. I stared into the flames as they licked the black sky, impatiently waiting for her. My hands tingled at the thought of touching her, of kissing her, of doing all of the things I'd imagined doing to her.

The zipper of the tent stole my attention. Bonnie stood there, staring at me. I was the *exception*. I sat up, resting one of my arms on a knee. *Alone*. Finally. I wanted to finish what we'd started this morning, what we'd started all of those weeks ago in that alley. She crossed toward the fire, her breath fogging on the chilly air. I was anything but cold.

"The Kid's asleep," she said, her voice breathy.

"Good," I said gruffly. I caught her by the wrist, and with one quick tug, she dropped onto a knee before me. Her blue eyes darkened as I lifted a hand to her cheek. She crawled toward me until there was less than a hair's breadth between us.

"Rule breaker," she said, her breath hot on my lips. Her voice was low and husky. I leaned forward, bypassing her lips to brush my mouth against her neck. Bonnie's head tipped back, a moan escaping from deep in her throat.

"You said I was an *exception*," I said against her pounding pulse. I ran my hand down her throat, reveling in her smooth skin. It came to rest at her neckline, stroking the smooth skin of her breast. "So, which is it? Do I break your rules or am I an exception to them?"

"Yes," she breathed.

Bonnie's hands found my shoulders, but they didn't stop there. She raked her nails down the center of my chest. I tensed at the enticing contact, tangling my fingers in her dark hair. Tension had been building for weeks now. Bonnie's breath hitched, and something sparked between us. She wanted me. I was her exception. Our passion flared to life, and my mouth crashed down against hers. I wasn't gentle. I needed to taste her, needed to feed this sensation raging out of control within me. She whimpered into my mouth, and I swallowed the sound. I consumed her.

Every look, every touch, every moment. With each desperate, clinging breath, she got closer. Arching her back, wriggling her hips, yielding to me in ways I'd scarcely imagined she ever would. She would be the ruin of me, and if this was what it felt like, I would happily let her be my destruction. We twisted until she was beneath me. Her hair splayed against our bedding, her eyes glazed in desire. She reached for me then. Even if she destroyed the Jesse who'd made that long journey from Montana, she would rebuild me into a new man.

The fire Bonnie had started back in Vegas raged out of control. We collided together in an explosion of sparks and flame. She clung to me, fisting her hands in the front of my shirt. I hooked one of her legs around my waist, settling deliciously against her.

It could have been minutes or it could have been days. I'd lost track, and I'd gladly never find it again.

Animalistic groans came from the back of Bonnie's throat as my hands explored every curve and hollow of her body, committing her to memory. My hand slipped beneath the fabric of her shirt, cupping her breast. Her back arched into my touch, pressing her breast further into my hand. I pulled back to watch her expression. My thumb brushed a quick circle at its peak, her body shuddering in pleasure.

Bonnie had scorched herself like a brand on my skin in that alleyway. Now I would finally return the favor.

CHAPTER SEVENTEEN

# BONNIE

E VERY TOUCH, EVERY KISS, every breath felt new and thrilling, as if I'd never experienced any of these things before Jesse. His hands were on my breasts, teasing and exploring with equal parts adoration and fervor. Until he'd wrenched an anguished moan from my mouth. I wanted to feel him. I wanted to feel his body on top of me, inside of me, behind me. I wanted to feel the heat of his skin, sliding against mine.

The rasp of his callused hands slipped from my breasts to stroke the midsection of my torso. Long, elegant fingers tracing the curve of my ribs and the flat planes of my stomach. Then back again. The friction was maddening, a shiver of pleasure racing up my spine. I couldn't catch my breath. I *needed* to feel him.

I reached between us, fumbling with his belt as the fire burning low in my belly blazed out of control and threatened to reduce me to ash. His hand pulled my wrist away. I whimpered into his mouth.

"Not yet," he said, his deep canyon voice forcing my eyes to his face. "For weeks, all I've thought about was what I wanted to do to you when I had you beneath me again." He changed his position, his wicked hand sliding down the length of my body as I squirmed beneath the friction of that motion. "First," he said, kissing my open mouth and popping the top button on my jeans, "I'm going to touch you." He slid the zipper down slowly. *"Everywhere."*

Then that wicked hand disappeared beneath the waistband of my jeans.

My entire world narrowed to the place where he touched me, slick heat flaring bright within me. The evidence of my desire flooded over his fingers, and a satisfied smile curled deep across his mouth. He stroked me, his eyes cataloguing each jerk of my hips or muffled groan. Until I was lost, mindless and adrift, being dragged along as his motions came faster and faster. Tossing my head back, I barely muffled the loud moan that ripped free from the back of my throat. I squeezed my eyes shut, writhing beneath his touch as my heart slammed against my ribs. My hips bucked, and I made breathy, desperate noises as I raced towards the peak of my pleasure, begging him to let me fall over.

"No," Jesse said, his voice a hard growl. "Look at me. I want to watch you."

His hand slowed. My eyes shot open in desperation, and he raced me to the edge of my oblivion. He cradled my face, guiding my gaze until all I could see was the blue fire of his eyes as I tumbled. I bit back my scream of release into a choked cry as pleasure shuddered through me, until I was pliant in Jesse's arms, sinking in a trembling heap onto the bedding. His hand slid free from my jeans. I reached up to him, kissing him softly.

"We aren't done yet," he said as soon as I pulled back. A self-satisfied grin curled on his mouth. "I'm going to taste every inch of you and show you *exactly* what you missed on that train."

"Oh," I said, still trying to catch my breath.

"Then, when you think you're spent, I'm going to give you a real reason to bite that lip of yours." He leaned forward to bite my bottom lip gently.

"Were you expecting me to argue?" I asked. He laughed against my neck as his mouth left a hot trail down to my collarbone. His stubble scraped against my too-sensitive skin, still flushed from moments before.

*Click.*

The soft sound almost didn't register. Almost.

"Jesse," I whispered as the barrel of a gun came into focus above us. He stilled, his entire body taut in an instant. Where a second before there'd been stifling heat, suddenly I was plunged back into reality and the frigid night air. It must've been the cold that made my body tremble involuntarily.

"Get up," an unfamiliar voice said. From my view on the ground, I couldn't make out the man's face. Jesse moved slowly, deliberately, pushing to his feet and angling his body between the barrel of the gun and me. My mind went blank. *A weapon, I need a weapon,* I thought desperately, but I immediately dismissed the idea. It wasn't just me alone anymore; if I made any sudden moves, the man would shoot Jesse, and a bullet wound at this range would be catastrophic.

Just the thought of that paralyzed me with fear.

"What d'ya think, Sean?" the man asked, looking Jesse up and down. "One in the knee? He'll have a limp, but he looks strong enough that the workhouses in New York would still pay for him."

"You could've let him finish," another voice said. A tall man with a bright smile stepped from the darkness just beyond the campfire. His smile was cold and lascivious as he stalked toward me in loping strides. "Look at this one. She'll be worth a pretty penny."

*Slavers.*

I refused to let my eyes wander back to the tent. It took every ounce of self-control inside of me not to check if they'd discovered where The Kid slept. The tall man, Sean, raked his eyes over my disheveled clothes and swollen mouth. He scrutinized me until his expression faded into one of hated recognition. Dread unfurled within me.

"It's you!" he said, something dark in the cadence of his words. "The bitch from the wanted posters. Because of you, there have been slave revolts along our route. I don't usually sully the merchandise, but I think I'll make an exception." His eyes darkened in a way that was too familiar, and the echo of the broken little girl I once was raged forward. Suddenly it was like I was back under that bed as the men broke down our door.

*"Look at you," a man said, but all I could see were his boots shuffling closer to my mom's bare feet, the laced edge of her skirt resting just above her ankles.*

*"Looks like she was just waiting for a real man to show her a good time," another voice said, the edge of something dangerous in the words.*

*Small and quiet. Mommy told me to be small and quiet.*

"It'd be a shame to leave her so unsatisfied, wouldn't it?" The man's words snapped me out of my memory and plunged me back into the danger I faced here. Now.

"If you touch her, I'll fucking kill you." Jesse's deep canyon voice rumbled through the air.

"Tough words," the man with the gun said, pressing the barrel flush to Jesse's forehead and walking him a few paces away from me.

I scrambled, trying to get my feet underneath me so that I could run. Before I could even rise all the way, the tall man threw me down bodily. My head cracked against the ground, and a high-pitched ringing sounded in my ears.

*"No! Please!" my mom screamed as she was thrown to the floor. She scrambled with large, dirty hands that ripped her dress open. All of her struggles were futile; the man tore the lace edge of her night dress off, exposing her skin to his punishing touch.*

I'm not her.

His hands reached to me, and instead of swatting at them ineffectually, I raked my nails down his face, aiming for his eyes. His skin caught beneath my nails, and dark lines of blood followed them. He roared, his fist thudding against my face. Stars exploded behind my eyes, and his hands ripped my shirt, bruising my skin while he explored. I tried to blink away the disorientation of the blow.

"Not the face!" the other man called, chuckling.

"You'll pay for that, bitch," my attacker said, shuffling to loom over me. Fear forced my thundering heartbeat into my throat, choking me. A sob escaped, and the tall man grinned wider, encouraged by the weak sound. I pushed against him, but he was immovable, my struggles amusing him.

*They pushed up her skirts, and I squeezed my eyes tight. I was all alone in the darkness now, surrounded by the sounds of my own terrified breaths, the clink of a belt buckle, and Mommy's crying.*

"Stop!" I cried, tears tumbling unbidden to drip unattractively off of my chin. He fumbled with his belt buckle. Using his weight against me, oppressive and suffocating, he pushed my jeans lower as he moved to position himself between my thighs.

"Please," I sobbed. The desperate plea wavered in the air before a gunshot pierced the night.

*Jesse.*

My tears fell faster, the realization rattling me to my foundation. They shot Jesse. I renewed my struggle, even if it was pointless. Suddenly, the man's weight was ripped away, and the cold night air rushed into the empty space where he'd been moments before.

Thoughts formed and shattered in the seconds that followed. My hands shook so badly it took me two tries to pull my jeans up and fasten them. The sound of a fist slamming into flesh resounded around me, but I couldn't focus on anything. Rolling to my side, then struggling to my feet. Each motion felt too heavy. Too slow.

The man with the gun lay in a dark pool of blood. I swung my eyes over to the struggling figures on the ground; Jesse's broad shoulders shifted as he brought his fist down again and again. Relief threatened to knock me back to the sand. *Alive*, he was alive.

I crossed to my saddlebag, pulling the M9 out with more effort than it should have taken. The weight dragged my arm down in a way it never had before. My eyes burned with tears that rolled down my cheeks, making tracks in the desert dust coating my skin. The tent flap was open, and I shuffled on legs that were too heavy to peer inside.

The Kid was gone.

I took a moment, only one, to gulp in a steadying breath. I had to swallow down this numbness that held me fast in its grip. When I opened my eyes, I assessed the area. There'd been a struggle, and The Kid was dragged south.

*My mother's eyes were wide and unseeing, and I couldn't stop screaming. The same large, dirty hands that'd hurt her reached under the bed and dragged me out. Wrenching my arm so hard it went numb. I kicked and clawed and never stopped screaming. I just wanted to wake her up. She had to wake up. She couldn't let them take me. Why was she letting them take me?*

I stumbled as I began to jog, nearly falling before I managed to get my feet beneath me. Another gunshot rang out behind me. Jesse called my name. He would catch up, he was fast, he always caught up to me. My feet pounded harder against the ground. Dark shapes in the distance caught my attention. It didn't matter that my lungs felt like they were going to burst. All that mattered was The Kid.

I promised him that nothing bad would happen while he was in my care.

I *promised*.

Another man was dragging The Kid towards a wagon, a knife flush against The Kid's throat. Something inside of me snapped seeing him like that. With a flick of my finger, the safety was off of the M9. I slowed my running to a jog.

"Stop right there, you sick son of a bitch!" I shouted, the words raw and deadly.

"You come any closer and I'll kill him," the man said. He pressed the blade of the knife harder against The Kid's throat. The Kid's body tensed, and he hissed in fear, fat tears wobbling in the corners of his eyes. I leveled the M9 at the man. Jesse reached us a moment later, panting, skidding to a stop beside me.

"Get," I growled, teeth bared as I shook with a rage I didn't know I was capable of. "Your dirty." I took another step, watching as the man's eyes widened. "Fucking hands." I adjusted the sight of the M9 right between his eyes, hand steady for the first time. "Off of my Kid."

"You wouldn't da—"

His words cut off when I squeezed the trigger. The world exploded around me. His arm fell slack before he slumped to the ground. The Kid rushed forward, slamming into me and burying his head against my stomach, wrapping frantic arms around me. I buried my trembling fingers in his hair, the M9 dropping to the dust. Whatever strength I'd gathered to chase The Kid down evaporated as soon as he was in my arms.

"Kid, I—"

But I fell to my knees before I could warn him. My trembling hands ran over his face and his neck, checking for wounds that weren't there.

"Did he hurt you?" I asked, my voice a garbled mess. He shook his head, and my bottom lip quivered. I pressed the heels of my hands to my eyes, but it didn't stop the tears. The weight of this night slammed down on me with full force. I clutched my stomach, as if that would plug the flood of bitter memories that'd haunted me my entire life. I understood now. I understood why my mother didn't fight harder that night, why she'd endured the worst kind of violence.

Love. She loved me enough that even the thin prospect of my safety made her sacrifice everything. *For me.* The same way I would have tonight for The Kid. My sorrow carried me away, and I crumpled. I mourned for the mother I'd lost, and the woman I could have been.

Jesse's arms were around me before I could rake in another ragged breath, lifting me onto feet that wouldn't support my weight anymore. His fingers tangled in my hair as he pressed my cheek to his chest, the steady thump of his heart a soothing rhythm. My body shuddered with wracking sobs, and I clenched his shirt in my quaking fists. I couldn't hold myself upright, but that didn't matter to Jesse. He held me tight until my tears slowed and my breathing normalized. His callused hands were soft against my face, wiping away the wetness.

He stood there in the darkness, holding me together while I fell apart.

## CHAPTER EIGHTEEN

# JESSE

AN HOUR PASSED. EVERY sound in the darkness, from the crackle of the fire to the shuffling of some distant creature in the desert, sent panic straight to my heart. Each time, I reached for Bonnie's M9, secured in the waist of my jeans. I'd picked it up in the aftermath of the attack. I'd managed to get The Kid settled down in the tent, his fingers white-knuckling the handle of his sheathed knife. Then there was Bonnie, sitting on our messy bedding in front of the fire, staring blankly into the flames.

"Here," I said in a quiet voice, holding out one of my extra shirts for her. She didn't move, didn't even look at me.

With gentle hands, I reached for the hem of her ruined shirt, slowly sliding the fabric over her soft skin. Skin that I'd only just been allowed to explore freely. My eyes roved across her chest, checking for injuries. How much time passed since the two of us were getting lost in one another beneath the stars?

I eased my shirt over her shoulders. My hands shook as I buttoned it up the front. When I reached the top button, she gripped my fingers tight. I looked up at her from where I knelt, trying to read her mind.

"I thought they killed you," she whispered. Her voice was harsh against the silence.

"They didn't," I said, lifting my hands to hold her face. I stared into those frightened blue eyes, reassuring her with my own that I was okay. I was worried about her. Since meeting Bonnie, I'd never seen her strength waver. She was constant; I could always count on that. Looking at her now, I didn't see any of that strength. I saw a terrified young woman who'd been beaten and nearly raped. I didn't regret killing either of them one bit.

There was a cut on her cheek. I pressed my lips to her forehead, promising quietly that I would return. I moved silently through the camp, gathering her flask, a canteen, and her torn shirt. When I made it back, I knelt in the same place. I ripped strips from her ruined shirt, then soaked one with alcohol.

"Look up," I said, finally turning to her. I tipped her chin toward the firelight to give myself a better view. "It's gonna sting."

Bonnie took in a sharp breath as I dabbed the cut on her cheek.

What would have happened if I hadn't killed him? Would they have taken us all? Suddenly, I thought of the warning from the other day when we filled our canteens at that well.

*Best be careful; there's slavers out in these parts.*

Only I hadn't worried about slavers. All I worried about was getting my hands on Bonnie. I'd already had to wait all day after she told me she wanted to make an exception for me.

I was angry at myself, I realized. Because I wanted to explore Bonnie's body, we were nearly captured, killed, or worse. I lowered my gaze, unable to look at her for the shame in my chest. This was my fault.

"It doesn't need stitches," I remarked, grabbing another strip. I poured water on it, then turned to her hand. Beneath the blood on her nails, her porcelain skin was unharmed. With her wounds cleaned, I stood to ready the camp so we could leave at first light.

Bonnie reached out and grabbed my wrist. "Jesse," she whispered, her grip almost painful.

"Yeah?" I asked, a pang in my chest at the panic in her eyes.

"If you hadn't been there, he would've—" She stopped, choking the words back. I knelt in front of her once more, dropping the supplies to the ground. I took her head in my hands and leaned close.

"But I was there," I whispered, so close I could feel her short breaths on my lips. "Okay? We can't think about the what-ifs. I was there. We stopped them."

"But The Kid—" Bonnie said, her voice cracking on his name.

"Bon—" Tears sprang up in my eyes at the emotion in her voice. "I know," I said, trying to push back the fear in my own chest. "I know."

I wanted to ease that terror I saw in her eyes, could feel rolling off of my shoulders. I leaned forward, pressing my lips to hers. I cupped her cheek with my hand, gentle, soft. Unlike the way I'd touched her earlier, before the attack. Her breath was hot on my skin as I broke away from the kiss. She twitched toward me, almost as though she wanted to kiss me again. I pulled back, staring into those fearful eyes.

I knew what she was trying to do. She was trying to get me to distract her.

I wasn't up for the task. Not now.

"We're okay," I whispered, crushing her against my chest.

We settled onto the bedding, and I held her tight for what felt like hours, until she managed to doze into a light sleep. I could tell by the short breaths she took. I wouldn't sleep.

I didn't know if I'd ever be able to sleep again.

Just as the eastern horizon began to lighten, whimpering caught my attention. This time it wasn't her. The sound came from the tent. I disentangled from Bonnie, careful not to wake her. Then I took broad steps toward the tent opening. The Kid thrashed in his sleep. I climbed inside and shook his shoulder.

"Kid," I said.

Harry's eyes, a mirror of my own, filled with terror. He blinked a couple more times before that fear faded and he realized it was just me.

"It's okay. You're okay."

The Kid slammed against my chest, his arms wrapping tight around me. He'd seen more in these past months than I wanted him to see in a lifetime. I crushed him to me, letting him lean on me for as long as he needed.

"It's okay. I'm here," I said.

"Where were you?" The Kid asked against my chest, his voice small and accusatory. I pulled back from him, brow furrowed.

"What?" I asked.

"When they took me. Where were you?" He sniffed and wiped at his runny nose. My stomach flipped. After all this time, I didn't think he needed me. He depended more on Bonnie; she was always the one he ran to. I'd never realized that maybe he depended on my solid presence just as much as hers.

"I'm sorry, Kid. One of the guys had a gun on me. I came as soon as I could," I said. The man's dead eyes staring into the starlit sky flashed through my mind.

"How did that happen?" The Kid asked, eyes horrified. I couldn't explain why I'd been distracted. "You were kissing Bonnie again, weren't you?"

"Harry—"

"No! You left me alone. Again!" he shouted, then exited the tent, flap closing behind him and leaving me speechless.

I took a minute. Just one, to sit there, the terror and near-tragedy washing over me. I bit my bloodied hand to hold back the unnatural scream threatening to rip out of my throat. I rocked back and forth.

My brother hated me. Because I'd allowed myself to get distracted.

Honestly, I hated myself too.

When I climbed from the tent, The Kid sat beside Bonnie, who was awake and only halfway listening to him. Her arm was around Harry's shoulders. She looked up at me, and I frowned. I went about packing up camp, trying to keep myself busy while my brother refused to acknowledge me. I poured water from a canteen to clean the blood from my hands.

"What does your scar say?" The Kid asked as I began deconstructing the tent. I looked toward them.

"Huh?" Bonnie asked.

"Your scar," The Kid said, pointing to the gnarled, pink skin of her arm, barely visible above her rolled-up sleeve. "It looks like it spells something."

I knew the answer to The Kid's question. I'd figured it out what felt like forever ago. By the way her features screwed up, I knew her scar was the last thing she wanted to talk about.

"Time to go. Kid, can you roll up those bedrolls?" I asked, turning from them. I secured the tent in place on Eagle's pack, then gathered up the small items. I kicked dirt over the fire, watching the flames die, smoke curling on the gentle morning breeze.

By the time the sun appeared over the eastern horizon, we were back in the saddle. My brother opted to ride with Bonnie, to no one's surprise. We were barely on the trail for five minutes when I tugged on No Name's reins.

A wagon rested in the middle of the path ahead of us. The same one that man pulled The Kid toward last night.

I climbed down from my horse, shotgun at the ready. I scanned the area in case there was anyone else waiting for unsuspecting victims. As my sight settled on the wagon, I realized it wasn't empty. The thing itself was raggedy, with patched wheels and different-colored boards. One thing was for certain: the metal cage was fully intact. Through the open door of the cage, I spied someone with blonde hair, fast asleep in a corner.

"Is it a child?" Bonnie asked, her voice strained. I lowered my shotgun, my hands still in place in case the person posed a threat.

Then a quiet, fearful voice came from within the wagon. "Jesse?"

Familiar eyes flashed at me from beneath a mess of blonde hair. *But the church . . . the padlock. No one could have survived.* I took in breath after ragged breath. My knees buckled as she crawled on clumsy hands and knees. My old world and my new one suddenly crashed together in a violent whirlwind of flames and smoke. How was she *here*? My shotgun hit the ground with a muffled *thunk* as the woman bolted out of the cage and ran straight at me. I unconsciously wrapped my arms around her as she whimpered into the front of my shirt.

"It's okay," I said. Bonnie's stare burned against my skin.

"Clara?" The Kid asked, incredulous.

Clara Higgins. The woman I'd been meant to marry, before everything changed. She didn't die in Montana. She was here, somehow, in the back of a slaver's wagon. She'd been taken as a slave. Not burned alive. She shook against me. I finally looked at Bonnie. Words failed me. I couldn't handle much more this morning.

When Clara finally pulled back, I took in her features. There was a bruise beneath her right eye, a cut on her chin. Fresh anger burned within me as I tried not to imagine what those men had done to her. Clara's eyes widened as she took me in, her tan skin slightly paled.

Bonnie cleared her throat. "Let's head back to Lamesa. I think she could do with a shower and some rest."

Then she turned her back on me before I could speak. While nothing had changed about the way I felt for Bonnie, the appearance of Clara could change everything. We both knew that. Bonnie headed back to the horses.

"We should take the wagon," I said, noticing a small pistol on the seat. I picked it up and tucked it into my waistband. "It could be useful. When we get back to Lamesa, we can find someone to break the bars." We needed to focus on getting back to Lamesa. I watched Bonnie mount her horse. Clara sniffled at my side.

I couldn't think about the look Bonnie'd given me, or how Clara clutched my arm as I helped her into the wagon behind me. Bonnie took No Name, and The Kid climbed on Eagle, letting out a happy shout at getting to ride by himself for the first time.

Once we set out, Clara spoke. "I thought you were dead," she said. *I thought they killed you*. The echo of Bonnie's haunted voice as we sat beside the fire earlier sent a shiver down my spine.

"Strangers burned down the farm. We barely got out alive," I said. A leaden lump formed in my throat as I thought about that night. "I thought you were dead, too. The church. Your house. Everything was on fire. They chained the door."

"They took me," she said, her voice haunted. When I looked at her, her eyes were clouded. I recognized that look. I'd looked that way for weeks after we left Montana. Sympathy flared bright in my chest. Would it have been better if she'd died instead?

"Do you know anything about the people that took you?" I asked. Maybe Clara could give me answers to the questions I'd had in the months since my parents had died.

"No."

She didn't offer anything else.

We rode in silence, setting a quick pace in the hopes of reaching Lamesa before night-fall. I'd catch myself watching Bonnie as she steered ahead of us. She knew Clara and I were engaged. I'd told her as much on the train. The fire had freed me from that obligation. Even though I tried to catch her eye, Bonnie never looked back while we rode. Uncertainty settled in my gut, leaving me with a bitter taste in my mouth.

I drove the wagon in silence, the rising sun at our backs. I couldn't speak; I could barely breathe.

All I could think about was how Bonnie had become pliant beneath me by the fire last night. How her soft body fit perfectly under mine. How she'd looked at me as I brought her to the edge and took her over it. *She* was what I wanted, but was she what I needed?

From the beginning, I'd compared Bonnie to Clara, how different they were. For the two of them to occupy the same space made my head spin. I couldn't quite reconcile the confliction in my chest.

Finding Clara changed nothing about my feelings for the dark-haired thief. But it might have changed everything for Bonnie.

CHAPTER NINETEEN

# BONNIE

*M*Y NAME IS BONNIE. *I'm a fugitive on the run from a man named Jones. I was attacked last night, but I escaped. Jesse found his fiancée alive—*

No. Fuck. I kept my eyes trained forward and started again.

*My name is Bonnie. I'm a fugitive on the run from a man named Jones. I was attacked last night—*

It took physical effort to push away the memories. A bright smile, too wide in the darkness. Hard hands pulling down my jeans. Gunshots piercing the night. Fragments of terror lingering in the recesses of my mind, preying on the fear I tried desperately to banish. I gripped the reins so tight it hurt, attempting to stop the tremors in my hands. I could still feel the unwanted touches on my skin, like a phantom, heightening my revulsion. I bit my bottom lip, hard. The pain reminded me I wasn't back there. I was *here*, in the saddle, with the sun beating down.

I ached to glance at Jesse, to take a better look at the woman who'd appeared out of nowhere, as if straight out of the morning mist. A beautiful blonde mirage of feminine fragility. Unkind thoughts warred with empathy; after all, we'd both been attacked by those men. She was probably struggling as much as me, if not more. It wasn't her fault I'd broken all of my rules for Jesse.

It wasn't her fault I'd fallen in love with him.

*My name is Bonnie. I'm a monster.*

I fell in love with him and it almost got us killed. It was made alarmingly clear last night that my feelings for Jesse were destructive and I needed to forget them. Every time we got close to each other, danger followed. Sixgun. Crater beasts. Slavers. I keep thinking by staying with them I was somehow keeping them safe, somehow helping them. The truth clanged through me like a discordant tone: if it weren't for me, they wouldn't have been in danger in the first place.

We stopped for lunch earlier than I thought we would, but I wasn't feeling the passage of time normally either. It could've been hours later than it felt. Everything was distorted, as if I were seeing it from a great distance or looking up on a misshapen world from the bottom of that lake. I stayed apart, shaking my head when rations were passed my way. I couldn't eat. I could barely breathe. Jesse tried to catch my eyes, but I wouldn't compromise today.

Instead, I busied myself with repacking one of the saddlebags. A hard rectangular object caught my attention. I'd almost forgotten. Pulling out the scuffed harmonica, I made my way over to The Kid, who glowered into his lunch, and handed it over to him unceremoniously.

"What's that?" he asked.

"I forgot to give it to you. Just somethin' I picked up," I said, watching as his eyes brightened with the fervor of his insatiable curiosity. Something dark eased inside of me, seeing the familiarity in his expression. Last night hadn't broken his spirit, at least.

"You really got this just for me?" he asked, looking at me expectantly. I just nodded, the words stuck fast inside my chest. Clearing my throat unattractively, I schooled my face into careful indifference as The Kid blew into the harmonica.

"Why don't you go show Jesse?" I asked, and The Kid's face fell.

"I don't want to," he said, staring down at the harmonica.

"Why not?" I asked.

"He wasn't there when I needed him," he said. I pulled his chin up until he stared straight into my eyes.

"Don't ever say that again," I said, my voice firm enough that it captured his attention. "What's rule number three?"

It took him a moment to remember but he squared his shoulders and held his eyes steady in confidence. "Keep your word. Outlaws may steal, lie, or cheat, but when we make a promise, we keep it," he recited, and I offered him a small smile in response.

"I promised you nothing bad would happen. Jesse knew that, and he trusted me to keep you safe," I told him.

"But—"

"No. No buts. Rule number seven: no one gets left behind. We never would have let them take you. Jesse fought off *two* of those men so I could get to you. You're lucky to have him," I said, holding his gaze until he nodded. I ruffled his hair affectionately. "Now, go make up with your brother."

He stood then, bounding over to Jesse, blowing off pitch notes and offering a goofy grin. My eyes lingered too long, and Jesse caught them across the space. His eyes softened in gratitude. I tipped my head down, turned away, and repacked Eagle's saddlebag so that we could leave. It was the least I could do, to try to fix the damage I'd caused.

The afternoon ride was less tense, the deafening silence from before broken by The Kid's bad harmonica playing and normal chatter. It almost felt like any other ride through the desert with them. Except that occasionally Clara's too-sweet voice would answer The Kid's questions and remind me she was here. Jesse's fiancée. The woman he was going to marry.

I barely knew what it meant to be in love, only that the words had fought hard to tumble from my mouth last night. With his hands on my skin and my tears mirrored in his eyes, I'd nearly died keeping them to myself.

Now, they didn't matter.

The sun dipped below the horizon as we made our way back into town, avoiding the worst parts since we were familiar with the gang territories here. The Kid swayed in Eagle's saddle, refusing to admit he was tired because he didn't want to give up his newfound responsibility. Without words, Jesse and I fell into our routine, finding a clean inn and tying the horses in front of it. Jesse helped The Kid out of the saddle and let him lean against him on weary feet as I finished tying the knots, patting Eagle's neck affectionately.

Clara watched, her brown eyes dark and calculating. An echo of the strategic glint I'd often seen in Jones's gaze when he searched for weaknesses to exploit. I shook the thoughts away as soon as they entered my mind. Clara didn't know me; of course she'd be cautious.

As we bought the room for the night, I noticed the pool tables on the far side of the bar and the raucous laughter splitting the air. The woman behind the bar kept staring at my cheek, then glancing over to Jesse.

We shuffled up to the room, and once there, The Kid tucked himself into the covers of one small bed and I ran my fingers through his hair until his breathing was deep and even. When I knew he was fast asleep, I turned dull eyes on Jesse and Clara, who were standing there awkwardly, staring at each other. I let out a weary sigh before turning to Jesse.

"Get out." His gaze snapped to mine, confused. "Clara and I need a few minutes. Wait outside," I said with no room for objection. He swallowed hard, taking off his cowboy hat and ducking his head before the door clicked shut behind him. Pulling my pack off the floor and onto the bed, I turned to her, watching as her fingers twisted nervously in the fabric of her skirt.

"Did they—"

I couldn't finish the words. Instead, I crossed to her and offered her what was left of my peppermint soap and some soft sleep clothes. She stared at the offered items, confused for a few minutes, her eyes regarding me suspiciously.

"You must've been through a lot. If you need new clothes, we can get some in the morning, but this may be more comfortable to sleep in. You can shower if you want. If they . . ." I bit my lip and steeled my nerves. The memories of too-wide smiles and hard hands on my skin left a bitter taste in my mouth. "If they forced themselves on you, I have an herbal tea that will keep you from having a baby. Just let me know."

"Why are you being nice to me?" she asked, tone accusatory. My spine stiffened at the animosity in her voice. She crossed her arms over her chest as she waited for my answer.

"You're important to Jesse," I said, because it was the only answer that didn't remind me of how powerless I'd been last night. The encroaching darkness already set my nerves on edge. As if the men we killed would be able to materialize from the shadows in the corners of the room. She took a step forward, crowding me, her too-sweet smile turning feral in the dim light.

"You care about him, don't you?" she asked. I didn't answer. I didn't deny it either. Holding her stare for a few seconds too long. Until she could see clearly the answer in my eyes. "Let's get one thing straight: Jesse is going to marry me. Whatever your past with him is, there are promises between us."

*There are promises between us.*

Something Jesse and I never had. Promises. There were only deals, with time limits, and rules between us. Rules I'd broken. I smiled at her then, sarcastically, retreating behind the walls I thought had broken down for good. I turned my back on her with an incredulous shake of my head. Pulling out my shorts and a new top, cut low in a clingy black fabric, I changed quickly. A soft knock sounded on the door. Jesse, worried about what was taking so long. I don't know how I knew it was him by the tentative sound alone, but I did.

"You can come in," I called. The door cracked open before he slipped inside. His blue eyes blazed at me as I studied my reflection in the small, clouded mirror in the room. The cut on my cheek was red and angry, blue-tinged bruises mottling my cheek surrounding it. I swore softly beneath my breath, digging all the way to the bottom of my bag, where a small tub I rarely used lay hidden. Unscrewing the cap, I patted some of the cosmetic onto my skin with the pad of my middle finger. Jesse watched my every move. I saw him from the corner of my eyes.

"Your shirt is on your bed," I told him, because his intense study was doing nothing to help my concentration. "Thanks for the loan." Without another word I turned for the door.

"Where are you going?" Jesse asked, following closely behind, reaching out to grasp my wrist gently. I shook his hand off, aware that Clara marked the motion with her too-strategic eyes.

"To get into trouble," I replied in a clipped tone.

"Haven't you had enough trouble lately?" he asked. I chuckled darkly, walking around him to the stairs, taking two of them at a time until I reached the landing. In two long strides, he was beside me as I walked into the bar. Leaning provocatively over the bar-top, I smiled disarmingly at the attractive woman serving drinks. Her curly hair bounced prettily around her face as she walked over. Jesse tried to catch my eye, but I ignored him.

"Hey, sugar," I said in a breathless voice, my smile widening at the pink flush on her cheeks. "You think you could spare a bottle of whiskey for me?" I bit the corner of my lip and reached out to wrap a finger around one of her curls before letting it go.

"I'm not really supposed to—"

"C'mon," I said, my voice a little breathy. "Do you *always* do what you're supposed to?" She giggled and snuck a bottle onto the bar-top before being called away by a man with a long beard on the other end.

"Bonnie, listen—"

Jesse's deep canyon timbre held a note of serious intention I was wholly unprepared to deal with. It didn't matter if he wanted to let me down easy, now that his sweetheart was back, or talk about the attack. Tonight, all I wanted to do was forget. I popped the cork out of the bottle with my teeth and turned it up for a few long seconds. The burn settled deep into my blood. I coughed, blinking back the water in my eyes. Reaching over the bar, I placed a glass down in front of Jesse.

"Listen," I said, focusing on the harsh lines of his face. "I didn't come down here to *talk*. If you're staying," I poured some of the whiskey from my bottle, "have a drink. Otherwise, you can go back to Clara upstairs."

His hand wrapped around the glass, fingers clenched tight at the mention of Clara's name.

"It's not what you think," he said. I leveled him with a withering glare, then turned my attention to the room, eyes scanning the faces in the crowd. They caught on a man in a cowboy hat in the corner who lifted his glass to me. Jesse's voice died beside me.

"Fine. What kind of trouble are we getting into?" he asked, swallowing the whiskey down and holding his glass out for more. I raised an eyebrow at him, then poured. Leaning closer to him, I pointed with the bottle to the other side of the room, filled with people drinking and playing pool at the tables in the corner.

"You wanna run a con?" I asked conspiratorially.

"What do you have in mind?" Jesse asked, sipping the alcohol in his glass.

"Well, first you need to learn to pick a mark," I told him, scooting closer, the familiar heat from his body relaxing my muscles unconsciously. He chuckled against the rim of his glass; he'd been one of my marks not so long ago. His arm slipped around me as he leaned in closer.

"It's all about the details," I said. I took another large swallow of the whiskey, letting it loosen my tense shoulders. "First, figure out what kind of mark you want. Tonight, we need someone with money to lose, a little gullible, not too shrewd. Then you find the details that fit that criteria." Jesse hung rapt on my words, shifting closer the longer I talked.

"Try it," I challenged. He turned to the room, his eyes scouring the faces of the patrons too obviously. I laughed then, until I felt moisture in the corners of my eyes. Jesse looked at me with confusion clouding his bright eyes.

"What?" he asked.

"Not like *that*. You can't just openly stare at people like you stare at me. They'll notice, and it'll defeat the purpose." I tipped the bottle up to my lips again.

"You notice? When I stare at you?" he asked, his voice deeper than before. I cleared my throat, taking a large, bracing swallow of the whiskey.

"Every time," I said. He didn't seem to have anything to say to that. Instead, he leaned forward, tightening his arm, slung along the back of my chair.

"See those guys in the corner?" I asked, my voice strained. I tipped my head toward the group of four men.

"They're too drunk, spent too much money, and not cocky enough." My eyes slid over the way the dark-skinned man rested his hand on the chest of another. "And I don't think I'm the right kind of temptation anyway."

Jesse made a sound in the back of his throat, like he hadn't recognized the smoldering heat between the men before I pointed it out. I took another long swig from the bottle and assessed the rest of the room.

"Them," I said, my voice low. His eyes followed mine until he saw the two men at the pool table in the corner. Eyes bright, a full bottle barely touched between them, with boots that looked new and expensive. "They have money to burn and have been smiling at a few girls who haven't given them the time of day."

"What's the play?" he asked, his voice hot in my ear.

"You know how to play pool?" I asked, and he shook his head. "Good." I grinned wide. "I do."

Shoving off of the barstool, I reached for Jesse's hand, and he took it as I dragged him forward. He tugged me back before we could cross the room too far. Indecision flared in the bright blue of his eyes, a question on his mouth.

"Just follow my lead, okay?" I asked. He let me drag him the rest of the way. As we got closer I let out a high-pitched giggle, stumbling into Jesse's chest. His arm wrapped around me easily. I stared up at him, pouting.

"Baby, *please* teach me how to play," I said in an exaggerated whine. Jesse sighed, a long-suffering sound.

"You're too drunk," he said, lying easily. The same way he'd lied to Sixgun all those weeks ago. I *knew* he would be good at this.

"If you won't teach me, maybe one of these other cowboys will," I said, petulant and taking another swig of whiskey. It was an exaggerated gesture, made to look like I'd taken a *much* larger swig than I had. I hadn't eaten anything today, after all, and I needed to keep my wits about me.

"Fine," he groaned, leading me forward with a hand tucked into the back pocket of my shorts. We racked the table, and I took the cue in my hands, holding it completely wrong. Jesse drank from his glass and stared into the corner, seemingly bored as I brought it *too* far back. I knocked one of the guy's drinks off of the table, sending it crashing to the floor.

"Hey!" our first mark said. I turned, off-balance, with an apology on my lips. "Watch what you're doin'."

"Sorry, man, she's had a bit too much," Jesse said from over my shoulder, slinging his hands around my waist comfortably.

"How can I make it up to you?" I asked, eyes wide. They stared at me, taking in the long expanse of leg accentuated by my shorts and the cleavage clearly visible in my tight shirt. I bit my lip innocuously. "We could play a round with you!" I jumped a little on the balls of my feet.

"No, that's not—"

I turned in Jesse's arms, shooting him a wicked grin before putting my hand down the front pocket of his jeans. I slid my hand down greedily, lingering in places that forced a cough from his throat, until I found his money. Jesse's eyebrows raised, and that wasn't all. I turned back to the men as Jesse shifted uncomfortably behind me. Offering them the four brass bits I'd stolen.

"Is this enough for a friendly bet and to replace your drink?" I asked, my voice still in that high-pitched whine. They stared back at Jesse's flushed face and chuckled, nodding in acceptance.

We played for a while, the men giving me tips while watching me shimmy around the table, leaning provocatively in my shorts. I missed every time, pouting and teasing Jesse in between. He found any excuse to touch me, his fingertips running on the back of my neck or slinging an arm around my waist. When the game was finally over, the marks were drunker and more flirtatious than before. Making comments about their *pool sticks* and how I could grip them. I giggled mischievously, wiping my mouth on the back of my hand after bringing the bottle to it. Their gazes lingered there.

"I'm havin' so much fun. What about another round?" I asked, turning back to Jesse and putting my hand into his other front pocket. He was more prepared this time, until I ran my hand along the hard length of him through his jeans. My hand came back empty.

"Sorry fellas," I said, my eyes falling to the floor. "Looks like he's outta money." With a shrug, I turned from the table, pulling Jesse with me by our joined hands.

"What are you doing?" he whispered in my ear.

"Wait for it," I said. A moment later, before we could get too far away, the men called out behind us.

"We could bet something else!" the other mark said, unwilling to see me go.

"Yeah? Like what?" I asked, feigning innocence. They spoke in low tones, and Jesse put his hand on my waist, almost in warning.

"What about if we win, you come back to the room with us?" he said finally. Jesse's hand gripped my waist tighter. I looked back at him, eyes flashing in warning not to ruin the hustle.

"And if we win?" Jesse asked, his voice deep. They smacked a heavy purse onto the table, arrogant since they'd won the first round.

"This enough?" one asked. I nodded slightly, a signal to Jesse. He accepted, shaking hands with the man before we racked the next game. I smiled wide, ready to spring the trap we'd laid. I took my pool cue and lined up the first shot, my finger placement perfect. Leaning deep over the table. Before I took the shot, Jesse pressed his hips against my ass, leaning over until his chest was flush against my back.

"I hope you know what you're doing," he said. The words were hot in my ear, his hand slid down the curve of my ass slowly, his fingers trailing along the skin at the edge of my shorts. I shivered, a breath shuddering from my chest as the memory of where those fingers had been last night nearly made me miss the first shot.

I broke the formation of the pool balls with a *clack*, watching as several of mine rolled into the pockets at the sides. In a matter of four moves, I'd cleaned up the rest and won the game. The men stood in drunken shock as I leaned against the pool cue, studying my progress before taking a victorious gulp of the whiskey, languishing in the burn that settled in the pit of my stomach.

"Beginner's luck?" I asked, with a self-satisfied grin as Jesse retrieved the money from the table. He slid an arm around my waist, pulling me away before they could object too heavily.

Stumbling into the other room together, I laughed more easily than I thought I'd be able to, the whiskey loosening my reactions. Jesse took the bottle from me, drinking deeply before handing it back. Something easy settled in his eyes as he stared down at me in expectation. I pressed my thighs together, remembering the way he'd run his hands all over me while we played. As if it were as natural as breathing. As if he didn't have promises with another woman upstairs.

The thought of Clara made me drink more, until I forgot her again. Until the only thing that mattered was the way Jesse looked at me as we lingered in the stairwell that led to the rooms.

"I *knew* you'd be good at the hustle," I said, a note of pride in my voice and only a slight slur in my words. "You lie surprisingly well for an honest farm boy."

He took the bottle back, grinning. The men from earlier complained loudly. I gripped Jesse's forearm and jerked my head up the stairs.

"Let's get outta here before we get into *too* much trouble," I said. We shuffled up together, until we were almost back to the room. I wavered in the hallway, not wanting the night to end. It'd been *fun*. I hadn't thought about the attack or Clara or the darkness that'd stalked us along the way. Only Jesse and the light in his eyes.

Instead of moving closer, I leaned against the railing, enjoying the cool air on my flushed face. Jesse looked at me curiously, pressing his back against the wall opposite me. His eyes made me squirm, the heat in my belly flaring to life beneath the smooth confidence in his gaze. He knew what I looked like when I was lost in the throes of passion now. *Look at me. I want to watch you.* The memory of his words shuddered through me.

"What if I'm no good at being an honest farm boy?" Jesse asked, the words a dark rumble between us. Lilting in that perfect deep canyon timbre that made my thighs quiver. His eyes roved over my body, liquid heat flooding through me as they lingered in places he'd touched and tasted. They traced down my neck, where he'd run his mouth in that alleyway in Vegas. Over my breasts that I'd pressed into his hands beneath the stars last night. Settling for a brief moment between my thighs. A shock of desire lanced through my entire body before those discerning eyes rested on my flushed face.

There were a million reasons I could think of to walk away.

Instead, the space between us disappeared as we collided. The bottle crashed to the floor, forgotten. His mouth was on mine, and I drowned in him. I cried into his mouth, and he dragged me closer. My fingers buried into his hair, his tongue slid against mine in a fury. Like a dance, we moved together, I pressed my body into his, and he slammed me against the wall in a rough push that forced every hard part of his body against every soft curve of mine.

He tasted like whiskey and sin, and I couldn't get enough.

His mouth left mine to rasp his stubble and lead hot lips in a trail against the skin of my throat and collarbone, then lower to my exposed cleavage where his teeth scraped against my flesh. I moaned his name and a sound tore from the back of his throat I'd never heard before.

"Don't stop," I gasped as he stood, chest heaving.

"I hate these *fucking shorts*," he said, his words wrenched from somewhere primal. He gripped my shorts tight in his firm hands, pulling my hips forward to feel every hard, *delicious* inch of his cock for me straining against his jeans. I groaned, despising the cumbersome layers between our bodies.

"I thought you liked them," I said, smiling breathlessly at him.

"I'd like them a lot more on the floor," he growled, bending his head to catch my mouth again. His hands slid over the curves of my ass, lifting me until I wrapped my thighs around his waist.

*Oh fuck.*

I could feel the entire length of him, exactly where I wanted him to be. My hips ground against him. I tossed my head back as he pressed against me even harder. All thought shattered. His tongue traced my pulse, and I pulled his hair, desperate for him.

"The room," I managed between heaving breaths as his hands and hips forced a choked scream from me. "We have to get to the room." I wrenched his mouth to mine again, tasting deep that whiskey and sin flavor.

His body stilled, muscles tense. I pulled my head back to catch my breath. Not understanding his sudden hesitation.

"I can be quiet," I said, misreading the stillness. "Or I can bite a pillow. The Kid sleeps like a rock, it'll be—"

All at once I remembered.

*Clara.*

Her name rang through me and settled like a stone in the pit of my stomach. We couldn't go back to the room because his fiancée was waiting in bed for him. Suddenly, what'd felt more right than any casual night of passion twisted into something cheap. Of course he tasted like whiskey and sin; he was drunk with me instead of the woman who would be his *wife*.

"Put me down," I whispered. I dragged in harsh lungfuls of air, attempting to still my riotous heart. I braced myself against him to put my feet back on solid ground as the cold night air rushed into the inches between our bodies. His hands were in my hair; he tried to guide my eyes up to his. He leaned down to capture my mouth with his again. I pulled back, something sharp twisting in my chest as I denied him.

My chest heaved, either from our passionate actions or the effort it took not to let the heat gathering in my eyes turn into tears.

"Bonnie—"

"It's fine, Jesse," I said, my voice too raw.

"It's not that I don't want to. *Fuck*, you know I want to," he said. I closed my eyes against the shame coating my skin. Of course that was what he wanted.

"It was a mistake," I said, leveling him with a direct stare. My words hit him like a physical blow; his body recoiled from them. He furrowed his brows in confusion, shaking his head as if he couldn't accept them.

"You don't mean that," he said. I clenched my jaw against the pathetic words rising into the back of my throat. *I love you. Choose me. Don't leave me alone again.*

"Of course I do," I said, an incredulous, drunk laugh catching on the tears at the edge of my voice. "What are we even doing?" I asked, stepping away from him. "You *barely* know me."

"I know you better than you think," he said, his words angry.

"No," I said, taking another step back. "No, you don't. I'm just another whore in a hallway keeping you from a good woman waitin' for you. Go back to your fiancée, Jesse. She won't leave you, but I'm going to."

"I don't believe you," he said, closing the distance between us. He towered over me, but I stood my ground. The scent of him, the warmth of his skin, the desperation in his eyes . . . it was all too much.

"You don't *believe* me? I've said it repeatedly since we met. This is temporary. One day soon, I'm going to ride away. I've never lied about that," I said, the truth of the words hanging low in the space between us. A dark omen, like black storm clouds in the distance, promising the arrival of devastation.

"You made an exception before. You can do it again," he said. I couldn't decipher the edge in his tone. If it was angry or frustrated or upset. Maybe he didn't know either.

"No. I can't," I said, my words clipped. "You *know* that. And why would you even want me to?" His brows furrowed, and he reached for me then. I took a tentative step back, certain that if he touched me, my argument would crumble away like dust. "I sat with you in Santa Fe and watched you cry over the woman in that room. You said you'd give anything to see her again. And she's here. On the other side of that door."

He ran a frustrated hand through his hair, groaning through gritted teeth. "Home. I wanted home. She's *not* home for me," he said, blue eyes pleading with me in the darkness.

"I should've never made an exception for you," I said, the words untrue. He leaned against the wall, mouth open but with no words left to try to convince me to stay. Part of me wanted him to try anyway. I nodded at his speechlessness, blinking hard to rid myself of tears I wouldn't allow to fall. I walked away without looking back.

If I'd looked back, I would've let those traitorous words fall from my mouth to rid him of the betrayal in his beautiful blue eyes.

*I love you. Choose me.*

*Don't leave me alone again.*

## CHAPTER TWENTY

# JESSE

THE WORDS LEFT UNSAID burned on the tip of my tongue as she walked away. She disappeared among the busy crowd below. I put my head in my hands. How had everything gotten so fucked up? I'd tried to tell her what I felt. She didn't want to hear it. I'd tried to show her. That wasn't good enough either.

I ran my fingers through my hair, pacing across the landing. I wanted to march downstairs and demand she listen.

But I wouldn't.

She'd made her mind up.

*I should've never made an exception for you.*

Before I realized it, I punched the wall. The wood cracked beneath my knuckles, and I pulled back, clutching it with my other hand. The door to our room squeaked open, and I peered over, finding Clara standing there. I turned my back, unable to look at her. It wasn't her fault that I didn't want her anymore.

"Jesse? What's going on?" she asked.

"Nothing, Clara. Go back to bed," I said, turning to the railing that overlooked the main floor. I stared into the crowded room but couldn't find her.

"Come to bed," Clara said as she walked over to me. She took my arm. I hesitated, not wanting to go to bed. Not without Bonnie. Not after knowing what it was like to sleep with her in my arms. But she didn't want me. Not anymore.

I let Clara guide me inside the room and watched her shut the door. She tried to move me toward the empty bed, but I shook her off.

"What is it?" she asked, her voice almost too sweet. As though I was used to the harsh words and bitter tone of the woman downstairs.

"I'm just tired," I said.

"Then come to bed."

Clara climbed between the sheets, dressed in the clothes Bonnie'd given her earlier. I knew they'd smell like her. I couldn't be anywhere near that right now.

Without a word, I kicked off my boots and grabbed one of our packs. I put it near the window and lay down on the floor, feeling Clara's eyes on me the entire time.

I didn't sleep. Not for hours. Then the nightmares started again.

Images flew through my mind. Sixgun with his belt around Bonnie's neck. The man who'd taken The Kid. The first man I killed. The second. Bonnie, walking away from me. Over and over.

When I snapped awake, it was barely dawn. My shirt was soaked through with sweat. I sat up, taking inventory of the two bodies in the beds. Neither of them was Bonnie. I put my boots on, then tucked the pistol I'd stolen from that slaver in the back of my pants.

The bar was dark when I made my way down to the first floor. We had things to get done. If I couldn't tell Bonnie how I felt, and if she was so determined that this thing had an expiration date, then I needed to start planning for that eventuality. As I walked to the exit, the barkeeper whistled to get my attention.

"You left somethin' down here," she said, motioning with her head to the end of the bar.

There she was, seated on a barstool, alone, her head down on the hard surface. Bonnie had fallen asleep down here. Dull pain ached in my chest at the sight of her.

"She's not mine," I said, putting my hat on and walking out the door.

A few men milled out front, holding cups of coffee. Their eyes tracked me as I walked to the wagon. We needed to get these bars off. We couldn't have people thinking we were slavers. Which, by the look they gave me, was exactly what they thought.

I headed down to the blacksmith with the wagon. For a few copper bits, he let me borrow his handheld torch. The work was slow, and my hands were covered in burns by the time I finished. Eventually, the bars were off of the wagon, left behind with the smith who told me he could repurpose them. As I climbed into the wagon, a man walked up.

"You better watch yourself," he said. "Slavers don't like to be stolen from." Unconsciously, I put my hand on my pistol.

"Good thing these slavers are dead," I said. The man's eyes grew wide. I clicked my tongue, snapping the reins, and the horses took off, back down the main drag.

We needed to leave before anyone came looking for that wagon. The Kid stood next to Eagle, helping Bonnie with the saddlebags by the time I returned. Clara stood to one side, changed back into the filthy dress she'd been wearing when we found her. The purse at my side with the winnings from our con last night weighed heavily on me as I looked at Bonnie.

Her hair was pulled back, and she'd changed out of those provocative clothes. She wouldn't look at me.

That was probably for the best.

"Jesse!" my brother shouted as he caught sight of me. He climbed up in the wagon. I was glad he wasn't angry with me anymore, even if it was only because Bonnie told him to apologize to me. "Can I drive?"

I shrugged. "Sure. Why not?" I'd rather have the silence of riding my horse alone today. I handed the reins to him and climbed down from the wagon.

"Clara, we should get you something else to wear," I said. "C'mon." Without looking at Bonnie, I took Clara by the hand and led her down the street, remembering the shop that Bonnie had gone into when we were here before. The dress she wore was ragged; the skirt was torn and covered in dirt.

I immediately regretted walking into the shop with Clara. Her eyes grew wide with an excitement I remembered seeing on her face on market days when a traveler would bring fruit in the summer months. She'd wanted some of everything. I was usually the one paying.

"Just one," I told her. She turned to me, her eyes sparkling. She trailed a finger down the middle of my chest.

"I'll let you watch me change if I can have more than one," she said, her voice low with promise. Once, I would have jumped at the opportunity. I grabbed her hand before she reached my belt.

"Just. One," I said firmly, turning my back to her. She huffed and walked off toward the curtained changing room.

Another hour passed before we walked out of the store, Clara in her new dress and boots. She clutched my arm as I noted the position of the sun high in the sky. We were already so behind schedule this morning that I was sure we'd be sleeping on the road tonight.

"Finally," The Kid said as we walked up. I mumbled an apology, refusing to look at Bonnie, who sat next to my brother in the wagon.

"Let's head out. We've already lost too much daylight," I said. Before I turned to climb up on No Name, I dared a glance at Bonnie. I shouldn't have. Because her eyes were so intense as she stared at me in silence. I couldn't tell what she felt; I didn't like that. I liked that I could read her emotions most of the time. I liked being able to tell her thoughts just by looking at her. It was why she'd never be good at playing cards. Her poker face sucked.

Except today, it seemed, she'd learned how to wear one.

"Thank you for my new dress," Clara said, using her fingertips to turn my head toward her. She leaned up, pressing her lips to mine in a quick kiss. It was different from the quiet kisses we once shared. It felt . . . wrong. My eyes went to Bonnie the moment Clara pulled back. Her steely gaze faltered for half a second. Jealousy flared, bright and prevalent in her dark blue eyes. Then the emotion disappeared, and her poker face returned in full force.

"Clara," I said, staring pointedly at Bonnie. "Ride with me."

Clara's eyes sparkled as she climbed down from the wagon. I helped her onto my horse and settled in front of her on the saddle. If the only way to get to Bonnie was to show Clara affection, I'd do it.

By the time we cleared the edges of Lamesa, it was the middle of the day. I cringed every time Clara gripped me. The wrongness of her touch was amplified the longer she clung to me. At first, our progress was slow going as The Kid learned how to steer the wagon. Eventually, he found his stride. Still, we couldn't ride full out, as we had with just the two horses.

I'd glance at Bonnie every once in a while, finding her eyes straight ahead. I guess we weren't talking anymore. Even if she was calling me an idiot or *farm boy*, I missed her acknowledging my existence. The insults were better than the cold shoulder.

"Do you remember," Clara said, her head perched on my shoulder, "that night in your barn?" Her arms tightened around my waist. I closed my eyes, wishing I *didn't* remember that night. Clara's voice was low, but not low enough that the others couldn't hear if they were listening.

"No," I said, trying to inflect in my tone for her to shut up. Apparently, Clara couldn't take a hint.

"Remember when you said you wanted to have a dozen kids?" she asked. I stole a glance at Bonnie. Were her hands gripping Eagle's reins tighter?

"No," I said, my voice louder. "I don't." I remembered when she snuck out to the farm and we stayed up talking on quiet nights. At least, she would talk all night. I would put in my two cents between kissing her, tell her what I thought she wanted to hear. All with the end goal of getting her dress off.

I might have said I wanted a dozen kids with her. That didn't mean it was true.

"Yes, well, we didn't just talk in that barn. Did we?" she asked, tossing a grin at me. Her voice seemed louder than before.

"I said a lot of things back in Montana, Clara," I said, lowering my voice. "In case you haven't noticed, we aren't *in* Montana anymore." When we stopped tonight, I decided, Clara was going to ride with The Kid. Making Bonnie jealous wasn't worth *this*.

Sometime later, when the sun dipped low against the western horizon, Bonnie finally spoke.

"We won't make it to the next town tonight." Her voice startled my ears; the harshness of her tone gave me a strange sort of comfort.

I didn't respond. Instead, I steered No Name to the side of the trail, finding a clump of trees and bushes where we could make camp tonight. The three of us—me, The Kid, and Bonnie—went about our normal routine, unpacking the saddlebags, feeding and watering the horses, building a fire, passing around rations. I was exhausted, but I knew sleep wouldn't find me tonight.

Once everyone settled in, I made for the wagon.

"Why aren't you sleeping with Bonnie?" The Kid asked, noticing my bedroll still wrapped up on its own. I stopped, the tension whipping my body straight. "You always sleep with Bonnie."

I pinched the bridge of my nose, letting out a low breath. He didn't know any better. *It's not The Kid's fault.*

"Someone's gotta keep watch, Kid," I said, my face flushed. I spared a glance in Bonnie's direction and found her staring back at me. Her eyes mirrored the longing in my chest. My stomach flipped as I remembered how she'd gone pliant in my arms last night. If only I'd have been able to get those shorts off.

No. She regretted it. She didn't want me.

I walked to the wagon where we'd left it, checking our surroundings constantly. We couldn't have been that far from where we were attacked. Someone had to stand guard. I didn't want to be plagued by nightmares again anyway.

When even the crackling of the fire stopped, I found myself on my back in the bed of the wagon, staring up at the stars in the sky. Every time I tried not to think of Bonnie, I thought of Bonnie. Of last night and the night before. Of how she'd looked at me from across the fire. Of that first day, in Vegas.

She consumed my every waking moment, and I'd let her.

What would it be like when she left? Would her eyes follow me everywhere I went? Would her words haunt my every move?

Sometime in the middle of the night, I caught myself dozing. It was only when cold, wet drops fell on my face that I blinked awake. I sat up, confused. I looked up at the sky and could no longer see the stars.

Rain. In the desert.

I laughed. The deep, booming sound came from within my chest and spilled out of my mouth. Rain. In the fucking desert. If that wasn't a sign from some higher power, I didn't know what was. I wasn't sure if it was the reminder of home, or of the way Bonnie smelled, or just the irony of it all, but I laughed for a long time.

By the morning, it wasn't funny anymore.

The downpour had lessened to a light rain. But the damage was done. We set out in the early morning, but didn't make it very far. The wheels of the wagon kept getting stuck in the mud. The horses were unsettled. They wanted to stretch their legs, but they couldn't. We were restless. By the afternoon, The Kid and I were covered in mud. Bonnie, too. But not Clara. Instead of helping, she either sat on one of the horses or in the wagon itself. The Kid was so frustrated after a particularly sticky hole that he pushed Clara right into the mud.

As I stifled a smile, I thought I heard Bonnie laugh next to me. Though we hadn't spoken, it was the closest we'd been to one another. I looked over at her. She turned to me, a satisfied grin on her lips.

"Bonnie, I—"

"Harry! What would your mother say?" Clara said, attempting to climb out of the hole she'd fallen into. My brother stood on the wagon's edge.

"Is my mom here?" he asked, hands on his hips.

"What?" Clara asked, attempting to brush her hair out of her face but smearing mud on her cheek instead.

"Do. You. See. My. Mom?" The Kid asked, slowing his words down in a way that reminded me of how Bonnie used to talk to me, at the beginning. Before things changed with us.

"Of course not," Clara said, rolling her eyes.

"Then it doesn't matter what she'd say, does it?" He stuck his tongue out at her. Clara darted toward him, but The Kid jumped back, forcing the wagon to stick further into the mud. He darted over the seat, and then jumped onto the ground to plant himself at Bonnie's side. Attempting, and failing, to hide my smile, I walked around the wagon, my boots squishing in the mud.

"Here, let me help," I said, offering her my arm.

"Thank you, Jesse. At least *one* of you James boys was brought up right," Clara said, grabbing my arm. I pulled her out of the hole. It made a disgusting squelching sound. "My boot!"

Sure enough, one of her feet was bare as she moved away from the mud hole.

I laughed. Blatantly.

"We aren't gonna get out of this until it dries out," I said, turning to look at Bonnie. Her eyes were bright. For the first time in two days, it felt like it had before. Before the attack, before she rejected me, just . . . before. When it was still the three of us.

Sometime after the fire went out that night, I spied movement from my perch in the back of the wagon. My back straightened as Bonnie came into my view. She climbed into the wagon and settled by my side, silent. I recognized the tense set of her shoulders and the way her eyes couldn't quite settle.

As I opened my mouth to ask if she couldn't sleep, she handed over her flask. We passed it between us a few times. She shivered beside me. I grabbed my blanket and wrapped it around her. I was afraid if I said anything, she'd storm off again. Instead, I remained silent, and Bonnie settled against me. Eventually, we both dozed off. For the first time in days, the nightmares stayed away.

When I woke, Bonnie's scent enveloped me. Her small body was warm against my chest. I smiled into her hair, pressing my lips to the top of her head. She let out a contented sigh.

Nearby, someone cleared their throat. I picked my head up, finding Clara and The Kid standing at the foot of the wagon. The former's arms were crossed over her chest, and fury was written in her eyes. Bonnie moved beside me, suddenly realizing we weren't alone.

She mumbled an apology and pulled out of my arms. Before I could protest, she hopped over the side of the wagon and walked off toward the horses.

I ran my hands wearily over my face, tired of her walking away from me. Even if she didn't want to talk, she needed to listen. The next time I had her alone, I would finish saying the things I'd wanted to in Lamesa.

An hour later, we were able to get the wagon out of the mud. By then, the trail dried enough so the horses' hooves didn't sink all of the way down. The afternoon sun finally peered out, and we were well on our way.

A town appeared in the distance after we stopped for lunch. The trees thickened up to the north, and we rode along the line of them until we were nearly upon the town.

Bonnie put her hand up, and we all stopped.

"Do you hear that, Kid?" she asked. I looked toward my brother, watching as he squinted.

"Is that running water?" he asked after a long pause.

Bonnie gave him an encouraging smile. The Kid bounded from the wagon, leaving it behind to break through the tree line. I shouted after him to slow down, but he was gone. I climbed down from No Name and tended to the wagon and horses. Bonnie walked off after my brother, leaving Clara and me alone.

"Jesse," Clara said beside me. I glanced up at her for only a second while I worked to untie the horses from the wagon.

"Yeah?" I asked. She put one hand on my forearm and tugged the leads from me with the other. I looked up at her, confusion flooding through me. She tipped my head down, her eyes resting heavily on my lips.

"What are you doing?" I asked, trying to shake her off.

"It's okay, they're gone," she said, before pressing herself into my chest. Panic seized my chest. I gripped her by the shoulders to put distance between us.

"What are you doing?" I asked again.

"I wanted to kiss you. Like we used to. We're engaged, remember?" she asked.

I knew this conversation would happen eventually, but I hoped we wouldn't have to have it. I dropped my hands from her. I wanted to be gentle, because this was Clara. She'd always been sweet to me, but I had a feeling kindness wouldn't get through to her.

"Listen, okay?" I asked, speaking in an even tone. "Whatever we had in Montana . . . It died the night of the fires. It was a different time and place. I don't hold you to any of those promises."

Clara's eyes were wide as she stared at me. "But—"

"I'd appreciate it if you would give me that same respect," I said. Then I turned away to finish untying the horses. If there was fresh water nearby, it would be better to let them drink from it.

"It's Bonnie, isn't it?" Clara asked, a harsh edge to her words. I let out a sigh and ran a hand through my hair.

"Does it matter?"

"I see the way you look at her. You used to look at me like that," Clara said, crossing her arms over her chest.

"No," I said, pointedly. "I didn't." I guided the horses by their reins toward the sound of rushing water. It wasn't fair of Clara to hold me to anything I said back home. Times changed; situations changed. The sooner she understood that, the better. I wouldn't leave her on her own. That wasn't the right thing to do, but that didn't mean I had to keep promises made by two dumb kids who didn't know any better.

As I broached the tree line, laughter sounded above the rushing water. It brought a smile to my face, much as it had back in Flagstaff the first time I'd heard Bonnie laugh. The stream was nearly ten feet wide and must have been a couple of feet deep, judging by how high it came on her legs.

Legs that wrapped around my waist a few short nights ago.

I pushed the thought away, but my traitorous eyes refused to cooperate. They trailed the pale expanse of her legs. Suddenly, I was back beside that fire, except the clothes were gone and my head was between her thighs.

"Jesse!" The Kid shouted, catching sight of me. I grumbled beneath my breath.

I had to talk to her.

I led the horses to the edge of the stream, tying off their reins on a nearby tree. No Name and Eagle were upstream. I glanced behind me, barely making out the shape of Clara in the wagon.

"Get in! The water's cold!" my brother said, falling backward and making a big splash. I smiled, thinking of our day at the lake and how damn near perfect it was. Until Bonnie rejected me and we fought. A frown crossed my face.

The mud we'd been in the past two days crusted over my clothes and much of my skin. It would be nice to have a hot shower, but a cold stream would do for now. I kicked off my boots, specifically *not* looking at Bonnie as I undressed.

Even at its deepest point, the stream barely reached past the middle of my thighs. I focused on cleaning the dirt off my skin, eventually soaking my clothes at the water's edge to clean them as well. The water was cold, just the shock I needed. To get clean and to *not* think about Bonnie and how little she wore.

Of course, that was until my brother decided to go taunt Clara and left us alone. Why did he do that? It was like he wanted us to get into trouble.

I spared a glance at Bonnie. She sat in the shallow water, running her fingertips back and forth along the surface. I was about to look away when her blue eyes captured me.

"A dozen kids, huh?" she asked, that familiar teasing edge back in her voice. I let out a breathy laugh.

"You know how guys are," I said, taking broad steps toward her in the water. I settled down about a foot away. "Say just about anything to get a pretty girl out of their dress." I shrugged.

"I don't, really," Bonnie said. "I've never been in a relationship."

"Wouldn't recommend it. They're not fun," I said, chuckling.

"I don't know. The tension, the suspense. The 'will they, won't they?' Will they kill each other first?" Bonnie said. "Seems like it could be pretty hot."

"I guess it could be," I said, staring into the water as it rushed away from us. "If it was the right person." I glanced up at her. *Bonnie* was the right person. Not Clara.

"If those dozen kids were as cool as your brother, I could see how you could convince someone to settle down," Bonnie said, blinking up at me through her eyelashes. There it was again. That longing. Not desire, not lust. Longing. I felt it echoed in my chest.

Every single day she'd been out of my arms was full of that longing for her. Each night when I fought against sleep or had nightmares, I remembered how she'd soothed them just by being there. Waking up with her in my arms this morning nearly made me forget her harsh words from the bar that night.

"He is pretty great, isn't he?" I asked. My gaze lowered to her lips. I inched forward to kiss her but stopped myself. I couldn't. Not with everything left unsaid. "Bonnie, what you said the other night . . . that it was a mistake. If that's how you feel, I'll respect it. But if it's not . . ."

There they were. The words I'd left unspoken. If she didn't feel the same about me, then I'd learn to let it go. But, if there was even the slimmest chance that nothing had changed, I wasn't going to let it pass me by. Bonnie's gaze fell to the water. She shifted, as though she were going to stand. Which meant she would walk away.

"Of course it was a mistake," she said. "For so many reasons. Clara, for one. But there are others. I keep putting you and The Kid in danger. Sixgun, the attack. If you hadn't been with me, it wouldn't have happened. You deserve a measure of peace, Jesse, and I can't give you that."

Her words struck me right in the heart. How had I missed it? Of course Bonnie felt like everything was her fault. I did, too. I reached up, taking hold of her hand.

"I understand why you must hate me. It's not fair of me to keep doin' this to you," she said, the words barely audible over the water rushing around us. Her eyes fell to our hands.

"I don't hate you. The attack was my fault as much as yours. We got caught up, but I don't blame you for any of it," I said, glancing to make sure we were still alone. "But I don't think it was a mistake. You and me. This . . . thing." I didn't know how to put my feelings into words. "I . . . want you. I don't want some whore in a hallway, or a girl from my past. I want *you*." That ache in my chest returned. She wasn't looking at me.

Bonnie finally brought her eyes to mine. Though I could see the open longing reflected back at me, there was sadness, too. "One day soon, I'll have to leave. I don't have a choice. You know that," she said.

I did. I knew that our time together had an end date. I knew that she couldn't just stop. She *didn't* have family or friends or anyone that could keep her safe.

Except me. And The Kid. We could be Bonnie's family.

We could protect her. Keep her safe from the madmen chasing her. I knew nothing I said would change her mind. Not right now. That didn't stop the trickle of hope that found its way into my heart. I reached over, brushing a stray lock of dark, wet hair behind her ear. She leaned her cheek into my hand. We shared a small smile. My eyes fell to her lips once more.

"Can I kiss you?" I asked. She nodded, her arms sliding over my shoulders to hook around my neck.

"Okay," she whispered against my lips. I pulled her to me, shifting her in my arms until she straddled my lap in the cold water. Our lips touched in the faintest of kisses.

"Jesse!" The Kid's voice cut above the rushing water. I pulled back from Bonnie, turning toward him. "Clara saw y'all kissing. Said something about leaving." Amusement lit up his eyes, and he bounded away from the stream.

I pressed my forehead to Bonnie's. "Guess I should go make sure she doesn't get herself killed," I said, not moving an inch. I leaned forward, capturing Bonnie's mouth with my own in a heated kiss. She rolled her hips against my hardening cock. I groaned into her mouth.

"You're wicked, woman," I said. Then, regretfully, I disentangled myself from her and headed toward the bank. After drying off and changing into clean clothes, we made our way back, Bonnie's hand in mine.

Clara stood at the tail of the wagon, stuffing some of the food into the small bag I'd carried from Montana. She froze at the sight of us, anger flashing in her eyes before she tossed the bag over one shoulder. I dropped Bonnie's hand.

"Where do you think you're going?" I asked.

"Leaving," she said, refusing to look at me. I snatched the bag away. "Give it back."

"If you want to leave, then go, but you're not taking this bag or anything in it," I said. Clara glared at me, grabbing for it again. I held it out of her reach.

"Give it back," she demanded.

"It's not yours," I said. "You have two choices. You can go off on your own, or you can sit your ass in that wagon and let us get on our way."

She huffed, glaring from me to Bonnie and back to me. I lifted my eyebrows in a silent challenge. She cursed beneath her breath and climbed into the wagon. The Kid took up residence in the driver's seat.

I turned to Bonnie, who was smiling at me. There'd been no love lost between the women. I started to turn away when a figure broke through the trees near the stream. A man rushed forward. He clamped a hand over Bonnie's mouth before I could shout. She screamed against his hand. He dragged her backward, narrowly avoiding the knee Bonnie drove up between his legs. I took in the man's dusty cowboy hat and familiar face.

"Let me go!" Bonnie screamed.

"Goddamnit, Bonnie, you didn't have to bite me!" the man shouted. Suddenly, I remembered why he was familiar. This was the same man who had tried to steal Bonnie in Flagstaff before we escaped. Will Ellis.

I grabbed the pistol from my waistband, aimed it at him, and pulled the trigger.

## CHAPTER TWENTY-ONE

# BONNIE

F OR A SOLITARY MOMENT, time stood still. The booming strike of the gunshot reverberated in my ears and my mind refused to follow or acknowledge what happened next. There was no pain, but the thud of the bullet finding flesh recoiled through me as Will fell. *No.* Years of separation and betrayal that'd loomed dark between us evaporated like smoke as I witnessed the pain in his eyes.

"*Ay dios mio!*" Will shouted, clutching the bloody wound on his shoulder. "What the fuck is wrong with that *pendejo!*"

Will's familiar rolling voice, his lean form writhing in agony on the ground—it churned my stomach. *No. Not Will.* I dropped down beside him, trying to pry his hands away from the wound to assess the damage. Had the bullet hit an artery? Did we need a tourniquet?

All at once, he was just my friend again, bleeding on the ground.

Jesse was beside me in an instant, gun trained on Will's prone form. Will glared into the barrel. All I could see was red as I tried to staunch the bleeding.

"Put it down!" I hissed at Jesse, but the gun never lowered.

"We don't have time for that!" Will ground out through clenched teeth. He gripped my shirt tight and pulled me forward. "I came to warn you. My father's waiting in that town to ambush you. You have to *run*, songbird."

A loud buzzing sounded in my ears. Sixgun was *here.* I leveled panicked eyes at Jesse, my own fear mirrored back at me. I swallowed down the terror threatening to swallow me whole and set my jaw.

Muffled shouting drifted toward us in the distance, someone signaling that they'd spotted us. My breath became ragged and I clenched my fists to still the tremors working down my arms into my fingers. Jesse looked to me, frozen in place by the same panic that seized me. We had to *move*. Now.

If Sixgun caught me, there was no telling what retribution he would carve into my skin this time. My defiance on the train, the bullet I'd buried in his knee, his obsession with me. The consequences of that night would be the perfect storm of horror and blood.

I pushed the thoughts away as I struggled with Will's obnoxious bulk until I'd managed to get him off the ground and leaning on me.

"We're not taking him with us," Jesse said, incredulous. His eyes were confused and shocked, but I didn't have the time to explain. Will and I were bound together by ties stronger than blood. No matter what happened, we would always fight for each other.

"Like hell we aren't," I said, grunting as I struggled to shove him into the wagon.

"He just tried to drag you away. For all we know he led them here," Jesse argued, reaching for my arm. I dropped Will heavily into the back of the wagon. He groaned as he landed on his wounded shoulder. Whirling to Jesse, my heart in my throat, I squared my shoulders.

"Rule number seven!" I shouted. "No one gets left behind."

Jesse pointed angrily at Will. "He's not *one of us*!"

"Either he comes, or I stay with him," I said, voice firm. We stared at each other for a tense moment; a muscle twitched in Jesse's jaw.

"Fine!" He shouted, hands gesturing wildly. He swung his leg back onto No Name and with a hard pull, forced the horse around.

"Fine," I said. I mounted Eagle and dug my heels into her side. I caught a glimpse of riders in the distance, a familiar black cowboy hat among them. A weak sound clawed its way from the back of my throat.

"Kid! How fast can you make that wagon go?" I asked. He grinned wide beneath the brim of his hat, whipping the reins furiously. The horses thundered back down the path we'd just come from. We kept a reckless pace, unable to hide our tracks in the drying mud. We veered off the main road and took a trail covered with rocks and small shrubs. The wagon bounced and jostled so hard, I was afraid it would shake apart. With each turn the riders fell further behind us, but they never stopped.

Will wasn't faring well in the back, if the string of bilingual expletives was any indication. The worst ones he shouted in Spanish, thankfully. At least The Kid wouldn't learn any *new* swears. Clara'd been in the back of the wagon when I shoved Will inside; I'm sure his colorful language and openly bleeding gunshot wound were doing wonders for her sense of safety.

The landscape blurred around us, shifting from the open expanse of nature to the crumbling remains of an abandoned town. Burned out buildings and cracked asphalt slipped away as Eagle soared over the terrain with each shuddering slam of her hooves. She flew over the ground, driving her legs down so powerfully it propelled her into a speed I'd only felt hints of on our journey so far. As if she could feel the threat behind us. As if she were protecting me the only way she knew how.

A looming gate holding back a sea of rusting cars towered ahead. A white $X$ marked the gates, a symbol indicating the presence of an undesirable sanctuary.

"There!" I shouted to Jesse who'd easily kept pace on No Name. Sixgun wouldn't look for us in the fringes. He wouldn't expect me to be crazy enough to ride into a place that dangerous, even to outrun him. My mouth went dry and my hands shook so violently I could barely hold on to the reins. There was no other choice. If we didn't do something, he'd catch us, and I *knew* what he'd do to Jesse and The Kid if that happened.

We thundered through the gates. I yanked up hard on the reins, Eagle skidding to a stop inside the junkyard. I extended the M9 in front of me, scanning the area. Fires burned from several metal cans. The people surrounding them turned to us, slinking out of the shadows. Some were barely more than skeletons, wrapped in scarred skin that stretched too tight over their frames. Others with blue stained lips moved in jerking movements.

"Sanctuary!" I shouted, chest heaving with adrenaline. With a *clack, clack* Jesse chambered a round in his shotgun beside me. "We need sanctuary!"

The silence seethed with malevolent intention. It had a sentience that promised violence and blood. I knew what they saw. The supplies, the weapons, the horses. We had too much they wanted. Too much they'd kill for.

"It's you," a voice said from the darkness beyond a tower of rusting cars. A tall dark-skinned man stepped from the shadows. At first glance, he wasn't an undesirable: no scars or deformities, not an addict by the pink shade of his lips. He was strong and healthy. His eyes fixed on my face with a warm smile. I tipped my gun down, but didn't lower it completely. I didn't know this man, didn't recognize him.

He pointed off to the right, and I found hundreds of wanted posters plastered over a section of the chain link gate. Thousands of my own eyes staring down at us. I swallowed down my trepidation, eyebrows knitting low in confusion.

"What is this?" I asked. More people filed in from the twisting paths through the junkyard. More people who *weren't* undesirables. Not from what I saw.

"You saved us," he said, arms relaxed by his sides. My eyes dropped to his wrists, scarred in thick, uneven bands. "You started the slave revolt that liberated us. We've been taking down your posters as we come across them."

A woman with a bright-eyed toddler came forward. Her rounded face flushed, her eyes welled with unshed tears. She was familiar, but I couldn't quite place her. A shocked sound of recognition fell from my lips. When I'd last seen her, the curls framing her face were limp with neglect, and her eyes had been dull and haunted. I lowered the M9 incredulously.

"You killed the man who raped me, and freed us from the back of a wagon. I never thought I'd see you again," she said reverently.

"*Please*," I begged. "We need help."

Without another word, the dark-skinned man walked to the horses. He directed us further into the junkyard where we couldn't be seen from the street. People parted around us. I shared a heavy glance with Jesse who kept the shotgun at the ready. The undesirables retreated from around our wagon, slinking into the shadows as if they'd never been there at all.

We dismounted slowly. The woman from earlier letting her toddler pat Eagle's neck for a moment before facing me. I studied the child, a girl with bright eyes and a wild smile. A question I didn't dare ask hung heavily between us. The woman nodded before kissing her daughter's temple.

"My name is Talia. This is Mercy," she said. A fractured smile crossed my lips.

"Mercy. I like that," I said quietly.

"They won't bother you," the dark-skinned man said from beside Jesse, motioning toward the shadows. "We'll keep them away."

The Kid bounded over with excitement flaring bright in his eyes.

"So, is this domestic terrorism?" he asked, grinning. I rolled my eyes and chuckled, ruffling his hair affectionately. Will's throaty groan tore through the comfortable silence. Relief washed over me now that the immediate danger was behind us.

Jesse wasn't concerned with the precarious safety we'd managed to find. He swung down from No Name, and walked around to the back of the wagon, leveling his shotgun at Will's chest. I pinched the bridge of my nose and called to The Kid.

"I need you to start a fire and get the med kit and canteen. Can you do that?" I asked. He nodded, his grin widening. I walked towards Jesse, whose blue eyes hardened in the afternoon light, trained on Will's every move as he struggled to sit up. "At ease, soldier," I said softly, my hand resting on Jesse's forearm for a long moment. Finally, he lowered the shotgun enough so I could face Will.

"What are you still doin' with this guy?" Will asked, jerking his head toward Jesse. "I mean, he's hot, I'll give you that." Will's warm brown eyes slid over Jesse's long legs and broad shoulders before focusing back on me. "But he's so *violent.*"

I stifled a grin, but it found its way onto my mouth anyway. My farm boy, *violent.* I guess it was true, considering the men he'd killed not long ago and the violent encounters we'd had along our journey. For some reason, I'd never thought of Jesse that way. Maybe because I felt safe with him.

"Why're you following us?" I asked, stamping down the moment of levity. This was Will; as much as I wanted to trust him, I didn't know if I could.

"I've been tracking you for months. Trying to get to you before my dad. There are things we need to talk about," he said in a low voice. His brown eyes lost their usual playful warmth. His gaze flickered to Jesse behind my shoulder.

"Then talk," I said, resting my hands on my hips.

"Alone," he pressed.

"Anything you have to say, you can say in front of Jesse," I said, stepping back to stand shoulder-to-shoulder with Jesse, who glanced at me.

"Well, isn't that just *adorable,*" Will said, swinging his mocking gaze between us. "Seriously, this has nothing to do with your . . . who exactly is he to you? Fuck buddy?"

Who was Jesse to me?

The question ricocheted through my mind, distracting me from Will's unique brand of annoyance. He wasn't my lover. Well, *not yet,* anyway. We weren't friends. He was someone who'd killed for me. Someone who stole my breath with a glance. I was in love with him, but what he'd said back at that stream was *I want you.* What did that make us, exactly?

"Will," I groaned, running a weary hand down my face at his lewd suggestion. "Just spill it already, or I won't sew up the hole in your arm, and I'll leave you here to bleed out."

He opened his mouth to say something else but, after studying my serious expression, snapped it shut again.

"Whatever, it won't make much sense to *Jesse* anyway," Will grumbled petulantly. "I left the crew."

The words stilled me, and my arms dropped to my sides. Even from here, the tattoo on his neck stood out against his bronze skin, as it had in Flagstaff. A hanged man. Jesse kept flicking his eyes between us as we held a tense stare. No one left the crew. Not alive, anyway.

"W-why would you do that?" I asked, stepping closer to him. He shifted on the back of the wagon, hissing as it jostled his injured arm.

"*You*," he breathed out incredulously, eyes soft. "I left the crew for you."

I opened my mouth, but no words came out. He'd signed his own death warrant *for me.*

"My dad took a job up north, and Jones made me a full-fledged Hanged Man. Honestly, I think he was just pissed he wouldn't have his resident psychopath to instill fear," Will said, running a shaking hand through his dark curls. "When he got back, he was acting really strange. Cagey. Like he was *afraid.*"

The hair on the back of my neck stood on end. Anything bad enough to make a sadist like Sixgun scared set my nerves on edge.

"I caught him talking to himself in his tent. He kept saying the same things, over and over. *Didn't find it* and *I had to burn it all down* and *it'll be alright as long as I get Bonnie.*"

Sixgun rarely did jobs for anyone but Jones. It wasn't uncommon, but the circumstances were unusual at best. Will's eyes were dark and troubled, but something stuck out in my mind.

"Where did you say this job was?" I asked, my voice careful as I regarded Jesse over my shoulder for a long moment.

"Somewhere in Montana. Why?" Will asked, but my mouth went dry all of a sudden.

*I'm scared of the fire . . . How do you know what burning flesh smells like? . . . Same thing that happened to my parents, fire . . . I buried them myself . . .*

Every moment of painful remembrance flooded me at once. Jesse recovered more quickly than me. As Jesse raised the shotgun with deadly intention, I stepped in front of Will to halt the dark impulse in Jesse's eyes.

"Move out of the way, Bonnie," he said, no hint of the deep canyon timbre I loved so much in his hard words.

"No," I said, my voice gentle. I stepped closer until the barrels of the gun were flush against my stomach.

How many times since I'd met him had he waded into my darkness and pulled me back? I gripped the barrels and pulled until Jesse's grip loosened, and I took the gun from him. He didn't look at me once. His eyes trained murderously on Will, chest heaving. Before I could reach out to him, soothe the ragged edges of the past, he was punching Will's jaw with a thud.

"Jesse!" I called, dropping the shotgun.

"Who was he working for? Your son of a bitch father killed—"

"Jesse!" I shouted, gripping his arm tight so he couldn't bring it down on Will's face again. The Kid stood by the wagon, watching the scene unfold with wide eyes. Innocent eyes that didn't know Will was talking about the events that led to his parents' deaths.

"Motherfucker! Seriously, Bonnie, control your fuck boy, would you?!" Will said, pressing his free hand to his face. "How does he know anything about that shithole town in Montana?"

I pressed my entire body against Jesse's as he lurched forward again. My hands gripped his face until I could pull his eyes to mine. They were dark and furious in an expression I'd never seen before. We stayed that way until his breathing slowed, the way he'd done for me before.

"Your name is Jesse James," I said. He swallowed hard.

I hoped I was enough for him.

"Did you hear what he said?" he asked through clenched teeth. I nodded, pressing my lips to his quickly.

"I heard," I said, brushing my fingers through his hair and cradling his face gently again. "Your name is Jesse James. You're an outlaw. And your brother is watching *everything*." I pressed my forehead against his as he fought for self-control. He gripped my waist hard, holding me tight. I let him. I let him hold me as tightly as he needed. Until he was more settled on his feet and the edge of desperation faded from his eyes.

"Kid, why don't you and Clara unhitch the horses and water them?" I asked. He rolled his eyes in response.

"Is this because you used to kiss Will but you kiss Jesse now?" he asked. I glared at him, eliciting a scoff and he turned his back. "Fine! But if she doesn't do her part, we're leaving her here." He turned then, and I thought I heard him grumble, "I'm never kissing *anyone*," under his breath as he left.

"Wow, neat trick," Will said in a sarcastic tone that grated on my last nerves. "You got one that'll get him to *stop fucking punching me*?"

I turned, marching over and pressing a hand against the bullet wound in his shoulder until he screamed so loud I thought it might break my eardrums.

"You're lucky I didn't let him shoot you again," I said. He glared at me, teeth clenched.

"You aren't listening to me, neither of you," he said when he'd finally shaken off the worst of the pain.

"Whatever my dad was sent to retrieve, he *didn't get it*." He turned serious eyes on me. Eyes I knew all too well. "Bonnie, he's dangerous normally, but *scared* . . . he's like a cornered animal."

Only a matter of weeks ago, he'd nearly strangled me on the floor of a train car and enjoyed it. I couldn't imagine what might terrify a monster like him.

"He was raving. I know he likes your pretty skin, even if you aren't a *gringa,* but this was different," Will continued, causing my eyebrows to furrow deep on my forehead.

"I think we've all had enough of your talkin' for a while, Will," I said, crossing to help him from the back of the wagon so I could tend to his wound. Apparently, Jesse hadn't heard enough of Will's bullshit. As I helped him over to the fire, Jesse peppered him with questions. Reminding me of The Kid.

"What was he looking for?" he asked. Will spat blood out of his mouth and glared at Jesse in response. "I knew I recognized the brand on his neck. What does it mean?"

"I'm not tellin' you anything, *pendejo*," Will responded. I unbuttoned Will's shirt. He grinned at Jesse over my shoulder as I helped him undress. I thumped him with my thumb and forefinger between the eyes.

"What did he call me?" Jesse asked darkly.

"Stop that." Will who only grinned wider. "He called you an asshole," I told Jesse flatly, helping Will remove his sleeve from around his wound.

"Fuck you," Jesse muttered as I assessed the damage to Will's arm.

"Maybe later," he said, winking.

"It's through and through," I said, reaching for the canteen to clean the area.

"Stitches or fire?" I asked. Will sighed heavily.

"Well, I know how sloppy your sewing skills are," he said. I grimaced; cauterizing would hurt worse. I reached for my knife, but Will's hand gripped my wrist tight.

"Wait. Help a guy out, would you?" he asked, his brown eyes warmed in mischief. He bit his bottom lip. I sighed.

"Where are they?" I asked, familiar with his vices.

"Front pocket," he said, grinning at Jesse. I reached into the front pocket of his jeans quickly and fished out his cigarette case. Pulling one out, I lit it from the fire and offered it to him.

"I fucking hate you," Jesse mumbled. I glared at him over my shoulder.

"You aren't helping," I said stiffly.

"You're a goddamn angel, *mi cielo*," Will said, inhaling deeply while I prepped my knife, placing it in the fire. He leaned forward and brushed a long strand of hair behind my ear tenderly. From the corner of my eye I noticed Jesse tense, his eyes marking the motion.

I retreated then, not sure what to do with myself while the knife heated enough to cauterize his wound. Both men glared at one another silently until The Kid stomped over, arms crossed over his chest. I hadn't seen him aggravated before; he was usually the one *doing* the aggravating. A metallic grinding whine reverberated from the other side of the junkyard. I looked up, but The Kid waved off my concern.

"Clara walked off," he said. I turned to Jesse with a pleading look. Even though what he'd just learned was hard, I needed him to be the partner I'd relied on all these weeks and help me through this.

"Can you go round up the dairy maid?" I asked. The Kid sat heavily, as close to Will as he could. Jesse's eyes slid to Will once before nodding and standing swiftly. He pulled me to my feet. In a moment, his hands gripped my hips and pulled me flush against his chest. The suddenness of his actions shocked me into breathlessness. He leaned down, his mouth hot on mine. I made a soft sound against his lips, and he pulled away, leaving me unsettled on my feet.

"Ugh, not again," The Kid said grumpily behind me as Jesse walked in the direction Clara disappeared. Will inhaled deeply, letting the cigarette smoke curl around his bronze skin. He joined me in watching Jesse walk away, letting out a low whistle. As soon as Jesse was out of earshot, he turned to me.

"When do we leave?" Will asked. The Kid made a surprised sound.

"It's not that simple," I said. I knelt in front of the fire again and adjusted the knife in the flames. "I made a promise to get them to Fort Hood."

"Rule number three of being an outlaw: keep your word," The Kid said, staring up at Will with a mix between adoration and smugness in his expression. Will turned to him, blowing a ring of smoke in his face. I glared at him, but The Kid was fascinated. "Can you do that again?"

"I tell you what's simple, songbird. My dad is comin' for you, and he's closing in. I have an in with some people in St. Louis who've run up against Jones's men before. We can be there in a couple of weeks if we travel hard and light," he said, but I was already shaking my head. "*They* can keep you safe."

"I made a promise," I said, pulling the knife out by the hilt, the blade red. Will swore. He braced against my shoulder and sucked in a few sharp breaths to prepare himself for the pain. As I pressed the sizzling metal to his skin, an inhuman howl dragged begrudgingly from between his teeth. "Almost done."

"That's so cool! Can I do the next one?" The Kid asked. I scoffed at him, incredulous.

"No," I said simply, pushing my hair behind my ears. I tried not to notice the pale pallor of Will's normally-bronze skin or the tremors in his hands.

"Hey, kid," Will said, not realizing that was his preferred *outlaw* name. "Keep me distracted for this next one."

"Okay!" The Kid said, his eyes bright. "How?"

"I don't know, just talk to me," Will said. I snorted. If there was anything The Kid was good at, it was talking. Jesse and Clara walked back, appearing from behind the remains of a crushed van. Jesse's eyes turned to Will, who'd tossed the nub of his cigarette into the fire. Clara, however, stared at Will in a different way. I understood the heat in her eyes as she trailed the long lines of his exposed bronze skin and the sculpted bow of his full lips. Will was handsome. He didn't let you *forget* that he was handsome.

"Can I ask you questions?" The Kid asked. Will offered him a short chuckle. I smiled affectionately. I knew what it was like, being charmed by The Kid.

"Sure, anything you want," he said as I put the blade of the knife back in the fire and cleaned the exit wound.

"Why doesn't Jones just give up on catching Bonnie already? He seems kinda stupid. She's made it all this way. Why does he care so much?" The Kid asked. My hand stilled.

Had I forgotten to breathe? My stomach dropped to the ground. Will laughed darkly, and I cleared my throat in warning.

"Well, that's an easy one," Will said. I fumbled with the rag in my hand. Panic surged up my spine.

"Will, don't—"

"She belongs to him," Will said with a shrug. "It's a hanging offense."

"Shut *up*—"

"What is?" The Kid asked. I scrambled for the hilt of the knife, hoping if Will was screaming, he couldn't spill my secrets.

"She's a runaway slave, Kid." The campsite fell silent, an oppressive absence of noise that caused a tremor in my hands. Hot tears welled in my eyes, and I refused to look anywhere. At anyone. Especially at Jesse.

"Didn't y'all know that already?" Will asked, confused. I pressed the blade hard against his shoulder, enjoying his tortured scream and the sizzle of his skin. Probably too much. Heat crawled up my neck and settled behind my eyes. I closed them tight and strangled the urge to cry. Pushing to my feet, I fought the need to run pulsing through my veins.

Jesse'd never looked at me like a slave. A part of me never wanted him to know. Will turned, an apology hanging on his lips. I shook my head to stave off his words.

"Bonnie, I didn't know—"

"I pay my debts," I said, louder than I intended. I felt their stares on my skin, like the unwanted caresses I'd endured my whole life. Marking me in ways I would never be able to unsee. Will's eyes widened at my words, and he stood, reaching out to me. I shoved him back, hard.

"I keep my word!" I shouted, an edge of hysteria coloring my voice as I pounded a fist into Will's immovable chest. He stood there, stoic, and let me. I hit him again, and again, and again. Until my fists ached and my words broke on the breeze.

Jesse's familiar hands were on me, pulling me into his arms. Arms that'd always made me feel so safe.

"I'm an outlaw," I whispered, all the fight seeping from me as he held me tight. I buried my face in his chest, raking in ragged breaths, trying to remember where I'd hidden my strength. "I'm an outlaw."

"You're an outlaw," Jesse breathed into my hair, holding up my bent frame until I could scrape together enough courage to lift my head high once more.

"Let's take a walk," he said. I nodded, hiding my tear-stained cheeks from the others as he led me down a winding path deep into the abandoned heart of the junkyard. I mopped at my face with the sleeve of my shirt as we walked.

"I can punch Will in the face again if it'll make you feel better," Jesse said after a while. I gave him a short, tearful laugh.

"Don't tempt me," I said quietly. After a while, I stopped walking and sat on the cracked leather of a bench seat that'd been ripped from the frame of a vehicle, staring into the distance. Silence stretched between us as he joined me.

"Why didn't you tell me?" he asked softly. I shrugged, staring at my boots. His arm came down around my shoulders, and I leaned into that spot the crook of his shoulder where I fit so well. The place that made me feel safe when I was tangled together with him at night. He inhaled deeply, and I gathered my courage.

"You didn't see a slave when you looked at me," I said. He tipped my chin up to meet his eyes.

"I still don't," he whispered. "You know this doesn't change anything. Not for me." He said it with the same conviction with which he said everything. In the deep canyon timbre I loved to listen to. He made everything sound easy, feel easy. He saw the broken parts of me and didn't run.

"Is that why you do it? The slave revolts, the people you've killed, the horses in Vegas . . . because you were a slave?" he asked. I sighed, trying to order my thoughts.

"Freedom isn't something that anyone should be able to take away from you," I said. Not sure if it was an answer to his question. It was the only one I had.

"We won't let them do it to anyone else. I promise," he said softly. My heart squeezed in my chest, and the words clawed their way forward, barely restrained. *I love you.*

"The night my mom died," I said instead. His thumb brushed my cheek. "Slavers broke into our house. After they raped and killed her, they dragged me from under the bed and threw me into the back of a wagon. Jones met them on the road and bought me."

Jesse was quiet, steady. He didn't falter at my words. He let them sink into his skin, sharing my burden.

"The night *we* were attacked," I said, and his shoulders tensed. "If it wasn't for you, I would've ended up just like her." He pressed his forehead into mine, and his fingers buried in my hair.

"I never would've let that happen," he said. I nodded, my nose brushing against his. When he said anything with that unwavering conviction, I believed him.

"I know," I said. He paused then, his eyes suddenly pained.

"Bonnie, I have to ask, you and Will—"

"I told you, we aren't like that. Not for a long time now," I said in a rush. "Turns out my type happens to be *you*, farm boy."

His eyes fell to my mouth, but I couldn't wait. I kissed him, crushing my body into his until I straddled him and his back was braced against the leather seat. My hands ran up his thighs, and he moaned into my mouth. He raised onto his elbows, reaching for me as I pulled back from his mouth to drink in his desire-darkened eyes.

"Jesse James, you have taken every opportunity to put your hands all over me," I said, my fingers running up the length of his chest to the buttons on the front of his shirt. He smiled beneath my mouth, and I bit his bottom lip gently. "It's *my* turn."

I fumbled with his buttons, impatient, as the hard expanse of his chest was bared to me. He was beautiful. Chiseled perfection, just like I'd thought since that first day. My fingers traced his open mouth and down the stubble of his chin, then followed the pounding pulse in his neck as his Adam's apple bobbed. My hands spanned wide on the broad expanse of his shoulders before they followed the midline of his body, stopping to explore the dips and hollows of his abdomen. I pressed a hot kiss to his chest as my hands fumbled with his belt buckle.

"*Fuck,*" Jesse groaned, the sound dragged long from his throat as I popped the top button on his jeans and carefully slid his zipper down. I smiled wickedly at him, remembering how lost I'd been to his touch not so long ago. I reached down and took him in my hand, not for the first time marveling at the size of him.

He made a sound in the back of his throat that sent a shudder through my whole body. I stroked him, relishing the feel of him in my hand, like silk slipping over steel. As the friction and intensity increased, he swore and grabbed my hips with hard hands.

His chest heaved, and his hips bucked beneath me. It was exhilarating to have this much power over him for once. He cried out my name, and his hands bit into my flesh punishingly before he shuddered beneath my touch.

He pulled me down for a hungry kiss, his tongue diving into my mouth with ruthless intention. Instead of being satiated, he began to stiffen again in my hand. Somehow, I'd only made him desperate for more of me.

"Jesse! Bonnie!" The Kid called, too close for us to ignore.

"The *worst* timing," I breathed into his mouth as his head fell back onto the seat while he adjusted his clothes before his brother came around the corner.

"There you guys are," The Kid said, ignoring how flushed and disheveled we looked. "Will said I could smoke one of his cigarettes if you said it was okay."

"No!" Jesse and I both shouted, sharing a sly smile before we stood and followed a complaining Kid back to camp.

That night, after rations were handed out, Jesse and I rolled out our bedding together. No pretenses of sleeping separately anymore. Will bedded down in the wagon, his arm in a makeshift sling. Clara slept in the tent with The Kid.

Jesse and I took the first watch. As we lay down that night, tucked comfortably in each other's arms, we spoke softly to each other. Even though we were surrounded by the others, it felt like we were alone.

"We're almost out of supplies," I said into Jesse's chest, and he rumbled a sound of sleepy acknowledgement. "Are you okay?" I knew he would understand that I meant about his parents. He'd learned something hard today and hadn't been able to talk about it for fear of his brother discovering the truth. Even if we couldn't talk openly right now, I wanted him to know I would share his burdens too.

His arms tightened around me as if to anchor him. His nose buried in my hair for a few long moments. When he pulled back, I stared up at him, expecting I would be able to read his expression. Instead, he slid his mouth against mine without urgency. He kissed me slowly, thoroughly. As if he just needed to drown in the taste of me. When we parted, he ran his fingers through my hair. That was the only answer he gave me.

The sun had barely risen when I woke the next morning. Taking a cursory look around the camp, I noticed no one else stirred. I drank in the sight of Jesse's sleeping face; I could stare at his contented expression for hours. But I wouldn't. I kissed his neck until he woke. He made a sleepy sound in the back of his throat, and I ran my hands over his chest and lower. Just as I stroked his morning erection through his thin sleep pants, he cracked open bleary eyes.

"Everyone's still asleep," I whispered against his skin. Confusion clouded his pretty blue eyes, and I grinned. "We're *alone*."

He blinked himself into waking rapidly before he rolled me against the ground and settled on top of me. His mouth was on mine a moment later, hands exploring my curves.

"You sure?" he asked, the words tight. I nodded as his hands plunged beneath my shirt to cup my breasts. *Those wicked hands.* I gasped into his mouth as he teased my nipples to hard points. Tugging insistently, I guided his hand down past the waistband of my sleep pants so he could feel the evidence of my passion soaking the fabric. I felt the curl of his satisfied smile against my mouth.

"I'm not," Will said from across the fire, stilling us both. *Fucking Will.* I closed my eyes and tried to swallow down the bitter disappointment.

"Let me fucking shoot him," Jesse mumbled against my neck. I laughed and pressed another kiss to his mouth.

"You've already done that. It didn't get rid of him," I said. He ground his hips against mine for a second so I could feel just how badly I hated Will this morning.

"I'll use the shotgun this time," he said.

"I mean, no one said you had to stop," Will said shoving his hat on his head. I made a disgusted sound, watching the amused grin deepen on his mouth.

"Let's get up before Will tries to join us," I told Jesse. He moved off of me so that I could sit up.

"I hate you so much," Jesse said to Will.

"You just need to get a room, with a lock," Will said standing and crossing to light a cigarette. He handed it to me. "You look like you could use one more than me, *mi cielo.*" A long silence ensued where Jesse and I glared at Will and he stared back at us, unaffected.

"So, serious question," Will said, leveling his eyes at us both. "Is the blonde single?"

"Yes, but keep your grimy hands off of her," Jesse said. I couldn't tell if he was being protective or jealous.

"What? You want 'em both?" Will asked, looking from me to Jesse.

"No. I just don't want your hands on her. She's too good for you, *hombre,*" Jesse said, pushing a frustrated hand through his hair.

"Well, you see, *gringo,* I won't have to put my hands on her at all—"

"Don't say it," I groaned, burying my face in my hands.

"No one can help but fall for—"

"*Please* don't say it," I groaned into my hands.

"The Ellis charm," he said proudly. I inhaled deep on the cigarette, coughing at the harsh smoke filling my lungs. Will smoked cheap tobacco.

"Bonnie didn't," Jesse said, self-assured.

"She fell for it enough to wind up in bed with me," Will retorted. I threw the cigarette at him, making him twist away from it so he didn't get burned.

"Yeah, notice she didn't make that mistake twice," Jesse retorted.

"She never does," Will said, smirking. "Clearly you don't know her that well."

Jesse and I shared a smile. Will, observant as ever, noticed the look between us and whistled low. He stared at me in shock. Rocking back on his heels, he stood and stretched his good arm above his head. Clearly he wasn't going anywhere, so Jesse shuffled out of our bedroll to start waking the others and packing up camp, adjusting the front of his sleep pants as he went.

"You haven't fucked him yet?" Will asked as soon as Jesse walked away. I laughed, *really* laughed, as Will flopped down beside me.

"You jealous?" I asked. Will nodded.

"Yes, *look* at him. Why *haven't* you fucked him?" he asked. Just having him here like this put me at ease.

"You better stop flirtin' with him," I said, poking him in the chest. Will's grin only widened.

"It's so much fun; he just gets his feathers all ruffled," he said. "Though mostly because of *you,* which isn't as much fun."

"Will," I said, my tone serious, and his eyes roamed over my face. "I broke my rules for him. *All of them.*"

"I know," he said, kissing the top of my head.

"Okay, now get up and help pack camp," I said, pushing the covers off my legs and standing swiftly.

"Oh, right," Will said, leaning back onto the bedding and lowering his hat to cover his eyes. "About that. *Someone* shot me, so unfortunately, I only have one arm."

An hour later we were packed and on the road again waving goodbye to the smattering of people who'd come to see us off. Talia and Mercy among them, watching us disappear with wide smiles. The Kid asked Will so many questions, I worried he would hyperventilate. Will sat close to Clara in the back of the wagon, attempting to teach her words in Spanish. He said they were terms of endearment, but they weren't. It might've scandalized her to know their real meaning. Jesse rode close to me today, our weapons ready at our sides for whatever came next.

For the first time, I knew I wouldn't have to face it alone. Not anymore.

## CHAPTER TWENTY-TWO

# JESSE

F ROM OUR DEPARTURE THAT morning, the heat consumed us. Almost as though Mother Nature was making up for the couple days of rain we'd gotten. The sun burned hot on our skin. Even my hat and the handkerchief wrapped around my mouth and nose weren't helping.

I kept No Name near Eagle to be close to Bonnie. Her old pal Will brought some difficult information to hear. I tried not to worry about Sixgun and his bunch of brand-toting followers, but as the sun beat down on us, it was all I could think about.

*Whatever my dad was sent to retrieve, he didn't get it.*

Who sent Sixgun to Montana? What was he looking for? Then there were the remarks about finding Bonnie. None of it made sense. Bonnie had nothing to do with Montana. Except for her ties to Sixgun. Sixgun and his men were hired out by someone else. But who?

I stole a glance at Bonnie. Her brows furrowed, and she worried her bottom lip between her teeth. Something bothered her. She caught me staring at her and smiled. The corners of my mouth twitched up at the thought of getting her alone again. Last night, I'd set out with the intentions of reassuring her that her being a runaway slave didn't matter to me. I'd never expected for things to get so heated.

I wasn't complaining, either.

The only complaint I had was that Will Ellis was awake when everyone else was asleep and ruined what could have been a perfect morning for us.

I looked at Bonnie again, not bothering to hide the hunger in my eyes. There was *a lot* more that I wanted to do with her before I'd find satisfaction.

While the others sat in a circle near the horses when we stopped for lunch, I rummaged in the back of the wagon. Our supplies were growing low. I dumped out the contents of all of our packs, sorting through what remained. We were good on water after the stream, but all that remained of our food from Lamesa was a single chunk of hard bread, half a bag of jerky, and a few moldy strawberries that must have fallen out in Bonnie's bag.

We now had five people and four horses to feed. No matter what, we'd have to stop in the next town.

"What're you doin'?" Bonnie asked from my side. I glanced at her, not realizing she'd snuck over. She moved in front of me, bending over to reach into the wagon. Her ass rubbed against the front of my jeans. Suddenly, I wasn't worried about food anymore. I put my hands on her hips and leaned down so that when she tried to stand up, her back was against my chest. She made a sound low in the back of her throat.

"Wishing we could ditch the others for a while," I said in a deep voice, pressing my mouth to the side of her neck. She leaned back, grinding my cock.

Bonnie turned in my arms, and then she was kissing me. I lifted her up onto the edge of the wagon. Her legs wrapped around my waist, and I was already reaching up the front of her shirt.

Someone kicked the side of the wagon, shocking me out of my Bonnie-haze. I looked up to see Will, settling his hat on his head and grinning.

"We're losin' daylight. Probably should get going," he said. I scowled at the satisfaction on his face as he walked away. When I looked at Bonnie, she burst into laughter. A smile crossed my face at the beautiful sound.

Yet again, cockblocked by Will Ellis.

I pressed a final kiss to Bonnie's mouth and straightened her shirt. Then I reached down to pick up my forgotten hat. I went back to combing through our dwindling supplies.

"We have to stop in the next town," I said as we mounted up for the next leg of the journey.

I worried about the potential gang presence in any nearby settlements. We were left with no choice. We would have to take our chances.

As buildings appeared in the distance, Bonnie motioned for us to slow our pace. "We're stopping here for supplies." She spared a glance at me before turning to the others. "Be on your guard. If you see any Crimson Fist or Hanged Men, keep your eyes low and don't be suspicious." She tugged the hood of her shirt low over her face.

"You have enough money to feed all of us?" Clara piped up from the back of the wagon.

"Sure." I laughed. I knew full well that even though we'd won a bunch of money that last night in Lamesa, it wouldn't be nearly enough to stock up for the rest of the trip. Oddly enough, I was okay with following whatever plan Bonnie came up with. Strange how things changed.

Clara giggled behind us. I turned to see Will leaning in to whisper something in her ear. I opened my mouth to say something, but Bonnie cut me off.

"You know, you shouldn't encourage Will. If you keep gettin' worked up, he's just gonna keep flirtin' with you," Bonnie said in a low voice.

"Why would he be flirting with me?" I asked, brows furrowed.

It was only when Will glanced up and saw me looking at him that I understood. He winked at me before turning back to Clara, smiling smugly. I remembered the two men in the pool room of the inn back in Lamesa.

"Never mind," I said quickly, turning my attention forward.

Bonnie drove us hard to cross the distance into the town. The afternoon sun beamed from high in the sky as we neared it. I double-checked that the pistol was secure at my waist and tucked my shotgun in the space beneath No Name's saddle and the blanket protecting his back. As soon as we were in sight of the town, I noticed men posted near a large gate. They wore strange patches on their shirts.

Their eyes tracked us as we passed through the open gates, though none of them tried to stop us. I closed ranks, steering No Name closer to Eagle. I felt the eyes of the men behind us still watching. We stopped in front of a building marked *hotel*. Bonnie and I dismounted at the same time.

"Stay here, Kid," Bonnie said over her shoulder. I stepped in front of her, putting my hands on her hips.

"Careful," I said, pressing a quick kiss to her temple.

I watched as she crossed the street toward a couple of guys in uniforms outside of the hotel. They stared at her with barely veiled distrust.

All around us, the town was busy with foot traffic. People walked about, laughing and talking in excited voices. I watched them carefully, checking back every few seconds on

Bonnie. Something was going on at the other end of town. Within minutes, Bonnie was back at my side.

"Town's heavily policed," she said. "I don't know that we'll be able to run a scam here. There's a festival or somethin' going on."

"A scam?" Clara asked.

"Shh!" The Kid said.

"Yeah. Me and Bonnie here are damn good at it, too," Will said.

"I don't know, Will. Jesse might be better at the hustle than you," Bonnie said. The look of surprise on Will's face mirrored on my own. I slid my arm around Bonnie's waist; it was such a natural thing I didn't realize I did it.

"Not possible," Will said with a grin. "After all, I have the Ellis charm."

"Anyway," Bonnie said, glaring at him. "The next town is two days' ride. We don't have enough food to get there." Her words were directed at me. I knew that we had bits saved up from the pool game, but money was a valuable resource, and we couldn't spend it all.

"If you hadn't lost your touch, *mi cielo*, you might have noticed the warehouse two blocks down," Will said, picking at his fingernails with a pocket knife. "You're going soft. I'll take Montana with me to go scout it out."

"Wait, what?" I barely got the words out before Will pulled me away from Bonnie and down the street.

"Songbird's pretty face is a little too noticeable for this kind of work," Will said, giving my bicep a squeeze. I looked up at him in surprise. "And we need to have a conversation. *Mano a mano.*"

"I've got nothing to say to you," I said, yanking my arm out of his grip.

"Well, I got plenty to say to you, *pendejo*. So even if you don't talk, you need to listen." He put his good arm up in front of me, stopping to peer around a corner. After a second, he seemed satisfied, and we kept walking. He tipped his hat at a pretty woman walking past.

"You need to back off of Bonnie," Will said. My eyebrows shot up on my forehead. He had some nerve if he thought he could tell me what to do, especially when it came to her. I hadn't fought so hard for Bonnie to just give up because some asshat from her past told me to.

"And what are you going to do if I don't?" I asked. Will stopped, shoving me against the nearest wall.

"Bonnie isn't just some woman you can chew up and spit out," he said. "She's not like Blondie. She's sensitive to people. I let her get hurt once. I won't let it happen again."

"I don't like your tone, Ellis," I said, fighting hard against my *violent* tendencies. "I'm not like you or *your* crew. I don't intend on hurting her."

"You sure about that?" he asked.

"What the fuck are you talking about?" He didn't know me. He didn't know how I felt about Bonnie. He sure as hell didn't have a right to decide who she spent time with.

"I've known Bonnie my entire life," Will said, giving me a hard glare. "She's *never* put herself at risk like this before. Falling in love with you is gonna get her killed." He shoved off of the wall and continued walking down to the street, leaving me behind, speechless.

*Falling in love with you.*

In love? With me? Bonnie?

No way. I started walking again, doubling my pace to catch up to him. There was no chance in hell Bonnie had fallen in love with me. It'd taken everything I had just to get her to give me a second look.

"Bonnie isn't in love with me. What are you talking about?" I asked.

"Keep watch," Will said without answering and darted between the buildings. I glared at his back as he disappeared. Before I could take off after him, a man bumped into me. He murmured an apology and headed down the street. I gathered myself, remembering that I was here to do a job. I glanced up and down the lane, checking for men with guns. There were a couple on a roof down the street, but so far, they weren't concerned with me. I turned toward the nearest building, pretending to relieve myself to appear less suspicious.

A minute later, Will returned, looking at me like I was crazy. "What're you doing?"

"Blending in," I said. Will scoffed.

"Bonnie says you're better than me. Please," he said, heading back up the street.

"What did you see?" I asked him as we neared the main drag.

"Locked," Will said. "No guards. I saw crates of food from the windows. We'll need a key." I followed his gaze as we approached the hotel. "I'm guessin' one of the guards in uniform will have it on them."

Our horses and the wagon were parked on the side of the hotel. The two of us wandered in, finding our companions seated in the back of the room.

I stopped, Bonnie's eyes finding mine instantly. They seemed brighter as she stared at me. Not so much midnight blue, but the blue that I imagined was the color of the ocean.

Will kept walking, but I stood there, staring back at her. My heart seemed to fly on its own, and it was all because of that look.

*She loved me.*

The world turned upside down, but not in a bad way. The fire had upended our lives, destroying everything we'd ever known. Now, the world was being put back together. Almost as if Bonnie loving me righted the terror of it all. Like the smoke was finally clearing, and she was what waited for me on the other side.

It was exhilarating.

A waitress bumped into me, jolting me out of the moment. She apologized, but I didn't pay much attention. I crossed the room to where my four companions sat, taking the only empty chair left between Bonnie and Clara. I reached under the table and tangled my fingers with Bonnie's, giving her hand a quick squeeze. Will relayed the information about the warehouse to them.

"Jesse," Clara said to my right. I turned to look at her. "You're going to get killed. This place is crawling with guns."

Bonnie scoffed into her glass from the other side of me. Clara leaned forward onto the table.

"Did I say something funny?" she asked, her tone black. Clara had never spoken to anyone like that before. Her mouth puckered at the edges, and she narrowed her eyes. Before I could question that menacing look, Bonnie downed the rest of her whiskey and turned to look at Clara.

"I haven't heard anything come out of your mouth that *wasn't* funny, dairy maid," Bonnie said. "Have you taken a look around lately?" Sure enough, there were a couple of men in uniforms across the room. I'd marked at least a dozen of them on our walk back from the warehouse.

"I'm not stupid," Clara said blackly, leaning back into her chair. I signaled the waitress for another round of drinks. "Obviously you don't know this town is full of Black Judges. Slavers. Didn't you see the shackles on those patches?"

"Fine. If you're so smart, how do you propose we get enough supplies to last us to Fort Hood *without* running a scam?" Bonnie asked. I gave her hand a squeeze, but she ignored me. The Kid and Will both stared between the women, amused as they watched the conversation.

The waitress dropped off the round of drinks. Clara sat beside me, silent, until finally she said, "Well, we could whore you out. You play that role with Jesse easily enough."

Will reached over and pulled the brim of The Kid's hat over his eyes.

"To have a dozen kids, you have to wrap your legs around him first, you frigid bitch," Bonnie said, knocking back her drink. She leaned across me toward Clara, eyes dark. "Where'd your bruises go?"

I hadn't thought about Clara's injuries since we found her. To be honest, I'd lost track of the days, but I remembered her having a bruise under one eye. I noted the lack of imperfections where they'd been before. Clara's cheeks reddened under my gaze.

"Maybe we should whore *you* out," Bonnie said through clenched teeth. "It seems you have a talent for lying. Insecure men like liars."

I put a hand on the small of her back and leaned in.

"Those uniforms are watching us," I said quietly.

Sure enough, the two men across the bar must have sensed the tension at our table. They were trying to pretend like they weren't watching, but I knew better. I'd learned from Bonnie how to covertly watch a stranger across a crowded room.

"If you don't like our plan, Clara, then you should leave," I said, pointedly. "We're in a town now. You don't *have* to come with us."

"Yes," The Kid said, punching the air victoriously. Clara's flushed cheeks paled as she looked directly at me.

"Where am I supposed to go?" she asked.

"Not my problem. Unless you shut up and let us get on with it," I said, turning back to Bonnie. "We're gonna have to move fast. What's the plan?"

Some of the anger receded from her eyes. Instead, Bonnie's jaw clenched, her eyes shifting the way they always did when she was planning a con. She was silent, contemplating our next move.

Whatever it was, I didn't care. All that mattered was that we would do it like everything else. Together.

## CHAPTER TWENTY-THREE

# BONNIE

"R UN THIS BY ME again," Jesse said. I pushed my hair behind my ears, staring pointedly at Will. He stood, promising to show The Kid more smoke rings outside and pulling Clara with him.

"It's not a big deal," I said, pressing a hand to his chest, which he covered with his own. "It's a classic honeypot scheme."

"Yeah, I just don't like the part where it's *your* honeypot we're using as bait," Jesse said, his eyes drifting down to rest between my thighs. "Or the fact that you're going unarmed."

"Listen," I said, pressing a quick kiss to the spot beneath his ear to silence him. "We have all the players we need to run this con. Will is our spotter; he's useless with the heavy lifting because of that arm, but he's observant and obnoxious enough that no one will suspect him of having an ulterior motive. He'll find our mark. The Kid can drive that wagon like the hounds of hell are chasin' him, which is exactly what we need: for him to position the wagon before going to the festival with Clara. Once it's loaded, he can get it out of town without trouble. I'm the bait, so all I have to do is be alluring."

"What about me?" he asked, his hand resting on my thigh. My smile extended to my eyes.

"You're the ringleader," I said. He stared, waiting for an explanation. "This is *your* con, farm boy. I won't need a weapon until we lure the mark from the festival, where you'll be waiting. That's how I know it'll be fine. You're my backup."

He kissed me hard, stealing my breath, until Will sent The Kid in to break it up.

An hour later Will parked the wagon in front of an alleyway so I could change away from prying eyes. He'd dragged Jesse off to a shop while I scouted the area and briefed everyone on their prospective jobs, taking special care with The Kid, who beamed. He was so excited to commit a crime it was laughable.

When Will and Jesse came back, Clara handed me the small tub of cosmetics. I used it to hide the greenish-yellow tint lingering on my cheekbone from the fading bruise. With one last glimpse at my reflection in the small mirror that Will pickpocketed somewhere along the way, I sighed. We hadn't spoken much, sticking to short practical conversation as I changed. Her pinched expression made her unhappiness at the situation clear. I sighed, stifling the urge to run a hand through my hair.

"I'm sorry," I said. Her eyes shot up to mine, wide with shock. "If him choosing me hurts you. I don't know what you've been through—"

"No. You don't," she said in a clipped voice. Taking a deep, steadying breath, I continued.

"If it makes a difference, he made the decision on his own. I tried to keep my distance because I didn't want to come between you." Her pursed lips twisted into a sneer of disgust. Her brown eyes flashed, darker than I'd seen them.

"You think I don't like you because Jesse wants to fuck you?" she asked, a bitter laugh coming from her mouth.

"Let me clear it up for you. I don't like you because you're *reckless*," she said, her words clear and concise. "I get you. You're used to being alone, so you take risks. But you aren't alone anymore, are you? You're dragging Jesse and Harry along with you. One day those risks are going to get them hurt, or worse."

My mouth hung open in shock, a thousand excuses coming to my mind. Each one flimsier than the last. I thought about the danger we'd encountered so far. Was Clara right?

"I won't let anything happen to them," I said, the words weak. She huffed, crossing her arms over her chest.

"We'll see, won't we?" Then she turned her back to pack the items we'd used in the saddlebags. A clear indication that she was finished with this conversation.

"I mean, you just have muscles *everywhere*," Will said from the other side of the wagon. I stifled laughter, glad for the sudden lightheartedness.

"Hurry up and finish with the buckle," Jesse grumbled blackly.

"Keep your hands off, Will!" I called, laughing. I gazed at my mother's hair comb. I hadn't worn it since *that* night. Today, I wanted to feel beautiful. I pulled my hair away from my face and secured it with the comb.

"Just his gun holster, unfortunately," Will called back to me.

The people here were organized and efficient. They didn't want some sloppy half-dressed whore at their party. They wanted a beautiful woman, who didn't know she was beautiful. Understated, yet eye-catching. I adjusted my breasts in the dress I'd bought all that time ago in Lamesa. The blue fabric made my blue eyes stand out against the dark shock of my hair, which was falling prettily around my face. I didn't know what'd possessed me to buy something so impractical. When I'd seen it, something inside of me had lurched, and we'd had money to burn then.

I imagined this was the kind of woman I might have been if life had been kinder to me. A woman unburdened by the deep scars that'd hardened my heart for so long. Maybe this was how I would feel all the time around Jesse. Beautiful.

"Are you done yet?" The Kid asked impatiently, blowing into his harmonica in a grating tone.

"Yeah," I called, my eyes on my boots. This was the only part of my outfit that wasn't quite right, but I needed to be able to move quickly. The wagon pulled forward.

"Woah, Bonnie," The Kid said. "You look like a girl." I raised my eyes to see everyone staring at me. A flush rose in my cheeks. Will recovered first, stepping forward with a tub of a pink cosmetic in his hand. He pressed some onto my mouth, and I rubbed my lips together self-consciously.

"There, now you're perfect," Will said. I hadn't dared to look at Jesse yet; for some reason I felt suddenly shy.

"She's already perfect." Jesse's deep canyon timbre rumbled through the space between us. My eyes drank him in slowly. His hair was slicked back from his face, his cheeks clean-shaven, highlighting the chiseled angle of his jaw. A leather holster wrapped around his broad shoulders, accentuating the muscles that moved beneath his tight shirt. He looked like the outlaw I knew he'd always been. His blue eyes blazed, the hunger in them stark and devastating. I shifted on my feet, but he'd already crossed the space to stand in front of me. His familiar heat washed over my exposed skin.

"There isn't enough time, lovebirds," Will said impatiently behind us. Even though we both knew he was right, neither of us pulled back right away. Instead of the multitude of things I wanted to do, I nodded and walked up the lane leading to the festival. Jesse grabbed my wrist and pulled me back, catching me against his chest and dragging my mouth against his for a searing kiss.

"I don't really mind the kissing anymore," The Kid said, loudly enough to hear over the pounding of my heart. I laughed against Jesse's mouth, and he let me go. I walked on unsteady feet towards the festival, Jesse's fingers tangled loosely with mine.

We dropped our hands as music and laughter filled the night air, warm from the sweltering heat only hours before. Lanterns were lit and hung in strings along a large dance floor, and a band played on well-worn instruments. There were a lot of uniforms here. Too many, almost. I glanced at Will, who nodded briefly before fading into the crowd to find our mark. The Kid blew into his harmonica, and Clara scowled, which was nothing new.

"Ask Clara to dance," I told Jesse. He chuckled, until he realized I was serious.

"No," he said simply, crossing his arms over his chest. The movement sent a flex down his muscles, rippling beneath his tight shirt. I sucked in a steadying breath. Jesse caught me staring and flexed his biceps with a grin.

"I need to make my rounds, and Clara needs to stay out of trouble. You can watch me better from the dance floor than from here," I said, making my case. He grumbled, ducking his head to whisper hot words in my ear.

"I only want you," he said. I bit my lip to contain my smile, and Jesse's eyes fixated on my mouth.

"Even if I step on your feet?" I asked.

"Especially then," he said, his hand slipping down my waist to settle firmly on my ass. "It gives me another reason to hold you tighter."

"Jesse," I breathed shakily. "Behave yourself."

"I'll see you soon," he said, the naughty tone in his voice turning serious.

I pulled out of his arms and steadied myself, studying the people here. Most of the soldiers were either on duty or scanning the area, assessing for threats. Each potential mark primed and ready for danger. That made it more difficult, but not impossible. Pulling my shoulders back, I walked through the crowd, much as I had in Vegas. Catching and holding the gazes of different men as I passed, letting them trail the swishing motion of my skirt or appreciate the long, pale curve of my calves as I twisted through the crowd.

From the corner of my eye, I noticed Jesse and Clara dancing, their movements stiff and formal. The edge that'd been in Clara's eyes for a while now softened considerably. Something pulled tight within my chest, seeing them together like that. Jesse had almost married her. Though Clara was clearly not meant for the life of an outlaw, he'd seen something worthy in her once.

Several men approached, smiling too wide or fumbling over their requests to dance with me. I politely turned them all down, increasing the mystery of my presence. Several of them asked to bring me glasses of punch, but all I could think about was the blazing heat in Jesse's eyes when he looked at me in this dress.

Eventually, I accepted one of the offers and was dragged by my hand onto the dance floor by a young, dark-skinned soldier when Jesse's deep canyon timbre rumbled straight through me.

"May I cut in?" he asked, not waiting for an answer. With a hard pull, Jesse spun me into the cage of his arms, trapping me flush against him. I swallowed at the devastation of the desire in his eyes. When he looked at me like that, I was helpless. It was a look that promised ruin and greatness in equal measure. He noticed everything from the rapid pulse beating a staccato rhythm in my neck to the breathy gasps I couldn't contain. His iron arm slid around my waist as he spun us expertly to the lively music. My heart lurched as he dipped me low before dragging me back against the dizzying heat of his body. I clung to his broad shoulders.

"You're getting better," Jesse said, his words causing the hair on the back of my neck to stand on end.

"I had a good teacher," I choked out before his wicked hand at the small of my back began to dip too low. I pulled it back into position, enjoying the flicker of frustration in his confident eyes.

"We're on a job, farm boy," I said, reminding him gently. He sighed, putting some much needed space between us as we finished the dance.

"I know," he said regretfully. As the song ended, he stepped away to bow his head in a chivalrous gesture. Will came up to his shoulder and whispered in his ear. Jesse pulled me off the dance floor and motioned with two fingers for me to lean in. The warm scent of him enveloped me.

"The tall one by the punch bowl. Keys on a ring at his belt. Dark hair, missing a bar on his patch," Jesse said. I brushed my hand against his quickly before turning to make my way to the punch bowl, fanning my face.

The mark was older than Jesse, late twenties or early thirties. No wedding ring, thankfully. He stared down the front of my dress as I poured a glass of punch. I watched the couples in silence next to him, pretending not to notice. His hands shook before he tapped me on the shoulder.

I offered a pretty smile and looked at him through my lashes, the way I'd seen Clara do when she attempted to look particularly innocent. In another five minutes, we laughed together, and he asked me to dance. He held me as if afraid I would disappear the moment he let me go.

"I know this seems *fast*," I said, shuffling closer to him as he spun me in the same circle over and over again on the dance floor. "But I can't help feeling that I've never met anyone quite like you before."

He swallowed hard. "Do you want to find somewhere *more quiet* where we can talk?" he asked, voice catching on the words. I dropped my eyes demurely, nodding in shy capitulation. *Men were such idiots.*

He led me swiftly off the dance floor and back towards the main part of town. I didn't worry when he twisted and turned away from the lights and noise; I knew Jesse was tracking my every move. I felt his eyes on me like a guiding hand. The man pulled me into a darkened alleyway, pressing me firmly against the wall. He leaned down to press his mouth to mine. I turned my face away, but his mouth came down sloppily on my neck.

With a thud, his body crumpled against me to fall in a heap of long limbs. Jesse replaced his pistol into the holster beneath his arm before bending down to collect the keys on his belt. He took my hand, and I let him help me over the man's prone body. We turned the corner, hand-in-hand, wild smiles on our faces as we ran for the warehouse.

"Hurry, before he wakes up or someone finds him," I said. We broke into a sprint as we weaved our way through the side streets until we reached the main road in town. A voice echoed down the lane. I yanked hard on Jesse's hand to stop him from barreling straight into a patrol. In a rush, he slammed me against the wall, shielding me with his body. Our chests heaved. The edge of wild abandon slipping through my blood was enough to make me forget everything except his skin on mine. There was a savageness in Jesse's eyes that mirrored deep down in my marrow. It made me feel dangerous and *free*.

The men turned the corner and saw us, but we didn't care. Jesse kissed me like a dying man. My hands buried in his too-slick hair, messing up the neat way it'd lain earlier. His hands were on my hips, my breasts, my ass.

"What're you two—"

Jesse's only response was to lift me until my legs wrapped wantonly around his waist. His hand ran up my thigh, lifting my skirt, and I moaned into his mouth. They laughed, wolf whistling and turning to patrol in a different direction. Jesse pulled back just enough to see my flushed cheeks and swollen lips.

"Do you have *any idea* how hard it was to see you in the arms of another man?" he asked, his deep voice thunderous against my neck.

"Probably as hard as it was for me to see you dancing with Clara," I said breathlessly against his skin. Kissing his jaw and tasting his skin.

"You told me to—"

His words were muffled against my mouth. I was lost to him. I was so lost to him. He ground his hips against mine. All I thought about was how badly I wanted to love him with my whole body. After lingering for far too long, I pulled back, trying to gulp in lungfuls of cold night air.

"The warehouse," I said. Jesse slapped a flat palm against the wall on one side of me. I kissed him and we nearly lost ourselves again. As he lowered me to my feet, we both wavered towards each other.

"We're almost done," I said, struggling to catch my breath. "And when we get back to camp, I'm going to mount and fuck you until you can't walk tomorrow." The shock in his expression made my grin widen on my mouth. A deep hum of pleasure rumbled from his chest as I twisted away.

We made it to the warehouse moments later. Jesse fumbled with the keys, and the door swung open easily on well-oiled hinges. The wagon was in place at the end of the alley. We packed supplies quietly; Jesse handed them out to me, and I stacked them silently, keeping an eye on the roofs for armed patrols.

Jesse carried the last box of supplies to meet me at the wagon. I pulled the keys from his hand and walked to the open door. Peering inside, I noticed familiar dark shapes along the back wall. Too familiar. Rings of rough, beaten metal attached to the ends of long wooden poles. For transporting unruly slaves by the neck to market. Rows of munitions in the back corner. Though the thought of stealing an assault rifle was tempting, my stomach churned in disgust. Whatever this town had done for their tentative safety, it was at the expense of people like me. I lit a lantern with shaking hands. Jesse slid his arm around my waist from behind and whispered in my ear.

"What're you doing?" he asked, motioning back in the direction of the wagon.

"Burning it to the ground," I said with all the hatred that'd been beaten into me before tossing the lantern inside. In the same corner where the munitions were stored. Let God forgive them, if he existed, because I wouldn't. Jesse realized quickly what I'd done, and we ran to the wagon. We scrambled up and spurred the horses forward as fast as they could go. The wagon thundered down the main street to our designated meeting place, rattling so hard I was afraid it would shake apart.

Will whistled, the signal that they were in position. Jesse stopped the wagon short, and moments later, Clara and The Kid were handed up into the wagon. Clara settled in the back between the boxes, and The Kid joined us on the front seat.

"We have to get out of here," I said, loud enough to set Will's nerves on edge as he fingered the handle of the pistol at his side.

"What did you do?" he demanded. Before I could answer, a loud boom shook the ground beneath our feet, and the crackle of flames sounded in a deafening roar as the night grew bright with the blaze. The pop of gunfire sounded behind us and from the left. I slid onto the ground, holding my palm out for the M9, which Jesse handed over without a thought.

"Will, take Eagle and No Name," I commanded. He nodded, swinging into the saddle and riding swiftly into the night.

"I'll lead them away," I said, eyes wild. Jesse swung down beside me and nodded to The Kid, who whipped the reins hard against the wagon ponies, disappearing into the night.

"Will knows to take care of them," I said. Jesse nodded as we assessed the crowd of soldiers rushing towards us. I squeezed off two shots, and one of the soldiers from a rooftop on the left fell with a crash.

"Run!" I said. We ran around corners and ducked below awnings until the open desert stretched before us. The *tat-tat-tat-tat* of continuous gunfire sounded loud in my ears as I focused all my energy on controlling my breathing and driving my legs into the ground. Every muscle screamed, but I pushed myself faster still. A woman began to catch up, and Jesse shot her; she fell with a cry.

240

We plunged into the darkness, unable to see more than a few feet in front of us. The lack of visibility would only help as they aimed those high-powered rifles at us. Jesse was faster than me, but he kept a steady pace to stay level with me. A bullet whizzed by my ear, and another thudded into the dust at my feet.

"Run ahead!" I choked out between ragged breaths, but his hand grappled through the darkness to find mine and grip it tight.

"I'm not leaving you!" he shouted.

We barreled on, hurtling out of control, barely one step ahead of certain death. I reached behind me and shot again, without aiming, desperate to slow our pursuers. We almost didn't see the canyon. I slid to a stop, but my momentum nearly sent me over the edge. Jesse's arm shot out to pull me forcefully from the abyss below. Staring down into the blackness below and back over my shoulder, I turned fearful eyes to Jesse. Dread settled like a stone in the pit of my stomach.

"There's water at the bottom," I gasped, my chest heaving. "No way to tell how far down or how deep."

The panic in his expression faded into resolution as he arrived at the same conclusion. We were going to be shot by the angry militia closing in on us, or we could plunge into the unknown together. Either way . . .

We were going to die.

## CHAPTER TWENTY-FOUR

# JESSE

W E COULD EITHER STAND on this cliff and die bleeding out, or leap into the unknown. There was no guarantee we would survive. By the dread reflecting back from Bonnie's wide blue eyes, she knew it, too.

It was now or never.

"Any last words?" Bonnie shouted. I barely heard her above the popping of gunfire and my pulse pounding in my ears.

Our journey flashed through my mind. Vegas, Flagstaff, the train. Lamesa. That night by the fire. Slavers. Playing pool. Her hands and the sinful things she'd done to me. Images of these past weeks filled me with emotions that I didn't know if I was ready to acknowledge. Everything was suddenly so clear to me.

Bonnie and I were the same. No matter how hard either of us denied it, fighting against being together was useless. I was lost to her. I'd been lost to her since the moment I saw her beautiful blue eyes. Why did it take us hanging on the edge of a cliff for me to realize it?

"Nope," I said, tugging her into my arms. I stared into her dark blue eyes. If this was our last moment, I wanted it to be worth something. I'd told her I wanted her, but it was more than that, more than her body. I wanted all of her: her brilliant mind, her quick tongue, how I could never guess what she would do next. Even the harsh tone of her voice when she called me an idiot. I wanted everything with Bonnie.

She threw her arms around my neck, and I covered her mouth with mine. At least if we died tonight, I knew the journey would have been worth it. Somehow, through this insane trip, I'd found someone that I couldn't live without. I held her tight, never wanting to let her go. She had to know. She had to know this wasn't some temporary thing between us.

That even though her departure loomed if we survived tonight, there was no chance in hell I would let her leave. Bonnie's mouth opened beneath mine, and I deepened the kiss, tucking my hand into her hair.

*If only we had more time.*

A shot rang out loud enough to send us reeling apart. I watched her gaze fall to the dark canyon below.

"Together?" I asked. Bonnie brought her beautiful eyes to me. She reached over, tangling her fingers with mine as we stepped closer to the ledge.

"Together," she said.

Then we leapt.

The air rushed past us, and time moved in slow motion. If we made it out of this, I promised myself, I would tell her. That I would do whatever it took as long as it kept us together. If she wanted to go to St. Louis, to that gang-less haven, I would follow her. Even if it meant never finding my uncle. As long as I had Bonnie and The Kid, nothing else mattered.

We just had to survive this first.

Our joined hands broke apart as we crashed through the surface of rushing water. My lungs burned as I fought to hold my breath. I opened my eyes, searching desperately for any sign of her, but all I could see were shadows. I kicked against the tide, hoping that I was moving up and not further into the depths.

I broke the surface, gasping desperately for breath. I tried to call out to her but choked around water burning my throat.

"Jesse!" Her panic-laced voice sent relief through my heart. I sputtered, forcing the rest of the water out of my lungs. Finally, she spotted me. "Don't scare me like that!" I followed her toward the shore.

I gripped onto a large rock at the edge of the river, my eyes never far as she managed to get up onto the embankment. She rolled onto her back. Her chest heaved. I pulled myself up and over the boulder, then scrambled to her side. Her eyes opened, finding mine, and a wave of relief pulsed through my veins. I splayed out beside her on the ground.

Bonnie burst into laughter.

Just like all those weeks ago on the train, I did too.

"We should be dead," Bonnie said, her eyes meeting mine.

"Maybe we are," I said.

My smile fell away as I looked at her. Most of the makeup was gone. Her lips puckered, still a little pink even though I thought I'd kissed it all away earlier. The water in her hair gave her that wild look I loved so much. I lifted my hand to her cheek.

"Robbing you was the best thing I've ever done," she whispered, her hands reaching up to grab the front of my wet shirt. I opened my mouth to speak but never got the chance.

Bonnie yanked me down. Our mouths crashed together, lips slicking in a rush as I swallowed her gasps. I rolled on top of her, as I'd done just this morning, remembering the way she reacted beneath my hands, and how crazy that damn dress had been driving me all night. I didn't want to wait a goddamn second more before I explored the rest of her.

When I broke my lips away, Bonnie's chest heaved with ragged breaths. I kissed along her jawline, nipping at the soft skin of her ear. Her hands gripped the back of my shirt. I pulled back long enough to yank off the wet gun holster, then let her pull the fabric off of me. I pulled down the top of her dress, baring her breasts to the night air. Her pale skin glistened in the moonlight as I moved my mouth across her collarbone and over the swell of her breast. I lowered my mouth to her nipple, teasing it with a swift flick of my tongue. Her hands tugged my hair as she moaned my name into the night.

One of my hands gripped her right hip, hooking her leg up around my waist. I slid my hand higher, peeling the layered skirts back from the smooth skin of her legs. She squirmed beneath me. I smiled against her breast. My fingers hooked into the waistband of her underclothes, tugging them down. I brought my mouth back to hers, slowing my movements. I didn't want to rush. I wanted to show her that I didn't just want to fuck her. I wanted everything with her in a way I'd never considered with anyone else.

Bonnie's skin burned against my fingertips. Her nails raked across every inch of my skin, sending pleasure coursing through me. I'd never felt this way before, not just by simple touch. I took my time, sliding her underclothes over her boots and tossing them away. I pressed a kiss to her lower belly; her body tensed beneath me. I smiled against her skin.

My lips trailed across to one of her thighs, agonizingly slow. She bucked her hips up towards me, her body impatient. I liked that about her. She didn't hide from what her body needed. I separated her thighs with my shoulders. She was bared to me in the night air. She was perfect, every slick inch of her. Her back arched, the swell of her breasts and planes of her stomach highlighted by moonlight, urging me to continue. I flashed a wicked grin, reaching up to entwine my fingers with hers. Then I kissed downward, taking a moment to bite the inside of her pale thigh. She moaned into the night air; the only other sound the rushing water behind me.

I picked up my eyes to watch her, propped up on her elbows. I smiled, but her patience snapped and she tugged our entwined hands to still me.

"I want you inside me," she begged, trembling underneath me. The sight of her shattered what little control remained. Her skin flushed, eyes glazed in passion. She was so beautiful like this it almost hurt to look at her. "Please."

I had to have her. I couldn't wait. There would be time for taking it slow later.

I slid up the length of her body to press another kiss to her lips. Bonnie dragged her hands over the broad planes of my chest, fingers grasping at my belt. She undid my belt buckle, the metallic clang of it sounding through the night. She shoved at my jeans, struggling to peel the wet denim from my skin. I pushed them down, the cool night air sending goosebumps across my skin.

Bonnie pulled me down, resting her forehead to mine. For a moment, our breath mingled, hot and full of longing. I slid one of my hands down her side, positioning myself between her legs. I gripped her skin when my hand reached her left hip.

A sharp cry of pain came from between her lips.

I stilled. When I looked down, there was a dark stain on the fabric of her blue dress. I looked at my hand; moonlight showed me thick, red blood. I rolled back onto my knees, pulling the dress up. How had I missed this?

"You're hurt," I said. Blood seeped from the wound.

"Must've been grazed in the water," Bonnie said, lying back as she pulled her dress into place.

I shuffled around on the ground, yanking my pants up and then finding my discarded shirt. I wrung as much of the water out of it as I could, then pressed it against Bonnie's wound. She hissed in pain.

"We need to get you to camp," I said.

How much blood had she lost?

Guilt wracked my shoulders as I helped her to stand. I wasn't going to let anything happen to her. Not now. Not after everything we'd been through. I kept a tight grip on her waist, and she lifted an arm to rest on my shoulders.

We had planned to meet the others on the east of the town before we got separated. After grabbing my gun holster and slinging it over my shoulder, we set out. I quickly lost track of how far we walked; all of my concern was for Bonnie. It felt like a thousand miles passed as she helped me navigate by the stars. Eventually, her words faded into silence and her head rested heavy against my shoulder. With each step, her feet grew clumsier.

"Bonnie," I whispered, lifting my shoulder to get her attention. She picked up her head, her eyes barely opened into slits. I had to keep her awake. "Tell me what your favorite food is."

It would be up to me to make sure that we made it out of this alive.

"Hm?" she asked.

"What's your favorite food?" I asked.

"Strawberries," Bonnie said with a sigh, her head falling back to my shoulder again.

"Tell me a story. Like you tell The Kid. Something you've never told me," I said, forcing my tone to remain even. I was terrified, but I couldn't let her know that. We were going to make it to camp. We had to.

"Two bits," Bonnie said after a long moment of silence.

"What?" I asked.

"That's how much I'm worth." She sounded drunk. My brow furrowed as a heaviness settled on my shoulders. She was worth so much more than that. "Jones was lookin' for that stupid gun. He was hagglin' over the price and had 'em throw me in for an extra two bits of silver." She paused, licking her lips as though she was thirsty. "After what happened with Beck, I started plannin' my escape. It took a year before she got word to me that she was in Vegas with Murph."

Bonnie groaned beneath her breath as we started moving uphill. I tried slowing my pace to compensate, but it wasn't helping. She cringed with every movement.

"Seven months after that, I was almost ready. Jones started losing it, bad. He would look at me and say strange things. He would ask me when our dad was comin' home. Or if I'd seen a TV show that night." A dark laugh bubbled from between her lips. "Then he'd catch himself and beat me until my bones hurt."

Anger flared in my chest for a man I hoped to never meet. The things Jones did to her, the things he did to other people. I'd never understand it, and I didn't want to. All I wanted was to keep her safe and to keep her in my arms. Bonnie dug her feet in, stopping our progress as we approached a ridge.

"I can't—" Her knees shook. Blood flowed down her left leg. *Fuck.*

"It's okay," I said, sweeping her carefully into my arms. Warm blood slicked against me as I cradled her to my chest. "I've got you." I pressed my lips to her temple. When I pulled back, her eyelids fluttered shut.

"Hey," I said. "Don't fall asleep. What happened next?" She nodded in response, her lips moving without sound for a moment.

"I knew I couldn't wait any longer," she said. She tried to swallow, but I could hear her struggle with it. "He brought me to his tent to punish me one night. Instead, I knocked him over the head with this . . . thing . . . I don't know what it was . . ." I focused on my steps, on my breathing, on *her* breathing. She fought back against the darkness threatening to consume her. She always fought back. It was one of the many things I loved about her. "I grabbed Selene and whatever I could fit in my pack and ran." She gave another dark laugh. "I didn't even have any water."

We reached the top of the ridge, and I stopped, my eyes widening as the world opened up beneath us. It was hard to tell where the land ended and the sky began. The view was the most beautiful thing I'd ever seen, aside from the woman in my arms.

How could I ever have thought that Montana was where I was meant to be?

The earth spread out before us, barren, but beautiful in the moonlight. The sky was an endless expanse of stars. It reminded me of my own mortality. That I was small in the scheme of things. Insignificant.

I opened my mouth to tell Bonnie about it, but her closed eyes sent panic through my heart.

"What happened after you left, Bon?" I asked, forcing my words to even out. I didn't want her to know how scared I was. She blinked her eyes open, leaning her head farther into the spot between my neck and my shoulder.

"Those goddamned wanted posters Jones put out happened. I was going to leave town before he caught up. Then I met you."

A smile crossed my face.

"I couldn't turn away. I had to know you."

Bonnie looked up at me with resignation in her eyes. I gave her a bittersweet smile, knowing to high hell that if we didn't get her to camp, she wouldn't make it past the morning. She'd lost too much blood.

"You *hated* me," she said. I chuckled at her words.

"I did," I said. "But, as it turns out, getting robbed by you was the best thing that ever happened to me, too."

I pressed my lips to her forehead; her skin was warm, too warm. We'd be lucky if the wound wasn't already infected. I didn't know what I was doing. I kept going, trying to think of something to say to keep her awake. Her eyes closed, and panic rose into my shoulders again. My arms shook from trying to keep her steady. The blood from her wound made it hard to keep a steady grasp. I had to shift her weight more onto my shoulder so I didn't lose my grip.

"Bon, wake up," I said in a quiet voice. She didn't acknowledge me. "C'mon. Wake up." I shrugged my shoulder to make her lift her head. It didn't work. Instead, her head flopped lifelessly back.

My heart plummeted into the pit of my stomach.

We'd come too far for it to end like this. My arms, shaking from the strain, tightened around her, keeping her close to my heart. I pressed forward, not knowing if we were even going in the right direction anymore. She needed help. Fast. If Bonnie died, then what was the point to the endless miles of wilderness and countless dangers we'd faced? I couldn't imagine a world where someone so stubborn and strong didn't exist. I didn't want to live without her fierce heart and sharp tongue. The very thought of having to tell The Kid that Bonnie died wrenched a sob from within my chest.

He couldn't lose anyone else. *I* couldn't. I lost everything in Montana only to find a better life with Bonnie. She was the one who had saved me when my own grief over my parents threatened to consume me. She frustrated me to no end sometimes, but she made me a better man. She showed me how kindness and compassion helped to soften the jagged edges of life. She picked me amongst a sea of strangers back in Vegas. I chose her now.

I would always choose Bonnie.

I dragged in ragged breaths as I ignored my own quaking legs. I wouldn't stop. I wouldn't give up. I couldn't.

*Because I loved her.*

Every step was fueled by that realization. I loved Bonnie, and I would do anything if it meant being able to save her.

I allowed myself a quick break, long enough to stand still. "C'mon, Bon," I whispered, leaning down to brush my lips to her forehead. "Don't leave me. Please." My eyes heated, and tears spilled over onto my cheeks. I couldn't lose her. I adjusted my grip, clutching Bonnie tight against my chest. I pressed my forehead against hers.

"I love you," I whispered.

Everything was silent, save for her shallow breaths and my pounding heartbeat. The blood on her legs turned cold, coating the skin between us. My life narrowed to a single point. Bonnie. Everything came back to her, to that moment in Vegas when she could have just watched me walk away but chose not to. She didn't know it, but she saved me that day, too. Not from anyone like Sixgun or a crater beast, but from myself. From destroying myself with grief over the loss of my parents, with anger at being left to take care of a child when I barely felt like more than a kid myself. Bonnie had taught me how to live. She had to survive. That was what she was good at, wasn't it?

"Bonnie!" I picked up my head as shouting echoed from a distance.

The Kid. I swore, then forced myself to take a step. Then another. I set off toward my brother's voice, trying to quicken my pace. Bonnie made a low noise with each impact of my foot on the ground. I followed the sound of my brother's voice, until we broke through a tree line.

"Jesse!" The Kid shouted, running for us.

Relief flooded through my chest. Will ran toward us as well. They hadn't been captured, and they were in much better shape than us. Adrenaline fueled each of my steps. The Kid stopped short at the sight of Bonnie's limp form in my arms. His face paled.

"What happened?" he asked, not hiding the fear in his voice.

"She got shot," I said, groaning as Will took Bonnie from me. My knees quaked as I compensated for her absence. "Kid, get bandages and alcohol and water."

My brother dashed away. Clara came up asking questions, but I brushed past her, moving toward where Will set Bonnie on the back of the wagon. I shoved him out of the way and leaned over her, putting a hand to her cheek.

"Bonnie, c'mon, wake up," I said, fighting back tears again. I cradled her head in my hands. Her eyes fluttered open, the lines of her face made harsher by the light of the campfire. "I need you to stay awake."

"Is she gonna be okay?" The Kid asked, returning with supplies in hand.

"She's gonna be fine," I said, turning to Will. Even if I wanted to stitch her up, I knew my hands would be too shaky to do it. I didn't know the guy. I didn't trust him. But I needed him to save Bonnie's life. "Please."

Without a word, Will took off his hat and got to work. I grabbed a blanket from one of the bedrolls and used it to cover her as Will cut her skirt away with a knife.

"Is the bullet in there?" he asked.

"No, it grazed her," I said. My legs shook beneath my weight. I sat on the edge of the wagon and gripped one of Bonnie's hands in both of my own. She squeezed my fingers weakly. She fought to stay awake.

"Fuck. She needs fluids," Will said, his sleeves rolled up. Dark blood covered his hands.

I grabbed the canteen and poured some water in her mouth. She struggled to swallow, but opened her eyes to look at me. I brushed the hair from her face and kissed her forehead.

"Why are you wet?" Clara asked.

"What?" I asked.

"You're wet."

"Oh," I said. "That. We jumped off a cliff into a river to escape those people."

"Cool!" The Kid said, climbing up the other side of the wagon to sit by Bonnie.

Then she screamed. Will shushed her, comforting her as he dragged the needle across her wound again and again.

"*Esta bien, mi cielo. El dolor es fugaz.*" He whispered the words softly to her, and she stopped screaming.

I lost track of how many times Will punctured Bonnie's skin in order to piece her back together. Seconds, or minutes, maybe hours later, she hissed between her teeth as Will poured alcohol over the stitches. Then he stepped away. She tried to sit up, and I helped her, keeping the motion fluid so she didn't injure herself further. I offered her the canteen, but she shook her head. I extended my hand to Will.

"Give me your flask."

He did it without a word. I unscrewed the cap and poured some into her mouth. She blinked at me, her eyes brighter as the alcohol settled into her veins.

"Jesse, where's your shirt?" Clara asked, arms crossed over her chest. I looked down for the first time, realizing I'd left my bloody shirt back on that embankment. When I looked at Bonnie, I couldn't hide my smile.

"Are you okay?" I asked her. She nodded, her eyes full of gratitude. But also the love I'd first seen at that hotel. The Kid slid into my view.

"So. You jumped off of a cliff," he said, his eyes full of awe as he looked between us.

"Yep," I said, not looking away from Bonnie. There were so many things I wanted to say. But with everyone watching, it didn't feel right.

"Got some bad news," Will said. "I had to put one of the horses down. It broke a leg."

"Which one?" I asked, searching for No Name and Eagle. Thankfully, they were both on the other side of camp. It was one of the horses from the wagon.

"I rode too close to The Kid and the horses spooked. One of them caught on a big root at the edge of the trees when they had to veer away," Will said.

Bonnie tried to stay awake, but her eyes grew heavy. I grabbed another blanket from the bedrolls and put it under her head.

"Get some rest," I whispered, pressing my lips to her cheek.

I turned to the others. We had a problem. No Name and Eagle were too strong to pull the wagon. I opened my mouth to start barking orders, but could see the fatigue written on their faces.

"Let's get an hour or two of sleep. Then we'll figure it out," I said. I found my pack and pulled out clean clothes, only to realize I was covered in Bonnie's blood. Horror seized my heart. I needed to get it off. Someone shoved a canteen into my hands.

"Here, clean yourself up," Will said. I looked up at him, and concern reflected back at me in his gaze. I poured water over my chest, scrubbing away the crusted blood from my skin.

"Thanks," I murmured. I rubbed my hands together, forcing the sight of Bonnie's limp body from my mind.

"She lost a lot of blood," Will said before lighting a cigarette. "Like . . . a *lot* of blood."

"Is she going to be okay?" I asked, sliding a clean shirt over my head.

"It's too soon to tell." Will took the canteen from me. I expected him to leave, but he stood there, staring at me with angry eyes.

"What?" I asked as I kicked off my soiled jeans.

"I told you back in that town. You're gonna get her killed," he said. His face shifted, his dark eyes fading from anger to pain. "Maybe you'll save her, too." The sincerity in his voice hit me squarely in the chest. I couldn't find the words to express my gratitude for what he'd said, or for saving Bonnie.

"What did you say to her?" I asked, remembering the smooth Spanish words he'd whispered to Bonnie. "To get her to calm down?"

*"It's alright, my sky. Pain is fleeting."* Will brought his gaze to mine. "We've had to put each other back together a lot." I didn't doubt that. With a nod of respect, I slipped on my clean pants. Then I glanced toward Bonnie's still form.

"Truthfully, will she be alright?" I asked him.

"The next couple of days will be touch and go. She needs to eat. Red meat especially, as much as we can give her. We need to keep her bandages clean. I don't have anything to help her if it gets infected," Will said, shifting his weight back and forth.

"Thanks," I said, tipping my head toward him. I respected him for how he took care of Bonnie. We both loved her. I couldn't hate him for that. I grabbed one of the oversized t-shirts we'd picked up somewhere along the line and a fresh pair of underclothes for Bonnie. I walked back to the wagon and sat quietly beside her.

"Those for me?" she asked. I hadn't realized she was awake. I nodded, once again helping her sit up. I eased off the ruined dress and put the dry clothes on her as carefully as possible. I started to climb from the wagon to let her rest, but she reached out, grabbing my wrist.

"Please don't go," she said, her voice barely a whisper.

With a nod, I moved behind her, sitting with my back against the stolen crates. She leaned between my legs, resting her head against my chest. I brushed some of her matted hair away, pressing my lips to her temple. I held her, not tight enough to hurt her, but enough to let her know I was there.

"We can't stay here," she said after a while. Her voice startled me into alertness. "Coyotes are gonna come when they catch the scent of that horse." Suddenly, I had an idea about what to do with the horse.

"I know," I said. "But you need to rest."

"We need to keep going," she said. Neither of us moved as I sat there, holding her, lips pressed against her hair.

"Just let me hold you," I whispered. "Just a little while longer."

What I'd wanted to say was that I thought I'd lost her. That I couldn't live without her. That even if it meant I *was* a dumb farm boy, I'd do anything for her. *Had* done anything for her. The words fell short on my tongue.

"It's gone," Bonnie said after a long moment.

"What is?" I asked, lifting my head up from hers.

"Her comb," Bonnie said. Her mother's comb. The one she'd held onto for all these years. "It's somewhere at the bottom of that river now."

I frowned. "I'm sorry, Bon," I said.

"I thought I'd be upset if I ever lost it," she said quietly. "Instead, I feel lighter somehow." She shifted slightly, snuggling further into my embrace. Within minutes, her breathing evened out. I buried my face in her hair, thankful she was alive in my arms.

The eastern horizon began to lighten a while later. I hadn't slept, but Bonnie did, and that was well worth the exhaustion. I managed to pull away and guide her down into the bed of the wagon without waking her. Then I went about the camp waking everyone else up. We had work to do.

Over the next couple of hours, we went through the stolen goods, repacking the food into our saddlebags. We found a couple of spare lengths of rope as well as a good knife. Since we couldn't take the wagon, we'd have to load down the three horses. The Kid and I made good work of the dead horse, teaching Will how to properly slaughter an animal. Luckily, one of the barrels from the warehouse was full of salt, so we were able to preserve the meat. Bonnie needed red meat, Will said.

When she woke up a while later and offered to help, I insisted that she rest. I wasn't sure if that made her mad, but I didn't care. She didn't need to overextend herself.

"Kid, you're on Eagle. Clara, with Will. He'll need the extra hand," I said once we'd finally packed the horses down with our supplies. There was something like respect in Will's eyes as he nodded back at me. "I've got Bonnie." I looked at her. She wore a pair of my sleep pants.

Three horses for five people weren't nearly enough, but we'd have to make do until I could come up with another arrangement. We set out, leaving the wagon behind with the supplies that we couldn't carry. I led the way on No Name, silent, keeping one hand on the reins and my other arm securely around Bonnie on the saddle in front of me.

It was slow going. Each time I tried to push faster, it put more stress on Bonnie. The Kid tried to keep spirits up, but after a while, he was quiet, too. I tried not to fuss about her each time she moved. I had a feeling she didn't want somebody making such a scene over her. I kept my arm steady around her, not caring whether it annoyed her.

"What was it like?" The Kid asked. "Jumping off the cliff?"

"It was fun," I said, not sure that I could quite capture the rush of adrenaline and the things that followed right after. We'd gotten lucky.

"Except for the whole getting shot part," Bonnie said, a smile breaking across her face. It was good to see her humor return.

We rode until Bonnie told me she couldn't keep going. We'd have to stop every couple of hours. When we'd get back up, exhaustion lined her face. She didn't complain once, but she needed rest. We all did.

By Bonnie's quiet estimation, we had less than three days to Fort Hood. The desert stretched on around us. It felt like we may never get there.

Then, around midafternoon, buildings appeared. A town. We could stop and Bonnie could get some rest before we made the last leg of the trip.

"Hey," I said, gentle in her ear. I motioned with my chin ahead of us. She saw it, too. I glanced over at Will, who had Clara latched onto him in the saddle. I couldn't tell if he minded or not. Bonnie nodded, and I steered our group toward the town. In less than an hour, we came across more modern buildings. It reminded me of Roswell: eerily quiet and abandoned. Broken glass littered the street in front of stores. There were charred ruins of what might have been a school.

We climbed down at the end of town. I helped Bonnie off of No Name, taking extra care to be mindful of her stitches. I was pretty sure I annoyed her with all of my fussing. When I turned back to No Name to get something out of my saddlebag, I saw it. Pop had a picture of one pinned up in the barn back home. There might have been paint in some fancy color on it once, but now it was faded away to a gray frame, hints of red rusting around its edges.

An old truck, more beautiful than I could have imagined.

I dropped No Name's reins and wandered over. It was a sturdy truck; the frame was all steel. Older than the car Pop had kept from before the Culling. I knew everyone was watching me, but I didn't care. This was something my father had only dreamed of.

I walked around to the driver's door and opened it. The keys were in the ignition. I tried to crank it, but it wouldn't start. After popping the hood and bracing it up with an old metal pipe, I began to poke around inside.

I barked a laugh. A broken belt. That was an easy fix.

Once I did, we'd make it to Fort Hood in no time.

## Chapter Twenty-Five

# BONNIE

Pain became me. My entire body throbbed in time with my pulse, driving me to madness. My stomach thrashed, threatening to spill its contents every few minutes between spells of cold sweats in the midst of the sweltering desert heat. I sat on the crumbling asphalt and tried to keep my vision focused as Jesse tinkered with the crumbling metal horse. I knew they were once called *cars*, but honestly it was how I remembered what they did before sitting in the middle of roadways like the skeletons of great beasts.

The heat worsened everything, but I kept my face impassive. Jesse was already so worried about me. It was a sight to behold how easily he fit into the role of leader. Even managing to wrangle Will's unruly personality into usefulness.

Cold sweat broke out on my temples, and the ground beneath me felt as if it were moving, rising and falling like rolling hills beneath me. Everything was hard. Sitting, riding, walking, but it was harder to sit here and watch as Clara doted on Jesse. Her eyes slid to mine as she crossed to hand Jesse a canteen. *Bitch.*

Will sat next to me, long legs splayed in front of him as cigarette smoke curled on the stagnant, wind-less air. The heavy smell of tobacco made my stomach thrash harder.

"Is there anything else I can get you, Jesse?" Clara asked in her too-sweet voice. It made me sicker than my blood loss, and I stood, clenching my jaw tight as my stitches pulled taut with the movement.

"No," Jesse said, reaching for his belt. "I'm about done."

The sound of his buckle clinking reminded me of last night, of how desperate we'd been on that embankment. Of how it'd felt so good to have his hands and mouth on my body. I didn't even realize I was bleeding out. My head swam.

Will was at my side instantly, his hand steadying me. I hadn't realized I'd wavered on my feet. I shook him off with a surly glare and started down the main road away from everyone else.

"Where are you going?" The Kid asked, and Jesse's protective gaze froze me to the spot.

"Exploring," I said, worried that if I said too much, my voice would wobble and give my weakness away. Jesse moved, crossing the space between us. As much as I longed to lean into the strength of his embrace, I also needed space.

"I've got her, Montana," Will said, crushing his cigarette beneath his boot and gripping my arm tight. "Just keep tinkering with your *machine*."

"Can I go with them?" The Kid asked. I smiled, motioning him over with a flick of my head.

"Maybe you should help your brother instead," Clara said, bitchily.

"Nah, he's good," Jesse replied.

The Kid made a vulgar hand gesture he'd no doubt learned from Will. Anger flared to life inside of me, exacerbated by the pain in my side. I'd honestly tried to be understanding. I knew she'd been taken from Montana and her cushy apple-pie life, where women were delicate feminine examples of virtuousness like she tried to be. I also knew that she and Jesse had made promises to each other that he'd broken. She was hurt, jealous, and probably felt alone.

But no one came between me and The Kid.

"I said he could come," I snapped, my voice cracking through the air like a lightning strike. Clara's face reddened and her knuckles bleached white as she clutched her skirt. I shouldn't have enjoyed the stricken look in her eyes as much as I did. The Kid was unfazed, sticking his tongue out at her as he ran over exuberantly.

"Y'all can gouge each other's eyes out later. C'mon," Will said, pressing a hand to my back to guide me forward. We walked in silence for a while, not acknowledging how heavily I had to lean on him as soon as we were out of Jesse's sight. The Kid pulled his harmonica from his back pocket and blew an off-pitch tune.

"Why'd you have to do that?" Will asked after a minute.

"Do what?" I asked, not sure what he was talking about.

"Antagonize Blondie. I mean, the way you and Jesse are together, it can't be easy for her to see. She thought she lost him, you know. All this time, she thought he was dead," Will said, his voice more serious than I'd heard it in a long time.

"What is it with you and her? She's not the kind of girl you normally go after," I said. He stifled a grin that I saw anyway. He shrugged, but his dark eyes warmed at the mention of her.

"The modest thing is hot," he said. "It's like she's a present you have to work hard to unwrap."

I rolled my eyes. After another few moments, biting my thumbnail down to the quick, I stopped to catch my breath and take a long look at Will.

"What did you mean? *The way you and Jesse are together?*" I asked, my mind reeling. Will laughed, a breathy, incredulous sound. He stared at me as if he didn't recognize me before pushing some of his midnight hair from falling into his eyes.

"*Mi cielo*, you look at that man like you're dying of thirst and he's a full canteen. It's obvious you're in love with him," he said. My mouth dropped open, ready to deny it, my heart thudding hard against my ribs. Only I couldn't. I'd known for a while now the way I felt about Jesse wasn't something one night of passion would ever be able to satiate. It wasn't about his body. It was about his character. He'd stood tall beside me, held me together when I threatened to fall apart, and last night . . .

Last night he'd saved my life. Again.

"Is it that obvious?" I asked in a horrified whisper. Will kissed the top of my head and urged me forward. "Do you think Jesse knows?"

Will gave a long-suffering sigh.

"I think being around the two of you is nauseating," he said. "But, you know, in a good way. It's nice seeing you happy."

The Kid called out to us, ducking below a half-crumbled wall into a building nearby. Will and I had been through so much together. Unspeakable things endured only because we had each other to lean on, to break in front of, to put each other back together. I thought he'd betrayed me, turning me over to Jones and his father. But, if that was the case, why was he here now? Why had he left the crew and put a target on his back for me?

"Why'd you do it?" I asked. "I *have* to know, Will. Why did you turn me over to Jones?" He ducked, hiding his eyes with the brim of his cowboy hat. His breath hitched, and I gripped his arm tight. Tipping his hat up revealed the glassiness in his dark eyes that he fought to control. "*Please.*"

"I wasn't the only one who saw you help Beck." He gulped, swallowing his emotions down hard. "I knew if Jones found out, he'd kill you."

"He almost *did* kill me," I argued.

"I went to my dad. I told him to convince Jones to let him do the punishing," Will admitted, blinking hard. Realization crashed through me. He hadn't betrayed me at all. He'd risked everything to keep me alive. My breath stilled.

"Will, I *hated* you. I thought . . . I thought when I told you I didn't want us to be together that you—"

"You *should* hate me," he said, his words hard. "I gave you to him. Fuck, I let him *carve* you."

I knew better than anyone the toll Sixgun's brand of cruelty had taken on Will. Years of torment, physical and psychological, instilling a guilt rooted so deep that trying to remove it would kill him.

"I forgive you," I said, my words soft.

"You can't. You can't just—"

"Why not?" I asked, cutting him off.

"Because you got hurt and it was *my fault*. You can't just forgive me. It can't be that easy," he said, incredulous.

"I've learned the right thing is rarely easy. But I forgive you anyway," I said, hugging him tight. His hat fell to the dust as he squeezed me back, careful of my wound. His shoulders shook with silent sobs.

"Bonnie! Are you kissin' Will now, too? Quit it!" The Kid teased. A brilliant grin crossed his mouth, reminiscent of Jesse's.

"We're not!" Will and I both shouted, giggling tearfully. The Kid bounded over as Will retrieved his hat, holding a book out to me. The cover was cracked and faded, the pages warped from exposure to the elements.

"It's about Bonnie Parker; will you read it with me?" The Kid asked. I wavered on my feet, and Will wrapped an arm around my waist.

"I can't, Kid," I said, ruffling his hair as we headed back. It took longer than I wanted to admit to get back. I'd overdone it. By the time Jesse and the truck were in sight, my side throbbed so bad it was the only thing I could think about.

Then a rumble tore through the air, like a crater beast roaring to life, and suddenly I forgot about the ache in my side. Shuffling toward the metal beast, my eyes fell to the tangle of gears and whirring pieces inside of it. Jesse smiled at me, and I leaned against the hood too heavily.

"I've never seen a machine from before the Culling working," I said in awe. He smiled wider at the expression on my face.

"Wanna go for a ride?" he asked. I wrapped my arms around his broad shoulders to steady myself. I nodded swiftly, and he helped me slide onto the seat. Then he slammed the hood down and climbed into the snarling machine beside me. The inside was hot, even with the windows rolled down, but the heat didn't bother me as badly as before. The dashboard displayed gauges of colored lines and numbers that meant nothing to me.

"How the hell did you do this?" I asked, watching him pull roughly on a lever, and the whole frame lurched forward. I let out a short yelp that forced a rumbling chuckle from Jesse.

"Pop taught me everything he knew about cars," Jesse said, shifting the gear as we picked up speed. His hand rested on my knee, and the contact distracted me from the ache in my side. The excitement in his voice was familiar. He ran away with his words the same way The Kid did, his mind moving faster than his mouth. It was endearing to see how similar they could be. "He had this old car in the barn, said it was the one they used to move everything after the Culling. By the time I was fifteen, he taught me how to take apart the engine and put it back together. I'll show you when we go—"

Jesse stopped abruptly, his brows furrowing deep. I stared at him expectantly.

"To Montana," he finished. I shouldn't indulge him, I knew that. It would only hurt us both later. After nearly dying in his arms, though, I needed the dream as much as he did.

"What's it like in Montana? I haven't really been anywhere but the desert," I asked, thinking my heart might burst. The corners of his eyes folded deep with his smile, and he stared at me for a long moment before turning his eyes forward.

"Well, it's colder," Jesse said. "The trees are taller than the tallest building you've ever seen." He turned the wheel as we made our way to the other edge of town and just drove. "In the summer, we swim in ice-cold creeks fed by the snowcaps on the mountains."

"What's a snowcap?" I asked. He wrapped his arm around me.

"It's when the snow piles high on the mountains," he said but noticed my confused expression. "Frozen rain. It's beautiful. You'll love it." I motioned to the abandoned building The Kid had ducked into earlier. It'd be a good place to camp for the night. Jesse turned the wheel again in the direction I indicated. My eyes strayed to the buttons on the dash, wondering what they were all for. Instead of asking, I pressed them. Most of them

259

did nothing. Until suddenly music blasted around us. I jumped, hissing as the jerking motion forced pain all the way down my leg.

"Maybe we should get you settled so I can go back for the others," Jesse shouted over the loud music. I nodded but wasn't really paying attention. I laughed, staring incredulously at the dash of the truck where music appeared from thin air, like magic. Like in the fairy stories my mom used to tell me.

"You aren't going to believe this," I said, loud enough to be heard over the drums. "But I know this song!" It sounded different, more energetic and upbeat than when my mom would sing it at home, but it was definitely the same. I sang along for a while, until Jesse slowed the truck and turned to stare at me. The look in his eyes made me forget the words as he cut the engine and we were blanketed in silence.

"What?" I asked, breathless.

"You're beautiful," he said simply, in the certain way he said everything. My heart raced, and I kissed him with a breathy groan.

"You have to stop sayin' stuff like that or you're gonna make me wanna pop my stitches, farm boy," I breathed against his mouth. He kissed me again, quickly, before pulling away to help me out of the truck. We walked into the building slowly, dark hallways echoing with our footsteps as we passed beneath the faded eyes of kids that were likely long dead. Everything felt solemn here, beneath the fine layer of dust and memories.

Jesse pushed into a room with long leather couches, cracked and fading from exposure to the light but still comfortable enough. After he'd scouted the area and deemed it safe, he went to gather the others. I slept, for how long I didn't know, lulled by the silence. When I heard Jesse's truck rumbling back, the sky was ablaze with the setting sun. Had it taken that long, or had I slept through multiple trips?

Will and The Kid burst in a few moments later, one with a flask and the other with a book. The Kid sat at my feet, begging me to read the book again. I ignored him.

"Time to clean your wound, *mi cielo*," Will said, shaking the flask as Clara and Jesse came in a few minutes later. Clara had a sour look on her face, as usual.

"Are you and Will going to kiss again?" The Kid asked, staring pointedly at Jesse, and my eyes slid to Jesse's.

"We *hugged*, Kid. I wouldn't kiss Will if you paid me," I said, laughing as Will clutched his chest dramatically.

GUNS & SMOKE

"You're fucking mean, *mujer*," Will said as I pushed my pants down so he could get to my wound. It was red and angry, the stitches holding together swollen, puckered flesh. Disgusting. "That's gonna be another nasty scar." He pressed the alcohol to the wound as gently as he could, but a pained gasp wrenched from me before I could bite it back.

"Son of a bitch!" I swore, biting the inside of my cheek as the pain pulsed with my heartbeat. Clara glared at my foul language.

"Sorry," Will said, grimacing as I breathed through the stinging until it lessened. "It actually looks good, all things considered."

"Bonnie, will you *please* read this book with me?" The Kid asked again, and I ruffled his hair absentmindedly. He shifted on the couch and jostled me on my sore side. I choked out a cry before he moved away.

"I'm fine," I said, staring pointedly at Jesse, who'd begun to walk over.

"I want you to read this with me," The Kid said again, and I looked down at his excited face.

"I can't, Kid," I said, turning back to watch Will fixing my bandage.

"Bonnie, please—"

"Oh my God!" Clara shouted in frustration, flinging her hands in the air. "Would you give it a rest already?! She can't read you the damn book! She can't *read*. They don't teach slaves how to read."

Tension snapped tight within the room. Will finished and stepped away from me, pity clear in his dark eyes. I bit my bottom lip to stifle the unkind words on my tongue. She didn't know my insecurities; she wasn't trying to exploit them.

"You can't read?" The Kid asked. His words were colored with judgment, the kind only thoughtless kids with no knowledge of social niceties spoke aloud. His words forced shame, like a blade, deep into my ribs. "Even little kids know how to read."

I couldn't look at him. I couldn't handle the disappointment I'd become to him. I swallowed down traitorous tears and shoved off the couch, fleeing on clumsy feet down the hallway. As the last rays of light faded from beyond the dirty windows, I lost myself in the maze of the building.

*Stupid.*

I found my way, clutching my throbbing side into a room with shelves piled high with books. As far as the eye could see. A dark laugh bubbled from between my lips as I fumbled through the drawers of a desk in the corner of the room. A bottle clinked as I slammed one

261

open, and though I couldn't read the label, I knew it was something that would numb the pain.

*Stupid.*

I walked among the shelves and drank deeply, groaning at the burn as it slipped down my throat. One of the walls had fallen away, and as I slid down a long row of shelves to sit heavily on the floor, I heard the cooing of birds nested amongst the shelves. The irony astounded me. Here I was, surrounded by books and not able to read a single one.

*Stupid.*

Jesse wouldn't want me to go to Montana with him now. Sure, it was an impossible dream at best. Even that was tainted by my shortcomings. I could almost see it, the derision on their pious townsfolk faces as Jesse introduced the ignorant slave girl he'd spent a wild summer with. Laughable.

"There you are." Jesse's voice rumbled through the room, and for some reason I wanted to giggle. So I did.

"Here I am," I said, waving the bottle at him before bringing it back to my mouth. I looked at him only to see his eyebrows raised in my direction.

"Hitting it a little hard, don't you think?" he asked, trying to mask the worry in his tone.

"Nope," I responded. "Drink with me." He sat next to me, eyes flicking to my wounded side.

"What is it?" he asked, holding his hand out for the bottle. I laughed, my lips clumsy.

"I don't know, can't read the label," I said, snorting. "It tastes like . . . clear."

"It's vodka," he said after taking a sip, then put the bottle out of my reach. He stared at me for a while, as if expecting me to say something. "They didn't mean anything by it."

"It's not like what they said was wrong. Can't risk us slaves gettin' any *dangerous ideas*. Better to keep us stupid," I said, blowing a stray strand of hair out of my eyes.

"You aren't stupid," he said, reaching a hand to my cheek. I knew Jesse didn't think of me that way; he'd told me so before. I carried this shame a long time before him, and it would remain until the day I died.

"Jesse?" I asked after a long time, both of us sitting in comfortable silence. He responded with a *hmm* sound as he brought the bottle back to his mouth. "Can I ask you a favor?" There was a smallness to my voice that seemed to alert Jesse that this moment, this request, was no simple drunken favor. He straightened, looking at me with blue eyes that I could drown in. I tried to stay composed but had to force the words out.

"Will you tell me what my scar says?"

## CHAPTER TWENTY-SIX

# JESSE

B ONNIE WOULDN'T HAVE ASKED if she wasn't sure. My heart pounded in my throat. I brought one of her hands to my mouth, kissing the back of it. I kept our fingers locked together as I rested our joined hands on my leg.

"It says 'Jones,'" I told her, trying to convey the words I couldn't say. She wasn't his property. She wasn't something he owned. She was her own person. She was smart and cunning, kind and beautiful. She was everything I'd never imagined I would have. I loved her. Bonnie's eyes fluttered closed, and she pressed her head back against the bookshelf.

"Of course it does," she whispered. I squeezed her hand.

"You remember when you asked me what I'd do if I had a day to myself to do anything?" she asked, her voice quiet. I nodded. "I said I would read. You asked me why, and I didn't tell you." I watched her eyes close, and she let out a long breath. "I'd read anything I could get my hands on."

I didn't understand it, then. There were a lot of things that I hadn't understood at the time. Through this journey, Bonnie had given me pieces of herself, things that may not have made sense in the moment, but that made sense now.

"I'm a survivor," she said. "That's what I do. I survive. For as long as I can remember I've had to fight every single day just to keep goin'." She seemed to choke on the next words. "I wanna be smart. Smart enough to figure out a way I don't have to fight so hard anymore."

I put an arm around her shoulders, tucking her into that space made for her.

"We can figure that out. Together," I whispered.

"I just wanna feel like I'm worth more than the two silver bits Jones paid for me. Like I'm worth more than that damn gun," she said, the words heavy on her tongue. I watched her expression fall.

"I wish you could see what I see when I look at you," I said, tipping her chin up to make her look at me. "You're worth *so* much more than some gun. You *are* smart. You're the smartest person I've ever known. You're also kind, and dependable. You'd do *anything* for The Kid, more than me sometimes.

"And Bonnie, I—"

She cut me off. Her mouth covered mine, and in an instant, it was like we were back on that embankment. Only, we weren't. I tangled one of my hands in her hair, wishing that we were back there, that she hadn't been shot, and that we could be alone forever. I pulled back, pressing my forehead against hers.

"Bon, your stitches—" I said.

"I know," she whispered, her eyes still on my lips.

"You're drunk."

"Drunk or not, I still want you," she said. I groaned regretfully, feeling the pain so starkly in my jeans. I wrapped my arms around her, tugging her into my lap, knowing that if I did nothing else for the rest of my days, I would die a happy man. I balled my hands into the fabric of her sleep pants, forcing myself *not* to rip them off of her soft curves. Her breasts pressed into my chest, and she broke her lips away to trail hot kisses along my jawline.

When I tried to pull back, she reached a hand down between us to keep my attention. I wrapped my arms around her back, holding her flush against my chest. The world seemed to shift around us. I could easily get lost in her, in this moment.

It'd been like this with Bonnie since that first day. Somehow, I managed to put an inch between us. She whimpered as we pulled apart.

"Bonnie," I said, reaching up to brush her unruly hair out of her face. Our hot breath mingled together, lust evident in both of us. "We can't."

With an insufferable groan, she pulled away. I adjusted my arms around her, holding her against my chest as we had in the wagon in those hours when I still wasn't sure if she'd make it.

"Tell me a story, Jesse," she said, her words quiet. I pressed my lips to the crown of her head, inhaling her familiar scent. *Home.* In such a short time, this woman had become my home. I drew lazy circles on her back. Storytelling was never my strong suit. I wouldn't deny her anything.

"It was market day," I said after pressing another kiss to her head. "Me and Pop went every Sunday we weren't stuck in the fields. All of the usual folks were there. Clara and her family. The old man who worked the farm near ours, some that came from hours away to trade their crops. There was a little old couple that made the most beautiful things by whittling wood. Not that I could ever afford them."

I clenched my jaw at the memory of *that* day. The one that changed everything. Bonnie tipped her head back enough to press a kiss to my lips, as if she sensed it was hard for me to talk about. She always seemed to know everything about me without ever saying a word. I let out a long breath.

"This day was different. There were two men I'd never seen before, sitting on a wagon made out of an old truck bed. One of them wore a ragged trench coat. They had these markings on their necks—" Suddenly, I remembered why that marking was so familiar. "It was the same one that Sixgun has. That crooked flower." I should have connected it sooner.

I refocused on the library, on Bonnie in my arms. I pressed my lips into her hair again.

"Pop didn't like it when strangers came through. I was going to talk to Clara when they stopped me. They weren't selling anything. Instead, they were recruiting men to go to California for work. It seemed like a dream come true. All I ever wanted was to get out of Montana," I said. "Pop interrupted us, apologized for me like I was a dumb kid. On the way back to the farm, I tried to tell him I wanted to go with them. I could go out, travel, like I always wanted to. Then when I got back, I'd take over the farm, marry Clara, pop out some kids, whatever he wanted me to do. I just wanted this *one* thing."

I was so angry at Pop that day. The devastation of his loss fell heavy on my shoulders as I sat there, holding onto Bonnie. I didn't realize I was shaking.

"What did he say?" Bonnie asked, pulling me back to her. I swallowed around the hard lump in my throat.

"He said there was no way in hell he was letting me go off with men like that," I said, feeling the silent tears spill onto my cheeks. "I told him I hated him and ran off into the woods as soon as we got back to the farm. I waited to go back until I knew he was in bed.

"When I finally made it home, Mom was up, but all she said was goodnight. I don't know if Pop even told her about the fight," I said. My bottom lip quivered at the memory of my mother in her nightgown, seated in her rocking chair near the fire. Bonnie reached up to my face, using her thumb to gently brush away my tears.

"That was the night those men burned down our house," I said, the words a vice around my throat. "I never said I was sorry. I never told him that I didn't hate him." I gripped onto Bonnie more tightly than I should have. She tensed beneath my touch, but she didn't make a sound, as if she knew how much I needed to lean on her.

"He knew, Jesse," Bonnie said after a long moment. "I promise. He knew."

The silence grew around us. Bonnie tucked her face into the crook of my neck, planting gentle kisses there. Eventually, she fell asleep. Her soft breaths were what eventually lulled me into my own dreamless sleep.

Morning light filtered through the opening in the cavernous library. I blinked awake, realizing it was late. Though there was an ache in my back from sleeping sitting up, I felt Bonnie's weight against my chest, and a smile crossed my lips. The Kid's loud voice echoed from somewhere inside the school.

"Bon," I whispered, pressing my lips to the top of her head. "Wake up." While I could have stayed curled with her like that forever, we had to get moving.

There was an impending sense of dread around my heart. We weren't far from Fort Hood, and Bonnie's promise to get us there weighed heavily on me. I hadn't told her yet that no matter what happened, I wouldn't be letting her go. That I didn't care if we found my uncle or not; I was staying with her.

Bonnie's blue eyes opened, sparkling as she looked up at me.

"Hi," I said, leaning down to kiss her.

"Hi," she said.

*This* felt right in a way that nothing else in my life had before. Everything about it, everything about *her* made me feel like we would be okay. This awful world that scarred each of us in different ways didn't feel so frightening when I held her. She was warm and pliant in my arms, a small smile perched on her soft lips. I leaned down again, covering her mouth with my own.

"They're up!" The Kid's voice echoed through the room. Bonnie pulled back, but she didn't look away; she just stared at me.

"Sun's been up for a while," The Kid said. "We should probably get on the road." Finally, I looked at my brother.

"Since when do you make the decisions?" I asked, laughing.

"Since the two of you decided to find a room to kiss in all night and sleep late," he shot back at me. My eyebrows lifted as I looked at Bonnie.

"You're a bad influence on him," I said with a smirk.

"Me? He's just like *you*," Bonnie said.

I enjoyed having her in my arms so much that it physically hurt when we separated. If she hadn't been the one to sit up to grab her boots, I may not have had the strength to get up myself. I stood, stretching out the pain in my back. Maybe we'd get the chance to sleep in a bed when we got to Fort Hood. I'd had enough of sleeping on the ground to last a lifetime.

"What I wouldn't give for a cup of Quanah's coffee right about now," I said, giving Bonnie a wry grin.

"I wonder if they have coffee in Fort Hood," my brother said, eyes lit up.

"'Course they do," Bonnie said as she stood. "All of the towns have had it. You just can't have none."

"Why not?" he asked.

"Because you're a maniac on coffee," I said. "Did you think we were drinking whiskey in the mornings?"

"Well . . . yeah," The Kid said. I turned to Bonnie.

"He thinks we're alcoholics," I said, incredulous. I flicked brim of his hat. It slipped from his head, landing in the dust-strewn floor. He grumbled beneath his breath as he picked it up.

A smile plastered across my face. We left the library, my fingers entwined with Bonnie's, toward Will and Clara's voices. They seemed to be in good moods. Clara didn't have the usual scowl on her face. Will put his hat on, looking at us as though he were gauging something between me and Bonnie.

"What?" I asked.

"Nothin'," he said, laughing beneath his breath.

Will wasn't as bad as I thought. He'd come through when I needed him, when it came to saving Bonnie. I'd always be grateful for that.

I went over the plan for today. If we pushed it, we might make it to Fort Hood by late tomorrow. We loaded some of the extra supplies from the horses into the bed of the truck in the hopes of lightening their load so we could make better time.

"Jesse, can I talk to you?" Clara asked as I tied down the last of the supplies. I glanced toward Bonnie, who sat inside the truck.

"Sure," I said, walking beside her. When we were out of earshot, she turned to face me with serious eyes.

"I just wanted to talk to you about . . ." Her voice trailed off as she glanced in Bonnie's direction. When she looked at me, there was resolution written on her face. "I know that you don't feel for me the way you used to. I just want you to know that no matter what happens, I'll *always* be here for you."

Confusion flashed through my chest. "Where is this coming from?" I asked.

"Bonnie. I understand that you really like her, but she's not one of us," she said, her words measured and even.

"Have you thought maybe that's what I love about her? She's nothing like home," I said, picking each word carefully. She stared at me; I couldn't read the emotion in her eyes. "I always talked about it, and you would laugh like it was silly. That life isn't mine. It never was." Clara's arms crossed over her chest; she glanced behind us at our three companions, who were pretending not to watch.

"I don't want her to hurt you," she said. Something in her eyes told me the words were true. I looked back to Bonnie, sitting in the driver's seat in the truck and talking to The Kid. She glanced up, meeting my eyes. A smile formed on her lips.

"That's not something you need to worry about," I said, returning Bonnie's smile. With one spare glance at Clara, I walked away, fully embracing her as my past, and the beautiful dark-haired thief as my future.

We got on the road shortly after. It was much later than I intended, but letting Bonnie get extra rest helped. She seemed more like herself as we rode together, just the two of us. Music played out of the speakers, and we enjoyed being together. I'd catch her now and then, humming along. There was one song in particular that she seemed to really enjoy.

This felt right. Her beside me, my arm tucking her against my side. Just the wind in our hair and a tune on the breeze.

We rode until dark. Even though the truck had lights, I knew it would be better to let everyone rest. The more time I could give Bonnie to recover before whatever lay before us, the better.

I propped the hood of the truck up, using the dim light of the fire to check the belts. I had to get the truck to Fort Hood. Bonnie couldn't ride a horse yet, and I wanted to make the rest of the trip easier on her. I checked the tension of the belts.

"Farm boy," Bonnie said behind me. A smile crept across my face as I turned to her. She held out a canteen. My heart skipped at the mischief in her eyes. I took the canteen and downed probably more than I should have.

"Thanks," I said, wiping my mouth with the back of my hand.

"How's she holdin' up?" Bonnie asked, moving beside me in front of the open hood.

"Pretty good. There's an oil leak, and I'm worried that belt won't hold, but I think she'll get us there," I said. Bonnie leaned into me, and I wrapped an arm around her waist.

"How're you doing?" I asked.

"Sore, but I'm almost back to being me," Bonnie said.

"Which version of you? The one that robs me or the one that kisses me?" I asked. She leaned up on her toes, pressing her lips to mine.

"The one that robs you," she said with a grin, snagging the canteen from my hand.

Behind us, Clara and The Kid broke into laughter. I turned around, watching as Will seemed lost in telling them a story. It was nice, for what it was worth, seeing all of us together like this.

"I'm gonna get some sleep," I said, motioning to the bed of the truck with my head. Without a word, Bonnie looped her fingers with mine. I took both of our bedrolls and spread them out over half of the back, then changed into comfortable clothes. I'd had enough of sleeping in jeans. By the time we climbed up, Will's story was done and the rest of them seemed to be settling in as well.

Bonnie got comfortable first, then I tucked in behind her, resting a hand on her thigh. She scooted back against me, wiggling her ass in all the right spots.

"Bon," I murmured with a smile. "Don't start something you can't finish."

"Who said I can't finish it?" she whispered, her voice breathless.

"I did." I took her hand in mine. "You need to heal." She shifted onto her back, grimacing at the pull of her stitches.

"You need to stop worrying so much," she said, her lips inches from mine.

"Trust me, when you're healed, I won't hesitate to get you naked," I said, forcing down the rising heat in my stomach. If it wasn't for her injury, I'd have already done it. I didn't care that the others were twenty feet away.

"Is that a promise?" she asked, her eyes sparkling at me.

"No, it's a threat," I said, smiling. I captured her lips in a long kiss. When I pulled back, I roved her features, from her darkened eyes down to her swollen lips. *God*, she made it so hard. The heat of her skin seeped through the layers separating us. I tucked her dark hair behind her ear, cupping her cheek in my palm. At least that meant she was feeling better.

"You know," she said, her voice low and husky. "There are *other* things we can do besides sex." Her hand grazed the front of my sleep pants, a smirk crossing her lips. She leaned forward, pressing her mouth against mine as she gripped my cock through the soft fabric. I shuddered at the contact.

"You're wicked," I said against her mouth.

"You could touch me, or kiss me, wherever you want," she whispered, trailing her lips across my jaw as her hand slipped beneath the fabric of my pants.

"Bon," I croaked. "Not fair—" She ran her hand up the length of me. If she didn't stop, I *would* end up ruining her stitches. I reached down, taking her hand firmly in mine. Bonnie's head fell back onto our bedding. Her hair splayed out around her, creating a dark halo around her face.

"I've never met a man who cockblocks himself," Bonnie said. Even though there was a frown on her face, her eyes reflected amusement. I kissed her again, willing my pulse to calm down, as much as I didn't want it to.

"Listen," I said, pulling back from her. "There's something I need to tell you. You don't have to say anything right now. I need you to know that I'm not going to give you up when we get to Fort Hood." Her mouth opened, but nothing came out from between her lips. Her eyes were wide and full of surprise. "Rule number three. Keep your word. And my word is that I want to be by your side. No matter what."

"But, your uncle—"

"We'll figure it out," I said, lowering my head to the makeshift pillow beneath hers. "Now get some sleep."

We set out first thing in the morning. Bonnie pulled out her map beside me in the truck, guiding me as promised all that time ago. At breakfast, we passed around a loaf of bread and freshly roasted horsemeat. We didn't speak much as the day grew hot. I'd catch myself watching Bonnie from time to time. She liked the music, a lot, and if it made her happy, I didn't care what we listened to.

At times, she extended her fingers out of the window, letting them trail in the wind. Every once in a while, I'd catch her looking at me. She would lower her eyes, smiling.

There were decisions we needed to make, but that would come later. I wasn't ready to tell her goodbye, and my only hope was that she wasn't either. If she decided that, after everything, she wanted to go her own way, it'd be hard for me to handle. I didn't expect to find Bonnie all of that time ago in Vegas. I'd be damned if I'd let her walk away without making it difficult for her.

We didn't stop except to relieve ourselves. The sun floated across the sky, eventually lowering back toward the horizon behind us.

Bonnie pulled her map out again. We approached a major highway. As soon as I veered the truck onto it, we passed a sign saying we were ten miles out.

Damn. We were almost there.

The anticipation in me grew with each passing mile. If we found my uncle, I hoped he would be able to make sense of this mess we'd found ourselves in. Not only the fire, but the gang that started it, and how it related to Sixgun. There was something more going on that I couldn't possibly understand.

Buildings popped up around us as we got closer. Bonnie stopped me from veering off of the highway by pointing to a crumbling bridge ahead. She sat beside me, helping me navigate as the world grew dark around us.

We started seeing signs for the base. My stomach thrashed as I followed the directions, taking my time to make sure that we were going to the right place.

Night engulfed us as we pulled to a stop near what looked like an old guard house missing its roof. I climbed from the truck, noting fires through the open gates. People milled about near the guard house; some carried guns, others nursed bottles. Most of them didn't even look our way. Bonnie linked her fingers with mine, providing silent support like she always did.

Will, Clara, and The Kid fell in behind us. For a military base, security was pretty lax.

"What the fuck, guys?" a woman shouted. Most of the people stood straighter as a woman with dark hair and skin came forward. She, too, carried a gun, but it was more military grade than the others. "You're just *letting* people walk in here now? Come on!" One of the men murmured an apology, but didn't so much as look at us. The woman approached, exhaustion evident in the deep lines of her face and her tired eyes.

"Who are you?" she asked, turning to me. She held the gun steady, pointed at the ground, but I recognized the tension in her shoulders. She wouldn't hesitate to shoot us.

"I'm looking for Michael Kincaid," I said.

"What do you want with him?" she asked, her gaze marking each of our faces.

"He's my uncle." Something like recognition flashed through her eyes. She glanced back to her guards before slinging her gun over her shoulder.

"You must be Jesse. I'm Gabriela," she said with a nod. "I'll take you to Mickey."

Relief poured through me as she turned and started walking. Without a word, Bonnie grabbed the reins of No Name, and Will and Clara began to guide the others.

"Kid, let's ride in the truck," I said, giving him a grin. He bounded toward the driver's side.

"Can I drive?" he asked with his usual wide-eyed excitement.

"Nope."

I noted the stares as we idled behind Gabriela. The people milling around the gates parted, watching us the entire time. Whereas I would have expected distrust and suspicion, I found vague curiosity. They seemed to be sitting around, just waiting for the next thing to come along. I parked the truck as the woman walked up to a rectangular building without windows. The doors were made of steel.

As we approached, Gabriela stopped outside. "First door on your left, you'll find him. What shape he's in this time of night, can't tell ya."

Bonnie's eyes lit up as she stepped toward the woman. "Is that an M4?"

"Military issue," she responded with a grin.

"Can I hold it?" Bonnie asked. I'd never seen her so excited.

"Maybe when you're older," Gabriela said. With a sarcastic grin, she left us alone.

"Let's go find your uncle, farm boy," Bonnie said, grabbing me by the hand. I pulled open the heavy door, which led to a dimly lit hallway. Bonnie and The Kid shuffled in behind me. There were old photographs lining either side of the hall. People in uniforms, in tanks. I couldn't fathom what life was like when there was an actual military.

"Liar!" Someone shouted from the far end of the hallway. "You cheatin' asshole!"

Before I could reach the door, a man was thrown bodily into the hallway. Another man walked out and spat on him.

"I've had it with your bullshit, Kincaid. Get the fuck outta here!" He walked away. I looked at the man on the floor. He smelled of cheap liquor and cigarette smoke. A red mark stood out on his cheekbone, and he was unconscious.

"Kid, meet your uncle," I said.

## CHAPTER TWENTY-SEVEN

# BONNIE

"I s he dead?" The Kid asked, staring down at the heap of a man crumpled on the floor. His blonde hair was lighter near the temples and in his beard, but the resemblance to Jesse and The Kid was startling.

"No," I said, sighing deeply. "He's just drunk."

Jesse bent down to pull the man's arm over his shoulder, and I moved to his other side, intending to take some of his dead weight onto my own.

"What do you think you're doing?" Jesse asked, his eyebrows furrowed.

"I was going to help you—"

"If you pop a stitch, it won't be because you're carrying this drunk asshole," he said, a wicked grin curling at the corner of his mouth. *Oh.* That grin promised the kinds of things that had me clenching my thighs together. I moved away and let Jesse struggle with carrying the man onto the front steps of the building, my skin suddenly flushed and warm.

From the corner of my eye, I noticed the woman who'd led us into the compound with the M4 slung along her back. I raised my hand to wave to her but pulled my arm down quickly as my stitches pulled tight. We caught her attention anyway and she turned towards us.

"Hey," I said as she approached, her dark eyes trained on the man lying at Jesse's feet.

"Oh, Mickey." She sighed, reaching down to brush the hair from his eyes in a tender gesture that surprised me. "What have you gotten yourself into now?"

"I'm assuming this happens a lot?" I asked. She turned to face me, nodding slightly. There was a deep sorrow etched into her expression, one that solidified with time and worry.

"Where's he live?" Jesse asked.

"Yeah, c'mon, follow me," Gabriela replied. Jesse hauled the man up before dropping him haphazardly into the bed of the truck. I slid into the cab, wrapping an arm around The Kid's shoulders as he hopped up next to me. Jesse cranked the engine, and I rested a hand on his knee. His eyes fell to mine, and I offered him a strained smile. These people were heavily armed and defensive, and no matter how friendly Gabriela seemed, I hadn't forgotten about the assault rifle strapped to her back.

Will and Clara led the horses beside us as we made our way through the winding compound. Will bent low to Clara and whispered something in her ear with a grin. Her mouth dropped open in shock, and she hit his shoulder. I rolled my eyes; leave it to Will Ellis to make inappropriate jokes surrounded by military-grade assault rifles.

Eventually, after the truck's loud engine garnered many incredulous stares, we pulled up to the largest house I'd ever seen. The compound was like a heavily fortified town. Places to gather, makeshift marketplaces, even what looked like a school. The house in front of us, though in disarray, could have sheltered a decent-sized gang comfortably.

"*This* is where he lives?" I asked as Jesse cut the engine and we shuffled out of the truck. I scanned the dormers on the second story, but there were no lights on.

"Mickey is the commanding officer here," Gabriela said. I moved in front of her before she could climb the stairs to the front porch, and she bristled, her shoulders tight.

"Before we go any further," I said, crossing my arms defensively over my chest. "Mind tellin' us who the fuck you are?"

She laughed, a throaty sound that was surprisingly pleasant. She held a hand out to me that I stared at for a long moment before taking. She had a firm grip and looked me in the eyes, something I appreciated.

"I take care of Mickey," she said. Jesse pushed past us, *Mickey* slung over one shoulder and snoring. "When he lets me." Her eyes followed the man's progress wistfully, a note of longing I knew too well in her voice. In fact, Gabriela reminded me a lot of myself. Strong, direct, and clearly pining for a man that didn't put her first.

*Rule number three. Keep your word. And my word is that I want to be by your side. No matter what.*

Jesse's words echoed in my ears as we filed inside, Will and The Kid bringing in our packs and tossing them unceremoniously onto a leather couch. The Kid had three of them stacked on his back, grumbling that he was going to shoot Will in the other arm.

"His room is the last one down that hall to the left," Gabriela directed Jesse, who disappeared with the drunk man in tow. She watched after them before turning to me. "There're enough rooms for you all to stay in. They aren't used by anyone anymore, not since people started leaving the base."

"Leaving?" I asked.

"After a while, people want to start families and settle down somewhere quieter. Where they aren't fending off gang members at the gates," she explained, motioning for me to join her as she walked into the kitchen. She pulled a bottle down from one of the cabinets and a couple of cloudy glasses.

"Can't they have both?" I asked, thinking of The Kid. We'd managed to travel so far, through gang territories, facing every danger imaginable. Together. Jesse's words came back to me again. The hope of finding someplace where we might all be together, safe, a family of sorts, flared bright in my chest. Gabriela poured some of the golden liquid in our glasses and raised hers to me.

"No," she said simply. "Not from what I've seen."

She downed the alcohol, grimacing as Jesse made his way into the room to stare between us. Gabriela set her glass down, but I stared into mine as Jesse crossed to me, pressing a kiss into my hair.

"So, you're Jesse, huh?" she asked before I handed my glass over to him and he drank what was inside. "Mickey told me a lot about you, and your mom."

"I never knew I had an uncle until a few months ago," he said, careful with his words as The Kid wandered into the room on weary feet. He crossed to me, leaning his head against my stomach as I brushed my fingers through his hair.

"He yours?" Gabriela asked, staring from The Kid to me and Jesse. I smiled softly.

"Yeah, he is," I said. Jesse's lips were in my hair again, his breath hot on my ear. My heart thudded painfully against my ribs. Would I have to leave them soon?

"He wasn't always this bad off," Gabriela said, capturing my attention once more. "After the Culling, he took the base over. He kept so many of us alive. But in recent years, our numbers have dwindled, and there hasn't been as much to do. It's when he has too much time to think, to *remember*, when he gets into trouble."

If there was anything Jesse and I could understand, it was how hard it could be to face down the demons of your past. I looked up at him, seeing the same understanding etched in his blue eyes. Gabriela sighed, shifting on her feet.

"I'm sure you're all tired and you need to get him to bed," she said, looking down at The Kid again with that same longing expression in her eyes. "I'll check on y'all sometime tomorrow." Then she left with a small wave.

"C'mon, Kid, let's find you somewhere to sleep," I said, motioning to Will and Clara as we searched through the rooms on the first floor. One room had two twin beds in it, with a small table in between. I settled The Kid in there, glaring at Will until he threw his pack at the foot of the other bed. I could've sworn I heard him grumble something in Spanish that sounded an awful lot like *cockblocker*.

Clara disappeared down another hall, and Jesse and I were left alone for the first time in a while. He pushed open a door near the end of the hall. A large bed rested in the corner with a desk settled beneath a window that showed the night sky beyond. Jesse went in first, dropping our packs onto the bed as I shut the door behind me. I flipped the lock on the door with an audible *click*.

Jesse's eyes found mine in the darkness, and I smiled, my lips curling slowly on my mouth.

"We have a door with a lock," I said. Jesse didn't hesitate; in a moment, he crossed the room, and I was in his arms. His mouth seared across mine. I gasped into his mouth as the pleasure of being pressed against him lanced up my spine. He pulled away, cradling my face with one of his callused hands.

"Did I hurt you?" he asked. I shook my head, pressing insistent hands against his chest until the backs of his knees bumped against the mattress. He lost his balance and sat heavily, but I didn't stop. My mouth met his in a fury, only stopping briefly to pull his shirt over his head and fling it to the floor, forgotten. Moonlight streamed in through the window, highlighting the hard planes of his chest. I remembered what I'd thought the first time I'd seen him shirtless in the daylight by the lake.

*I wanted to lick every curve and dip on his chiseled body.*

My mouth trailed from his lips to trace his pounding pulse before dipping lower. I pressed a hot kiss to the skin covering his thundering heart before smiling at him with lascivious intention.

My tongue flicked out of my mouth as I tasted the heat from his skin. A smooth groan slipped from between his lips. I reached his hips and the steep valley of muscles that seemed to curve towards the waistband of his jeans. I raked my nails gently down his hips, popping the top button of his jeans. I bit him softly on the skin above his waistband.

"Bonnie," he gasped. I pressed his zipper down slowly, until the whole hard length of him was freed from his pants. Jesse's hands fisted into the rough-hewn quilt below him. I stroked him until his hips squirmed beneath my touch. When I thought he was almost lost to my touch, I replaced my hand with my mouth.

I groaned, the sound reverberating around him and forcing a cry of pleasure from his mouth. He was intoxicating, his every reaction urging me on. Jesse swore, his hips bucking forward and his hands tangled in the long tendrils of my hair. As his body shifted beneath me, his groaning became more choked, and his fingers tightened against my scalp. It felt so *good* to know that his pleasure was at my mercy. Good enough that I sped up my motions until he was crying out his release into the still night air.

He fell back onto the mattress, chest heaving as he struggled to regain his composure. I stood before him, wiping my mouth on the back of my hand. In one swift motion, I pulled my shirt off over my head, unclipping my bra at the back before dropping it to the floor.

"Take your pants off," I ordered, my voice a husky rasp. We'd waited so long. So many times, I'd wanted to give him my body, to feel his rough hands on every part of me. To fall into exhausted bliss next to him after a vigorous night of mindless pleasure.

I wanted more now.

He flung his boots off and shoved at his jeans, fumbling as they caught on his ankles. He reached for me, his hands on my arms as I climbed over him in all his beautiful nakedness.

Now that we'd finally made it, things were about to change. Jesse wanted to stay with me, but I couldn't be responsible for putting The Kid in danger. I'd started wanting things that day at the lake, and it hadn't stopped there. I wanted to drown in the taste of Jesse, to be wrapped in his arms every night, to lean on him when things got hard. Even as I lay dying in his arms, all I'd wanted was more time with him. There were so many things I was uncertain about. I didn't even know how much time we had left together. If there was anything I knew with certainty, it was that I wanted *this*. I wanted all of Jesse.

I kissed him hard, sure that the taste of him would banish the doubts lingering in my mind. His hands slid up over the curves of my ass and traced my spine. He cupped my breasts, teasing my nipples to hard points until he'd wrenched a desperate moan from deep within me. Then, as I'd done to him earlier, he replaced his hands with his mouth.

I cried out into the night, my hands buried into his hair. It was too much. I was too lost to him to hold back anymore. The words rose up within me, and I stifled them by leaning to press my mouth to his in a hopeless rush. His hands fell to my sleep pants, fingers curling around the waistband to slide them down my legs. He moaned my name. Heat gathered in my eyes.

"Jesse, I lo—"

"You're bleeding," Jesse said, cutting off my reckless admission with an edge of panic in his harsh whisper.

"What?" I asked, but he pushed me gently off of his lap and laid me down on the mattress. He fumbled with a lantern on the side of the bed, until suddenly light flooded the room. I covered my bare chest with an arm as he shoved on sleep pants. He pulled bandages from my pack. I sighed, seeing the small crimson stain soaking into the fabric of my pants.

"Does it hurt?" he asked, pushing my pants down until the bandage was visible.

"No, I was distracted at the time," I grumbled. Jesse offered me a disappointed smile that I returned in kind. He peeled back the bandage and cleaned my wound. All the while, he hunched over me, nearly naked. I watched the muscles move in his shoulders as he cleaned away the blood. The careful concern in his expression and the delicate way he touched me only made me want him more.

"It just pulled them tight, you didn't pop any of them," he said, discarding the bloody bandages and opting for clean ones.

"Bloody gunshot wounds are such a turn on," I groaned, turning my red face away from Jesse.

"Trust me, bloody wound or not, you're still sexy," Jesse said, pressing a soft kiss to the skin above my bandages before pulling my pants back up. He passed me my shirt, which I pulled on over my bare breasts. Jesse stretched out next to me, his fingertips running over my shoulder. A shiver ran down my spine, and I tucked in against him. He hadn't slept much since I was shot, and I could see exhaustion written clearly in the lines of his face.

"We should get some rest; it's been a long time since we had an actual bed to sleep in," I murmured against his chest. We adjusted until I was pressed tight into that spot on his shoulder where I fit so well. He leaned over to turn the lantern off and buried his nose in my hair, sighing like the weight of the world had lifted from his shoulders.

"We have time now, Bonnie. We don't have to rush," he whispered in my ear. I swallowed down my trepidation.

*Did we?*

Jesse's warmth and the strength of his embrace were too soothing to chase those thoughts. Instead, we fell asleep clinging to each other, our deep breaths synchronized.

It seemed as if it were only a moment later when I woke, the sun's rays barely peeking over the windowsill. Jesse's fingers were tangled in my hair, and his arm was slung over my waist, the other cushioning my head. We'd slept with our mouths inches apart, like lovesick fools.

*Who am I kidding? I am a lovesick fool.*

It took entirely too long to twist out of Jesse's arms without waking him up, but somehow I managed. Unlocking the door and shuffling out on bare feet, I walked to the kitchen, where Will leaned against the counter with a mug of coffee steaming in his hands. His eyes trailed from my braless breasts to the bloodstain on my pants, and he cringed.

"How many stitches did you fuck up?" he asked. His expression fell when I stole his mug of coffee with a dark glare in his direction and brought the bracing bitterness of the drink to my mouth.

"None," I said with all the hate in my heart. Will laughed, ruffling his dark hair and pouring himself another mug. "Glad I could amuse you."

"Sorry, it's just . . . each morning I keep expecting to see the both of you glowing and yet . . . still . . ." Will said, taking a long pull from his mug.

"I wish Jesse'd shot you in the hip," I grumbled blackly. Will held up his hands in surrender, stifling another chuckle. The truth was, my sexual frustration wasn't the only thing bothering me. My predicament and my feelings for Jesse left me feeling confused and oddly upended today.

*I want you. I want to be by your side. No matter what.*

Jesse wanted me, wanted to be *with* me. But he'd never said he loved me. My mind went back to the longing I'd seen in Gabriela's eyes last night when she looked at The Kid. The wistful way she spoke of settling down and leaving this place for a quiet life and a family. Was that what it looked like when only one person was in love? I worried my bottom lip with my teeth. Will stayed quiet, recognizing the confliction clouding my eyes.

"Whatever you decide, songbird, I won't leave you again," he said after a long time. Too long. I shook my head and offered a strained smile. Before I could say anything, a door shut loudly down the hall, and a few moments later Jesse shuffled in on bare feet. Still wearing only his low-slung sleep pants. His near-nakedness in the daylight startled me awake. His eyes were half-lidded, mouth still swollen from sleep as he crossed the room and plucked my coffee mug out of my hands. Setting it on the counter, he pressed me back against the cabinets.

"Why didn't you wake me?" he asked. He didn't wait for an answer. Instead, he bent low and covered my mouth in a bruising kiss. He swallowed down a muffled sound of surprise until I was clinging to him to stay upright. Then he pulled back just long enough to look down at me expectantly.

"What was the question?" I asked, breathless. He smiled.

"Why didn't you wake me?"

"Oh, right. You looked tired," I said stupidly.

"Mornin', Montana," Will said, overly chipper. Jesse turned, a confused expression on his face. "Been here the whole time." I cleared my throat awkwardly, wondering where everyone else was this morning.

"I was thinking," I said as Will handed Jesse his own mug of coffee and eyed his bare chest when he wasn't looking. "Maybe Will could take Clara and The Kid on a tour of the compound today. At least for a while, to give Jesse a chance to talk to his uncle."

"Wait," Will said, holding up a finger. "You're *encouraging* me to spend time with Blondie now?" A lopsided grin tilted his mouth in a way that meant nothing but trouble. I groaned, running a weary hand down my face.

"I'm going to regret saying this, but . . . yes?" I said, looking to Jesse for confirmation. After all, he'd been the one opposed to Will flirting with Clara.

"Have at it, my friend," Jesse said, taking a long sip of his coffee. "Just don't give The Kid coffee or chocolate. You'll regret it. Trust me."

Will's expression turned serious as he regarded Jesse, just a flicker before his normal mischievous glint returned to his dark eyes. It'd caught on the word *friend*. I tangled my fingers with Jesse's and pulled his hand up to my mouth for a gentle kiss.

The rest of the morning was a flurry of action. Waking The Kid and getting him ready to go with Will and Clara, getting dressed and stealing peeks at Jesse across the room, watching as the tension returned to his shoulders at the prospect of getting answers to his past. Before we knew it, I pulled Selene from my saddle bag and tucked her into my waistband.

"Do you think you're going to need that?" Jesse asked, his tone curious.

"No, but waking up a drunk with a hangover could get interesting, and I'm not takin' chances," I said stiffly. We walked to the end of the hall, and Jesse pushed open the door to find the man snoring with his mouth wide open and one arm flung over his eyes to block out the dim sunlight filtering into the room. It smelled like sweat and vomit in here. Jesse kicked the mattress, his uncle slumping to the floor and waking with a start. He came up swinging, a pocket knife in hand. I ducked, and Jesse shoved him back hard enough for him to fall back onto his bed.

"W-who are you and what're you doin' in my house?!" he shouted, his words lazy with sleep or drink, I couldn't tell which.

"I'm your nephew," Jesse said, stoic. The man lumbered onto unsteady feet and wavered close to Jesse's face, narrowing bloodshot eyes. He grunted in acknowledgement before his eyes swung over to me. They widened briefly, and he took a step forward before Jesse placed himself between us. An incredulous sound caught in the back of Mickey's throat, and he pushed Jesse out of the way to half-stumble down the hall towards the kitchen, where he immediately found the bottle of golden liquid Gabriela had pulled out the night before.

"Look, mom sent us here—"

Mickey had no intention of listening to Jesse. He popped the cork on the bottle, and I found myself pulling it roughly out of his hands. He stared at me in disbelief before reaching for it again, but I stepped back until there was enough space between us that he was forced to acknowledge Jesse.

"She did, huh? Where is she, anyway? Her and that son of a bitch Jeff didn't have any problem abandoning me to this shithole when they left," he said, a bitter chuckle booming from his chest. I poured him a lukewarm mug of coffee and set it in front of him, probably with a little too much force, as some of it sloshed out the sides.

"Watch your mouth," Jesse said in a dangerous tone. "There was a fire." He checked over his shoulder that The Kid and the others were gone. "She and Pop didn't make it."

Mickey's face, full of spite, fell into unimaginable sorrow. The difference was subtle yet devastating. His eyes, as blue as Jesse's, filled with tears wavering on his lower lashes. Something about seeing a man who'd survived the end of the world crying had my heart in my throat.

"A fire?" he said, the words a choked whisper. Jesse nodded solemnly.

"That's why we're here," he said, clearing his throat and clenching his jaw. "The last thing she said was to find you. There were these men, maybe a gang, but not one we've seen before. They came to Montana and burned everything down—"

"I don't understand," Mickey said, his head in his hands. He raised his tear-stained eyes to Jesse. "How did they find her?"

"Who?" Jesse asked, sitting heavily at the table across from him. "Who was looking for her? *Why* would anyone be looking for them? They were small town farmers, for fuck's sake."

Mickey turned and fixed me with a pointed stare.

"We're gonna need somethin' stronger than coffee for this conversation, sweetheart," he said, and I begrudgingly handed him the bottle I'd taken earlier. He poured some of the alcohol into his coffee and handed the bottle to Jesse.

"Your parents were goddamn heroes, kid," he said before taking a long swallow that stilled his shaking hands. I crossed to Jesse, putting a hand on his shoulder to let him know I was here. He put his over mine and pulled me onto his lap. Mickey watched our interactions carefully, his eyes sharp now that he'd had something to drink.

"Tell me," Jesse said, his voice commanding.

"Well, your dad was an agricultural engineer. He knew how to put things together and take them apart, and he applied that knowledge to large scale . . . well, *farming*," he said, breathing a laugh. "But not like your family farm in Montana, I'm sure. He was trying to solve world hunger."

Jesse trembled, and I remembered the stories he'd told us on the journey here about his father. Fishing with him. Working on the car. Going to the market. I tangled my fingers with Jesse's, and he squeezed my hand. His father was exactly who he thought he was, and so much more.

"He met your mom at a United Nations meeting, world leaders from all over the world there to hear him speak about how to feed everyone on the planet. Your mom was in the government; I barely even knew what she did. It was mostly top-secret." Mickey paused, taking another long drag from his mug and running the pad of his thumb over his bottom lip.

"All I know is that she found out about the Culling right before the first bombs fell. She got messages to everyone she could. They came to the base at Roswell but left before it was destroyed. She told me she had to go into hiding, that she hid something dangerous and there would be people coming after her. I was the only one she told.

"I don't understand how they found her. I don't understand," he said, his voice cracking on the words. I ran my hand on the back of Jesse's neck where he was the tensest.

His mother had risked her life to save people during the Culling and his father tried to feed the hungry his entire life. No wonder Jesse turned out so wonderful, with parents like that. Mickey mopped at his face, and Selene was beginning to dig into my sore side. I shifted on Jesse's lap, and his worried eyes found mine.

"It's fine," I said softly, pulling Selene from my waistband and sighing in relief. Mickey's hand was around my wrist a moment later, yanking me to my feet as he stared at the gun in my hand.

"Where'd you get this gun?" he shouted. I shoved a hand against his chest, which was surprisingly solid for a drunkard. Jesse was on his feet, scrambling to find a weapon.

"None of your business, you drunk piece of shit," I spat. He pulled on my arm again, and my stitches pulled tight. Pain flared in my side and I yelped. Jesse's fist came down hard on Mickey's jaw.

"Don't you *ever* put your fucking hands on her," he said. Just as Mickey dropped my wrist, Jesse threw him bodily to the ground. His arm was around me from behind, shielding me from the man staring incredulously up at Jesse from the floor.

"You're a Kincaid, alright. Got the same right hook," he said, pushing onto his elbows as he stared at me behind Jesse's shoulder.

"You kill him?" he asked, wiping the back of his hand across his bloody mouth. I stared at him in confusion.

"What?" I asked, swallowing hard.

"Phillip Jones. Did you kill him? You had to if you have that gun. I was there when he bought that for Emma; he wouldn't let it go without a fight," he said. The world spun, and the ground tilted beneath me. I hadn't realized I'd gone weak in the knees until Jesse's arm steadied me on my feet.

*Phillip Jones.*

I never even knew he had another name. *Phillip.* It sounded too normal for the monster who'd broken me for sport. My stomach thrashed inside of me. *I was there when he bought that for Emma.*

"M-my mother's name was Emma," I said, my voice barely above a whisper. I found it hard to focus on anything in the room. Mickey pushed to his feet. Jesse tensed, pulling me farther away from Mickey as he crossed into the living room. He grabbed a box from the top of a bookshelf leaning in the corner of the room. He opened it and rifled through what sounded like papers until he pulled out a photograph, one of the corners creased, faded at the edges. He handed it to me, and a strangled sound came from my throat.

There in the middle were two young men. One was clearly Mickey, nearly identical to Jesse with his bright blue eyes and lopsided grin. His arm was slung over a tall, lanky boy with short, clean hair and dark eyes I knew well. He and Jones were friends, comrades.

Worse still was the dark-haired girl tucked in tight next to Jones, her blue eyes wild with laughter. *My mother.* I couldn't breathe. My chest was so tight it hurt. Jesse looked over my shoulder to the sandy-haired woman and curly-haired man next to Mickey in the picture. I trembled in his arms.

"Why is my mother hugging Jones?" I asked. Jesse's surprised eyes turned up to me. "Why do you have a picture of my mother?"

"Kid," Mickey said, his voice full of sorrow. "Emma is Phillip's baby sister. Jones is your uncle."

I didn't realize I'd moved. All I heard was buzzing in my ears. It wasn't until I'd slammed the door shut to the room I'd shared with Jesse and the lock clicked behind me that I allowed myself to breathe properly. At some point I'd fallen to my knees but, through reckless tears, I studied her face in the picture still clutched in my hand.

Wild. Vibrant. *Alive.*

*"Did you see the new True Grit movie? They remade it! As if anyone could be better than John Wayne," Jones said. I stilled, afraid to say anything. But I didn't know who John Wayne was, and I'd never heard of a movie before. He'd said so many strange things lately. I turned slowly, watching as realization crept into his dark eyes, edged with madness. He pulled a belt off the table, still laden with a holster and extra buckles, bringing it down across my shoulders. Again and again and again.*

He thought I was *her,* I realized. The thought sobered me enough that I curled into the messy bed sheets that smelled like Jesse and folded the picture until all I could see was my mom's wild smile in the darkness beside me.

## CHAPTER TWENTY-EIGHT

# JESSE

MICKEY'S WORDS HUNG HEAVY like smoke on the air. I watched as Bonnie left, the picture clutched between her fingers. The two seconds I hesitated to follow her proved to be my mistake. By the time I reached the door to our room, she'd already locked herself inside. I knocked quietly, my ear pressed against the wood.

"Bon?" I called.

Silence.

I couldn't imagine what she was going through. Finding out that she was related to a psychopath was probably the last thing she expected today. I knocked again, but still no answer. I pressed my hand to the rough wood.

"I'm here. When you need me," I said quietly.

I waited another five minutes before leaving her alone. I promised her that we would be together through everything. Some things you have to go through alone before you can let other people in. The least I could do was give her that. If I learned that the sadistic bastard who raised me was an actual relative, I wouldn't know how to handle it either.

By the time I returned to the kitchen, Mickey sat at the table, his coffee long forgotten. He drank directly from the bottle, pictures and other items from the box strewn across the table.

I had a lot of questions, but I didn't know where to start. I sat across from him, then grabbed the bottle and took a deep pull from it. The liquor burned.

"What is this?" I asked.

"Only the best tequila from the Borderlands," Mickey remarked with a grin, yanking the bottle back. He lit a cigarette before grabbing one of the photos and passing it to me. It was another picture of my mother and the woman Bonnie said was her own. My mom

287

had an arm around Bonnie's mom's shoulders. They were young, carefree. As though they had no idea that the world was going to end.

Bonnie had told me about what happened to her mother, what she'd witnessed. It was hard to imagine the beautiful woman in the picture next to my mom had met such a terrible end.

"How did you know them?" I asked.

"Phillip and I were in the same unit. These are from Thanksgiving a couple of years before the Culling," Mickey said, sliding more photographs across the table. One of Mickey and Pop arm wrestling, while Mom cut a piece of pie in the background. They seemed so happy.

"I knew Emma had a kid. I never knew what became of her."

I watched Mickey's eyes flash to the hallway. There was something more in that gaze than curiosity. It was almost guilt and sadness. I frowned, wondering what life was like for the people in the pictures and how things would be now had the Culling never happened. Would I have met Jones in that life?

"Do we need to be worried about Jones coming here?" I finally asked, looking back at my uncle.

"No," he said, lifting the bottle to his mouth.

"Are you sure?" The words came from between my clenched teeth. If I ever had the chance to meet Phillip Jones, it wouldn't end well for him. Not after what he'd done to Bonnie.

"I told him I'd kill him if he ever came back here," Mickey said. "That piece of shit does nothing but destroy the people around him."

From the things I knew about Jones, I would say Mickey's assessment was correct. My uncle gathered the pictures and papers, placing them back in the box. He passed one of them to me before closing the box and returning it. Mom and Pop were embracing, staring at one another. She was in a white dress, and he wore a fancy suit. I recognized the picture. Pop had a smaller one of it in his wallet, which probably burned down with the rest of the house.

"It still doesn't make sense to me," I said, flattening the photograph on the table. "You say people were after them, but who? And what was she hiding?"

"Jesse, I don't know," Mickey said, taking a long drag of his cigarette. He exhaled the smoke on a long, suffering sigh. "She only told me what I needed to know."

My mother had worked in the government. It was a challenge to reconcile the idea that she may have been in a position of power with the woman I knew. She'd always been soft-spoken, firm when she had to be, but kind. What could she have been hiding?

I thought back to the day we picked up Will, when I'd learned that his dad was responsible for the fires. I grabbed an old piece of newspaper from the stack of them on the counter and a pen. I sat back down at the table and began to draw the pointed flower I remembered from Sixgun's neck.

"What do you know about this symbol?" I asked, sliding the paper across the table.

Mickey regarded it for a while, silent. Then he passed it across the table toward me.

"Nothing," he said.

He was lying. I knew how to be a good liar, and Mickey wasn't one. I could tell by the way his eyes shifted to the right as he spoke. I grabbed the paper and smacked it down on the table in front of him.

"The men who came that night had this symbol branded into their necks," I said, my finger coming down on the drawing with a loud *thunk*. "One of Jones's men has it, too. They weren't there on Jones's orders, though. Whoever it was, they were after Mom and Pop."

"This is a fleur-de-lis. Way back in the day, it symbolized French royalty," Mickey said, shoving the paper back across the table. "The people with these markings are a ruthless gang. That's it. They've never come here, and that's all I care about."

I let out a low breath. My head ached from the tequila. My parents were heroes. According to Mickey, they'd saved people during the Culling, and Pop had tried to save people long before that. I knew my dad was smart, given the way he could take a car apart and put it back together. How he always knew the right time to plant and harvest, even when others told him he was doing it too soon.

"You knew about me," I said. "Gabriela said you mentioned me." I'd always known I was born shortly after the Culling.

"That's right. Jeff used to make jokes all the time. That his parents missed a prime opportunity to name him Jesse James, after the most famous outlaw in the west. He and Anna made a bet that if you were a boy, that's what they'd name you," Mickey said. "She lost."

"Why didn't they stay and help more people, though? It doesn't seem like them to give up," I said. My parents were devoted people. From what I'd seen, and what Mickey had told me so far, it didn't make sense that they'd abandon their cause. Mickey's red-rimmed eyes looked heavily into my own.

"Anna almost lost you," he said. "They came to me, thinking it would be safe in Roswell until they got more people out, but they were attacked on the way. Jeff didn't want her to take any more risks. They left in the dead of night in his shitty old car."

"You said she hid something. What is it? Where is it?" I asked.

"I don't know," Mickey said, running a hand over his face wearily. "You should go check on your girl. I'm sure she's much better entertainment than I am." He let out a choked laugh before taking another pull from the bottle.

He wasn't wrong. I stood, tucking the photo of my parents into my back pocket. I needed a break. Talking about them was hard for me. I couldn't imagine what Bonnie was going through. The door was still locked when I reached the room. I grabbed my knife and wiggled it between the door and the frame. Eventually, it popped and I pushed it open.

Bonnie curled up on the bed, fingers clutching the folded photograph. I kicked off my boots and climbed in behind her. I slid one arm around her waist, tucking her against my chest. I smoothed her hair down and pressed a gentle kiss beneath her ear. Some of the tension went out of her body at my touch. I smiled against her hair. Knowing that my presence could help her through something difficult meant almost more than moments like last night, when we were entwined together. She shifted, rolling to her other side and burying her face in my chest.

I enjoyed it, having her there against me. I'd never felt so comfortable with a woman before. Maybe it was because, like her, all of my secrets were stripped bare, and she didn't judge me for them. I inhaled her scent deeply, my eyes closing as the word *home* echoed through my mind.

After a while, she let out a breathy laugh, then tipped her head to look at me.

"If the Culling had never happened, we would have still met," she said. A lazy smile crept across my face. She was right. An image of our two families, sitting together around a gigantic table with a bird as the centerpiece passed through my mind. It was a beautiful idea, this world without the Culling. Where we could have grown up like our parents, lived in relative peace, and maybe had the chance at finding one another under happier circumstances.

None of it changed that, against all odds, we *had* met in this life. I was grateful for it.

I slipped the photo of my parents from my back pocket, smoothing it down before holding it out for Bonnie to see.

"They'd have loved you. Mom, especially. She tried to be friendly with Clara, but I could always tell she wanted something more for me, even if she never said it." I tightened my arm around her, letting silence engulf us for another long beat. "I'm sorry about Jones," I said into her hair. "But blood doesn't mean family."

If there was anything I had learned on this journey, it was that people you never could have imagined could become even more important than the people you were related to. I thought about our ragtag band of people. We were an interesting group for sure, but they were mine to protect. In some way, the things we'd gone through brought us together.

I thought back to last night, when Bonnie had claimed The Kid as ours to Gabriela. I hadn't been able to express how much it meant to me to know that she loved my brother. Just like she loved me, though neither of us said it.

A loud crash sounded from down the hall. Moments later, The Kid came banging into the room.

"They're sleepin'!" he called out behind him.

"We're not," Bonnie said, lifting her head to look at him.

"Never mind!" The Kid said. I rolled onto my back to look at him, standing in the doorway.

"Did you need something?" I asked.

"Will said he was tired of walking around," he said.

Well, I guess it was time to get back to some semblance of normalcy. I still had questions for Mickey, but I had a feeling they were things he couldn't answer. We shuffled out of the room. I tucked the photo of my parents into my pack before following Bonnie. Mickey still sat at the table, staring between Clara, Will, and The Kid.

"Who's the kid?" he asked. I crossed to the cabinet to see if he had any food.

"That's Harry, my younger brother," I said, turning to glance at Mickey. "But don't call him that. He goes by The Kid. He's an outlaw, and he'll set you straight if you call him anything else." My brother gave a curt nod, sitting at the table beside Mickey.

"You don't look like my mom," The Kid said, wrinkling his nose, probably at the smell emanating from Mickey.

"Well, your mom got all the looks in the family," Mickey said. I gave brief introductions of Will and Clara before abandoning my hunt for food. With the meager rations we'd been living on, I was ready for a good meal. The Kid mentioned a place they'd seen up the road, so we set off.

For the first time, the urgency faded. We had no plan. I'd expected that when we found my uncle, he would know what to do with us, but I could see how hopeless he was. He didn't have a plan for his own life. How could he have one for ours?

I glanced over at Bonnie as we ate hot bacon sandwiches, wondering where her head was at.

"How's your bacon?" I asked, flashing a grin at her. Bonnie narrowed her eyes playfully and took another large bite of the sandwich instead of responding.

Here we were, on the verge of the unknown, and yet neither of us broached the subject of the end. She tangled her fingers with mine beneath the table, and I smiled at her. The Kid chattered on about all of the stuff they'd seen while exploring the base.

"I watched this guy clean his rifle. Will says he was really slow," The Kid said, looking at Will with admiration in his eyes. He turned to Bonnie then. "Will you show me how to clean a gun?"

"Sure, Kid," she said, her eyes shimmering in his direction as she took a sip of her drink.

The interactions between them had initially scared me. Back in Vegas, when The Kid looked up to her, I was wary of her motivations. But now, sitting at Fort Hood, in some semblance of safety, my heart beat a little more quickly in my chest at the care she showed him.

I couldn't let her go. I hoped she couldn't let us go, either.

After we finished lunch, we headed back to Mickey's house. Gabriela was there, trying to get him to sober up. She showed us to the backyard, where a small range was set up for target practice and a table for playing cards.

"Wanna see how a real outlaw does it?" Will asked my brother.

Bonnie sat at the table, the M9 disassembled in front of her. I stood back, happy to watch for a while.

"Rule number eight, Kid: know your weapons. If it's supposed to keep you alive, you should know it inside and out," she said, folding a bandana. Then she tied it around her head. Once it was secure, Will waved a hand in front of Bonnie's face. Her hands fell to her sides.

"How long do you think it'll take her, Montana? A minute? Two? I'll bet you a pack of fresh rolled cigarettes she can do it in less than a minute," Will said, smirking in my direction.

"You shouldn't be allowed to bet," I said to him. "You have an unfair advantage." I lifted my eyebrows in challenge at him.

"I'll take that bet, then," Clara said, moving to stand next to me. "I say it takes her a minute and a half."

"What're the stakes?" Will asked, lifting his eyebrows suggestively at her.

"Whatever you want," Clara said with a wink. I ran a hand over my face.

"You might regret that," Bonnie said.

"God. Stop flirting. Let's start!" The Kid said, bouncing on the balls of his feet. Will handed him his watch.

"Ready? Three, two, one—" Will let out a loud whistle.

Bonnie began assembling the M9, her fingers moving faster than I could keep up. The pieces slid into place expertly, one after another, until she slammed the clip in.

"Thirty seconds!" my brother said, letting out a loud whoop.

The display set the mood for a happy afternoon. I watched as Bonnie showed her skill with knives. With each flick of her wrist, a knife slammed into the bull's-eye of her intended target. Mostly, I watched her with The Kid. How she was always patient with him, making sure that he understood not only how to do it, but why it was important to do it safely.

Will and Clara were off to one side. He was teaching her to shoot. At least, I thought that was what he was doing with his hands all over her hips.

For the first time in weeks, I sat back and watched. I wasn't worried about dangers that could jump out at any moment, or gun-toting madmen. I wasn't worried about the fire that had changed our lives forever.

*This* could be a good life.

Bonnie caught me watching her from time to time, a smile finding its way to her face. She was totally in her element. While I wanted to imagine that this could be our lives, I also knew that she'd never settled before.

Was this any different? Was this sliver of peace enough to tempt her to stay?

As though she could sense my trepidation, Bonnie crossed to me, planting herself in my lap as I sat in a chair at the table. The Kid tossed knives, missing even the closest target. I rested one of my arms over her legs, tipping my head up to press a kiss to her mouth.

"You okay?" she asked, her arms hanging loosely around my neck.

"Yeah," I said, glancing between Will and Clara and my brother. "Wanna get out of here?" I gave her a lopsided grin. We could sneak out and they'd never know it. Bonnie climbed out of my lap.

"Where are we goin'?" she asked.

"To find some trouble," I said, winking at her. A grin lit up her beautiful face. I took her by the hand and led her back into the house. She clutched my arm as we walked toward the front. I pulled the truck keys from my pocket, swinging them on my index finger as we made our way into the kitchen.

Then I stopped short. Mickey sat at the table, Gabriela beside him. He slumped forward, fresh tears on his cheeks. Gabriela gave us a forced smile. Then Mickey noticed us, his eyes showing me how lost he was to the drink.

"I never knew she had another kid," Mickey said, seemingly losing himself to another sob.

"You wouldn't have," Bonnie said beside me. "There was no way for her to tell you." Mickey looked up at her, eyes rimmed in red.

"You're sure they're dead?" he asked, the words hard as though he didn't want to believe what we'd already told him.

"I buried them myself," I said, tension building in my shoulders once more.

"Buried who?" came a small voice from behind me.

*Fuck.*

I closed my eyes as I dropped Bonnie's hand and turned to my brother, who clutched the entryway to the kitchen.

"No one—" I lied.

"Liar. Who'd you bury? Was it the guys that attacked us?" he asked, in that way only an innocent kid could.

"Kid, I—" The words caught in my throat. An image of my parents' bodies, clutched together as the smoke rose above them, came to my mind. Up until now, I'd avoided having this conversation to shield him from the truth. I didn't want him to have nightmares like I did. I knew I'd have to tell him one day. I'd just hoped it wouldn't be any time soon.

I crossed to him, squatting down to his level. I put a hand on his shoulder. "Mom and Pop. They—"

"No, they're comin'. They'll be here," he said, shaking me off. "They'll find us. Mom promised."

My grief was a living thing, clawing its way up my throat.

"Harry—" I said, reaching for him again. He took a broad step back, eyes wide.

"You haven't called me Harry in a long time," he said.

"Kid," I corrected, trying to reach for him again. I knew that I needed to talk *to* him and not *at* him. Bonnie had taught me that. "They're not coming. They didn't make it."

"You're wrong," Harry said, his chest puffing out at me.

"Kid, I buried them. When I made you wait by the trees outside the house," I said. It hit him then. He took another step backward, right into the wall. I'd left him alone a long time that day, and he hadn't understood it then. His eyes grew wide, filling with tears.

He understood now.

"That's how you got Pop's ring," he whispered. My heart wrenched in my chest, and my knees crashed to the floor. I didn't know what to say to him. I didn't know how to help him through grief I hadn't even fully processed myself.

"Kid—" His name came out from between my lips, strangled.

"No!" He darted down the hall. Seconds later, the door to his room slammed. I hung my head, defeated. I'd betrayed him. I didn't know if it was something we would ever come back from.

Bonnie put her hands on my shoulders. I reached up to cover one of hers with my own, comforted by her touch. But I wasn't the one who needed her now. I stood, slowly, my own eyes hot.

"Go to him, please," I said, the emotions in my throat choking my words off. Without a sound, Bonnie nodded and pressed a gentle kiss to my lips. She squeezed my hands, then headed down the hall.

I turned back to the table, stealing Mickey's bottle of tequila. Then I walked out to sit in one of the rocking chairs on the front porch. I needed a minute. That was all.

## CHAPTER TWENTY-NINE

# BONNIE

I PRESSED MY FOREHEAD against The Kid's bedroom door and listened to his frantic sobbing for a long time. It was this part that I remembered the most, the chaos of grief as it crashed into you so hard that all you could do was sob as it swept you away. Only Jones didn't like it when I cried. He beat the tears dry, until they filled me up with a kind of poison that'd turned me bitter. So I let The Kid cry. When his sobbing ebbed, I knocked tentatively.

"Go away, Jesse!" he shouted, and something slammed against the door, shaking it in the frame.

"It's not Jesse," I said, my voice quiet and calm. He didn't say anything, but he didn't throw anything either. "Can I come in?" When he didn't answer, I cracked the door open and peered inside. He was curled around his pillow, face buried, shoulders still shaking. Instead of trying to talk him through his grief, I climbed into the bed beside him, the way Jesse had done for me earlier. I wrapped him in my arms. My fingers brushed through his hair until his tears started afresh. He turned swiftly and flung himself against me. I clutched him tight, wishing more than anything I could take this pain away from him.

It could have been hours, but I didn't move. I let him lean on my strength the way I'd leaned on Jesse's when I needed to fall apart. I pressed a kiss into his hair, and he raised his bloodshot eyes to look at me, sniffling.

"Bonnie?" he asked. "They can't just be *gone*."

Something sharp twisted in my chest at his broken words. I wiped the salt tracks from his cheeks and helped him sit up next to me. I blinked back the heat gathering in my own eyes and breathed slowly and deeply. The Kid mimicked me without realizing it until he looked steadier.

"They aren't gone, Kid," I told him. He gripped my hands tight. "You remember that day by the lake?" He nodded, his unruly blonde curls flopping into his eyes. I pushed them back. "You saw Jesse smile and you said he looked just like your pop."

"That doesn't count," he said, sniffling and dragging the sleeve of his shirt over his face.

"Yes, it does," I said, leaning forward. "I don't know what your parents believed, but I don't think the people we love are ever really gone. Just like you saw a shadow of your dad in Jesse that day, I'm sure Jesse sees a lot of your parents in you."

"What about your mom?" he asked. "Do you see her?"

"Every single time I look at you," I said, my eyes hot. His unwavering kindness and the burning curiosity in his eyes reminded me so much of my mother's goodness. Her unconditional love.

"She would have *loved* you," I said. He leaned back against the headboard. "Sometimes I think my mom and your parents brought us together because they knew we needed each other," I muttered. He nodded solemnly, as if that made perfect sense.

"You remind me of my mom sometimes, mostly when you're yelling at Jesse," he said, and a small smile curled on his mouth. "He *lied* to me." I nodded, my eyes falling to the quilt, tracing the pattern beneath my fingertip.

"He did," I admitted. "But what's rule number three?"

"Keep your word," he said, grumbling as he crossed his arms over his chest.

"Outlaws may steal, *lie*, or cheat. But always keep our promises," I finished. He swallowed down his tears. "Jesse made a promise to your parents, Kid. He promised to get you *here*. To keep you safe. He lied to you, but he kept his promise. You have to forgive him, okay?"

He hugged me again, for a long time, before nodding into my shirt.

"Promise you won't leave us, Bonnie," he said, the words small against my chest. I squeezed my eyes shut and clenched my jaw tight to keep from letting the hot tears fall from my eyes. I couldn't make that promise. I *couldn't*. Because I loved him, both of them, too much to put them at risk.

"I don't wanna lose you, too," he said. I kissed the top of his head and rocked him against me for a while, struggling for words.

"I'm not a sweater you flung off at bedtime, Kid. You can't lose me," I said, forcing a playful tone into my voice and struggling to regain my composure. He pulled away then, offering me a sad smile. It was a smile, nonetheless.

"I'm glad we found you," The Kid said, his voice uncharacteristically solemn. I opened my mouth but couldn't find any words.

*Found*. I'd been found.

Instead, I offered him a sad smile. From the corner of my eye, I noticed Jesse leaning against the doorframe and wondered briefly how much he'd overheard. I cuffed The Kid on the chin with a breathy laugh.

"Alright, handsome, stop charmin' me and go make up with your brother."

The Kid pushed off the bed and walked over to Jesse warily, eyeing him with his arms crossed over his chest. He squared off against Jesse, staring him down.

"I'll forgive you," The Kid said, his face a serious mask. "On *one* condition."

My mouth dropped open in shock. He was *extorting* Jesse emotionally. Maybe I had been a bad influence on him after all.

"Can I keep the horse we got from the wagon? Can I name her and everything?" The Kid asked, looking between me and Jesse quickly. "I want to be able to ride with y'all when we go on our next adventure."

Not if, *when*.

"Sure, Kid," Jesse said, crushing him tight to his chest. Until The Kid complained that Jesse was hugging him too long and squirmed away, shouting to Will that he needed help naming his horse. I shook my head, incredulous. His resilience astounded me. I unfolded from my position on the mattress and pushed to my feet, feeling shaken.

"That kid is gonna be all kinds of trouble in a few years," I said, smiling as I crossed the room to Jesse. I started to walk into the hallway, but Jesse stopped me, pressing me gently against the other side of the doorframe, keeping me trapped in the steel cage of his arms.

"Gonna be? He already is," he said. "It's your fault."

"Good," I said, proudly. "Every time he gives you hell, you'll think of me."

Jesse's eyes dimmed, turning dark at my words. I swallowed down the *many* things that'd been running through my mind for the last few days. He opened his mouth to say something, but Will's voice echoed down the hall, the back door slamming open and shut again. Jesse's attention was diverted for a second. I bit my bottom lip to keep the doubts sealed inside of me. When he turned his attention back to me, something in his demeanor had changed.

"Want to go for a drive?" he asked. I didn't. Not if it meant having the conversation we'd both been avoiding. Not if it meant leaving them. Instead of saying that, I nodded.

Gripping my hand, he led me down the hallway and out one of the side doors to the front yard. It was still littered with bottles and debris. He crossed to the truck and opened the door for me. My mind whirred, thoughts forming and shattering in the span of seconds as I slid onto the seat. He climbed in beside me, and as he turned the engine over, my heart leapt into my throat.

"I know what you want to talk about and—"

He leaned over and kissed me swiftly, silencing me as he shifted gears and backed out of the drive. We drove forward a second later, earning stares from everyone we passed. I pushed my hair behind my ear nervously, biting my thumbnail to the quick. *How was I supposed to say what I needed to say if he kept kissing me?*

He reached over, his hand covering mine. I pulled away. The lines around his eyes deepened, and he dragged his hand back, balled into a fist on his knee. I couldn't think when he touched me, and I needed to *think*. The truck pulled through the gate a minute later, and my heart was in my throat.

"Bonnie, I—"

"Let me talk," I said, my breath heaving in my chest. "If I don't say it now, I might not say it at all, and I *have to*."

Jesse slung his arm across the back of the seat and turned the wheel to park us just outside of the gate before turning his full attention to me. My pulse pounded in my ears, his eyes trained on me expectantly. He didn't rush me; he just waited until I was ready.

"Okay," I said, tucking my hair behind my ears. "I'm not *good* with words, so bear with me." Now I was stalling. The words strangled me; they were harder to say than I expected. "You've been saying a lot of things lately. You've said that you *wanted* me." He opened his mouth as if to add something, but I gave him a desperate look, and he ran a shaking hand through his hair. "You've said that we would figure things out *together*. You've said that you want to stay by my side."

Why was this so hard?

"Those are all really *nice* things to say. Things most women would kill to hear," I told him, swallowing down my painful awkwardness. "But the thing is, I learned early on in life not to depend on anyone. Because they would just hurt you, or leave you, or die." His eyes blazed in the fading light, something anguished in the depths of them. "Until *you*.

"You make me *want* things I'd given up on. And it's killing me, because I can't have them. You make me feel safe, and I'd forgotten what that even meant. Goddamnit, Jesse, you make me feel *free*.

"When you touch me—"

His hands were on my face, his thumb brushing the line of my jaw. A shiver raced down my spine, and my world narrowed to the contact of his skin on mine.

"When you touch me, the rest of the world fades to smoke. Until you're the only thing that's left, the *only* thing that's real. And if you ask me to stay—"

"Stay," he said, his voice the deep canyon timbre that unraveled me at the seams.

"It's not that simple—"

"Bonnie, you *have* to stay," he said, his forehead pressing hard into mine.

"Jones and Sixgun are comin' for me, and if *anything* happened to you or The Kid, I would—"

"I love you," he said, with the same conviction with which he said everything. I gasped, breathing in his warm leather and desert dust scent, tasting him on my tongue. "Damnit, Bonnie, *I'm in love with you*."

"You love me?" I asked, the words clumsy on my lips. He smiled at me, and the last of my resistance shattered as my arms curled around him. A wild smile spread across my mouth as I blinked back the heat gathering in my eyes. The tension had been building since we met all that time ago in Vegas, gathering like storm clouds over the open desert.

"I love you so much it hurts," I breathed against his mouth.

Then, the storm broke.

We crashed together, my mouth opening with a cry beneath his. He hauled me into his arms, settling me on his lap as we hurtled out of control. His wicked hands roamed over my curves without hesitation. Time slipped away from me, contorting the way it always did when Jesse and I were locked together like this. We could have drowned in each other. Heat crackled like lightning across my skin. His hands were beneath my shirt, cupping my breasts as I moaned into his mouth.

A loud wolf whistle split the air, male voices making lewd comments from the top of the gate. I pulled away from Jesse breathlessly; his eyes were so bright. An unapologetic grin slipped over his lips and his thumb teased my nipple before he slid his hands out from beneath my shirt. I kissed his wicked mouth again, lingering for a moment before I pushed off of his lap and settled beside him.

"We should probably drive a little farther from the gate," he said, clearing his throat and adjusting the front of his pants as he turned the engine over. The truck lurched forward as he pushed the gas pedal down hard. I was in his arms, my hands running over his chest, my lips tasting the skin beneath his ear, teeth tugging on his earlobe.

"How fast do you think this truck can go?" I asked, breath hot in his ear. His hand slid down to cover my ass, grabbing hard as a groan was wrenched from him.

"I miss those shorts," he said, his voice a rumble that shook me through to my toes.

"I thought you hated my shorts," I said, my hand slipping up his thigh as he pressed the gas pedal all the way to the floor.

"I hated not being able to peel you out of them," he said, switching gears as the truck flew over the crumbling asphalt. The sunset was a violent riot of color as we hurtled towards the horizon. It felt like I was flying. Jesse's hot mouth ran along my throat before turning back to the road.

A loud pop followed by a metal grinding sound echoed around us as the truck rapidly lost speed, black billows of smoke rising from beneath the hood. Jesse swore, turning the wheel until the truck finally rolled to a stop in a field of tiny yellow flowers. I tried to stifle the sound, but the laugh escaped anyway. Jesse turned incredulous eyes on me, but it only made me laugh harder. I bit my lip to keep the smile from spreading too widely across my face, and his eyes dropped to my mouth.

"You have no idea how bad I wanna bite that lip," he said. Suddenly I wasn't laughing anymore. My pulse pounded in my ears, and just like before, we folded against each other as if we'd rehearsed this a thousand times. His mouth was hard on mine, his hands firm as he lifted me onto his lap again. I fumbled with the buttons on his shirt, and he broke away, chest heaving beneath my hands. He opened his mouth to protest, but I kissed him again, hips rocking against his until I forced a choked groan from his mouth.

"If you say *we can't* or *we shouldn't* one more time, I swear I'm gonna—"

"I don't want to hurt you." He forced the breathless words against my mouth, his hand cradling my face. I finished with the buttons and slid the shirt over his shoulders.

"Idiot," I said, pulling back to tug my shirt over my head and tossing it to the floorboards. "You would never hurt me."

His blue eyes roamed my pale skin without restriction, lingering in places I didn't expect. Like the scar on my arm and the pulse thumping erratically in my neck. His fingertips brushed against my flesh, the touch so soft it raised goosebumps in its wake. They traced the jagged pattern of scars crisscrossing over my ribs reverently.

"Tell me," he said softly. I swallowed down my self-consciousness as his eyes mapped the area adoringly.

"Belt buckle. For stabbing a mark that got too close," I said between ragged breaths. He dipped his head down and kissed the scars. His fingers traced up my spine to the back of my left shoulder where his deft fingers found a round scar, raised and pink.

"Here?" he asked, without judgment or reprisal.

"Cigar. Just because," I choked out as he kissed the ugliness away.

When he reached the scar on my arm, I stilled, heart thundering. His fingers mapped the gnarled skin followed by the gentle brush of his lips.

I felt that kiss in every part of me.

"You're beautiful," he said, and I believed him.

"Make love to me," I begged. My fingers buried in his hair, raising those blazing blue eyes back to mine. I kissed him slowly as his hands unclipped my bra and pulled the straps from my shoulders. He wrapped a strong arm around my waist before shifting us together, pressing my back against the hot leather seat.

He raised his head to look at me, lost in desire beneath him, and pulled gently on my pants and underwear until I was naked below him. His eyes shifted to the bandage on my hip, but only for a moment. He leaned down and trailed his mouth down my neck. The contrast of his soft lips and the rasp of the stubble on his cheeks was a dizzying sensation. He sucked my nipple into his mouth until he tore a cry from my lips. Then he moved down the midline of my body, his tongue tasting my skin. My back arched to guide him lower, between my thighs, as I tucked my fingers firmly in his hair.

"You have no idea how badly I've wanted to taste you," he said, staring directly between my legs and inhaling deeply. "I want to drown in you." He nipped the inside of my thigh.

He stared up at me then, a smile curled onto that wicked mouth. His arms wrapped around my thighs and Jesse buried his face against me with a groan. My nails scraped against his scalp, and I moaned his name, begging for more, for everything. He devoured me like a starving man. His tongue paid special attention to the spot that forced a scream from my throat. Slick heat settled into my blood and grew hotter with every rapid beat of my heart.

"*Please,*" I begged him. "*Please.*"

I threw my head back, eyes closed in rapture, as my pleasure began to crest.

"No, you don't," he said, and the words rumbled against my flesh. "I want to watch you."

A moment later he raised his head, eyes dark with a hunger that threatened to consume me whole. He undid the front of his jeans, pushing them down hurriedly before settling the hard length of his cock *exactly* where I wanted him. I arched my hips impatiently, but he stretched his body long over mine, settling his weight on top of me. Our hot breaths mingled as he pressed forward slowly enough to draw out my pleasure. All while he watched my every expression. I gasped as the sweet friction took hold of me, hooking my legs around his waist until he was buried all the way to the hilt.

We paused, bodies tensed, *finally* joined together. I wanted *more*. I wanted to be closer, wanted him *deeper*. Wanted this to last forever. Until I couldn't tell where I began and he ended.

My nails scraped down his back, and he shifted his hips, building a steady rhythm. We fit together seamlessly, our bodies working in perfect synchronicity. I was *made* for this man. The slick heat in my blood flared into brilliant light as he guided us toward the precipice of a pleasure I'd never known before. I screamed his name, and he whispered mine against my hair, my impatient body arching to meet his. Hearts thundering, we writhed together as his control broke and he set a pounding cadence. Until I couldn't hold on any longer, until the heat threatened to consume me, then I was falling, faster and faster, and my mind shattered. With a harsh last push, he cried out into my mouth, and we both fell into a heap of sweat-slickened flesh. I trembled in his arms, and he pressed short kisses to my feverish skin, worried eyes finding mine.

His hands were on my face, thumbs brushing wetness from my cheeks.

"Are you alright? Did I hurt you?" he asked through heaving breaths. I shook my head, pressing a mindless kiss to his open mouth. "Then why are you crying?"

"I didn't realize it was possible to be this happy," I managed to say, and he kissed me for a long time. Until I was breathless again for another reason entirely.

"Let's see what I can do about making you that happy again," he said, his wicked grin curling onto his lips.

And he did.

Many times.

## CHAPTER THIRTY

# JESSE

THE SKY WAS PAINTED in dark oranges and reds when I stirred awake. A chill in the air made me tug up the blankets to cover myself and Bonnie. At some point during the night, we'd moved from the cab of the truck to the bed of it. I was glad we still had the bedrolls.

Bonnie folded against me, her back flush against my chest. I curled around her, hoping that our shared body warmth would shake the chill. She stirred long enough to arch her back and then went still once more.

I couldn't have gotten more than a couple hours of sleep. I'd give up sleep altogether if it meant I had more nights of *that*. Of worshipping Bonnie's body to the brink and over it again and again.

I'd been with women before, but it had never felt like *that*. I'd never felt so seen by a person, so loved. Ever since Vegas, I'd wanted her body; there was no denying it. I hadn't realized how much I'd wanted her heart.

Now that I had it, I was never letting it go.

One of my hands trailed lazily across the plane of her stomach and up her side. My touch was gentle. I didn't want to wake her up. Yet.

My deft fingers slid up to her neck, then across her shoulder and down her arm. I entwined my fingers with hers, inhaling the scent of rain and salt on her skin. I hadn't had nearly enough time to worship her body. With the sun rising, I knew that we'd eventually have to return to the base, but I wasn't ready yet. I wanted to keep her to myself a while longer.

I let go of her hand, my fingers finding their way across her thigh and around to her ass. I smiled into her hair, drawing lazy circles along the curve of it. My lips found the soft spot beneath her ear. I kissed her gently enough that it would start waking her up. Then my hand moved to the apex of her thighs, my fingers exploring her already slick core.

Bonnie took in a sharp, sleepy breath. I smiled against her shoulder, watching as her eyes fluttered open. She leaned back into me, suddenly remembering I was there. A lazy smile found its way to her lips. She opened her mouth to say something, but I didn't let her. I covered her mouth with my own, my hand still working slowly between her legs. She rolled to her back, giving me better access, and her hands found purchase in my hair.

I picked up my pace, enjoying how her hips bucked against my hand. I smiled, pulling back to trail kisses along her jawline. She took in a sharp breath and whispered my name into the silent morning. I flicked my tongue across her skin until I reached her breasts. My teeth paid gentle attention to her nipple until it stiffened into a peak. A moan slipped from between her lips, sending goosebumps prickling along my flesh.

I could do this all day.

In the past, with women the goal was to get mine. With Bonnie, it was different. Sure, it was nice, but it wasn't necessary. There was something about how intimate this felt that gave me the satisfaction I needed.

Bonnie's breaths came in short gasps, her hips bucked against me. She pulled my head away from her breasts and pressed a hot kiss to my lips. Her skin was moist with sweat. I could tell by the look in her eyes what she wanted. I'd have more time to play later.

I moved back behind her, my hand reaching for her thigh and lifting it to give me the access I wanted. I pressed kisses to her shoulder blade as I pushed into her. Her wet heat enveloped me, consuming my body as she'd consumed my heart. She was more than I could have ever wanted. No one could ever compare to Bonnie. Her hand fisted my hair again, locking me against her. The first few times last night were rushed. I wanted to take my time, wanted to enjoy the soft curves of her body, how she met my enthusiasm with equal fervor.

She was fire. She was chaos. But she was *mine*.

Bonnie reached back, her nails digging into my thigh as I quickened my pace. It would leave a mark, but I didn't care. I kissed her neck, grazing my teeth along the sensitive skin there. She grabbed my head and pulled me to kiss her, slowing my movements. We parted for just a moment, and then Bonnie turned toward me, shifting her weight on top of me. Within seconds, the tables turned, and she straddled me.

She sat straight up, her hips setting a rapid pace. Her entire body was on display, her hair waving in a gentle morning breeze. I reached up, teasing her breasts as she ground herself against me, the friction bringing us higher and higher. The sunrise peeked over her shoulder, painting the sky in an explosion of golds and oranges.

Before long, we were making noise loud enough to wake up the entirety of Fort Hood.

I reached a hand between her legs to the sweet spot there, and she cried out, her thighs clenching against me as her pleasure crested. I watched, a contented smile on my face as she slowed to a near stop.

Then, taking her into my arms, I rolled her over, her back pressed into our bedding. I kissed her long and slow, pulling almost all of the way out before slamming back into her. She whimpered against my mouth. That familiar pressure built low in my belly. I broke my lips from hers, biting down on her shoulder harder than I intended. My release took me, stars bursting in my vision. Chest heaving, I slowed to a stop, my entire weight fitting perfectly against her.

When my breathing evened, I pulled back long enough to lay beside her in the bed of the truck. I kissed her again, brushing her unruly hair out of her face.

"Good morning," I said, the first words I'd spoken since last night. Bonnie brought a hand up to my cheek.

"You bit me," she said, the corners of her mouth turning upward. I grinned and kissed her lips.

"Yeah, sorry about that," I murmured against her mouth. When I pulled back, a brilliant smile crossed her face.

"Why? I liked it."

I barked out a laugh. "I'll remember that," I said, kissing the soft spot beneath her ear. Bonnie raised her eyebrows at me.

"I bite back," she said, her eyes glimmering at me.

"Good," I remarked.

I wanted every morning to wake up next to her like this. I wanted to drink coffee and have breakfast with her and The Kid. I wanted to be with her, wherever that may be. If she wanted to travel the world, we'd go.

"They're probably worried about us," I said, unable to hide the smile on my lips. I knew we would have to go back soon, but not yet. Bonnie stretched, her breasts pressed against my chest. I ran a hand down her back to her ass, giving it a gentle squeeze. She settled into the blankets and closed her eyes.

"Probably," she said.

This could be dangerous, I realized. Because I didn't want to get up, and I could tell Bonnie didn't either. I chuckled.

"We should figure out what's next," I said. Bonnie's blue eyes blinked open. "You know, if we wanna stay here, or go somewhere else."

"Well, I just wanna stay here," she said, snuggling further into my neck. I brushed a kiss against her jaw.

"You know what I mean," I said. "Fort Hood . . . or somewhere else."

There were a lot of things up in the air right now. I'd thought that when we met my uncle, he would be able to give me a new goal. Now that we'd made it, I wasn't sure what my purpose was. I'd never planned on him *not* knowing what to do. Instead, all Mickey wanted was to drink his sorrows away.

"We could make a life here," I said, my eyes glazed over as I thought back to yesterday afternoon, with everyone hanging out in Mickey's backyard.

"You want to make a life with me?" Bonnie asked, trepidation and excitement warring in her eyes.

"Mickey said Jones wouldn't come here, if that matters. He said he'd kill Jones if he tried." I hoped that would at least give her some measure of comfort. I also knew that she'd never settled in one place. "Or . . . that city—"

"Jesse," she said. "Shut up." She smiled before kissing me. "I don't care. Not as long as I'm with you."

Maybe in some ways, I'd become her home like she'd become mine.

"God, I love you," I whispered, wrapping my arms around her. I kissed her again, unable to stop my cock from hardening already. "But if we don't get up, we'll never make it back." Bonnie groaned, burying her face in the crook of my neck. She hooked a leg over mine.

"Not yet," she said, kissing my neck. Her fingertips played with the hair on my chest. It would be all too easy to fall into her, but we had to get back.

Begrudgingly, I disentangled myself from Bonnie. She staged a silent protest while I gathered our scattered clothes and dressed myself. I tried to start the truck, but it wouldn't even turn over. When I lifted the hood, the char marks on the engine told me everything I needed to know. Bonnie joined me, slipping on her shirt as she looked beneath the hood.

"What is it?" she asked.

"It's done," I said. "We'll have to walk." I took her hand in mine, and we headed off. The sun was getting high by the time we reached the gates. A couple of cheers sounded from the guards, but we ignored them. Instead, Bonnie and I shared a smile and kept walking. We ran into Gabriela as we approached Mickey's house.

"Hi, I brought breakfast," she said, slinging her gun over her shoulder. "Bonnie, I wanted to talk with you. Do you have a minute?"

Bonnie glanced at me and shrugged, releasing my hand. I kissed her quickly, then watched as she walked away with Gabriela. She, at least, seemed like a good person. She had to be in order to put up with Mickey.

Loud talking filtered out of the screen door before I made it into the house. I paused, smiling to myself. Bonnie hadn't said no when I'd told her we could make a life here. When I entered the kitchen, all conversation suddenly stopped. Will, Clara, Mickey, and The Kid stared at me.

"Where's Bonnie?" The Kid asked. I shook my head and ruffled his hair as I walked past him to see what was for breakfast.

"Talking with Gabriela," I said, filling up a plate with freshly made biscuits, bacon, and eggs. I turned back to the table. Everyone still stared at me. "What?"

"Good for you, Montana. Maybe now you won't have so many *violent* tendencies. I always thought all you needed was a good fu—"

Clara punched Will in the shoulder, motioning toward my brother with her head.

"Where were y'all?" The Kid asked. I stuffed my mouth full of eggs to give myself time to come up with an appropriate excuse.

"We went for a drive," I said after swallowing my food. "Truck broke down."

"And it took all night to fix it?" he asked, narrowing his eyes at me.

"Eat your breakfast, Kid," I said. He grinned in response.

"Mickey was telling us about the operations around here," Clara said. I appreciated her attempt to get the conversation going again. Mickey picked right back up. I ignored him and dug into my breakfast, eating until my belly was overfull, because we'd missed dinner last night.

I finished eating and, since Bonnie wasn't back yet, decided to take a shower. The hot water was a nice change from bathing in streams and lakes. My mind ran back to our night together under the stars, remembering all of Bonnie's little quirks, like when she bit her bottom lip. That *damn* lip.

A hand touched my back as the water ran down my skin. When I turned, Bonnie slid her arms around my waist, pressing her head into my chest. Pleasantly surprised, I wrapped my arms around her naked body. She pulled back a moment later, a mixture of mischief and want written in her eyes. I didn't believe she could ever stop surprising me. That just her very presence could set my soul ablaze. When I lifted one of her legs around my waist and kissed her, she whispered those words against my lips.

*I love you.*

The water washed over us like rain after a drought, cleaning away the dust and bringing in life anew.

We didn't have plans. It was nice, for once. We could enjoy each other instead of having to worry about danger lurking around the next corner. Once we were out of the shower, Bonnie talked about her conversation with Gabriela. I shaved the stubble from my chin, listening as she explained that Gabriela wanted to recruit us. I wasn't sure how to feel about that. I didn't want to end up like Mickey, but it would be nice to have a place to put down roots again.

"I mean, with extra defenses, we could make Fort Hood like St. Louis," Bonnie said, her voice animated with passion. She slipped on those shorts I loved so much. I appreciated the curve of her ass. "It could be a safe haven. Families could come here. We could reopen the school. Maybe set up a trading post. A market day." She realized I was staring at her and snapped her mouth shut. "What?"

"I love it," I said. I tugged her against me by the belt loops on her shorts. I'd never seen her so excited about anything. Her smile was infectious. My heart felt lighter in my chest, realizing that she *wanted* to stay here. With me. I tucked her wet hair behind her ear, giving her a swift kiss. Bonnie made a sound of disgust, wiping at the shaving soap I'd gotten on her face. I took her chin in my hand, then ran my tongue up the length of her cheek to wipe it away. She smacked me in the shoulder, making me laugh.

The Kid dragged us out back again a little later so he could get more practice throwing his knives. I sat at the table with a blank notebook and pencil I'd stolen from Mickey's office, watching as Bonnie corrected The Kid's stance and gave him advice on how to aim.

He was getting better. I pressed my pencil to the page, drawing for the first time in what felt like years.

"So, Montana," Will said, sitting in the chair next to me. "It seems we have the same taste in women, now that we've shared two of them." My eyebrows lifted as I looked at him. "It's the Ellis charm. Never thought we'd beat you and Bonnie between the sheets, but I guess some men just aren't as lucky as others."

"Congrats, I guess?" I said, glancing toward Bonnie once more. Clara was, surprisingly, absent. "But Clara and I never—" I shrugged. Will leaned forward, resting his elbows on the table.

"You mean you were going to marry her and have no idea how she was in the sack?" he asked, letting out a low whistle. "Brave man."

"Tell me something I don't know," I said, shooting a sarcastic grin at him. Will leaned back, an easy smile crossing his face.

"I just figured it was you who got there first," he said. "Bonnie has all her rules, but I only have one. No one's first and no one's last."

I barked out a laugh. He was funny, I'd admit that.

I went back to drawing, glancing up at Bonnie every few minutes to make sure I captured her just right. Eventually, Bonnie and The Kid settled at the table with us. Again, she started talking about her ideas for the base. I loved the way her eyes lit up with excitement. It reminded me of The Kid.

"There's a med bay. I mean, if we're stayin', I could talk to them about helping," Will said, knocking back what looked like Mickey's tequila. "My dad may take people apart, but I put them back together. It might be nice to do it somewhere that matters."

The conversation went on until late in the afternoon. When I finished my drawing, I went back into the house to check on Mickey. He'd been quiet lately. I found him in the living room, passed out. I kicked the side of the couch to wake him. He sprang up, looking wildly around the room.

"You alright, Mickey?" I asked.

"Jesus, Jesse, I thought you were a damn tango," he said.

"What's that?"

"Huh?" Mickey looked at me, a grim expression on his face. "Oh. Enemy."

"At least you didn't have your knife this time," I said, settling down on the coffee table. "Look, I know we kinda barged in on you here. But it sounds like we're staying. For a while at least. You think you can sober up?"

"Why would I do that?" he asked, reaching for the empty tequila bottle on the floor.

"Because we came all of the way from Montana to find you," I said, glancing over my shoulder to make sure we were alone. "You have an entire base of people looking to you to lead them. Maybe if you were sober you could?"

Mickey glared at me. "Why do you care?"

"Because you're family," I said. "We take care of family. We can't take care of you if you don't put the damn bottle down. I don't know what you've been through. I can't imagine what it was like during the Culling, but if you took *one* look around at the people who cared about you, maybe you'd understand there's more to life than the drink."

My uncle didn't speak. Instead, he got to his feet and headed toward the kitchen in search of another bottle. I let out a low breath.

We had time, right? Maybe I'd eventually get through to him.

## CHAPTER THIRTY-ONE

# BONNIE

I WAS SORE *EVERYWHERE*, and yet I couldn't seem to get enough time alone with Jesse. Every look, every touch, every hitch in his breath I was acutely aware of even if he was across the room. Logically I knew that eventually our passion would fade into a semblance of normalcy, but each time I started to push down my desire, his words echoed through my mind again.

*I love you.*

It would set my heart pounding erratically in my chest all over again, desperate to be close to him. As close as it was possible to be. As if the warmth of his body on mine solidified this new, bright feeling in my chest into a beam of light that banished the darkness of my past. Making way for things I'd never allowed myself before. *Dreams.*

The Kid and I walked back from the stables after tending to Eagle, No Name, and his freshly named horse, *Whisper*. I'd asked him what it meant, but he wouldn't tell me. The day was coming to a close, warmth lingering in the air as the light grew hazy around us. The Kid was oddly quiet, but in a comfortable way. I reached out and ran my fingers through his hair until he turned to look at me, smiling so wide it was a wonder his face didn't break in half.

"Hey, Kid," I said. He stopped and turned to me. "I have a confession to make. I broke one of the rules."

He stared at me expectantly.

"I'm in love with Jesse."

He chuckled, turning back to the path to Mickey's and continuing our walk.

"I already knew that," he said with a shrug, surprising me. "I just figured if it's the right person, it was okay to break the rules."

I smiled, wondering how he'd gotten so smart.

"So you don't mind that I'm stayin' for good, then?" I asked. That stopped him in his tracks, his back ramrod straight. In a moment, he hurtled across the space and wrapped me in his arms excitedly, nearly knocking me over in the process. "Watch the stitches, Kid."

"You mean it?" he asked. I nodded, laughing into his hair. "Have you told Jesse yet?"

In his excitement, he half-dragged me the rest of the way back to Mickey's. As I shuffled up the front porch steps, I looked around to the weeds and debris outside. Those would be the first to go. Starting tomorrow, I was going to put that drunkard to work, even if I had to hide all his tequila first.

"If you don't get in here quick, *mi cielo*, there won't be any dinner left!" Will called to me from inside. I realized that for the first time in my life, I didn't mind standing still, as long as I had these people standing with me.

Dinner was chaos. Will hogged the mashed potatoes; he and The Kid shouted over the table at one another. Clara kept trying to pull Will's attention away from the food, but that was one battle I didn't expect anyone could win. Gabriela told us about her extended family living in the Borderlands while Mickey sipped on his tequila instead of drinking himself into oblivion. Even though his face was ruddier than normal, he was in good spirits. I don't know that I'd ever laughed that hard before or smiled so freely.

Jesse held my hand under the table and found any opportunity to run his fingers over my thighs or press a kiss into my hair.

By the time dinner was over and the table was empty, the silence felt somehow obtrusive and wrong. Jesse went to help The Kid get ready for bed while Gabriela and I cleared the table. There were dark circles beneath her eyes, and I knew that Mickey hadn't been letting her get much sleep lately. With our arrival also came memories he'd tried hard to drink away.

"I'll finish up. You should get home and sleep. Mickey'll be fine tonight," I said, and she nodded, shuffling away on weary feet. I washed the dishes quickly, reaching high on my tiptoes to put a glass back in a cabinet that was *just* out of reach. A hand slipped around my waist as the glass was taken from me and placed on the shelf.

I turned in Jesse's arms, pressed between his hard chest and the countertop. His eyes were hungry when he looked at me. The expression said clearly that he knew what he wanted, and it was beneath my clothes. I pressed my thighs together to keep from squirming beneath his gaze.

"Those shorts are *killing* me," he breathed hot into my ear before tucking some of my hair behind it. I stared at him directly for a long moment and bit my lip. His breath shuddered. In a swift motion he swept me into his arms and carried me down the hall to our room, slamming the door shut with his foot before the lock clicked in place.

An hour or so later we lay together, naked and tangled in our sheets, his fingers tracing lazy shapes against the pale skin of my shoulder. I stretched over him to reach the bedside table and opened the small drawer there.

"I unpacked earlier," I told him, even though he wasn't really listening. Instead, he'd taken to staring at the curves of my ass that were now in his line of sight. "And I stole one of Will's cigarettes." I took the glass off the lantern on our bedside table and lit it quickly, inhaling the bite of tobacco smoke deep into my lungs. I offered it to Jesse with a grin, but he shook his head.

"Your loss," I said, inhaling again.

The curl of smoke was thick in the air around us. Pulling the sheet off the bed, I wrapped it lazily around my body before crossing the room to open the window. The chill in the early evening air raised goosebumps on my skin. The bite of the tobacco settled into my relaxed muscles as I finished the cigarette, flicking the end out the open window. Before returning to bed, I picked up a small bundle of books off of the desk with a grin curling on my lips.

"I have a surprise for you," I told him. He raised his eyebrows as I climbed back onto the mattress and crawled until I was tucked into the spot on his shoulder made for me. I handed him two of the books, and his eyes widened in shock as he recognized their faded covers.

"These are—"

"Your mother's books. I couldn't let you leave them behind. It's all you had left of her," I said, my voice soft. "I snuck them into my pack when you left the room."

His breath hitched and his mouth opened, but no words came out. I couldn't tell if that meant he liked the surprise or not. Opening the small book still in my hand, I turned the pages until I pulled out a tiny yellow flower I'd pressed between them.

"I have *one* more surprise," I said with a grin. He looked down at it in confusion.

"I picked it before we walked back to the base. To remember your truck by," I said with a giggle. Jesse groaned, his hands running over his face.

"I'm gonna miss that truck," he said, pulling the book from my hand and leaning down to press a hard kiss to my mouth. "But I'd burn that engine all over again." He tucked the flower between some of the later pages and looked down at the book in my hands. His eyes scanned the words, and I let my fingers trail over his arm to get his attention.

"What does it say?" I asked. He wrapped a lazy arm around me and adjusted so I could see the words on the page, even if they didn't mean anything to me. It was just how Jesse was, always considering me.

"It's a poem," he breathed into my hair.

"Hope is the thing with feathers," he read, his voice the deep canyon timbre that I loved so dearly. "That perches in the soul. And sings the tune without the words. And never stops." He looked down at me. "At all."

"The thing with feathers," I said, brushing my fingers over the words. "I like that." I ran my lips over the skin below his ear, smiling as he groaned. "Remind me that I need to talk to Gabriela tomorrow about getting more of my herbal tea." He tensed, looking down at me with concern in his blue eyes. I patted his arm softly, chuckling.

"Don't worry, farm boy. There's plenty of time. It seems what I packed got left behind with the wagon," I said, kissing him again until he looked less worried. "I'm impulsive, not reckless."

He nodded, his eyes on my mouth, still swollen from his attention. He rolled me back into the mattress, the books falling forgotten to the floor, settling on top of me as if we belonged together like this. All of my broken, jagged pieces were beautiful when they fit together with his. Like a stained-glass window.

"I'm yours, Jesse," I whispered against his mouth. He stilled at my words, thumb brushing against my temple. "You're an outlaw, Jesse James. *My* outlaw. And if there's anyone I belong to, it's you."

"I'm never letting you go," he said with his unwavering conviction. He kissed me, our bodies sliding together slowly, languidly, as we enjoyed each other without urgency or desperation. Until the night grew dark and our lantern burned low. Until we fell into each other's arms, completely spent and satisfied in ways I'd never imagined were possible before. The steady thump of his heart beneath my cheek lulled me into a sweet sleep.

The pop of gunfire woke us with a start.

In an instant, Jesse and I scrambled for our clothes on the floor. I shoved on my shorts and a shirt as a crash resounded from the front of the house. Panic seized hold of my heart as I shoved my boots on, hands scrambling for a weapon. I turned to Jesse, tossing him the M9 as I cocked the hammer back on Selene and he threw the door open.

The Kid cried out, and my heart lurched in my chest.

We hurtled down the hallway in a rush at the sound, not stopping to take note of the broken furniture and overturned chair. A shadow in the corner of my eye caught my attention. I whirled, an unfamiliar armed man raising his weapon to Jesse. I squeezed the trigger, and he dropped heavily to the ground, unmoving.

Jesse, always faster than me, was out the front door a few steps ahead, stopping short at the top of the porch steps. As soon as I stepped beside him, I realized why.

Sixgun and twelve armed men had The Kid kneeling on the grass, a gun pointed to the back of his head.

Mickey bled from a cut on his temple and was clutching an arm that was held at an odd angle, his shoulder too far displaced from where it should be. Will and Clara burst through the doors behind us. A strangled cry reached my ears, Will's steady medic hands leveling a silver pistol at his father across the way.

"Good. It seems I finally have your attention," Sixgun said, a sly smile spreading over his cruel mouth.

"Please," I said, breathless, my eyes on The Kid's face. He wasn't crying, but his expression was too tight and unnatural for his normally joyful face. As if he were trying everything in his power to keep from losing it. "Please, let him go. He's a *child*."

Sixgun laughed darkly, shifting his weight. Then I noticed the brace on his left leg, a souvenir from our last encounter. One I was sure he wanted vengeance for.

Jesse lurched forward bodily, the M9 extended, his blue eyes wild.

"Stop!" I shouted, shoving myself in front of him. I braced my feet against the ground, wrapping my arms around him as his chest heaved. "Stop."

Sixgun pressed the barrel of the gun harder against The Kid's head, forcing his gaze down to the grass in front of him. Jesse's mouth opened to argue with me, his eyes never leaving his brother.

"We know what he wants," I said quietly, the words hitting him like a physical blow. His eyes dropped to me then, and he shook his head softly. We both remembered what Will said as I'd tended his gunshot wound. *I've never seen him scared before . . . he kept saying it would be okay . . . that if he found you, it would be okay.*

"No," Jesse said, his voice dangerous as it rumbled from his chest to shake through my entire body. "No, there has to be another way." He wrapped an arm around me as if afraid I would disappear into thin air.

Before I could protest, Jesse's hard hands yanked me inside the house, the door slamming behind us. His eyes were a wild blue that broke my heart.

"You have to leave," he said, his words hot in the space between us. "Just go out the back—"

"Jesse—"

"Go to St. Louis. I'll come for you. I'll fix this. I just have to—"

"Jesse," I tried again.

"I can *fix* this. You just have to go. *Now!*" His hands were in my hair, eyes imploring me. The vision of his face wavered through a curtain of my tears.

"I'm done running," I said, the words a whisper that silenced him. "Even if I could, I wouldn't run from this."

"*Please*," he begged, his deep canyon voice breaking on the word. "I can't lose anyone else. I can't lose *you*." His lips trembled, and my tears spilled over onto my cheeks.

"I'll kill him, Bonnie!" Sixgun called from beyond the door, and I ran trembling hands over Jesse's sharp jaw and his beautiful, chiseled face. Mapping him with my fingertips.

"He has *The Kid*, Jesse," I sobbed. "*My* Kid. *Our* Kid."

He ducked his forehead down, and his mouth crashed against mine in a ruthless kiss that muffled a sob between our lips. I couldn't tell if it was his or mine.

"You can't lose me," I said, breaking away in a rush. "I'm *yours*." I scrambled with the gun in my hand, pushing it into his palm. He looked down at the small ivory-handled weapon that'd been my bargaining chip for so long. He fumbled with the ring on his finger, slipping it into my hand. A piece of him to carry with me.

"If you run, I'll kill him slow!" Sixgun shouted. I mopped the tears from my cheeks and took a shuddered breath. Before Jesse could convince me otherwise, I twisted out of his arms and flung open the door. I stepped onto the porch with every ounce of false bravado I'd gathered in my years on the run. Until I was level with Sixgun's mercilessly empty eyes.

"I have conditions," I said, spitting the words out with every bit of malice in my heart. "I'll come with you, but you have to let The Kid go, and when you leave, you don't *ever* come back here."

Sixgun's jaw clenched hard enough to tick a muscle in his cheek.

"Why would I negotiate with you? I have you outmanned and outgunned," he said, spitting into the grass. I smiled then, coldly, the expression exposing too many teeth to be considered anything other than predatory.

"Because I know you need me alive," I said, staring him down. He already knew from my attempt on the train that I wouldn't hesitate to take my own life.

"You wouldn't," he said.

"Fucking try me," I said.

"Fine, but my traitor son comes with you. There are a few lessons it's clear I haven't taught him yet." His eyes slid to Will on the porch. I glanced over briefly, reading the terror in Will's guarded expression. He wouldn't leave me again; he'd promised. If it meant keeping Jesse and The Kid alive, I would use that promise to my advantage now.

"He gets a full pardon from the Hanged Men," I said. Begrudgingly, Sixgun nodded. Will's incredulous eyes found mine, but a moment later, the fear I'd seen in them was masked with stoic indifference.

I wanted to sink into the safety of Jesse's arms. The wanting nearly unraveled me. I turned to him for one last look.

"I can't do this without you," he said. I swallowed down the tears threatening to fall.

"Yes, you can," I said with every bit of strength I had left. "You stand tall, Jesse James. Promise me—"

"*Anything*," he said, his voice breaking on the word.

"Promise me you'll look out for The Kid. The way no one looked out for me," I said. He nodded, his jaw clenched tight.

"We don't have all day, Bonnie!" Sixgun called. I squeezed my eyes tight for a moment, trying to find the strength to walk away from Jesse.

"I'll come for you," he said, conviction ringing true in his deep canyon timbre. When Jesse said it, I believed him. "I'll come for you and bring you home. I don't care what I have to do, or how long it takes."

The words steadied me, holding me together, the way he always did. I swallowed down my fear and held my head high, as a free woman. Jesse bent low and inhaled deep, drinking me into his lungs. I nodded, feeling colder without the warmth of his skin against mine. I turned from him then, tucking the ring into my pocket as I made it down the steps.

One of the Crimson Fist met me; his dirty hands gripped my arm and twisted it painfully behind my back. He walked me forward until I was facing Sixgun.

With a smirk, he gripped the back of The Kid's shirt and pulled him forcefully to his feet. The man holding me twisted my arm until I cried out, laughing cruelly behind me. Will was shoved bodily between us as two men searched him, pulling several hidden knives and his pistol from his body before they walked him toward the gates.

"Clara?" one of Sixgun's men asked from nearby. "What're you doin' here?" The blonde narrowed her eyes, staring across the yard. Recognition filled her expression.

"How does he know you?" Jesse asked. Clara regarded him for a moment before a cool mask slipped over her face.

"Haven't seen you since you hooked up with them slavers," the man said, a grin widening across his face. "Why don't you come with us?"

*Slavers.* The same slavers that attacked us on the road. I laughed bitterly, every suspicion I had about her confirmed.

"You fucking *cunt*," I shouted at her. "I knew you were a fucking liar!"

"What the fuck is he talking about?" Jesse asked her, a note of incredulity in his voice. She moved toward Jesse, and I wrenched against my captor, trying to break free.

"Don't you judge me, Jesse James," she said, her voice no longer sweet but cold and commanding. "I did it to get out. You should understand that." Without a second glance, she walked down the stairs, a smirk on her lips when she glanced my way.

"Good to see you, darlin'," the man said, putting an arm around her shoulders and guiding her after Will until they disappeared from sight.

Sixgun snapped his fingers, and a large man moved forward, toward The Kid.

"Can't have your little guard dog trailing me, now can I?" Sixgun said. The man roughly pulled The Kid from Sixgun's grip. He wrapped his hand firmly around my throat, making sure that I would watch. "Break his arm."

I struggled, but between Sixgun and the man holding me, it was useless. I kicked, bucking my entire body, lurching towards The Kid as Sixgun laughed at my terrified tears.

"You gave your word!" I shouted.

"I said I'd let him go; I didn't say I wouldn't hurt him," he said with a sly smile. The man brought a club down on The Kid's arm, over and over, until a crack sounded and The Kid screamed. I tossed my head, tears blurring in my vision at the sight of The Kid's blood. The man tossed him carelessly to the ground. The Kid clutched his arm as Jesse took the stairs two at a time to drop to his side.

"I'll kill you!" I screamed, snapping my teeth as his hand dropped swiftly from my throat. "Kid!"

But Sixgun's eyes were dark and cruel now.

"Shut the bitch up," he ordered.

Pain exploded in my head, and the world went black.

## Chapter Thirty-Two

# JESSE

Time moved too slowly and too fast, all at once. Stuck between the moments, I watched as Bonnie's head lolled to one side and The Kid cried out, clutching his broken arm. I froze, not knowing whether to follow Sixgun's man dragging her away or to help my brother. Blood glistened against her dark hair from the blow they'd delivered.

Suddenly, the world snapped back into place. Sixgun and Bonnie were long gone. Soldiers ran toward us, carrying rifles and shouting words I couldn't make out. Panic lanced up my spine. *Kid.* I rushed to his crumpled form. His small body curled around his battered arm, the same arm he'd broken when he was little. He screamed and writhed in pain. A knot formed in my chest.

How had this happened?

Gabriela moved to my side, assessing my brother's injuries. A couple of others carried a flat plank of wood. When they reached down to grab him, I shielded him with my body.

"No!" I shouted.

"Jesse," Gabriela said, yanking me back. I struggled out of her grip. "They're medics. They're here to help." She grabbed me by the back of my shirt, shoving me out of the way. I scrambled to my feet, advancing on her.

"How did they even get into the base?" I asked, the words bitter and desperate. One of the medics administered something from a small bottle by sticking a needle into my brother's arm. The Kid moaned in pain, then went still.

"Get him inside," Gabriela said, helping the others to lift The Kid. They retreated across the littered lawn and into the house. Her brown eyes were fierce as she turned on me.

"How the *fuck* did those bastards get in here?" I demanded. My hands shook at my side. From the corner of my eye, Mickey approached.

"Jesse—" he said, clutching his own injured arm.

"Don't fucking *Jesse* me. This is *your* fault!" I glared between them. "Your goddamn guards just let *anyone* in."

"Listen to me—" Mickey started.

"Fuck you," I said, picking up the M9 from where I'd dropped it in the grass. I stalked toward the stable, intent on getting No Name and leaving this fucking place. My uncle grabbed me with his good arm, wheeling me around to look at him.

"What are you doing?" he asked, eyes searching mine wildly.

"I'm going after her. Get out of my way," I said, venom dripping from my tongue. This was *his* fault. He'd gotten so lost in the bottle that he didn't take proper precautions for a place he was responsible for.

"You can't," he said.

"Don't you fucking tell me what I can and can't do," I said. I took purposeful strides, holding the M9 pointed at the ground. Mickey stalked beside me.

"You made that girl a promise," he said, moving in front of me. I stilled. For a man who was nearly the same size as me, he seemed small. I stared past him, toward the wide-open gates. Bodies littered the ground. The survivors milled about. A few carried the dead, but most of them just stood there. Instead of guarding the fucking base like they were supposed to.

"I promised I'd find her—"

"You promised you'd take care of The *Kid*," Mickey said, putting a hand up. "She didn't give herself up so you could get yourself killed and leave *him* alone."

Finally, I looked into my uncle's eyes; it was like looking into a mirror. They were the clearest I'd seen them in the days since our arrival, untainted by drink. I clenched my jaw, bidding the tears back. My eyes heated as I thought of the horrors I'd let Bonnie go right back to. My bottom lip trembled. I dropped the M9 into the dirt at our feet. The image of Mickey wavered as my eyes filled with tears.

"I can't lose her," I said, my voice breaking.

"You won't," he said, putting a hand on my shoulder. "They need her alive. Wherever they're taking her, she won't be harmed."

"But—"

"Your brother needs you more," Mickey said, his tone even. "When he's stable, we'll find her."

I stared at him, not understanding.

"We?"

Mickey nodded. "We take care of family." He gave my shoulder a squeeze. "We'll find your girl."

My jaw clenched, and I stared at him. I gave a curt nod. Mickey dropped his hand and stalked away. I remained, staring out at the gates. When we'd started this journey, I'd had one goal: to find my uncle. I'd found him, but I'd also found something more. Love. Family. Honor. All of it, in Bonnie. I wiped furiously at my cheeks as I picked up the gun, before making my way back to The Kid.

*Who are you?* Bonnie's voice echoed in my mind.

I'm Jesse James.

*What are you?*

I'm a motherfucking outlaw.

*What are you gonna do?*

I'm going to set the world on fire until I get you back.

Thank you for reading Guns & Smoke! If you enjoyed this novel please consider leaving a review on Amazon, Goodreads, or wherever you purchased your copy.

KEEP READING FOR AN
EXCLUSIVE PEEK AT

LEATHER
&
LACE

THE THRILLIING FOLLOW
UP TO
GUNS & SMOKE...

# JESSE JAMES

F UCK THE SILENCE.

Anything was better than the all-consuming, yawning darkness of my mind. The silence was filled with too many memories. Her beautiful voice twisted into wails. Bones cracking. How she pleaded for my life. My brother's life. For help.

Beyond the steel door of the old service station bathroom, a riot of clashing voices echoed and drowned out the commentator. The vibration of stomping feet and screaming voices shook the ground. Apparently, my opening act was just getting good. The thunderous roar soothed me, dragging me away from that insidious silence.

I wound the bandage around my bicep once, twice, a third time. The fresh ink had barely dried, and I wasn't about to fuck it up. I split the bandage with my teeth, tossing the roll into my bag.

No doubt my opponent tonight would be bigger than me. They usually were.

After all, everyone wanted a shot at beating me, and I was only in town for one night.

Mickey and I had arrived in Little Rock with the sunrise this morning, and we'd be gone by first light. We had places to go, things to do.

We had to find Bonnie.

I'd spent a month at the bottom of a tequila bottle after Jones's men stole her from me. It was only when my kid brother gave me a swift kick in the ass that I sobered up and made plans. Even now, three years later, the temptation to get lost in a bottle was strong. I shoved off the bench and paced the small room, forcing back the hopelessness at the edge of my mind.

We would find her. It was just a matter of when. If I didn't hold onto that hope, I'd have died three years ago.

A fist pounded against the door as the crowd roared. An unstable calm stole over me, as it often did before a fight. My breathing steadied, and the pounding in my chest steeled me as I pulled open the door.

*"C'mon, Jess," Mickey said a couple weeks after Sixgun stole Bonnie. I sat alone on the back patio of my uncle's house, trying not to think about the last time we were back here. I tried not to imagine Bonnie teaching The Kid to properly aim a knife at a target. I tried not to think about Will's attempt to teach Clara to shoot a gun. I tried not to think about Bonnie draped across my lap.*

*Thinking about what I lost hurt too much.*

*"I'm good." I tipped back the bottle of tequila I'd swiped from his kitchen. I didn't like the liquor, but it was all Mickey had.*

*My uncle sat across from me, blue eyes bright beneath furrowed brows. "I know what you're feeling—"*

*"You don't know a fucking thing." My nostrils flared as I shoved down my anger. But it was always there, just beneath my skin.*

*Mickey ran a hand over his face. "I know more than you think, Jess." Something unreadable passed through his eyes as he looked at his fingers and picked his nails. "You aren't the only person that's ever lost the woman he loves."*

*"No shit."*

*"So quit acting like the world is over."*

*"And do what?" I leaned forward, plunking the bottle on the glass table. "The Kid can't keep his eyes open for more than a few minutes because of the drugs. I can't go after Bonnie until he's okay. There's nothing else here for me."*

*I averted my gaze as hurt passed across his face. Guilt coiled like a snake in my throat, choking back the other harsh words threatening to spill forward.*

*"Why do you even care?" I asked after a tense silence.*

*"Because until you came along, I'd forgotten."*

*"Forgotten what?"*

*"What it's like to give a shit about anyone other than myself," Mickey said plainly. "We're family, Jess, and we take care of family."*

*The stinging burn of grief snuck up in my chest. I'd said that to him. Right before Bonnie was taken. I inhaled sharply, eyes slamming shut as I forced the emotion back. I couldn't lose my shit. Not now. Not in front of Mickey. Maybe not ever.*

*"C'mon," he said again, rising.*

*"Where are we going?"*

*"You'll see." He swiped the tequila from the table as he moved past me.*

*After I changed my clothes, Mickey led me down the main drag of the base. We walked in silence until he turned off the road toward a giant metal building. A long strip of aged asphalt spread out across the ground for what could have been a mile.*

*To the west, the sun dipped behind the horizon, its rays painting the clouds in bright reds and oranges. My breath caught as an image of Bonnie straddling me in the bed of the truck flashed through my mind. The bright hues of sunset caressing the lines of her face, making love to the soft slope of her nose and angle of her eyes just as I was making love to her. As if the whole world wanted to see the pleasure soaked in the depths of her eyes. And I was the only bastard lucky enough to witness it.*

*It was all we had. Those two nights.*

*Shouting sounded as we approached the building. My uncle grinned over his shoulder and led me into the open building. Most of the cavernous space was empty. Sound reverberated off the metal, making the place seem fuller than it actually was. A small bar lined the wall to my right. Several tables were arranged around an open square marked by orange cones. Barbed wire was slung between the cones. A man edged backward into the wire, cursing loudly as the barbs dug into the bare skin of his calf. Another man approached him with a menacing grin, taking advantage of the distraction. He delivered a swift uppercut to the man's chin, sending him reeling backward, his legs tangling in the barbed wire.*

*"What is this?"*

*"Fighting pits." Mickey grinned.*

*He introduced me to some of his friends, men and women who traveled the fighting circuit. After procuring a glass of tequila, Mickey chatted up his friends. But me? I watched the battle in the ring. I caught myself lurching forward with each desperate blow. Before long, I shouted alongside the other spectators.*

*"You good, Jess?" Mickey asked warily. I didn't realize I'd jumped to my feet as another round ended.*

*"Yep." I lowered into my seat.*

*As the night wore on, unspent energy tingled in my fingers. A guy twice my size had just knocked out his opponent. Blood tinged his teeth as he grinned at the crowd.*

*"Who's next?" he called.*

*An image of Bonnie's head lolling to the side filled my mind. I thought of my brother, just a sweet kid who may never fully regain control of his shooting arm. Guilt at not being able to protect them rose up in my throat.*

*I practically jumped into the ring.*

Screaming voices and a high-pitched whistle drowned out my thoughts as I walked through the smoky, pulsing crowd. The walls of the old service station were littered with graffiti and signs depicting a rather familiar likeness. A sly smile found its way to my mouth. They never could get Bonnie's eyes right on those old wanted posters. Though I focused on the rough-hewn ring, more than one person recognized me.

"Montana?"

"Is that *him*?"

"Oh my God, he's sexier than the posters!"

Ignoring the hands that reached out and the voices that shouted for my attention, I focused on breathing. A sick sense of relief coursed through me at the thought I would get a good night's sleep tonight. I'd found out after that first fight that my nightmares disappeared when I was too exhausted to think.

Fighting was my drug; I fell into it with reckless abandon. It was the remedy to my nightmares, the means to find Bonnie.

Heat radiated from the crowd as I climbed onto the platform made from an old highway sign. I unbuckled my holster, pausing to grip the ivory handle of Selene—the .22 pistol Bonnie'd given me for safekeeping. With deft fingers, I unbuttoned my shirt, to the excitement of the crowd. Wolf whistles and eager screams mingled with the electricity in the air.

"Give it up for Montana!" The already pulsing crowd exploded. A mixture of roars and jeers drowned out any coherent thoughts. I faced my opponent. He was only a few inches taller, his hair cropped close to his scalp. An ugly shadow blossomed on his cheek; yellow tinted the bruise, hinting it wasn't fresh.

Between us, a spotlight shone down on the aluminum sign, worn down over the years. The man sized me up as hecklers cursed my name.

You didn't become a well-known fighter without gaining a few enemies along the way.

Light flashed across my opponent's face as he stalked nearer. The tip of his nose hooked to the a little to the left, no doubt from too many breaks. In the crowd behind him, I caught sight of a man wearing a pair of aviators beneath a black cowboy hat. Panic gripped my heart.

*Sixgun.* The monster who stole Bonnie.

I lunged toward the man, not bothering to retrieve Selene. I'd murder the motherfucker with my bare hands.

"Hey!"

The announcer moved in front of me, momentarily distracting me from my mark. I shoved him out of the way, eyes flashing to the crowd, searching for the cowboy hat. A calloused hand gripped my bicep, twisting hard enough to elicit a hiss from between my lips. *My fucking tattoo.* I bared my teeth at my opponent and ripped my arm from his grip, punching his throat. He staggered backward.

The crowd exploded.

Desperation clawed up my throat as I wheeled around. Aviators. Black hat. Where the fuck was he?

"Montana!" the announcer shouted. I sidestepped him again. There were only a handful of cowboy hats in the crowd, and none of them were the dusty black I was so familiar with. "Get back to your position or forfeit!"

I clenched my jaw against the helplessness that coiled in my belly and spread outward. Maybe I'd imagined Sixgun. It wouldn't be the first time.

The announcer lifted his eyebrows, silently questioning whether I intended on throwing the fight. I ducked my head and moved back into place outside the ring of light. My opponent wrapped his fingers around his throat, glaring as he squared off. Fire coursed in his eyes; veins bulged in his neck.

"Sorry 'bout that," I said, my words barely registering above the crowd.

The man merely smirked at me, lips pulling away from his yellow-stained teeth. "I'm gonna murder you."

A cocky grin crossed my lips, and I lifted an eyebrow at him. We'd just have to see.

"There ain't no rules," the announcer said, having regained some semblance of control over the crowd. "First to yield, knock out, or die loses." His hard eyes darted between us. "Good luck."

"Fuck luck," I murmured.

A siren wailed. The man charged, surprising me with his speed.

5

Most of the fighters I faced underestimated me, and I used it to my advantage. My farm-toned muscles had changed. With targeted training over the last three years, I'd gained enough mass that I needed an entirely new wardrobe. Softness that might have layered my body hardened over time. Though I was just over six feet tall, most of the people I fought were taller, broader, maybe even stronger.

But strength didn't always win.

Texas fighters were ruthless and swift on their feet. They taught me to use my added bulk to my advantage, to trick my opponents with misdirection.

As the man advanced, I dodged his meaty fist and ducked beneath his arm. The crowd screamed as I delivered a swift punch to his kidney. A choked sound came from between his lips as he wheeled around. Sweat and fury lined his face. I shrugged, unable to help my smirk. Maybe if he'd listened to what people said about me, he could have been better prepared. I didn't fight for money or glory. I fought for something more. Something harder to achieve.

I fought to free my mind from chaos, left behind in Bonnie's wake.

From the moment I'd seen Bonnie's dark, pin-straight hair whipping around her beautiful face, I was done. I fell into her trap and kept falling.

A malicious grimace flashed across the man's face as I split my stance. I lifted my fists to protect as satisfaction warmed my chest. I'd angered him. I wouldn't feel bad about kicking his ass. My opponent circled the light, and I mirrored him, waiting for his strike. It was always easier to let the brutes tire themselves before knocking them out.

Anticipation tingled along my skin as predator and prey sized one another up.

Fuck this.

I wanted his skin to split beneath my knuckles. I wanted to distract myself from the dark blue eyes that haunted me night after night. If only for a moment, I wanted to remember what it was like to be worthy of someone like her.

Losing her was my fault. That fact rattled me all the way to my core. I'd struggled when The Kid and I left Montana, never quite feeling like I could take care of him. Somehow, I'd reached a place of peace within myself, a place he would be safe. Because he had Bonnie and me. Now all he had was me.

And I was a massive fuck-up.

I motioned for my opponent to come at me. He rounded his shoulders to make himself look bigger. I shifted my weight back and forth, feeling the bounce of the metal ring. The movement caught his attention, which gave me an opening to punch him in his left eye.

*I'm no angel, and I don't pretend to be. I'll do whatever it takes.*

If Bonnie taught me anything, it was that we did whatever it took to survive. I would do whatever I had to in order to get her back.

Jesse had been an honorable man; he'd tried to do the right thing.

But Montana? Montana didn't give a fuck.

As the man's hand reflexively reached for his face, I drove my knee into his gut. A whoosh of air spilled out of his lungs; I bit back a gag at the decay on his breath. He hunched over, but I caught him easily, letting him rest against my shoulder for a single breath. I shoved him away, satisfaction blossoming inside me as he stumbled. My chest heaved with the adrenaline coursing through my veins.

I motioned for him to come at me again. He staggered forward, movements sluggish as he attempted recovery. With a sweep of my leg, he crashed to the metal highway sign, a resonant *crack* snapping above the crowd. As the spectators roared, I drove my knee into his gut and covered his body with my own.

My knuckles ached as they bashed against the man's cheekbone. The pain was familiar, soothing in a way that it shouldn't have been. I reveled in it. In feeling something visceral and real before me, something I could touch, instead of the things that haunted me.

*Damnit, Bonnie, trust me! I've got you!*

Hesitant, dark blue eyes flashed through my mind. I could almost feel her delicate hand grasping mine as we jumped onto a moving train. What would my life look like now if Bonnie hadn't taken my hand?

I drove my fist into the man's nose. The crunch beneath my hands gave a sick sense of pleasure. Satisfaction roared in my chest. I reared my arm back, readying for another blow to his face. I wasn't even close to being done.

Rough hands grabbed me, dragging me bodily back from my opponent's form. I bared my teeth as another man wrapped his arms around me to secure my arms at my sides. I bashed my head forward against the first man, pain blasting behind my eyes as I made contact with his nose. He released me, hands immediately going to his nose.

Blood dripped down my forehead, sticky and warm.

I drove my elbow backward into the gut of the man holding me and delivered a swift right hook to his jaw, enjoying how he fell into the crowd.

"Montana's dirty!" a voice bellowed. I turned toward it. A man about half my size stood near the edge of the ring, holding what looked like an old bullhorn. His eyes widened as I lifted my brows in challenge. I lurched toward him, and he flinched backward, dropping the plastic thing to the floor. He staggered away and fled.

I grinned at the raucous crowd, extending my arms to beckon the next challenger.

A drunk stumbled into the ring. Their long hair was tied back with a leather strap. They drained the drink in their hand and slammed it to the ground. Shards of glass shattered against the floor of the ring; light bounced off of them, and dancing colors filled my vision.

A small, blue glass bead flashed through my mind. It had delicate whorls of silver carved into it.

*Something to remember me, or trade. If you're ever in a pinch.*

I'd carried that bead with me every day since. A year ago, when hope of finding Bonnie dwindled, I took some of my winnings to a jeweler outside of Dallas. He fashioned that bead into a ring.

It became a promise. To myself. That I'd find Bonnie and give her that damn ring if it killed me.

A cocky grin curled across the drunk's face as he staggered toward me. I landed a single punch to his face, and he went down. As I scanned the room for any other challengers, pain exploded in the back of my knee. I landed heavily on the aluminum, an ache lancing up my spine. I turned in time to see my original opponent, red staining his chin, as he lifted a booted foot.

Motherfucker wanted to play dirty?

So be it.

I hooked my arm around his boot and yanked him toward me. The man's massive bulk couldn't keep up. He crashed to the floor of the ring. I flipped him over and delivered a swift kick to his ribs, barely registering the crack of the bone.

Instead of the satisfaction of breaking him with my strength, all I saw was The Kid, writhing on the ground after one of Jones's men had shattered his arm.

*He has The Kid, Jesse. My Kid. Our Kid.*

Stumbling backward, I suddenly remembered the crowd watching this display.

"Montana, fuck, you won. C'mon!" the announcer said. I turned toward the man, finding two bouncers on either side of him.

I swiped beneath my nose, nodding.

I won.

So why didn't I feel like a winner?

I still didn't have Bonnie.

After scooping up my shirt and holster, I staggered away from the ring. People patted me on the shoulder as I passed, but I ignored them all. Instead, I focused on re-dressing and securing the holster and Selene at my side. My fingers wrapped around the cool, comforting handle of Bonnie's gun. I ignored the shouts of *fuck you!* from people who'd lost money by betting against me. Time slowed nearly to a stop as the bar slipped into my sight. I sidled up to it, ignoring the patrons that either gaped or jeered at me.

The bartender was at the far end, grinning at a woman wearing a red ribbon who leaned on top of the bar with a low-cut top. As I contemplated whether I should climb over the bar and get my own drink, a warm hand slid across my lower back. A pretty blonde woman shimmied up beside me, tucking her hand into my back pocket.

"Hey sugar," she said around the pop of chewing gum in her mouth. "I can help you clean all that blood off back at my place." Her eyebrows lifted suggestively.

I clenched her wrist, yanking her hand out of my pocket. I shrugged her off. "Go find some other dumb fucker."

The woman scoffed. I ignored her, whistling louder to get the bartender's attention. The man reached toward the whore, tugging on the end of the red ribbon around the woman's throat. He wasn't worried about anything but getting that whore alone.

Leveraging my weight, I jumped the bar, feet hitting the concrete floor lightly. Voices rose in dissension, but I didn't give a shit. I rifled through half-empty bottles arrayed on a cart. Because of Gabriela's family in the Borderlands, Fort Hood was rife with tequila. I couldn't remember the last time I'd had good whiskey.

Amber liquid caught my sight, and I plucked the bottle. The cap clattered to the floor as I upended it; the whiskey's bite made me grimace. It burned away the hazed edges of my vision. The room snapped into startling clarity. My gaze moved about as I hopped the bar a second time, whiskey still in hand.

Shouts erupted nearby. Someone slammed into my side, knocking me off-kilter. The bottle slipped and crashed to the floor, whiskey sloshing across my boots. The fighting pit around me faded, replaced instead by a landing at some inn in a nondescript town in the desert. Bonnie's hands tangled in my hair, teeth grazed across my mouth. I could feel her ass in those short shorts as she moaned against me.

*We have to get to the room.*

Desperate kisses filled my senses. I could smell the sand on her skin.

My heart ached. Three years. Three long years dreaming of stolen moments like that, when it was just Bonnie and me and our undeniable attraction. It was more than just physical. I missed her body, but I missed her sharp tongue and clever mind. I missed how she called me out when I was being an asshole.

I missed her in a way I never thought I could miss anyone. As though my entire body seized with a helplessness that left me frozen, teetering on the edge of shattering into a million pieces and being blown away on a breeze.

Could I last another three years without her? Hell, another day?

A fight broke out in earnest, snapping me back to the bar. I stalked away, gripping Selene as I shoved through the crowd. A familiar form hovered near the exit.

My uncle tipped his head up. Blue eyes like mine, sandy hair graying near the edges, and gray stubble lining his chin greeted me.

"Mickey," I said by way of greeting. His eyes were clearer than my own, the expression in them determined, a glint I hadn't seen in months.

"What?" I asked. "Is it The Kid?"

"No, he's fine," Mickey said. "It's Bonnie."

My heart stuttered in my rib cage. I reached for the front of his shirt, eyes widening as panic revealed the cracks in my controlled facade. He wouldn't say anything about her unless he had news. Mickey wouldn't fuck with me. Not when it came to her.

"We know where she is."

*We found her.*

Hot relief coursed through my veins, heating my skin and inflating my chest. It spilled out through my extremities. My vision wavered, eyes slamming shut.

*We found her.*

Three years of searching, of fighting, of reliving the best and worst moments of my life culminated in this single, solitary moment.

*We found her.*

Now it was time to get the woman I loved back.

# ACKNOWLEDGMENTS

Years ago, Lauren gave me inspiration dice for Christmas. I'd always wanted to be a published author. For a long time, the two of us did text-based roleplaying (shout out to all of our Souls friends!), but we never quite considered writing together outside of it.

"Let's write a short story," Lauren said the day she gave those dice to me. That night, Guns & Smoke was born. It wasn't called Guns & Smoke back then, and it looked very different. Thank God we cut the aliens. Also, we've never been very good at containing ourselves to "short."

Now, almost a decade later, I am so proud of the world we created and the work we've done to shape it into this story. Guns & Smoke is a labor of love that I feared would never see publication. But through late hours, long nights, and heated arguments (kinda like being married), my dream of becoming a published author has finally been realized. I am incredibly lucky to share this with one of my best friends.

I adore this world and the characters, and I hope you do, too.

Co-authoring a novel is equal parts genius and madness, as I think Abbie would agree. This not-so-short story birthed an entire world that I'll happily spend the rest of my life exploring through the unending cast of characters, places, and themes. So, never fear, there is a ton more where this came from.

Writing Bonnie has been an honor. When I first imagined her, this product of a corrupt and decaying society, she'd been subject to the absolute worst parts of humanity. It'd hardened her heart and forced her into being nearly as bad as our villains at times. She's not a likeable character, but that's what made me love her. Why should she have to be likeable for her to find someone who would see her and adore her exactly as she is? Why should she soften her edges just to make others comfortable? I love her for all the same reasons Jesse does, because she's direct, she doesn't flinch, and she never backs away from a fight. My hope is that Bonnie's character helps normalize strong women in society; to make them more understood and valued.

Of course, it takes a village to create a book & there are several people we owe thanks to:
-Thanks to Stefanie Saw, Artist and Owner of Seventhstar Art, who can be found at  for creating our amazing book cover.
- A special thanks to Alexandra Ott for her invaluable editorial services.
-Of course we want to thank Jonathan Sevier; Husband, Maker of Coffee, Breakfast & Bringer of Wine. We couldn't have done it without you.
-Our AMAZING Beta Readers: Sarah Frazier, Ashley Nelson, Tori Gerald, Meagen West, Alexis O'Neal, Amanda Boulos,  Susan Farris, Cat Bowser, Laura Fielder, Krista Metwally, Sarah Hart, Rebecca Bentley, Dawn Morgan, & Kalen Evans. Thank you for your feedback!
-Dr. Paul Garrett for his invaluable medical advice.
-Wesley Wayne Jenkins - for his love of westerns.
-Joshua Guillory for being an AMAZING ARC reader & finding all the typos.
-And finally, Sada R-tist, for the use of his artwork in our promotional materials.
We hope you continue with the series to find out what happens in the thrilling next chapter for Bonnie & Jesse.
Remember to keep your guns loaded & your flask full.

# ALSO BY LAUREN SEVIER

**Songs Series**
Songs of Autumn
Songs of Winter

**The Fool's Adventure Series**
Guns & Smoke
Leather & Lace
Chains & Reckioning

# ABOUT LAUREN SEVIER

Lauren Sevier lives a simple life in small town Central, Louisiana with her family and sweet Border Collie. She's a proud firefighter wife and mother to her miracle son, born through IVF after an eight-year battle with infertility. She works for a non-profit hospital in Cardiology. Writing and being in the service of helping others are her two passions in life.

She started writing song lyrics and poems on the front porch swing of her family home. She and her best friend get most of their inspiration on girl's night, after a glass of wine, or after watching movies from the early 2000's. They have plans to publish many series in the future together. However her passion is derived mostly from being a mother to her adventurous, imaginative, and affectionate son who ceases to amaze her every single day.

For more information, go to www.laurensever.com.

# Also by
# Abbie Lynn Smith

**The Fool's Adventure Series**

Guns & Smoke

Leather & Lace

Chains & Reckoning

# ABOUT
# ABBIE LYNN SMITH

Abbie Lynn Smith is an author of romance novels. She holds a Bachelor's degree in theatre, where she learned the art of storytelling. A lifelong resident of southern Louisiana, she is a lover of coffee, naps, and animals.

When not writing, she can be found spending time with her rescue dogs, Klaus and Mama.

Abbie is passionate about mental healthcare and believes that helping others with their own mental health battles is her small way of changing the world. Abbie grew up watching westerns with her grandfather, which partially inspired the setting of her co-authored debut novel, Guns & Smoke.

For more information, go to
www.abbielynnsmith.com

www.ingramcontent.com/pod-product-compliance
Lightning Source LLC
Chambersburg PA
CBHW031610100726
47898CB00006B/1735